The House of Broken Dreams

The House of Broken Dreams

By Anne Carden

iUniverse, Inc.
New York Bloomington

The House of Broken Dreams

This is a work of fiction. All of the characters, names, incidents, organizations, and dialogue in this novel are either the products of the author's imagination or are used fictitiously.
iUniverse books may be ordered through booksellers or by contacting:

iUniverse
1663 Liberty Drive
Bloomington, IN 47403
www.iuniverse.com
1-800-Authors (1-800-288-4677)

ISBN: 978-1-4401-2610-9 (pbk)
ISBN: 978-1-4401-2609-3 (cloth)
ISBN: 978-1-4401-2611-6 (ebk)

Printed in the United States of America

iUniverse rev. date: 2/20/2009

To my husband, Zack, for being my editor, my inspiration, and my best friend

To my children, Heather and Zack III, who taught me the joy of motherhood

To my daughter-in-law, Tennyson, who gave me the gift of grandchildren and is a gift herself

To my grandchildren, Seth, Talbott, Cole, and Halle, for walking me through innocence again

To Dianne, my sister forever, for always being my friend

To Elaine for encouragement, empathy, and faithfulness

And he that shuts Love out, in turn shall be
Shut out from Love, and on her threshold lie
Howling in outer darkness.

Alfred Lord Tennyson
(1809-1892)
From *To—*

The Graveyard of Broken Dreams

Love is dead:
His last arrow is sped;
He hath not another dart;
Go—carry him to his dark deathbed;
Bury him in the cold, cold heart—
Love is dead.

Alfred Lord Tennyson
(1809-1892)
From *The Burial of Love*

November 11, 1982

Laurel crouched to place a rose on her mother's grave. With a twig she dug a small hole in the icy dirt to anchor it.

"Mama, I really did love you," she whispered. "I really, really did."

All she felt in response was the deafening silence of the frigid air. Communicating with Mama wasn't any easier in death than it had been in life. Assaulted by overwhelming emptiness, she sank to the ground feeling the cold of the hard-packed earth seep through the wool of both her coat and her slacks. She hugged her knees to her chest as snowflakes pelted the bare skin of her neck chilling her to the bone. She shivered and with one hand turned her collar against the bitter wind. In the other hand she held a single red rose. One more to go, and it would be the hardest.

Every time she confronted the memories in this mountain graveyard they chilled her heart. Even the blanket of time offered little warmth to that bleak pocket of her life. She wished she could talk to Grandpa and Mama Rita, but they were gone now, too. She had placed the first two of her five roses on their graves. The third one went to Daddy.

She could still picture Grandpa standing at the rough-hewn lectern in the little white church that used to sit adjacent to this graveyard. He always led the singing. She could almost hear his uneven baritone booming the words to his favorite hymn. That hymn promised that the farther along you got in life the better you would understand its heartache. Grandpa had been a wise man, and he'd believed every word of that hymn. It wasn't that she didn't believe it, but she wished she could ask him why ten years wasn't far enough along.

Her family had never been normal; so maybe it would just take longer, and maybe someday she wouldn't feel this regret. Deep in her soul she knew that if she had to walk through those hard decisions again, she would make the same ones. Time had at least helped her sort through the broken dreams. She had turned them over in her heart and tried to find their roots, to see whose they were to begin with, but knowing their ownership hadn't lessened her loss. These were people she loved. This was her family.

She rarely told her story to outsiders. When she'd taken the risk, she could see the visible shock register on their faces. She could feel their judgment and their inability to empathize with her choices, but how could they know what it had been like living inside the heartache? How could they know how hard she had tried to save her family and how much courage it had taken to walk away from the carnage?

And she wondered why redemption came so hard to the wounded, why the choice to save yourself—to cease being a victim—came with such judgment from both the outside and from within. With every step of her emancipation had come the voices of reproach labeling her courage as selfishness.

Therapists in their manic need to categorize every honest emotion had sorted her overwhelming sorrow into the cubbyhole closest to psychosis. They hadn't wanted to understand it, and worse, they couldn't solve it. They'd labeled the whole thing dysfunctional: her, her anguish, her family. She hated that word—*dysfunctional.* There were better words to describe them, better adjectives more encompassing of what went wrong and less indicative of the careless psychobabble used to dismiss them.

Where did the heartache begin? How far back did it reach? She'd never been sure, so she had to begin with herself and her entrance onto the stage. Sometimes she believed that when she'd had the breath of life smacked into her that her first conscious thought had been one of guilt. That stinging blow to her backside, bringing on that first breath of life, was her punishment for emerging from her mother's womb of control.

Birth was a foreshadowing of days to come, for every step she took into the world and away from Mama's house she paid for with guilt and pain. It was the only way Mama knew to love—by controlling, demanding, and manipulating. It was the same with her brothers. She was just one of three.

Gene was Mama's firstborn. She had almost died giving birth to him, and so had he. He came into the world blue and cold, barely breathing. Mama had prayed in desperation for God to let him live. After much work by the doctors, Gene did live, but ultimately Mama believed that God had answered her prayer against his better judgment—that Gene had been born against God's will. They'd all heard that story for as long as Laurel could remember. How could her brother not be doomed to a self-fulfilling prophesy?

She opened the palm of her gloved right hand and watched the snowflakes drop silently onto the wool and instantly melt. Del, who was born in July 1941, had become a permanent part of their family in July 1944, when Mama's older sister and her husband were killed. A train had hit their car at a dangerous railroad crossing. Mama took immediate custody of her sister's only child. Gene remembered them all living with their aunt and uncle in Sunset Valley where the adults worked in a munitions plant. She couldn't remember life in the valley, and she couldn't remember when Del hadn't been part of their family. As far as she was concerned, he was her brother, not her cousin. Daddy had accepted him, too, as if he had been his own son.

Daddy had been inducted in the first pre-war draft of October 1940 and assigned stateside to the Army Corp of Engineers. He hadn't been allowed any furloughs during his first intensive year of barracks construction, but after that he had come home about every four months. She had been conceived on his first furlough in the fall of 1941 and was born nine months later in the summer of 1942. It had been a sunny June day. Daddy just happened to be home on leave. There were no labor complications and no health problems. So she'd even made her entrance trying out for the part of "best little girl in the world."

She blew at a drifting snowflake sending it airborne before it had a chance to land and melt on her glove. She'd been the obedient child who never made any waves, but no matter how good she'd tried to be, it was never enough for Mama. She could never make her proud of her.

After Germany surrendered in May 1945, Daddy came home permanently. Their family then settled back into the cabin on Sunset Mountain that Daddy had built for them before the war. Absence hadn't made the heart grow fonder with her parents. The separation had driven a wedge between them. They did nothing but argue. Daddy had plans to start a construction business using the skills he had honed in the army. He needed to go back to the relationship he and Mama had before the war, but Mama had learned to be independent. Neither of them could adjust to the changes in each other.

Laurel hadn't learned the full truth of the discord between them until eleven years ago, but she could mark the exact point when their marriage fell irretrievably apart. Maybe if she had heard and understood the content of their argument that day, she wouldn't have tried so hard to fix the unfixable.

She remembered that day in great detail. Gene was twelve, Del was seven, and she was six. Del and Gene were in the yard playing cowboys and Indians. Del crouched behind the family car to stalk their brother as she watched from the porch where she played with her doll. She could hear Mama and Daddy inside the house yelling at each other. When they had one of their fights, she and her brothers couldn't get far enough away.

It all seemed to happen in a split second but in slow motion. At least that was the way she still remembered it. Daddy abruptly stormed out of the house, his face red with rage, and headed for the car. Mama, her jaw set in that determined scowl of hers, followed. Daddy got into the car, but Mama got there before he could close the door. They scuffled over the keys, and before Laurel could even realize what was happening, the car lurched backwards with Mama still blocking the door. It was then that she heard Del's screams. She remembered running off the porch toward them. She saw Gene standing off to the side gaping at the site of their brother twisting in agony, his right arm caught under the right back tire.

Mama rushed around the car to bend over Del, and she started screaming at Daddy who had followed right behind her. "You did this on purpose, you bastard! You ran over him!"

"No. No, the car slipped out of gear. You know that!" Daddy sounded frantic. He bent down to Del who was sobbing uncontrollably. "Son, oh God, hang on!" Then he ran around to the front of the car and pulled it forward. When he turned off the engine and set the brake, he ran back around to where Del was lying with Mama hovering over him. Gene was standing nearby crying. Daddy gently lifted Del into his arms and spoke in a calm voice. "Gene, son, it's okay. Your brother's going to be okay. Open the back car door for Daddy, and you and Laurel get in front with Mama. Sarah, you have to drive us to Doc Edwards's place. Hurry."

Mama turned on her and Gene before they could obey Daddy, and she started barking orders. "Get in this car, Laurel

Elaine. Are you deaf? And *you,*" she pointed to Gene, "you're the oldest. You should've been watching him. This is your fault, you and your daddy and his hot temper."

She and Gene scampered into the car, and Daddy yelled at Mama as he cradled a sobbing Del in his arms. "Just shut the hell up, Sarah! For once, will you think about somebody besides yourself? Get us to Doc's place and lay off the kids. This is our fault—you and me—not theirs."

On that defining day their places in the family became indelibly stamped on their individual psyches, and never again did her parents express a trace of love toward each other. They just coexisted. They were like two oxen yoked together, never pulling in the same direction, only sinking deeper into the mire.

Gene, because he wasn't supposed to be born in the first place, became the convenient scapegoat doomed to always be in the wrong place at the wrong time such that the end results of their warped family dynamic could perpetually be dumped on him. Daddy became a workaholic, burying himself in his construction business. He never stopped trying to make it up to Del that he had been in the driver's seat of the car that had almost killed him.

Even though Del completely healed physically, his tortured psyche became the expression of the discord between Mama and Daddy. He'd been wounded as an innocent bystander in a war in which he'd had no part. Each side professed to love him, but they hadn't protected him from the fog of war, hadn't shielded him from the friendly fire. That was bad enough. But despite Daddy's loving attention, Mama made him believe that this horrible accident had happened because he wasn't a proper member of the family.

As for her place, Laurel became her family's audience, the onlooker who saw all sides of the disagreements, whose comprehensive perspective could have changed things. But Mama wouldn't allow the baby of the family that much credibility. Mama became the judge and the jury. From that point forward everything filtered through her even though she never had the objectivity to be fair.

Mama had been the one to search unceasingly for the next two years until she found a doctor brave enough to offer surgery to undo the country doctor's inept bone setting, which had left Del with a miserably twisted right arm. It was Mama who administered the months of rehabilitation afterwards, and it was Mama who dictated that Del reach her goal of using that arm without even a hint of evidence of his previous injury.

Laurel remembered Del's therapy well and how she'd hurt for his suffering. He would get frustrated when Mama made him fight the pain and do the arm exercises. He would cry and refuse to do it, but Mama wouldn't ease off. She soon learned that if she taunted him and made him mad, he would lift even the heaviest of the weights, glowering angrily at her. So, for Del, even that benign act bound him to Mama in a love-hate relationship.

Laurel couldn't comprehend what had attracted her parents to each other in the first place or how they could have negotiated a truce long enough to conceive either Gene or her. They had nothing in common, and they seemed to hate each other. Daddy had been quiet, hard-working, and introspective. Mama could have been Joan of Arc. She was liberated before they invented the word, and she was perpetually at war for some cause.

Laurel got to her feet, dusted off her coat, and pulled it closer to her body as she stepped to the other side of the plot to stand over the mound of Daddy's grave again. She gazed down at the rose she had already placed there. It wasn't a fitting tribute. Nothing was. She had adored this man. He lived on a pedestal, and she worshipped him from afar; but she had never expected him to solve her problems. He'd had too many of his own.

Did he know how much she loved him, how much she had cherished being his little girl? Did he know that every good thing that she was she got from him, that there would be a hole in her heart forever from losing him?

It wasn't that she didn't love Mama, but loving her had been painful. Love did strange things to Mama, and she didn't know how to accept it. To her, love was control. She had to be the ultimate authority in her children's lives. Everyone and everything else had to come second, even God.

She had finally ripped herself free from Mama's invisible cords of guilt, but she still bore the psychic scars of that amputation. Sometimes the phantom pains were hard to bear. Her brothers had been too entangled in their individual ways of coping with Mama's control to recognize the need for separate and healthy lives. They hadn't escaped the way Laurel had, and now in addition to her other wounds, she had survivor's guilt. She hadn't been able to help them. She couldn't make Mama change. She had tried.

It would have been simpler if she could have hated Mama, but she had come to realize it was the strength she got from her that had allowed her to survive her. And that was the tragedy of it all. Nothing in this world was ever all bad, and nothing was ever all good. In her family it always rained when the sun shined, and their rainbow got refracted away from them or completely absorbed by the energy of the opposing clouds.

Still, she had always looked for the rainbow, thinking it was the damning rain that caused their pain and that if they could ever stop the rain and let the sun shine all by itself they could find their rainbow. Her idealistic streak came from Mama, acquired either by association or in the DNA she had given her.

Granddaddy Cowan always told Mama she had her wagon hitched to a star. She had her goals, and she could have soared. She did accomplish amazing things, but Mama's problem in realizing her most important dreams came not in her vision but in her choices. She always willingly chose paths that kept her earthbound.

As Laurel rubbed the cold granite of the headstone that joined Mama and Daddy in death in an intimacy and peace they'd never found in life, she acknowledged that she hadn't always understood that about Mama. So, stuck in the mundane with all Mama's dreams languishing around her, she had felt duty-bound to play the surrogate and jump into that wagon and fly them all to the stars. She was the observer, after all. Hadn't she known what her family needed to be happy?

She had learned the hard way that the most vital part of her mother's failure lay in lack of commitment, that she didn't want to go anywhere and neither did the rest of her family. They might have been unhappy in the life they'd chosen, but they were firmly rooted in its familiarity while Laurel's soul had yearned to reach those heights Mama had pointed her toward.

For so many years Laurel's life had been an ongoing balance of helping her out-of-control family to survive and of trying to realize her own dreams. Many times she had feared that she would be grounded in the mire of their bad choices, but she had never wanted to choose between her dreams and theirs. Eleven years ago she had been forced to make that choice.

She crossed the path that separated the large expanse of the Harper plot and crouched to deliver her last rose. Tears blurred the inscription on the headstone, *Gene Sinclair Harper*, and her gloved fingers snagged on the etching in the cold granite as she traced them over the indentation of each letter.

"Everyone thought you were fearless," she whispered stroking her brother's name, "but you didn't think you deserved to live, so you just didn't care. You never stood a chance, did you? She made you believe you were born against God's will. It wasn't true. You were a gift. You were supposed to be loved and cherished." Warm tears trickled down her cold cheeks.

"I loved you, and I wanted to save you. I tried, but instead it was you who saved me. You gave me the courage to walk away. Rest in peace."

Chapter One

August 9, 1971

"Before we adjourn I want to remind you that our new lab chief starts tomorrow morning. Grady's going to be sorely missed, but he's found us a winner to replace him."

David half-listened as Stu rambled on about the new employee's qualifications. He tuned out most of his boss's words and concentrated on his notes. He wanted to be sharp today. He was assisting Miles on a frozen section at two o'clock.

Stu called these short meetings the "morning huddle." David thought of them as a waste of time, but it did keep them in touch with the daily functioning of the general lab. That was good especially when it involved a new chief. Still, it wasn't going to matter all that much to him, a lowly first-year pathology resident.

"Can you show our new chief around, David?" He suddenly became aware that Stu was speaking directly to him now.

"She's a very impressive young lady," Miles added. "Her name's Laurel Harper."

He snapped to full attention then, looking up from his notes. He felt like he'd been punched in the gut. It rendered him mute.

He glanced from Stu to Miles and then to Grady. *Laurel Harper? Did he really say Laurel?*

Grady flashed him a devious grin. What the hell was going on? Then Grady leaned toward Stu. "Why don't you let me take care of it? I'm sure David will get the opportunity to show her around." He smiled again. Oh, he was enjoying himself. Why hadn't he told him about this?

"Sure, no problem," Stu agreed good-naturedly. "It's just that she's David's age. I thought she might relate to you better, David. In fact, she trained here eight years ago about when you did. I was hoping you'd know her."

Did he know her? Oh yeah, but he didn't want to talk about it in morning huddle. Luckily, given Stu's short attention span, he didn't wait for a response. He dismissed them and left his office chatting with Miles about an autopsy he'd done the day before. Grady was making his escape right behind them.

"Not so fast, Grady. I'd like a word with you." He folded his notebook shut as he stood, slipped it into his lab coat pocket, and moved forward to confront Grady.

Grady paused in the doorway and flashed him a sly grin. "You do realize I've got a million things to do. It's my last week as chief tech, you know."

"I thought you were interviewing Gladys Pike for your position."

"But you said mousy Gladys could never handle this zoo."

"It's not like my opinion counts in all this."

"Why, David, I thought you, of all people, would be thrilled that Laurel's coming back."

"You could have warned me. Why didn't you say something?"

He shrugged. "Because I fully intended to hire Gladys, but then Laurel called a month ago asking if I had any openings. Given her experience as a chief tech she'd be a total waste in a mere tech position. Stu and Miles trusted my judgment, so I hired her."

"She's a chief tech now?"

Grady nodded.

"Where?"

"At Mountain General up on Sunset Mountain."

"Really? And just how long has she been there?"

"Since she left here."

"And you recommended her for the job, I guess, even though you told me you had no idea where she was."

"I did not. It appears she landed the position all by herself." He shrugged again. "As smart as she is, that shouldn't surprise any of us."

"But I was told five years ago that she'd moved away from Sunset Mountain to parts unknown."

"Well, somebody lied because she told me she's been there since she left here in the fall of '66."

"Does she know I'm on the pathology staff?"

"It was on the tip of my tongue, but the second I mentioned your name she told me you're ancient history and she'd prefer not to talk about you."

Yeah, he figured she'd say something like that.

"That means she still has feelings for you."

"I'm sure. Hatred, loathing, and contempt just to mention a few."

"That's not the way I read her. If I was going to be around, I'd see what I could do to mend things between the two of you."

"What makes you think that would be a good idea?"

Grady gave his shoulder a fatherly squeeze. "Since the day you hopped this circus, my young friend, you've had a burning desire for two things and two things only, going to medical school and Laurel Harper. Her burning desire was you. Granted, you were prone to frequent distraction by all the sideshows along the way when she was nothing but steadfast. But you've grown up a lot in the last few years. I believe you can handle this one on your own."

"You think so, huh?" He felt miserable, so why was he trying to pretend it didn't matter? Grady knew everything anyway. Well, almost everything.

Grady was still talking, so David focused his attention back to him. "I do need to warn you—"

"About what?"

"Life has pretty much stomped the sweet out of her, and things are a bit more complicated with her now."

"What do you mean?"

Grady sighed. "I really do have a lot to do, and I have to get going. You'll find out soon enough." Then Grady turned from the doorway, and the last thing David saw was the bald spot at the back of his head as he rounded the corner toward his office.

He lingered in the doorway thinking about Grady's parting words. How could things not be complicated? Just seeing Laurel again was going to be complicated, not to mention working with her, and the last thing he had a right to expect was that she'd be sweet about any of it.

He forced himself to get moving, and he made a quick detour through the lounge to the coffeepot. He needed a stiff drink, but coffee was going to have to do for right now. After being unreachable for five years, Laurel was coming back to City General. He couldn't believe it.

When David had finished his internship and become a pathology resident two months ago, Grady Banks' impending retirement and the search for his replacement had been the focus of his first morning huddle. The announcement hadn't upset him all that much even though the man had been his ongoing mentor since he'd entered the lab tech program back in 1963. But Grady was the job personified, and David hadn't believed he'd actually retire.

He took a sip from the Styrofoam cup he'd just filled from the full carafe and immediately fought the urge to spit the gosh-awful liquid back into the cup. Audrey hadn't made coffee worth a crap when he was a lab student, and she sure as hell hadn't improved in the eight years since. Most of the time it was at least drinkable, but this morning's offering was pushing it.

Coffee cup in hand he took a left outside the lounge and headed toward the morgue through the main lab office. He called to the secretary as he passed through, gesturing with his cup. "Someday, Audrey, you're going to sell this formula to Texaco, and I can say I knew you when."

Audrey giggled giving her gray-brown curls a jiggle. "Hey, David, guess what. Laurel Harper's coming back. You, Laurel, and me. It's going to be like old home week around here."

He felt that constriction in his gut again. It moved up to his chest and took his breath away, but he managed to keep his voice light. "So I hear."

"I hear she's got a kid now," Edna the other secretary piped up.

Thankfully, both lines on the main lab phone rang abruptly because he felt his knees go so weak he had to grab the door facing with his free hand to steady himself. He regained his composure while Edna cradled her phone between her cheek and left shoulder and jotted notes on the pad in front of her. Audrey placed her call on hold and rose to search through the file cabinet for a report. She glanced toward him again as she headed back to the call. He held up the coffee cup and forced a smile. "To old-home week," he said.

Chapter Two

"Well, that's the last of it." Betty Jo collapsed into the platform rocker, smoothing her palms over its maple arms. "I'm glad your apartment is on the second floor and not the third. Whew! We must've made ten thousand trips from my truck and your car."

Laurel retrieved two Cokes from the refrigerator in her cozy new kitchen, setting them on the drop-down bar that separated it from the living-dining area. She flipped the caps off the bottles and walked into the living area, handing one to her cousin. Betty Jo always exaggerated. They'd made around six trips apiece. Tops.

"I appreciate it that you got your friends to move the furniture for me." With the heavy stuff already in place she could get the apartment in order by noon. She would have plenty of time to pick up Gena at Mama Rita's and get her settled here before dinner. She glanced at Betty Jo. "I got the bedrooms and bath unpacked and arranged while you were gone to show the guys the shortcut back to the foot of the mountain. Thanks to you I'm way ahead of schedule."

Betty Jo took a sip of her Coke. "Thanks to Ben and Bobby having more muscles than brains, you mean."

"Twenty dollars apiece hardly seems like enough for them. Are you sure I shouldn't have paid them more?"

Betty Jo waved her hand in the air dismissively. "Nah, if you give the idiots too much, they'll just blow it on Sparky Hall's moonshine and end up in the ER at Mountain General."

Betty Jo was probably right about the moonshine. Ben and Bobby were Banjo Whitt's twins. Her brother, Gene, and Banjo were Sunset Mountain's most notorious drunks, and so far the acorn hadn't fallen far from the tree with Banjo's eighteen-year-old boys. Like her brother, when stone-cold sober the twins had been affable, even sweet, and she'd found herself wishing she could do something to avert their paths from disaster, something that so far seemed impossible with her thirty-six-year-old brother.

She picked up a small box labeled "living room" and went to sit on her patchwork patterned chair. She glanced around the apartment as she set the box on the coffee table. It was a nice place, and her Sears, Roebuck furniture fit well: her blue sofa with its tiny red flowers that looked so good with the patchwork and plaid chairs; the two solid maple step end tables; and the matching coffee table. Then there was her maple dinette set that fit perfectly in the dining alcove.

The rest of her furniture was used except for the mattresses, which also came from Sears. She'd put the mattress sets along with the other furniture on her charge account at separate times and paid them off within eighteen months of each purchase. She had bought Aunt Emmaline's old cherry bedroom suite: double bed, nightstands, dresser, and chest on chest. It was in fantastic shape, and she had gotten it for thirty dollars.

Two years ago when Gena outgrew her baby bed, Laurel bought her cousin Amelia's twin bedroom suite. It was solid mahogany, and the beds were four-posters with acorn spindles. She'd bought some purple eyelet at Chandler's Fabrics and made coverlets for them and matching window curtains. Gena had squealed in glee, which had made it all worth the effort. Purple was her favorite color.

The apartment was nice and cozy with new paint and freshly shampooed carpet, but the best thing about it was that it was immediately across the street from the hospital. The sprawling complex was four years old and had replaced the rows of shacks that used to line Tenth and Baldwin Streets, effectively taking City General Hospital out of the ghetto where it used to reside.

She glanced at Betty Jo who was now standing at the bar unpacking a box of kitchen utensils. "This is a nice place," she said to her cousin, "but I'll have to admit I'm going to miss my little house, my flower garden, my cute little backyard."

"And weeding and mowing your cute little grass. How could you miss that?" Betty Jo took a sip of her Coke, set it back on the bar, and bent to deposit some pots into a lower kitchen cabinet.

"It wasn't so bad. It was a small lawn."

"Daddy said Aunt Sarah had a cow when you told her you'd sold your house and were moving back down here."

"Mama had a cow when I bought that house in the first place. She never approves of anything I do."

"She cried and carried on and told Daddy how mean you are to take her only grandchild and move away."

Laurel rolled her eyes. "What does she think Julie and Amy are?" She got up to place Gena's most recent professionally made eight-by-ten-inch portrait on top of the television, padding it with a crocheted doily. Mama had made the doily back when her hobbies were less deadly than the games she now played with her health and the lives of her children.

Betty Jo shot her a mischievous grin. "Del's stepchildren don't count. They don't have Cowan blood coursing through their veins."

"Lucky them." Laurel bent to retrieve more items from the box on the coffee table. Then she moved to disperse some keepsakes to the left step end table on the level below the red tole lamp: Gena's baby picture and her silver baby rattle engraved with her date of birth and a carving of a chopping block complete with an ax and a miniature whiskey jug. Gene had carved that for her last Christmas. "Mama was overjoyed when Julie and Amy went to live with their real dad. They're both sweet kids. I don't know why she couldn't accept them. Daddy loved them."

"Uncle Sinclair loved everybody." Betty Jo unpacked the dishes Laurel had carefully wrapped, and she paused to glance up at her. "Well, except for Aunt Sarah. I don't think he liked her too much."

On the other end table beneath the glow of the brass pole lamp's bullet-shaped lights she set the Avon candle Daddy had bought her the last Christmas he was alive. Instantly an image of him flashed across her mind. He was dressed in a blue plaid flannel shirt and denim work pants. Daddy hadn't smiled much. He was the ultimate stoic, and it had been hard to tell when he was happy or sad. Maybe he was happy now. She hoped so. If anybody deserved to be happy, it was Daddy.

Betty Jo spoke again, and her conjured vision of Daddy evaporated. "Mama Rita told me that Aunt Sarah's been nagging you on the subject of Gena's daddy again and that Aunt Sarah thinks it's time you told her the truth."

She placed the red Fenton compote Mama Rita had given her on the end table on the level beneath the candle. "Which is exactly why I made this move. I'll tell Gena when I think she's ready, and I don't want Mama or anyone else on that mountain giving her their sordid version of it. Since I can't padlock their mouths, I had no choice but to move away."

"How are you going to keep Aunt Sarah from telling her when you visit? Or Del?"

"I won't leave her alone with either of them, and if Mama keeps this up, I just won't visit. I'm going to tell Gena when she's five anyway. I've been gradually preparing her for it since the day she was born, and I refuse to let this be done the wrong way. I won't have Mama traumatizing her."

"You do know that Aunt Sarah's going to have another deathbed crisis to get you back for this. She's overdue for one anyway."

Betty Jo, who was Mama's brother Nathan's child, was the only member of her family who ever openly addressed the opinion that Mama made her illness worse than it had to be. Consoling as it was to have someone else recognize the truth as she saw it, that didn't make Mama's situation any easier to take. "One day she's going to go too far, Betty Jo, and she won't be able to bounce back. I don't see how she's alive now, and every crisis she loses something. Sometimes I don't think I can take a second more of it. Her life didn't have to be this way." Her voice broke into a hoarse croak. She stopped and took in a deep breath. Every time she talked about this she felt as if she would suffocate.

She busied herself with stacking the emptied boxes near the door so she could carry them down to the dumpster. She laid the wreath she'd made of dried rosebuds and baby's breath on top of them. She'd tack it outside her door on her way to dump the boxes. She felt Betty Jo watching her. When she could breathe normally again, she spoke softly.

"I know everyone on Sunset Mountain blames me for Mama's illness. Well, Gene and I get to share the blame equally now that Daddy's gone. Gene hides from Mama in booze and drugs. I just physically run away. But not Del—oh, no. He's been right there molded to her will doing her dirty work ever since Daddy died. He's ruined his marriage. I don't know why Connie stays with him. She's miserable living in Mama's house."

"You have a right to your own life, Laurel."

"Mama doesn't see it that way. When I moved back home for that month after Daddy died, I couldn't take it. I paid rent, bought groceries for everybody, and paid the power bill; but it wasn't enough for Mama. She tried to control every breath I took. The minute those houses at the old army base went on sale I jumped at the opportunity. It may have only been six miles away, but it was enough. Until now, that is."

"I don't blame you for Aunt Sarah's illness, and neither do Mama and Daddy. You know that Mama Rita and Grandpa don't. Aunt Sarah wasn't happy even before Uncle Sinclair died. I could see that even though I was a kid, but, boy, she's self-destructed since his accident. Maybe there really was some love there."

"Or maybe it's just because Daddy got all the attention by dying, and she just couldn't stand that. I know she makes her condition worse than it has to be just for the attention she gets. Stupid me, at the beginning I thought I could get her the help she needed if I moved closer to her. But then how was I supposed to know dying would become a life pursuit for her?"

"How on earth did she and Uncle Sinclair ever get along long enough to have you and Gene?" Betty Jo had finished unpacking the kitchen already, and now she was kneeling to inspect the other unpacked boxes.

"Your guess is as good as mine about that." She squatted with Betty Jo near the six remaining boxes. "I'll put these records in the record cabinet if you'll put the books in the bookcase."

"Consider it done."

She pulled the three boxes of records over to the left living room corner where her stereo cabinet sat. The twins had hooked up the record player, tuner, and speakers before they left. She sat cross-legged on the beige carpet and started filing Gena's story-time records first. Betty Jo worked on the other side of the television, sorting Gena's Little Golden Books to the top shelf of her small bookcase.

"Are you excited about starting nursing school?" Laurel asked.

"Yep. I pick up my books and uniforms tomorrow. Classes start week after next. Thanks for getting me in."

"You're the one who aced the entrance exam. I didn't do anything."

"Sure you did. You gave me that glowing recommendation, which helps bunches because you're in big time with the head cheese—you know, on a first-name basis with the hospital administrator, the head nurse, and the director of the nursing school."

"I'm not so in. It's just that when you work together for five years building something from the ground up, you dispense with the titles. But I also knew Byron and Miranda from City General. He was an assistant administrator. She was second-shift nursing supervisor."

"Really? And now she's head nurse, and he's the big daddy boss."

"Yes. As for Hortense Foster, Byron coaxed her out of retirement with a nice salary package. His family owns the hospital. His dad owned the building when it was a 1920s resort hotel. When the hotel business dwindled to being open summers only, Byron convinced him to let him turn it into a hospital."

"I didn't know Mr. Laughlin was old money from out on the mountaintop. He doesn't act like most of those snobs."

"Byron had vision and a heart to go with it. He saw the need, had the money, and hired people he thought he could count on to help him make it work. You work harder when someone believes in you that much. I'm grateful to him for the chance to prove myself. I know he couldn't possibly identify with us have-nots, but he's so good-hearted you can't think of him as the enemy."

"If you ask me, he's got a crush on you. Did you ever date him?"

She shook her head. Byron had asked her out several times, but she had deftly refused. Why pursue something that was a dead end? Not that he wasn't desirable, but there was no future in it. He was a handsome guy and a good person, but their backgrounds were too different. And then there was the problem of not being able to feel anything for him.

"He's a friend, not to mention my boss," she finally said. "I couldn't accept a date with him."

"Oh, my gosh! That means he asked you out. Gorgeous Mr. Laughlin who's loaded to boot asked you out, and you didn't go?"

Betty Jo's probing smarted although Laurel knew she hadn't meant for it to. She chewed on her lower lip as she remembered acutely why Byron couldn't measure up, why no one could ever measure up.

Betty Jo paused in her task and straightened. "Sorry. I didn't mean to step on any graves. Daddy says I'm the Mouth of the South. I'll probably get my butt expelled the first week of school. If Hortense Foster is as crotchety and prudish as her name sounds I might as well not even start."

She had to laugh at both Betty Jo's unique way of expressing herself and her assessment of the feisty head of the nursing school. She loved Betty Jo, and even though she was eleven years younger, she was her best friend. She'd been smart and intuitive even as a preschooler. She picked up on things, and although Laurel had never discussed her deeply personal pain, Betty Jo knew. She connected the dots of body language, tidbits of information, and suppressed emotions like a psychic. She would make a great nurse. Tennie Foster was going to love her, too.

"Don't worry about Tennie," she said. "She used to be an army nurse. You can't shock or insult her."

"Tennie? Good, she's got a decent nickname. Now I won't have to point out that she'll never get a man with a frumpy name like Hortense. She's not that old and definitely not that ugly. She has a chance without that awful name."

Betty Jo placed a stack of textbooks on the second shelf of the bookcase then paused to leaf through a thick book Laurel recognized by size and color as her Todd and Sanford from medical technology training.

"You can borrow that book if you like. It's the best all around lab manual you can find. Read that and you'll be way ahead of your classmates when it comes to understanding the lab."

Betty Jo kept flipping. "I'll take you up on that. Looks like you've already taught me some of this stuff like blood typing and about white cells and red cells and how to do tests on pee pee." Betty Jo paused in her page-turning and pursed her lips. She strode over and tossed a piece of notebook paper into Laurel's lap. "But you probably want to keep this."

Laurel picked up the paper and turned it over to read the familiar poem written in neat cursive.

"Who's 'all my love, David'?" Betty Jo asked glancing sideways at her.

She shot her cousin an abrupt glance. Betty Jo paused briefly then cocked her eyebrow knowingly. "Oh, yeah, he's The One." She quickly went back to her task of loading the bookcase. "I was barely thirteen, but I remember The One."

Laurel felt a squeeze in her chest as she read the words of the romantic poem David had written for her the year she first met him. Then the familiar regret and pain came flooding back. She fought the tears. She was beyond this.

"Does he still work here?" Betty Jo asked with real caution in her usually impulsive voice.

"He'd be long gone by now. He started medical school two weeks after I left. Right after he married Marilee Baker."

"Men are lower than cow turds," Betty Jo muttered.

Chapter Three

David left the hospital at four o'clock and walked across Tenth Street. He entered the front lobby of Ridgeview Apartments and let the door ease shut behind him as he retrieved his mail from the rows of individually locked mailboxes just inside the door.

The cool air was a welcome relief from the ninety-eight-plus-degree temperature outside. He'd heard from Audrey that the heat index was 101 degrees today. August was like that in the Carolinas. He'd seen a bunch of empty boxes bulging from the dumpster behind the fence near the front entrance. Some poor tenant had moved into the complex in this heat. He sure didn't envy them that.

He'd lived here since the end of May when his salary as a resident had bumped his lifestyle up from the tiny furnished efficiency he'd had as an intern. The weather had been considerably cooler when he'd moved. He'd brought his bedroom suite from home. The rest of his furniture he'd bought from various relatives, or they'd donated them. His stereo had been the only thing he'd bought new. His furnishings were sparse, but everything had come together okay and looked fine to him.

Medical school had been expensive, but he'd worked as a lab tech part-time for living expenses, and thanks to Grady's efforts he'd gotten scholarships for full tuition. Now he was debt-free. Dad had helped with unexpected expenses, but he'd tried hard to manage without his funds. His father had grown up during the Great Depression and had worked hard all his life. David wanted him and Mom to enjoy the fruits of their labors in their senior years. They'd both worked hard, and they had a comfortable life thanks to good planning.

Mom couldn't understand why he didn't just live at home and had nagged him constantly about it. He'd turned a deaf ear though. He knew she meant well, but he'd be thirty his next birthday. Why would he want to live with a woman who used to pilfer his room and count his condoms? Not that he would have that problem now. He'd devoted so much time and energy to becoming a doctor he could qualify as a monk.

And to think he used to be notorious. When he'd returned to City General a little over a year ago to start his internship, he'd had to live down his reputation. The hospital gossips spent their idle time trying to figure out what had made him change his philandering ways, and the man-eaters were forever attempting to rehabilitate him by offering their services. The rest of the women tried to fix him up with their single relatives—everybody but Audrey.

Audrey knew what had changed him. She knew that although the grueling four years in medical school had been his dream, it was also his place to hide his broken heart. She also knew that he'd deserved it, but she'd been kind enough to be his friend.

He climbed the stairs and walked down the hallway to Apartment 210. As he slid his key into the door lock, he noticed a wreath on the adjacent door. When he'd left for work this morning it hadn't been there. The apartment's last occupant had moved out three weeks ago. Today's new arrival must be his neighbor, probably some poor slob of a medical resident moving up in the world like him. He was probably married thus the feminine door display. Guys didn't give a crap what their doors looked like.

Maybe he should go welcome them, but later—much later. He needed to unwind first, and it would help if he was in a better mood. He dropped his keys onto the kitchen bar and headed to his second bedroom turned office. He threw the mail haphazardly onto his desk. It was all bills and junk mail anyway. He set his stereo to play the 33-1/3 record already on the spindle, kicked off his shoes, and slumped into the desk chair. He leaned back and listened as the strains of Rachmaninoff's Concerto no. 2 filled the room.

He closed his eyes, and the memory of her filled his senses against the pathos of Moderato; Allegro. Why had he been such a fool? What was he going to say to her? Was she happy now, or was she just treading water like him?

He ran his fingers through his hair and sighed. It was too overwhelming, all of this at once: the sweet memories, the guilt, the pain, the thought of seeing her again, working with her. He needed a buffer. He got up and headed toward the antique icebox Mom had given him. He'd refinished it and made it into a liquor cabinet. Mom hadn't figured out what he was using it for yet. It was better that she didn't know. She'd lecture him about the evils of alcohol until he had calluses on his ears.

Well, he wasn't an alcoholic. He wasn't going to be an alcoholic, but he sure needed the comfort of a stiff drink right now. He pulled a glass from the top shelf and poured some J&B Rare, two fingers. He'd skip the water for this one.

He paced and sipped. He'd pulled Laurel's file before he left the hospital. He had every right. He *was* one of her bosses. As Edna had announced, she indeed had a child. She was listed right there in black and white as her dependent, a little girl named Gena Renee Harper.

Was Laurel married? She hadn't changed her name if she was or the child's. Laurel wouldn't have kept her maiden name if she'd married. She wasn't one of these bra-burning feminists unless she had changed. But why wouldn't she? It had been five years.

He took another sip of scotch and rolled it around in his mouth. When he swallowed, it felt warm going down, and the warmth slowly seeped toward his limbs relaxing him. If only it could warm his heart.

He tried to shake off the one thing that had been haunting him since he'd read that file. In addition to using her maiden name, Laurel had marked single, not divorced. The child had her last name. Her birth date was May 14, 1967. Their night of sweet passion had been August 13, 1966, almost exactly nine months before. Was this his child? They hadn't used protection. It had been too spontaneous and pure, but it had only happened that one time. Still, once was all you needed.

He'd replayed that night many times in the past five years. They had gone to a movie, and afterwards they'd parked at their favorite secluded spot by the lake. By that time he had known Laurel for three years, and even though they had dated off and on for that entire time, necking was all they had ever done. He'd felt she wanted more. He for sure did, but she wasn't the kind of girl to give in to her passions. Sex was special to her. It had to involve love and commitment. He'd respected that. He'd respected her, more than any girl he'd ever met.

He hadn't shared his dreams with many people, but he'd shared them with Laurel. He'd dreamed of becoming a doctor ever since he was a child. As the son of a pipe fitter that hadn't been a realistic goal, at least according to his ninth grade guidance counselor. The man had tried to discourage him, but not Laurel. She believed in him, more than Grady, more than his parents, maybe even more than he believed in himself. By their last night together he had already taken the medical school entrance exam and had been accepted for the fall quarter that was to begin in a few weeks.

"I'm so happy for you," she'd said softly, "but I'll miss you. Memphis is a long way from home."

He'd squeezed her close and nuzzled her hair just above her ear, breathing in her fresh, sweet scent. "I'll miss you, too. Maybe I'll kidnap you and take you with me."

He could tell by the way she pulled away a little that she didn't take those words as seriously as he had meant them. Ironically, it had been in that exact moment that he'd known for sure that what he felt for her was love.

Giddy from that sudden realization he'd grabbed her hand and beckoned. "Let's go look at the stars. It's a beautiful night."

She slid out of the car on his side. He opened his car trunk and retrieved a blanket and his portable reel-to-reel tape recorder. They found a spot at the crest of the hill overlooking the lake. He spread the blanket, and they sat down.

"You like Rachmaninoff, don't you?" he asked, reaching to place his recorder at the edge of the blanket.

She nodded and smiled. "He was one of the few composers who didn't put me to sleep in music appreciation."

"This particular piece is my favorite. I taped it from my record, so it's a little fuzzy. It's his Concerto no. 2." He'd reached to press the play button, and this same music he was now listening to filled the warm night air.

Maybe it had been the angst of the music or the way she was looking at him, her eyes soft in the moonlight, but he'd known by the time they'd listened to the first few minutes of the music that he couldn't leave her.

"We could get married," he'd said suddenly, surprising himself as much as he'd surprised her. "I love you, Laurel. I know that now."

He could read the shocked expression on her face even in the moonlight. She gazed at the blanket tracing her forefinger across the fabric. "What happened to the guy who wanted to play the field and have fun with all his other women? That guy who didn't want to get seriously involved?"

He moved closer, and with his free hand he tilted her chin so that she had to look at him. "That guy was a fool."

"I've been here for a long time, David. You've known from the beginning how much I love you. Why now and not then?" Her face was inches away. She looked into his eyes.

"I've grown up, baby. I know I've hurt you by being so unsettled, and I'm so sorry for that. Please forgive me. I love you, and I don't want to lose you."

"When did you all of a sudden decide this?" she asked softly. She was so cautious, but then why shouldn't she question his intentions? He'd been an irresponsible playboy for as long as she'd known him.

"When I realized that going to school is going to mean you won't be in my life. It's all I've thought about from the minute I read that acceptance letter and the only thing that puts a damper on this for me."

"You really mean that?" She was softening. He could feel it.

"With all my heart, and if I leave you, you'll still own my heart. Marry me, sweetheart. Go to Memphis with me."

"When?" She touched his face with her fingertips, and he could feel that they were trembling.

"As soon as possible."

"I'll go anywhere with you, David, as long as I know you love me the way I love you."

After that, one passionate touch led to another, and before he could think about whether it could hurt her or not, they were making love. He hadn't intended for things to get out of control, and that had made it sweeter. It had been so natural and so right to make love to her. It was serendipity. It was meant to be.

If he'd just dealt with his past before that perfect night such that it couldn't hurt their future … but he hadn't, and the next day it all came undone.

They made a date for the next morning to talk about wedding plans. It was a Sunday, and he planned to go by early to pick her up. When the stores opened in the afternoon they'd go shopping for the ring. He'd been giddy with happiness. He'd never known he could be so happy.

That next morning after he arrived at the hospital dorm where she'd lived since he'd known her, he waited in the living room, thumbing through the Sunday paper while the house mother called for her. That had been when he saw that damned announcement of Marilee's. Beneath her picture the caption read, "Marilee Baker betrothed to David Hudson, Labor Day wedding planned."

Shocked, he quickly scanned the announcement that listed a best man and groomsmen he didn't even know. He wondered what in the hell Marilee was up to. Then he remembered that the week before she'd mentioned fearing that she was pregnant. He'd figured her intern boyfriend must have knocked her up but wouldn't marry her, and she was trying to pin it on him to make the guy jealous.

It was so like her. She'd been a philanderer just like he was even from the beginning when he'd been stupid enough to trust her. After he'd learned what she was, they'd used each other. He'd been attracted to her looks, which had been an enticing mix of girl next door and Playboy centerfold. It hadn't taken him long to realize there was nothing attractive inside the pretty package, yet once he'd realized it, he'd kept dating her. It had been one of those male territorial things.

That morning he'd faced not only the stupidity but the immorality of his actions, and he'd been ashamed. It was going to cost him, too. He'd known that before it all blew up in his face.

As he read the last sentence of the announcement stating that the happy couple would reside in Memphis after the wedding, he heard a slight movement behind him. He turned to see that Laurel had entered the living room from the side hallway. Her face was ashen, and she held up the same announcement that was spread on the coffee table before him.

"Explain this to me, David." So much anguish infused her voice that it ripped at his heart.

He stood and met her halfway. "I did not propose to Marilee. I swear it."

"Then where did she get the idea?"

"She's using me to make her newest boyfriend jealous. I'm not even going to be here on Labor Day, and I've never met any of these people in this announcement, least of all my supposed best man."

"You know Marilee."

"But I didn't propose to her, Laurel."

"Then why is she doing this? If it's not true, why would she risk embarrassing herself like this?"

Seconds ticked by as he tried to think of a way to explain what he thought was going on without making things worse, but she misinterpreted that silence and went on the offensive.

"You can't marry both of us, David. Was this just a first-come-first-served offer, and she got there first?" Tears welled in her eyes. "You didn't want to be lonely while you were off in school studying, and you needed a woman for your off times? Or maybe last night was just another one of your conquests, and you never intended to marry me."

He placed his hands on her shoulders, and she looked up into his eyes, biting her lip. "That's not the way it is, Laurel. I love you. You're the only girl I've ever proposed to, and I had nothing to do with this announcement."

She glanced away from him. "She's a slut, you know, but then I don't guess that matters to you because she's so beautiful, like Marilyn Monroe, like a movie star. There should be some law that demands that girls like her are as ugly on the outside as they are on the inside. Then you wouldn't be fooled into thinking you could ever trust her."

"I know she can't be trusted. This whole marriage thing is her using me as her backup, but I never thought she'd go this far. She thinks she's pregnant, and she's using me as her cover."

"What?! When did you find out about this?"

"Last week."

"So you proposed to me so you'd have an excuse to give her because you know I'd never force you to go through with something you didn't mean to begin with. You wouldn't have to marry her and support your child, and you could be free to do what you always do. Is that it?"

"No, that's not the way it is. And in spite of what this stupid announcement says, Marilee doesn't want to marry me."

"What about her baby?"

"I'd stake my life on the fact that she's not pregnant."

"If you hadn't slept with her, she wouldn't have grounds to accuse you."

He was guilty of that, something he was sure she knew. He wanted to smooth things over the way he always did, clouding honesty with vagueness by neither admitting nor denying it. He'd wanted to take advantage of her forgiving nature, but the previous night had changed everything. He couldn't be that person anymore.

There was only one point in his favor in the whole mess. Even though he hadn't made it a practice to be morally responsible, at least he'd had enough sense to practice birth control. Finally, he responded. "I always used protection, and if she's even pregnant at all—which, as I told you, I doubt—there's no way it could be mine."

She went nuts then, not that he blamed her. "Do you think I want to stand here and listen to this after last night?!" she hissed. She crumpled the announcement and threw it at him.

"Laurel, please. Last night meant everything. You have to believe me."

"No, I don't believe you. This couldn't be happening if you really loved me. You couldn't have slept with someone else if you loved me the way I love you. I've wanted you for the past three years, but I didn't give in because it wouldn't have been right. Last night I thought it was right. I guess that proves what a fool I am."

"No, no, baby. No." He reached for her again.

She shook her head slowly back and forth and pulled away. Tears were trickling down her cheeks. "I don't regret it because I love you, and it was the purest thing in the world to me. I don't understand how something that pure could be wrong, but it had to be or this wouldn't be happening."

"This is happening because I've been immature and selfish. I just had to prove I was a man, and I've gone about it in all the wrong ways. Last night you taught me what love and being a man is all about. I meant everything I said to you. Please believe me, Laurel. I'm not going to marry Marilee. I didn't propose. I didn't even suggest it, and I didn't know she was going to put that announcement in the paper."

"What are you going to do about her baby?"

"I told you. If there really is one, there's no way it could be mine. I always used protection."

"And that's supposed to excuse you, I guess."

"No, but as wrong as my actions have been, at least I was responsible."

"We didn't use protection." Her lips trembled as she spoke.

"Because I love you, and if you're pregnant, baby, it's okay. We're one now."

"Oh, don't you worry." Her voice was so bitter it stunned him. "I've counted back. Last night was a safe time."

"What if you're wrong?"

"I'm not wrong. But on the million-to-one chance that I'm not, then it'll be my responsibility. I'm not Marilee. I don't trap people. And, just so you know, I don't want anything from you, and I don't want you anywhere near me."

"Laurel, please listen to me."

"No, you listen. You got what you wanted. It's over. You're free to be with your precious Marilee. Now go away and leave me alone." With that she turned and ran back down the hallway toward the stairwell before he could even react.

He'd decided to try to talk to her the next day after she had cooled down and after he strangled Marilee, but tragedy struck. Her father had been involved in a head-on collision and brought into the City General ER early that next morning. Laurel was so visibly devastated that he couldn't bear to add to her pain. He asked if he could do anything to help, but she had guardedly told him no.

"My daddy's going to be fine," she told him through clenched teeth. "God wouldn't take him away from me, too."

That week she sat with her father every day when she got off work. He knew because he checked every day. Sitting with ICU patients wasn't usually allowed, but the head nurse was a personal friend to Laurel and had made an exception. On Wednesday, August 17, two days after the accident and immediately after his doctors had charted that Sinclair Harper was out of the woods, he suddenly died. The funeral was held that Saturday.

Audrey had been like a trusted big sister to both him and Laurel, so he had confided in her about his proposal to Laurel and the whole Marilee fiasco. She had advised him not to attend the funeral service. "It'll only make it worse for her," she had said. "Give her a little time." But the time he had given her had been enough for her to disappear.

When she hadn't returned to work the next week, he went to the dorm to check on her. The housemother told him she'd moved out the day after her father's death. He'd thought surely she would have told Audrey where she was going, but she hadn't. When he'd asked Grady, he said that she'd resigned and moved back to Sunset Mountain.

He'd looked up her father's records and got her parents' phone number, but even there he came up against a brick wall. The short time he had left before school started ran out, and he had to get ready to leave. He mailed letters to her parents' address when he was in Memphis, but she never answered. It was as if she'd dropped off the face of the earth.

Today after seeing on her application proof that for the entire past five years she had been at Mountain General Hospital up on Sunset Mountain, a thirty-minute drive from the valley, he was angry with fate, with himself, and especially with God. Hadn't he begged for forgiveness? Hadn't he changed, and hadn't he promised he'd make it up to her if God would just let him find her?

Now, here she was after five painful years, his answered prayer, and he didn't have a clue about what to say or do. God certainly had a warped sense of humor.

Chapter Four

As Laurel moved forward in the line at the hospital cafeteria, helping Gena guide her tray and make her food selections, poignant memories threatened to breach the protective wall she had built around her heart. It hadn't helped that a couple of hours ago the occupant of the next apartment had been playing Rachmaninoff's Concerto no. 2. That had reduced her to tears even after all these years.

Maybe it was a mistake coming back here. Memories were everywhere. Aside from her apartment complex, which had replaced the shacks across the street from the hospital, everything looked exactly the same. The old dorm where she used to live had the same scraggly hedge bordering the same dandelion-filled lawn. The hospital lobby with its black-and-white tiled floor and especially the cafeteria hadn't changed a bit. Even the tables seemed to be in exactly the same positions.

The place was too familiar with all the scents she remembered of good food mixed with the underlying antiseptic smell and the staff in their lab coats and white uniforms coming and going, reacting to the oral paging system the way she once had. Although Mountain General had many of the same characteristics, given its turrets and its commanding views of both the east and west valleys, it had been a bit like working in a castle in the clouds.

Here at City General her memories were so interwoven with the background that it was difficult to separate them. At the table in the far corner she could almost see herself sitting over coffee with David, leaning toward him, drinking in his essence. She could almost feel the warmth of his hand on hers and the tingling sensation of his touch. She could almost see the smile that had reduced her to a mass of romantic giddiness and those intense blue eyes that had told her so many things that in the end hadn't been true.

Something deep inside ached at the loss even as her common sense told her she was better off with him in her past. Well, she was going to have to be strong. These were only memories, after all. David was long gone from City General by now. She hadn't heard from him in all the years since she had left, and she hadn't wanted to know about his life.

Grady had mentioned his name just once, but she'd set him straight and asked him not to mention him again. What was the point in rubbing salt in her wounds? She knew he was married to Marilee Baker. Hadn't she seen their engagement announcement in the paper the next day after David had proposed to her?

Abruptly she reprimanded herself. *Stop it. That's ancient history. You have responsibilities now. You have a life. Maybe not the one you hoped for, but some parts of it you wouldn't change for anything.* She glanced at the sweet four-year-old at her side.

"Mommy, can I have some red Jell-O?"

"It's 'may I,' and yes, of course."

"Do we get to eat here a lot? I like it."

"We can make it our treat." She reached to transfer the heaviest items off Gena's tray so she could carry it herself. She had literally jumped up and down in glee at the challenge of that, and Laurel wasn't about to discourage her. She didn't want to be like Mama. Mama had always discouraged independence.

She remembered the big fight she and Mama had when she had moved into the hospital dorm as a paying tenant in 1963 at the beginning of her medical technology training. The best excuse Mama could give for her disapproval was that it wasn't safe. A locked-down brick fortress with a live-in housemother as the door master wasn't safe? It had been safe alright, safely away from Mama's control, and that had been what she'd objected to in the first place. But Mama had no cause to worry. Wherever Laurel went in Sunset Valley, the mountain loomed dark on the horizon reminding her where she came from and who was ultimately in control.

"I want to sit by the window. Can we see our 'partment from there?"

"We sure can. I'll show you when we get settled at our table."

When she paid for their food, she recognized the cashier although she couldn't remember her name. Trixie or Pixie, maybe? They exchanged pleasantries, and she smiled as the lady gave Gena a lollipop for dessert, telling her how adorable she was. They headed across the room then, and she watched as Gena set her tray expertly on the table and crawled up into a chair perching on her knees.

"Honey, they have booster chairs. I can get you one." She moved the rest of Gena's food back onto her tray.

"I like sitting on my knees." Gena was already munching a roll. She could have reprimanded her for talking with her mouth full, but this was a new adventure. Gena was so excited, and she wasn't going to do anything to make it unpleasant for her.

Even though leaving the mountain was best in the long run, she knew Gena was going to miss Mama Rita and Grandpa and even Mama. She was just a baby. How could she know how dangerous Mama's manipulations were or how detrimental gossip could be? She wanted to make this move a good experience. Both of them had loved their little house on Sunset Mountain, and both had been sad when she'd sold it to move here and take this job.

"How about that big playground at our new place? We've got a big old slide and swings and a merry-go-round, and Saturday when I don't have to work we'll go to the pool. Would you like to learn to swim?"

Gena nodded her head of shiny brown curls. She had definitely inherited Mama's hair genes. Gene had curly hair, too, in the same shade of brown as her own board-straight hair. She didn't mind that she didn't have curls. They made her look frumpy, and for a while there, her shiny straight hair had won her stares of appreciation from the opposite sex, especially David. He loved her hair. He was always running his fingers through it and …

She sighed, laid her fork aside, and took a sip of her tea. Okay, maybe she could cut herself some slack. She was on hallowed ground. Maybe if she just let herself go ahead and reminisce, she could get this completely out of her system. But what was the point in remembering the good times when it had all been a lie? What was the point in loving someone who had moved on with his life? She shouldn't still love him, but she couldn't deny that she did. She would always love the man she'd thought he was, but that didn't change the fact that he *had* moved on. He probably didn't even remember that she existed, and he had probably long ago forgotten what had been the most important moment of her life.

Chapter Five

David was on call and had just finished running interference for a problem between an intern and the lab. It was only five forty-five. It had the potential to be a long night given this new batch of interns and the man-hating second-shift tech who was pulling a double shift tonight for the vacationing third-shift tech.

He dropped by the cafeteria to grab a hot meal. He wasn't in the mood to cook or have a sandwich back at the apartment, and hospital food was free for residents. Luckily, City General had good food. As he moved up to the checkout with his tray, Pixie, the aging red-headed cashier, was filing her frosted white nails but looked up abruptly. "Hello, Dr. David," she said as she quickly tallied his order and pulled the tape from her cash register. "Just sign and go, sugar. How's residency treating you today?"

"Better than internship, Pix. Not quite as freewheeling as my tech days, but good. I did grow up somewhere along the way."

"Have you seen who's back?"

"Who?"

He followed Pixie's index finger as she pointed across the room to a table near the window. He'd left his tray sitting on the checkout counter, a good thing for him because he might have dropped it. "Right there. And she's still got that hair."

And right there she was, Laurel, after all these years. She did still have that beautiful brown hair, and from her profile it looked like she hadn't changed a bit. His heart squeezed, and a myriad of conflicting emotions pulsed through him in unison: regret, shame, tenderness, desire, joy, hope. He willed his heart to slow its thunderous galloping. He'd actually learned to do that. Mind over matter. But his hard-earned willpower barely took the edge off this.

He signed his ticket and handed it to the cashier who was watching him. He forced a smile. "Well, guess I'll go say hello."

He picked up his tray and started moving away. Pixie grinned and whispered, "If plates start flying, I'll call the code team for you, sugar."

Did everybody know what a rat he'd been to her? Maybe they did. Maybe it was obvious, but they couldn't know the full depth of his sins. Only he and Laurel knew that. Well, it had been five years, and he'd grown up. If God was giving him another chance, and it looked like he was, he was for sure not going to blow it.

When he arrived at her table she was bent toward her little girl opening a milk carton. He couldn't see either of their faces. He took in a deep breath. Then it felt as if the words squeaked out of him, but when they reverberated back to his ears they sounded normal enough. "Hello, Laurel."

She turned abruptly, and two matching sets of blue eyes immediately zeroed in on him. The child's eyes were exactly the same shade and shape as Laurel's, and they were studying him intently.

He forced his gaze from Laurel and settled it on the child. He set his tray on the table and extended his hand to her. "Hello, young lady. What's your name?"

"Gena. What's yours?" She pumped the hand he had extended and smiled unguardedly the way Laurel used to smile at him.

He glanced back at Laurel. Her expression of surprise had turned to contempt. "May I join you ladies?" he asked.

"Suit yourself," she answered, but she couldn't have said *no* with any more disdain.

He pulled out the chair next to her and sat. Then he leaned across the table. "Gena, to answer your question, my name is David."

"Are you a doctor? Mommy says the men who wear white coats are doctors."

"Yes, I am, and I used to work with your mommy back before I became one. Didn't I, Mommy?"

Laurel glared openly at him now. "What are you doing here?"

"I work here."

"But—" She scanned him up and down, and she reached to tilt his name tag. "Dr. David Hudson, Pathology?" she read the tag aloud. She looked up into his eyes again, the look of contempt never once leaving her face. "You're a pathologist? You … you're my boss?"

"Stu and Miles are your real bosses. I'm just a first-year resident."

"And that makes you my superior." She squeezed her eyes shut and breathed in and out. She was counting to ten so she wouldn't scream at him. She used to do that all the time. Finally, she looked him straight in the eye, and he winced at the ferocity of her anger. "Why didn't somebody tell me?"

"Did you ask?"

"Why should I? How was I supposed …" She paused, counting to ten again, he guessed.

"Look, I didn't know you were the new chief until staff meeting this morning, which ought to tell you about my lack of power. And you were the last person I expected to see here today. I knew I'd see you tomorrow, but I didn't know that until this morning."

"Grady didn't say a word about you. But I guess that's my fault." She twisted her napkin around her fingers so fiercely they were turning white from lack of circulation. "I told him I didn't want to ever hear your name again."

He nodded and ran his fork through his mashed potatoes, suddenly not interested in eating. "I guess then he was honoring your wishes."

There was a long awkward silence, and it was Gena who spoke. "Mommy, why are you mad at David?"

Immediately she bent forward and patted Gena's hand. "Oh, honey, it's okay. I'm not mad at David."

"Yes you are, the way you get mad at Uncle Gene when he drinks too much bad stuff."

He didn't know about Laurel, but he didn't feel like lying to such a perceptive child. He began softly, "Mommy has a right to be mad at me, Gena. A long time ago I did some things I shouldn't have done."

"Are you sorry?" Those honest blue eyes zeroed in on him again.

"Yes. Yes, I am."

"Then, Mommy, you should forgive him. That's what Miss Emily says Jesus would do. And she says it's bad not to do what Jesus would do."

Laurel wouldn't even look at him, but he could sense her frustration. Regardless of what Jesus would do, she had a right to be mad at him for the rest of her life just for being so careless with her heart. He bent toward Gena again. "You know something, Gena. Your mommy's the nicest lady I ever met. I knew her for a long time, and she always does the right thing, so you don't have to worry. Okay? She's not going to get into trouble with Jesus."

Gena flashed him a brilliant smile. "Okay." Then she dug into her Jell-O, giggling at the way it jiggled when she jabbed it with her spoon.

Laurel softened a bit, but she didn't smile. Finally, she muttered, "Cool it with the charm. She's just a kid."

Coming from Laurel, no allusion to his charm was a compliment. She used to always tell him he employed it to avoid depth in relationships. He'd given that a lot of thought these past five years, and he'd had to acknowledge that it was true. He took a sip of his tea and turned to meet her angry gaze. "I'd like it if we could talk before you start your job. Maybe we could clear the air so we can at least work together. Maybe later, after dinner?"

"I doubt Marilee would like that. Isn't she expecting you to come home?"

"Marilee?" he said with all the contempt he felt for that particular blonde.

"Your wife," she said flatly.

He looked straight into her eyes. "I never proposed to Marilee, and I didn't marry her. We were polar opposites. We never agreed on anything and would have killed each other before we got the date selected."

"You'll forgive me if I have trouble believing that. You set a date. The announcement was in the newspaper."

"I tried to explain that at the time."

"That doesn't mean I believed you." She stabbed at her okra and shoved a dainty forkful into her mouth.

Gena announced abruptly that she was finished with her Jell-O. She smiled sweetly at Laurel. "I ate all my food. Can I—" She paused and grinned impishly. "I mean, *may* I eat the lollipop the nice lady gave me?"

Laurel smiled. "Yes, sweetheart, you may."

As Gena concentrated on peeling her lollipop, David pushed his uneaten tray of food away and leaned back in his chair. "Just so you know, Laurel. I'm not married, and I've never been married. I know you won't believe this, but for the past five years I've been as celibate as a monk."

"You're right, David. I don't believe that."

From then on he did all the talking. She didn't say much, but at least she listened when he told her that the lab hadn't changed much except for the pathology part of it.

"Stu's a strictly hands-on chief. He's done wonders for Pathology. Dr. Campbell let it stagnate. The department's better off with him retired to his stamp collection. It was all he did anyway."

She leaned to wipe Gena's sticky hands with a napkin she'd dipped in her water. Then she fished a Nurse Nancy Little Golden Book from her purse and handed it to Gena who became immediately engrossed in separating the Band-Aid from one of the pages.

"I haven't met the chief yet," she said flatly. "I interviewed with the assistant chief, Dr. Miles Ashley after Grady hired me."

He'd already seen that on her application. She'd requested a Saturday interview most likely to lessen the chance of being seen coming and going by the lab gossips.

"Miles is new to his position, too," he continued. "He's nuts, and he can be totally off the wall, but he knows pathology like the back of his hand. Expect unconventional from the word go with him. And Stu. He's one of those geniuses with no common sense and a short attention span. You'll like him better if you understand that."

"And Dr. David Hudson?" She said it so sarcastically he cringed. "What's he like?"

He was fresh out of cute comments to counter with. "I guess you'll just have to find that one out for yourself."

There was a long silence as she sipped her tea and Gena wiggled around in her seat. Finally, he spoke. "Where are you living?"

"Across the street in Ridgeview Apartments."

He perked up then. "They're nice apartments, and you can't beat the convenience."

"Speaking of that," she said abruptly, "we have to go. We just moved in today, and we need to get settled."

"Then let me escort you across the street," he offered. "I'm going that way."

Gena was immediately agreeable and let him stack her tray on top of his and carry it to the conveyer belt. Laurel, on the other hand grabbed her tray and Gena's hand before he could even offer to carry hers. Her anger was conspicuous, but she let him walk with them to their apartment.

What both amazed him and renewed his faith at the same time was the realization that came the moment they arrived at the door of apartment 212. Laurel and Gena were his new next-door neighbors.

Of course, when he pointed out the coincidence, Laurel got pissed and made the comment that one of them could most certainly arrange to move to a different section, but then Gena piped up, "Mommy, I want to live next to David. I like him." Laurel glared at him over Gena's head.

Since she was mad anyway and he'd just received a boost of faith, he decided to push a bit more. "About that conversation, to clear the air since I'm right next door, I don't see why we can't go ahead and talk."

"I do. There's nothing to talk about."

"Your anger says there is, and it's going to drive Stu crazy when he picks up on it. He likes to see everybody tiptoeing through the tulips. Maybe you haven't heard about that feel-good morning huddle he makes us have."

"All right," she said none too gently. "Eight o'clock, after Gena's bath and bedtime."

"But I want to see David, too," Gena protested.

"You can see him tomorrow, honey." Her voice with the child was sweet and gentle. "He's right next door. You've had a long, exciting day, and you need to go to bed on time."

At eight o'clock David sat in Laurel's living room nursing a bottled Coke while she checked one more time to make sure Gena was asleep.

She returned and sat beside him on the sofa. He noticed she was careful to keep a comfortable distance from him, but she was close enough that he detected the delicate scent of the Chanel No. 5 she wore. She'd always worn Chanel No 5, and every time he'd smelled it in the past five years, he thought he would die from missing her.

"I was afraid Gena would be traumatized by this move, but, thankfully, she considers it an adventure." Her eyes sparkled when she smiled. Tonight he had learned that this child could make her smile when nothing else could.

"She's a smart kid," he said.

"Yes, sometimes a little too smart."

"She looks just like you, Laurel. She's a little beauty."

She looked into his eyes for a brief second, and he knew that she doubted his compliment.

"How old is she?" He already knew from the application, but he wanted to see her reaction when she told him. Also, he was edging his way to the question he really wanted to ask.

"She turned four on the fourteenth of May," she answered without any emotion. Why had he expected her to reveal any feelings other than anger?

He mentally counted again. Almost exactly four years and nine months from that night. He took in a quick breath and asked the next obvious question. "Who's her father?"

At first she frowned at him as if she didn't understand the question, but a few seconds later she jumped to her feet and planted her hands on her hips. "Oh, I get it. You think because of what happened between us five years ago I went wild and loose. Well, you couldn't be more off base."

"Then answer the damn question, Laurel."

She grabbed the toss pillow from the sofa and threw it at him. "You insufferable jerk, I don't owe you any explanations about my life."

He intercepted the pillow, placed it on the sofa beside him, and stared into her eyes.

"What do you want from me, David? You went on with your life, so I had to go on with mine. Why are you acting like

I betrayed you? It was the other way around in case you don't remember."

"I remember," he answered softly, "but I tried to explain and make things right. I wanted to talk some more after you had some time to calm down. I wanted you to see the truth that it was you I proposed to, not Marilee. I'm not guilty of lying to you, Laurel. What I'm guilty of is not getting my past in order before I asked you to share my future. Don't you think I know how much all that hurt you? I wanted to explain so we could work it out, but you disappeared off the face of the earth."

"I've lived thirty miles away! It's not even long-distance!"

"I didn't know that," he snapped. He paused and made himself soften his voice. This wasn't the way he'd envisioned this meeting. "I tried to reach you. I swear to God, I tried. I called your parents' house right after you left the hospital and moved out of the dorm. When I was in medical school I sent you letters at their address."

"Liar, I never got them."

"I sent them, Laurel. For the whole first year of school I sent them, and they were never returned to me. When I called your house, some guy told me to get lost."

She had been pacing with her back to him, but she turned abruptly. "Who told you that? Who told you to get lost?"

"I don't know who he was. He said his name was Del. The last time I called, I got your mother. She told me you had moved, and she didn't know where you were."

She slowly sank back onto the couch, and she turned toward him. She looked totally defeated. "I want to believe you. It sounds like something they'd do, my mother and my brother Del. But what does it matter anyway, David? It's been five years."

"It matters because you hate me. Maybe I deserve that, but things weren't the way you thought they were five years ago. If they were, I'd be married to Marilee, and I'm not."

"But she was pregnant."

"No. She wasn't pregnant. I told you then I was certain that was a lie. She made that wedding announcement to make another guy jealous. To try to force me to go along with the farce she faked pregnancy. I didn't fall for it, so she was out of luck."

He glanced at her trying to gauge how she was taking this, but her expression hadn't changed. She busied herself stacking the three Little Golden books that were scattered on the coffee table. He reached to touch her upper arm, but she immediately shrugged away as if he'd burned her with a hot iron.

"Laurel, I'm not proud of the person I used to be. I had grownup aspirations and a high school maturity level. Because of that immaturity I didn't know how to handle what you and I had together. I was careless with it, and I took your love for granted. I didn't even know how much of a lie my life was until that night we made love. Until that night I didn't even know what love was."

She stiffened, and he knew he'd said too much too soon.

"I think you should go now, David." Her voice was barely more than a whisper.

He took in a deep breath and stood. He knew that stubborn expression, the tightened lips, the rock hard gaze, but he also saw the pain she couldn't quite hide. Why couldn't he have grown up sooner? Why did he have to hurt her so much just because his ego had to be fed? When he reached the door, he turned. "Laurel."

She lifted her eyes slowly to his in response.

"The way I hurt you was never intentional; but I'm so sorry, and I wish you could forgive me. It may look like I've moved on, but I'm stuck back on that hillside August 13, 1966, and no matter what I do with my life, it won't mean anything until I resolve that with you."

He had to leave after that because the knot in his throat threatened to erupt. He slipped into his apartment and poured his second neat scotch of the day. He had to relax so he could get some sleep, or tomorrow would surely do him in.

Chapter Six

The next morning Laurel went through her instruction sheet with Lucy Archer, the lady Grady Banks had recommended as a babysitter. She had already interviewed Lucy extensively a week ago. She met all her criteria for Gena's care, but you never knew with a total stranger if things would work out.

As she left for work she realized she'd worried for nothing. Gena and Miss Lucy hit it off immediately. Maybe it was because she was so much like Mama Rita: short, round, sweet, and bubbly. When she pulled her apartment door shut she heard Gena's happy giggles as she bounded into the kitchen to make cookies with Miss Lucy. She released a sigh of relief. Gena's care was a priority in this setup. If she wasn't certain she was well cared for, she simply couldn't do her job.

Once downstairs she stopped to glance at her reflection in the glass door before she exited the building. She'd managed to conceal the bags under her eyes with makeup. She hadn't slept more than two hours the entire night, and those had been from sheer exhaustion.

Seeing David so unexpectedly after all these years had been disconcerting, and no matter how hard she'd tried to be strong, the wall she had built to protect her heart had crumbled in the face of his presence. When he had touched her last night, she'd felt their old connection so strongly it terrified her. How was she going to handle working with him every day?

All she could think about, lying awake in her bed, was that he was just a partition away in the next apartment. When she'd closed her eyes she could see his handsome face: those clear blue eyes, that tiny dimple at the corner of his right cheek that deepened when he smiled. He still wore Canoe aftershave. She'd detected wafts of it as they talked. Even after he left it seemed embedded in her senses, and she couldn't willfully banish it. With that scent came unbidden memories of that night. She could almost hear his sweet, rich voice whispering how much he loved her, how beautiful she was, how he couldn't imagine life without her in it. It had awakened all her senses and threatened her self-control. Worst of all, she couldn't stop thinking about what he'd said as he left. It was unsettling, and she didn't know where to go from here.

Their entire conversation had played over and over in her mind, and she was so angry with Mama and Del that she almost called them at midnight to confront them about David's calls and letters. She didn't doubt David on that part of their conversation at all. It was the way Mama operated, and Del, who was such an extension of Mama. What right did they have to play God in her life?

She crossed at the light on Tenth Street and walked up the sidewalk toward the hospital's main entrance still thinking about David's revelation. She knew Mama and Del weren't trying to protect her. They didn't even know David, and their manipulations were never benevolent, especially Mama's. They were always about control. It was so like Mama to do whatever she had to do to keep her children close and anyone she considered an outsider away. She'd seen her in action too many times. She'd meddled in both her brothers' marriages, and Gene's had ended in divorce.

Laurel entered through the automatic front doors of the hospital and caught the closest elevator just before the doors closed, barely acknowledging the elderly operator and the crowd of employees already inside. "Two, please," she said. She would get to the bottom of this with Mama and Del, just not in front of Gena. The last thing she wanted was to put that sweet child though the hell-raising fights she'd witnessed, but Mama wasn't getting away with this one, not by a long shot.

Audrey Taylor was the first person who greeted Laurel when she stepped off the elevator and entered the main lab doorway across from it. When Audrey encircled her with an affectionate hug, she almost cried. Audrey knew her. She was better than family. It was an unspoken kinship, and this felt like her first day here back in 1963. It was as if time had stood still, and she almost believed she could go back and undo the last five heartbreaking years.

"Mr. Banks' office is where it always was, your office now," Audrey told her. "He's going to be here for the rest of the week to get you going."

"I understand he's planning to travel now that he's retiring," she said.

"Oh yeah, he's heading off in his camper, him and Lois, to see the USA, campsite to campsite. Personally, I can't see it."

"But hasn't he always enjoyed camping?"

"For weekends, not long trips. He's more one of them hotel travelers. Find that boy the first Holiday Inn. I don't think he's figured out yet they don't have vibrating beds and room service in the great out-of-doors. I'd love to be a fly on his tent when he spots his first bear. Law, wouldn't that be a hoot, Mr. Banks being chased by a bear?"

She laughed. "Audrey, you haven't changed a bit. How's your little girl?"

"Big. Begging to date. Scaring the fool out of us learning to drive."

"You'll live through it. If you didn't go crazy that week all of us students rotated through this office and managed to tick off every doctor in the hospital by hanging up on them or giving them the wrong report, you can survive anything."

Audrey was about to respond when Grady Banks appeared from the back entrance to the main lab. "Laurel, sweetie." His voice boomed across the room. Then he spoke to the totally bald man next to him who looked to be in his early fifties. "What did I tell you, Stu? She's much nicer to look at than me."

This must be the chief pathologist, she thought. She squeezed Audrey's arm. "Let's take a coffee break together later and have lunch together." Audrey nodded.

She walked toward Mr. Banks, and when she arrived across the room, she directed her comment to the man standing next to him. "You must be Dr. Stuart Spencer."

He extended his hand. "That I am, Laurel. Welcome aboard. I understand this is like coming home for you."

"Yes, Sir, it pretty much is."

"Rule number one, young lady, you don't have to call me sir. It's Stu. We're on a first-name basis around here."

"And we do a morning huddle now," Mr. Banks said with a mischievous twinkle in his eye. She was guessing he didn't care for the huddle any more than David appeared to. "I'm going to let you go solo on that. When you're ready, you can go with Stu. It'll just be you and the pathologists."

She continued to be greeted by the lab staff. Some she'd liked, and some she hadn't, especially the gossipy lab assistants. Many of them led lives that were nothing but ongoing soap operas and illicit trysts, yet they gleefully enjoyed the misfortune of others. They had certainly taken pleasure in gossiping about her three-year relationship with David. She dreaded having all that heartache dredged up again, but she knew it was inevitable.

When Celia, the Hematology supervisor, greeted her, she was shocked that Grady still kept her in that position. She had always liked the pleasant lady, and she was an excellent tech. What she knew, she knew well, but she had never been progressive enough to keep up with new technologies. And Paula Kelly was still one of the group supervisors. Paula was just plain lazy. Looking around her she realized that little had changed in the hierarchy of supervisors, which was both good and bad.

She would have to speak to Grady about this. Did the overtly bad supervisors have something on him that made him keep them in their positions, or was she missing something about their skills that his seasoned intuition hadn't? Grady was a people person, and he knew how to match a job with the right person. She'd ask his advice before she considered any change. She wanted to be fair, but she wanted to run a progressive lab.

She had greeted so many people her cheeks were aching from all the forced smiles when Stu finally rescued her. She followed him into the office marked "Chief Pathologist." It was Dr. Campbell's old office. Dr. Miles Ashley and David were already there, and both stood when she entered. She smiled in their direction carefully avoiding David's eyes.

Stu seemed a no-nonsense person because he got started immediately. He talked about areas that needed improvement and asked her opinion about them. She gave him honest answers. He seemed pleased although she doubted this was a test of any sort. She glanced quickly at David and saw that he was doodling on his notepad.

"This final matter we've discussed with Grady," Stu said, "but since it involves the women techs we'd like your opinion before we decide."

"Sure."

"Well, in some of the more progressive hospitals across the country the women have started to wear pants uniforms rather than the traditional dresses. Some female employees have made a request to wear them here. It's met with some resistance. Some of the old-school doctors think they're unladylike."

She glanced first at Stu and then around the room. She saw that David was now watching her, and that made her nervous—

but not because of the opinion she was about to express. Her job was the one place in this world where she felt sure of herself and the one place where she felt she belonged.

"My honest opinion? You're sure?"

Stu nodded enthusiastically, so she told him exactly how she felt. "I'd vote in favor of them. Nothing's more unladylike than having to practically stand on your head down in ER to get a specimen from a trauma patient exposing everything you've got to a sea of gawking interns who'll probably kill the next patient who comes though the door because the sight of a woman's underwear has suddenly reduced them to a bunch of giggling fourth graders."

Both David and Miles started laughing. Then David spoke up. "Stu, she's right. It happened when Laurel and I were students, and now eight years later, it's still happening. Speaking as one fresh off the intern rotation, you can trust her on that."

"Then pants uniforms it will be," Stu said smiling. "Thank you, Laurel."

After she exited Stu's office she detoured through the main lounge before meeting Mr. Banks in what was to be her new office. She grabbed a Styrofoam cup and reached for the coffee carafe.

"Stop." It was David's voice directly behind her. "Audrey's still making the coffee."

"Oh, no. Yuk," she blurted automatically, immediately flashing back to the many cups of Audrey's bad coffee they had shared as students. She turned and looked up at him, hoping he couldn't sense how uncomfortable she felt standing this close to him.

"You should make it your first duty as chief to remedy this."

When he looked down at her with a tentative smile, she realized he was treading softly with her. She glanced at the Styrofoam cup she still held clutched in both her hands. Was he really sorry for the way things had turned out between them? Was it the truth that he had loved her and not Marilee? He wasn't married. That meant something, didn't it? Or was he merely the smooth talking philanderer he had always been who had learned better excuses with time? A few awkward seconds ticked by, and she reprimanded herself. You can at least be professional, Laurel.

She made eye contact again. "Really? Does the central coffeepot fall under my jurisdiction?"

"I believe it does. In fact, I'll put a bug in Stu's ear to make sure it does."

"Why do I get the feeling the new kid on the block is getting the job nobody else can muster the courage to do? Are you guys afraid to tell Audrey how bad her coffee is?"

"Not me. I tell her every day. She just laughs at me."

Remembering how Audrey always used humor to dismiss criticism on nonessential things, she relaxed in the familiarity of that common ground between them. She felt herself smiling automatically, and she saw something in his eyes immediately acknowledge the change. "I'll see what I can do then."

If every task was going to be as easy as expressing her opinion and persuading Audrey to stop making coffee when she knew Audrey could care less about losing the privilege, this job was going to be a breeze, but she already knew from experience that this was the easy stuff.

Her conversation with Grady regarding the supervisors hadn't helped much. He'd made her feel sorry for Celia when he told her she had a disabled husband and three children to support. The weight of her responsibilities, he told her, made Celia concentrate her energies toward what she knew. Fear of failure made her reluctant to venture into the unknown. Grady hadn't had a problem with that since hematology was his first love, and he took care of keeping up with changes.

Paula, he told her, had a mentally retarded child who exhausted her. When challenged, she could perform well, but she was so lonely for adult companionship she talked rather than worked.

It wasn't going to be easy to accept stagnant and unmotivated staff members, but maybe she could find a positive way to encourage Celia and Paula. She most certainly wasn't going to be cutthroat and fire or demote them, and maybe that had been the point Grady had been trying to make all along. If you bought a machine, you expected it to work perfectly, but humans were far from perfect, herself included, with too many influencing factors that had to be considered.

She decided to make it her goal to inspect each lab individually in the four days before Grady left so she could confer with him about the setups, the staff, and any needed changes. She visited Bacteriology and Serology before lunch, consulting with the supervisors in those adjoining labs. Both Kate and Susan had always been efficient managers, and nothing had changed in that regard.

Kate could use a bit more tact in dealing with her students. Laurel remembered how abrasive she could be. Students might need a firm hand, but she remembered learning better from the more compassionate teachers. It was like Mama Rita always said: you caught more flies with honey than you did with vinegar. She would speak with Grady about Kate to see if he could shed any light on how to soften her.

In the afternoon she inspected the urinalysis lab. It was the smallest lab and an orphan in that it had no direct supervisor. Supplies for its testing were ordered through Chemistry, and techs and students rotated duties here. It didn't seem to have changed much since she was a student. In this lab both urine and stool specimens were analyzed, the latter for occult blood and ova and parasites.

The eight-by-ten-foot room had a stainless steel countertop and a sink on the long wall with a refrigerator above the left end of the counter. Its contents were accessible from both the urine lab and the specimen drop-off side in the outer hallway. A desk with a microscope, a centrifuge, and a drop-down stat delivery area lined the opposite wall. The entry door was on the short side, and on the wall opposite that was an eighteen-inch-square cubbyhole that opened to the main lab office where finished requisitions were stacked for the secretaries to separate and file.

Since a small sitting area was tucked just off the main lab office near the cubbyhole, conversations between the lab assistants could easily be heard without eavesdropping. Laurel was checking the procedure notebook when she heard one such conversation.

"I heard she's got a kid. I'll bet you it belongs to David Hudson. She's been nuts about him ever since they were students. He had a lot of other girlfriends, but they were together all the time until five years ago when she just up and left. He didn't miss many chances to score, and the kid's about the right age for that."

Laurel bristled. It may have been five years, but she recognized that voice. It was Trudy, the wild bleached blonde who had been rumored to be Dr. Campbell's lover back in her heyday.

"Trudy, not everybody is like you. Maybe she's divorced and decided to keep her maiden name." That voice belonged to Gail. She wasn't a floozy like the rest of them. "Anyway it's none of our business."

You've got that right, she thought.

"David is such a hunk. She couldn't be his type. She's too prim and proper." This voice she didn't recognize, but she sounded young. "A sexy stud like that needs passion. A good girl like her couldn't possibly know how to satisfy a man like him."

"Darlin', men like to add virgins to their conquests every now and then, but then they move on." Trudy's voice again. "Right after his last fling with Laurel, he dumped her. Then he got engaged to another girl who used to be a nurse here, the notorious Marilee Baker. That didn't last a week."

Laurel leaned against the counter as misery washed over her. How dare they reduce her life to such base gossip? She felt like screaming through the cubbyhole at them, but what good would that do?

Then she heard Gail's firm voice. "It didn't last with Marilee because David didn't propose to her in the first place. She made all that up to make the intern she later married jealous."

"How would you know that?" Trudy asked.

"I heard her bragging about it to another nurse. I was at her station charting. She was telling her friend how mad David got about that newspaper announcement."

"What exactly did she say?" The voice was Trudy's again.

"That David told her if he never saw her again, it'd be too soon, and that if he wasn't so stupid, he'd never have wasted his time on her. The little trollop thought it was funny that he got so upset."

"When was that?" Trudy asked.

"The day after that announcement came out in the paper. From what I hear he hasn't dated anyone since all that happened five years ago."

"Now, you couldn't possibly know that to be the truth," Trudy scoffed.

"It's what Dr. Connor said. He was David's medical school roommate, and they interned together. I heard him telling some little starry-eyed nurse who was drooling over David that she was wasting her time."

"Dr. Chad Connor, the surgery resident? That homely guy?" Trudy laughed. "He probably scared off all the women within a block of both of them."

"He's not homely," Gail protested. "He looks like Humphrey Bogart."

"Like I said, homely," Trudy mumbled. Laurel heard the clicking of a lighter, and the faint smell of cigarette smoke drifted through the cubbyhole.

"Anyway," Gail continued, "Dr. Connor said when David wasn't studying, he was working and that he wasn't the least bit interested in dating. I haven't heard of him dating anybody since he came back either even when he was an intern. He's changed. He's not on the prowl like he used to be."

"That's because he's been waiting for me." The young voice gave a low predatory growl. Hysterical laughter followed.

Laurel made herself concentrate on the last page of the procedure notebook. She flipped it shut and made a note to update it. It was too vague and sketchy. Abruptly she heard a distinctly familiar male voice, and her heart did an involuntary flutter. "Hey, Audrey, what's all that cackling about?"

"It's just the brainless wonders analyzing your love life," Audrey answered in a low voice.

"My love life? I haven't had one of those in quite a while."

"Yesterday's news, hon. They're taking odds on whether Laurel's little girl is yours and chewing over when and how it happened."

"What?!" There was a dangerously dark edge to David's voice.

"Don't go flying off the handle. That'll just make them worse. Something I can do for you?"

There was a long pause. She knew David well enough to know that he was trying to control his temper. Was he angry at an implication that could cramp his style, or was he trying to protect her and Gena?

"I need a favor," he said.

"Name it."

"Stu let me borrow his notes on abnormal liver tissue. Problem is, I can't read his scribbling, and I was planning to study them tonight. You don't seem to have a problem reading his stuff. Think you can decipher it for me and type it? It's ten pages handwritten."

"Consider it done."

Laurel resumed her task by moving to the next item on her list. She was checking the inventory of supplies when she heard the young female voice again, the one she couldn't identify, and it was coated with honey.

"Well, hello there, David. I thought it was you out here. Want me to type it for you?"

"He wants it before his residency's over," Audrey scoffed. "Anyway you shouldn't fool around with machines that have a higher IQ than you do."

"You don't have to be so mean."

"You don't have to be so obvious. The boy's not interested in you, honey. Does a brick building have to fall on you?"

"He has a mouth. He can speak for himself."

Laurel paused with the lower cabinet door half-open. There was a long silence, and she wondered what was happening. All she could see through the small cubbyhole was Audrey's back and the tiniest glimpse of David's arm covered by his lab jacket.

"I'm sorry. Exactly what am I supposed to be speaking about?" David asked.

"I'll translate," Audrey piped up sarcastically. "She wants to know if you want her body."

"Not in this lifetime," he answered quickly. "Oh, and a word to the wise, and you can pass this on for me: I'm not up for grabs; my past is my business; and if I ever hear of any of you gossiping about your new boss and her daughter again, I'll see that you're fired. Laurel is the best, and I won't tolerate anyone slandering her reputation." His voice moved away. "I'll pick that up on my way home, Audrey. Thanks. I owe you."

Nice, she thought, *very nice.*

At the end of her first day, before she crossed the street to her apartment, Laurel stopped at the bank of phones in the lobby. She started to pick up the first phone and insert her quarter, but then she opted for the privacy of one of the booths. She entered the first one, closed the door, inserted the coin, and dialed Mama's number. Del answered on the fourth ring, and she lit in on him.

"How in the hell do you expect me to remember a phone call from five years ago, little sister?"

Oh, he remembered all right. All she had to do was get past his good-old-boy bull crap. "What right do you have to screen my phone calls, and how could you insult people you don't even know, Del? What's the point? What about common courtesy?"

"Oh, did little Laurel miss a phone call from her long lost boyfriend? I probably should have let him talk to you. Maybe you wouldn't have ended up such an old maid."

"Shut up, Del. Let me talk to Mama."

She could hear his rat-a-tat laughing as he handed the phone over to Mama. She counted to ten. He made her so angry. Their relationship hadn't always been like this. The older they got, the more they disagreed.

Abruptly Mama's voice came across the line. "Laurel? How's my little Gena?" Her voice sounded weak and vulnerable, making Laurel cringe with guilt. But then she reminded herself what a supreme actress Mama was.

"Where are my letters, Mama?"

"What?" She was genuinely shocked.

How dare she not remember her life-altering manipulations? So, Laurel spelled it out for her in detail along with a vague recap of her conversation with David, the one where Mama had told him, in effect, that she'd dropped off the face of the earth. Knowing Mama, she could have been in the next room when the conversation took place.

"Laurel," Mama's voice sounded hoarse, "I don't understand." She made the tiniest of gasps then.

Laurel let out an exasperated sigh when she realized she'd been holding her breath in anticipation of exactly the reaction she'd received. Mama should get an Academy Award for her stellar performances. The tragedy of it was that she was killing herself and wounding everybody around her with them.

"Of course, you understand," she said.

"Good grief, what are you getting all worked up about?" Mama's voice was getting raspy now.

"Just stop it, Mama," she hissed. "What did you do with the letters from David? And don't lie to me! I know you."

She heard a rustling noise, and she could almost see Del moving Mama's breathing machine into place, getting ready to do a treatment so she could breathe easier. Damn it. Mama played dirty when she got caught red-handed.

"Del, get me … that tin … over there. I think some of … Laurel's papers … are in there."

"Later, Mama. We've got to give you a treatment first," Del ordered. Once again Mama was gasping for breath, and it was her fault.

She would never understand this woman who gave her life. She had plenty enough breath for criticizing Del's wife. How many midnight calls had Connie made to her crying her heart out because she couldn't take any more of Mama's verbal abuse?

She'd managed to keep Gena away from the worst of the turmoil with Mama, Del, and Gene, although she had heard some low-key arguments, more than Laurel had meant for her to hear. She knew she needed a balance for the sensitive and intuitive child, but balance was impossible in her unbalanced family. For Gena's sake she had buffered both of them against the caustic relationships. She took her to visit Mama once a week and more often only when guilt overwhelmed her.

According to Mama and Del, she was cruel and heartless. One of the new nurses at Mountain General had even taken her to task after one of Mama's deathbed crises. "Why don't you sit with your poor mother? Surely someone can take over for a little while down there in that lab," Patty Hodges had demanded just six months ago.

She was guilty of running away into her job, for sure, but she could have done worse things like Gene with his alcohol addiction that had recently escalated into drug abuse and Del with his inhumane dogfighting and God only knew what other shady endeavors. Sometimes she wished she could divorce them all.

She stiffened and resolved to see this through. "The letters, Mama, I want them. Gena and I are coming up Sunday to go to church, and I'm coming by to get them."

A second later she heard Mama gasping for breath, something she could have predicted and right on target. Then Del yelled into the phone. "That's enough, Laurel Elaine! She ain't talking to you no more!" After that, all she heard was a dial tone.

Chapter Seven

David had to exercise all his willpower to keep from taking advantage of living next door to Laurel. He longed to set things right between them, but he had seen all too clearly that he was going to have to give her some space and time. He just hoped the amount of time she needed wasn't forever. He comforted himself with the fact that he would see her every weekday morning at huddle, and he concentrated on making sure he was light and charming.

She'd arrived just this past Tuesday, and already she was running the lab as efficiently as Grady had. She'd learned some innovative things along the way, too, and she was more aggressive than Grady.

She immediately restructured the hierarchy of supervisors by appointing a section leader under each one. Celia in Hematology had the sharpest tech in the lab under her. Laurel changed job descriptions such that supervisors were responsible for ordering, scheduling, and machine maintenance while their section techs were responsible for new technology, the daily flow of testing, and quality control. Teaching was a shared responsibility.

He saw it as a stroke of genius. She was mending weak areas without the morale problem of demotions, and the raise in pay for the section leaders would more than pay for itself in increased competence and higher productivity.

Bacteriology students now had a choice between overbearing Kate as a teacher or her section leader, the ever patient Lorna Peal. She appointed Paula Kelly supervisor of the urinalysis lab pulling her from her previous position as group supervisor. Everybody knew Paula worked better alone when she couldn't yak with a co-worker. Her change of position had been a promotion and also an incentive to actually earn her pay.

Previously there had been four group leaders who were responsible for scheduling on their group's weekend rotation. Laurel abolished this position rotating the responsibilities to the section supervisors and leaders. It hadn't cost anyone a decrease in pay because all weekend group leaders had been section supervisors already except for Paula who was actually promoted.

According to Stu, Laurel had made the changes quietly going to each supervisor and presenting her ideas in a positive way. He hadn't heard anyone complain. Well, that wasn't entirely true. Some of the lab assistants were livid about the one change she'd made that affected them.

Grady's secretary, Mildred, had retired when he did, so Laurel chose Audrey as her personal secretary. Since the new position would give Audrey much more free time, Laurel added a duty to her job description that Mildred didn't have. Audrey was also supervisor over the secretaries and lab assistants who'd previously had no direct supervision.

David had learned about that change when Trudy confronted Stu to complain as he and Stu were walking down the hall headed to a conference.

Using her sexiest over-the-hill pout Trudy sidled up to Stu and began her tirade. "Dr. Spencer, I just heard that your new chief has made Audrey Taylor my boss. How dare she? Audrey's just a secretary."

Stu had paused to listen carefully as Trudy went on. "I'm not the only one who's upset. You just ask anybody. You'll be lucky if we don't all quit. Dr. Campbell would never have put up with this."

Not once betraying his concerned demeanor Stu replied. "Most likely because Dr. Campbell made the mistake of putting himself in a position such that he could be blackmailed. Rest assured that won't be happening again. I'm sorry. I can't help. I've already approved this position. Is there anything else?"

David almost laughed in Trudy's face at her attempt to seduce Stu. He wondered how long it was going to take her to realize that Stu was immune to sins of the flesh. The only flesh he got passionate about was embedded in paraffin, sliced into thin layers, and viewed under a microscope.

Unlike Trudy and her cohorts, Laurel functioned well inside the hospital's male hierarchy without having to play the coquette, and both Stu and Miles were completely taken with her abilities. He understood their admiration, but he couldn't separate his personal feelings from his professional ones if he tried. He didn't want to try. He was too happy to have her in his life again no matter how tentative it might be.

He'd had a hard time falling asleep last night because he couldn't stop thinking about the fact that yesterday had been the fifth anniversary of their passionate night, August 13, 1966. He wondered if she'd acknowledged it.

It was Saturday morning now, and he longed to see her and talk again; but he fought the urge to knock on her door and invite her and Gena to breakfast. He had the Pancake House in mind. He figured Gena would like that, but Laurel would suspect ulterior motives.

Acknowledging that she would be completely correct, he nixed the idea. Instead he ate a light breakfast of toast and coffee and browsed the morning paper. He saw that the St. Louis Cardinals were playing the Pittsburgh Pirates at Three Rivers Stadium that same day. He was pulling for the Cardinals. He loved baseball, but he hadn't been to a game in years. He had free season tickets to the local team's home games that he'd never used. He wondered if Gena liked baseball, but he guessed she was a little young for sports.

He tossed the newspaper aside, changed into his bathing suit, and headed down to the pool. He needed the exercise. Standing on the hard concrete floors in the morgue doing autopsies had made his legs begin to ache. Regular laps in the apartment pool were helping to alleviate that.

It was a quarter after eight so the pool was empty. Not even the lifeguard came on duty until nine. That suited him fine. He took advantage of the solitude and dove into the pool to swim repetitive laps. He was just beginning to get tired when he heard voices.

He glanced toward the sound and saw Laurel and Gena coming in through the gate. Laurel was carrying a large straw beach bag, and Gena hugged an inflatable purple hippo as big as she was. He swam toward that side of the pool, moved up to the edge nearest to them, and stood in waist-level water shaking his head to remove the excess droplets.

"Mommy, there's David!" Gena shrieked gleefully, dropping her hippo and tugging her hand free of Laurel's grasp.

He waved and smiled, but suddenly without any warning at all Gena dove toward him into the water. He saw an instant flash of horror spread across Laurel's face. Then the tiny child hit the pool sending water splashing all around her. Before she could sink past chin-level he scooped her into his arms and hugged her against his chest. She was such a wiggling mass of wet curls and giggles, he couldn't help smiling.

Instantly, with her beach cover-up still on, Laurel jumped into the water with them. She reached for the child. "Gena, are you alright?"

"She's fine," he said. "I grabbed her before she went under."

"That was fun." Gena giggled. "I want to do it again."

"No!" Laurel said quickly, but she softened her voice as she patted Gena's back while he still held her. "That's the kind of thing you get to do after you learn to swim, not before. Do you understand, honey? I don't want you to ever do that again until I say it's okay. Promise me."

"Ahh, Mommeee."

"I'm serious. If you can't follow the rules, we'll have to stop coming to the pool. Okay?"

"Ohhkaay," Gena pouted.

"We're lucky that David was here to catch you, or you could have been hurt." Laurel glanced up at him then. "Thank you."

Gena tightened her arms around his neck and pressed her curly head against his cheek. Warmth spread through him. She was such a sweet child.

"How about I ride you around the pool for awhile on that fine hippo you've got there, and afterwards Mommy and I can go over to the kiddy pool with you. Is that a deal if Mommy's okay with it?"

She nodded enthusiastically. He glanced toward Laurel, and she nodded. "Okay, let's just go grab the little guy and get started. What's your hippo's name?"

"Purple People Eater."

"Does he really eat people?"

"No," she giggled. "He's not real."

They sat on the rim of the children's pool watching Gena splash around in the water totally absorbed in sharing the experience with Purple People Eater. Other tenants had arrived along with the lifeguard, but they had the kiddy pool all to themselves.

Now that Laurel had removed her wet cover-up, he saw that she wore a two-piece turquoise bathing suit that showed off her stunning figure to perfection. He remembered instantly the way it felt to have her body beneath him, the tenderness and warmth of being inside her. When he felt himself getting aroused at the sweet memory, he discretely draped his towel across his lap.

"Gena's fearless, isn't she?" he said forcing his eyes to her face.

She smiled and lifted her eyes from watching Gena to his gaze. "Yes, a little too much for my comfort level sometimes." She wiggled her toes in the water and glanced down toward them. "I try not to discourage her. I have to set boundaries, but I want her to be her own person."

He wanted to ask again about Gena's father. He had to know, but the last time he'd done that she'd let him know it was none of his business. He didn't want to antagonize her. This chance meeting was too sweet, so he let it slide for now.

"You're good at this mommy stuff."

She swirled her ankles in the pool. "I don't know. It's scary. Sometimes it seems like I'm just bouncing off my mother, but the last thing I want is for Gena to be parented the way I was."

He was getting the strong impression that she didn't get along with her mother, but he decided not to pursue that either. He didn't want to spoil the moment with anything unpleasant.

"How did your first week as chief go?"

"A few problems but much better than I could have hoped for."

"Stu is embarrassing in his praise for you."

"He's nice, a good boss, but maybe just a little too paranoid that he's going to catch some disease."

He laughed. "And Miles is loose as a goose. He'd eat with one hand and do autopsies with the other if he thought he could sneak it past the old man. He'll be lucky if he makes it to forty. Of course, Audrey's putrid coffee will probably kill him first, which I seem to recall is supposed to be one of your priorities."

She turned to glance at him, and he cocked his eyebrow at her.

"She said you're the only one who complains." He knew she was trying to keep a straight face. Both of them knew that wasn't true.

"Yeah, right. Did you even talk to her?"

"It's taken care of, thank you."

"How did she take it?"

"She said she didn't want the job in the first place. She has enough to do, but it won't matter who makes it. It's the dirt-cheap brand of coffee, part sawdust, part dehydrated swamp weed, she figures. The old tightwad Dr. Campbell insisted on buying it, and Dr. Spencer didn't bother to change brands because the egghead would drink mud if she put it in front of him since he always has his head in the clouds. Her words, mind you."

"That's our Audrey."

"She suggested a coffee service, one she tried to get Dr. Campbell to use a long time ago. The coffee's good. It comes in measured packets, and their machine has settings from mild to strong. I requisitioned it Wednesday. They promised to have it up and going first thing Monday morning."

"Wonderful. You're great at this." He paused to watch Gena scoop bucketfuls of water over her hippo. Then he squinted back at Laurel, shading his eyes with his left palm against the morning sun. "I understand you were chief at Mountain General, too. When did you take that job?"

"I got so lucky with that. I heard they were turning the old resort hotel on the mountain into a hospital. A neighbor just happened to mention at my father's funeral home visitation that they had a sign posted at the entryway that all departments were hiring even though they weren't open. I needed a change, so I called about it."

She glanced over at him. She didn't say it, but he knew the change she'd needed was to get away from their past. She turned her glance toward Gena and continued. "Byron Laughlin is the administrator. Do you remember him? He used to be an assistant administrator here at City General."

"Yes," he answered. What he remembered most about Laughlin was that he had asked Laurel out several times. She'd declined saying they had nothing in common. He wondered if that situation had changed in the years since.

"Byron hired me on the spot just from the phone interview the next day. I had to give my notice here, of course, but Mr. Banks took my two weeks' vacation as notice."

"So Grady knew about the Mountain General job," he said. Grady had already told him that he didn't know. Why had he lied to him?

"No, I told him only that I needed to be closer to my family. I didn't tell him about already being hired at Mountain General. Only two other people had made applications for the chief's job anyway. They were straight out of school and hadn't taken their exams yet. I hoped three years experience would seem like decades compared to that, so I didn't give any references."

"I'm sure it helped that you're very smart, that you were the head of our class, and that you made the highest grade on our registry exam. That's common knowledge at City General. If Laughlin didn't already know that, he was deaf, dumb, and blind."

She shrugged. "What helped was Byron's vision. We were a ragtag team, all of us, from nursing supervisor all the way down to head of housekeeping and maintenance. He believed in us, so we did our best not to disappoint him."

He didn't like it that she was on such a cozy first-name basis with this guy, and he wondered exactly how important a part of that team he had been to her personally. And yes, damn it, he was jealous even if he didn't have a right in the world to be. But if she'd been involved with Laughlin, why had she come back to City General? According to Grady she had been willing to settle for a tech position. Maybe they had broken up, and now she had moved to get away from him.

"Looks like you didn't disappoint him," he said feeling resentful but keeping his voice light. "I read the recommendation he gave you."

"It was a case of The Little Engine That Could, pure and simple. Still, I can't tell you how many times I almost picked up the phone to call Grady for advice."

"Grady's a great guy. I wouldn't be where I am today without his support. Remember how he pulled strings to get me into medical school? I for sure didn't want to disappoint him. Talk about being terrified."

"You were born to be a doctor, David. There's no way you could fail. The gods would be angry." She didn't look at him when she spoke; but her voice was soft and serious, so he knew she wasn't being flippant. "I'm surprised to see that you're doing a pathology residency. You always loved surgery. You were looking at internship and residency in Memphis. What changed?"

"You know I've always loved pathology and that I preferred coming back home, but I figured most pathology department heads were like Dr. Campbell, which didn't make it all that enticing as a specialty, and, too, I figured he'd never retire."

"Me either," she said. "I was shocked when I saw a newspaper article on his retirement in the fall of 1968. It didn't say who replaced him though."

"When I came home on breaks, I always visited Grady. That Christmas of '68 Stu and Miles were here. Grady introduced me, and I talked to them for a long time. After getting to know them it was an easy decision to pursue pathology. They're both great teachers."

"How was school? Was it everything you hoped it would be?"

Everything, except that you weren't there with me. But he didn't say that out loud. "It was grueling, but I loved it. It was a humbling experience. I wasn't sure I could cut booking it in real academia. I took my education for granted and goofed off in college."

"I think it's a rite of passage to goof off in college, a part of growing up."

"You didn't goof off."

She twirled a finger in her shiny hair. "Because I couldn't afford to. I couldn't have gone to college if I didn't qualify for scholarships and loans. My dad could never have afforded it, and

I didn't want to make life any harder for him than it already was. He was such a good man. He didn't deserve that."

Instantly his mind flashed back to the day she had lost her father, and he remembered how sorry he had felt for her. She was sitting at his bedside in ICU when it happened. He had made it through the trauma of the accident, and according to Audrey the doctors had assured her family that he would pull through just fine. Instead he'd thrown a clot, and the Code Team couldn't save him.

He had been the lab part of the team, and he would never forget the look on Laurel's face when she realized her father couldn't be resuscitated, how she had turned completely ashen and leaned against the wall. He'd started toward her thinking she was going to faint; but Linda, the head nurse, got there first, and he backed off. He'd wanted so much to comfort her, but he was the last person she wanted near her. He'd already hurt her enough.

"Laurel," he began softly. "I'm sorry about your father. I never got to tell you that. I'm so sorry I couldn't give you the support you deserved, and I'm especially sorry for the reason I couldn't give that support."

She chewed on her lower lip and glanced toward Gena. "Losing him was hard enough, but once he left this world, it was like all the forces of evil were set loose. Now my family's self-destructing, and there's not a thing I can do about it."

She was quiet for a long time, and just when he didn't think she was going to say anything else, she continued. "I've tried to help, but it's like pouring love down a caustic drain. They never get filled. The love gets dissolved in the bitter acid. I've had to settle for saving myself and Gena. It was never the way I wanted it to be, and it's so sad."

He realized this for the rare and pure moment of trust that it was, so he didn't spoil it with words. Instead he reached to touch her cheek with his palm rubbing it gently. He was totally shocked when she leaned her face into his hand, and it sent waves of warmth though him.

Gena abruptly appeared before them leaning forward placing one wet hand on his leg and one on Laurel's. "I'm hungry. Is it lunchtime yet?"

Laurel reached into her bag and glanced at her watch. "It's almost ten thirty. Close enough."

"I have an idea." He glanced at Laurel. "I woke up this morning craving pancakes. Would you ladies do me the honor of accompanying me to the Pancake House? My treat."

Gena started bouncing up and down. "Yeah! Yeah!"

Laurel smiled at the child's exuberance. "Okay, let's go get changed."

Chapter Eight

On Sunday morning after she and Gena had breakfast with Mama Rita and Grandpa, Laurel guided her car over the dirt road headed toward the blacktopped mountain highway. She hadn't had time to find a church in the valley yet. Until then she would keep attending the little white Presbyterian church on the brow.

Almost a half-mile up the road, just past the sage grass field that marked the edge of Grandpa's land, she glanced toward the bare spot where her grandparents' church used to stand. An arsonist had burned the clapboard structure to the ground last December. Without funds to rebuild, the handful of congregants now met at her grandparents' home. She'd loved that church as a child, but it consisted only of older people now, and she wanted Gena to have friends.

The large expanse of the Harper Memorial Baptist Church graveyard stretched just past the bare area where the church used to stand. A glint of the morning sun bounced off the headstone of the first roadside plot: the Harper plot, Daddy's gravestone. She felt a squeezing pain in her chest as she remembered that awful day in ICU when she had watched him die. He wasn't supposed to die. She'd really believed that God wouldn't take him away from her, too.

A few yards from the end of the graveyard the road branched left toward Brown Town and continued right as Harper Hollow Road snaking up a short hill, then down past the long driveway to Mama's eighty acres and around and up another hill toward the main highway and the brow. A long row of white mailboxes mounted on a common weathered plank marked the fork. Brown Town Road, which ultimately led to Coal City, was even worse than this one. She remembered sitting in the back of the school bus, bouncing completely off her seat when Cade Parker, their driver, would hit an unavoidable rut.

She'd loved this community as a child, but the older she got the more she saw it as the root of her anguish. She kept moving farther away from it. Maybe it wasn't the place as much as it was the heritage that made her feel trapped, but it was hard to separate the two. There was a mindset here that led to heartache, an outdated allegiance to the past that wounded and imprisoned. The sense of loyalty to this land was the hardest thing for her to understand. The once lucrative coal mines had been abandoned almost two decades ago. After all-electric homes flourished, the demand for mountain coal had severely diminished. Coal City became a ghost town, and the railroad eventually ripped up the tracks that led up the mountain to it.

Although the land was still rich, only a few people farmed for a living. Those who had successfully lived off the land, her grandfather's generation, were dying off. Their offspring, thanks to the war, had seen that this impoverished pocket of Sunset Mountain wasn't all there was to the world. Their confusion as to what to do with that knowledge had spawned her generation in all its ambivalence. Maybe that was where she had gotten her vision. She'd often wondered why her aspirations were so different from those around her. Those her age had married in their teens, got stuck in a lifestyle they weren't equipped to follow, and claimed as their most valuable asset a land that no longer sustained them.

She could understand ownership of property. She'd loved having her little place, but it wasn't more important than having a nest egg for emergencies or for assuring good care for Gena. Mama, like most of her neighbors, sacrificed her basic needs for love of her land. She chose the pride of that ownership over common sense. It was the mountain way. Laurel hated being tied to the insanity. It was a legacy she did not want to perpetuate, and that made her a traitor. She didn't belong here, but then neither did she belong in the world she aspired to. The caste system of this mountain had always dictated her place. She was born and reared on its lowest elevation, the poor side, and the topography of the mountain itself formed a natural wall between her world and the one she aspired to.

Even her name labeled her indelibly a part of the mountain. The mountain laurel, for which Mama had named her, flourished without tending and blossomed into delicate star-shaped clusters every spring. It was a survivor like she was, maybe because all parts of it were poisonous to fend off predators. She couldn't help wondering if that was happening to her. Was her soul becoming poisoned? Her heart? Like Mama? She shivered. She hated that, like her birthplace, her name seemed to mark her fate and take away her choices. This wasn't who she was. Would she ever be allowed to be herself?

She glanced at Gena who was absorbed in the rush of wind on her face and in her curls as she took in the countryside around them, her cheek resting on tiny hands that clutched the open window. It was for Gena's sake that she was going to the mountain church. Gena loved Sunday school and eagerly bounced out of bed every Sunday. She delighted in hearing the Bible stories the preacher's wife, Miss Emily, told and illustrated by flannel graph. With her flannel easel background and her colorful fabric figures she made the Bible stories come to life.

Train up a child in the way he should go; and when he is old, he will not depart from it. Mama had been big on that verse from Proverbs, training her up in the way she should go. Had she departed from it? Had her night with David been a sin or just a bad decision, and had God punished her for it by taking both him and Daddy away from her? Had he filled her life with all this turmoil because of that one beautiful night?

That would be Mama's take on all of it, but she couldn't trust Mama's laws. They were too subject to change. She had been so shocked when she learned that Mama didn't always practice what she preached. She used half-truths and underhanded manipulations to rule her children. Gene called her the great god Mama. It was an accurate perception, and sometimes she feared that her resentment of Mama separated her from the real God.

For that reason, gathering with the people of God on Sunset Mountain hadn't been so uplifting for her. Her neighbors saw only the false front Mama portrayed. No one understood the problems of being her child, so why try to convince them otherwise? She did her true worship and seeking of truth alone Sunday mornings before Gena awoke.

Just this morning she'd read from Psalms, and verse 27:14 kept repeating in her head. *Wait on the Lord; be of good courage, and he shall strengthen thine heart.* Hadn't she been doing that? And things with her family had gotten worse. Then there was the matter of David. She knew she'd never stop loving him, but just because their paths had crossed again and he had said he was sorry, that didn't mean things could ever work between them.

Just like Mama he'd left out part of the truth, the most important part. If she'd known he hadn't completely severed his relationship with Marilee when he proposed to her, that whole night would have turned out differently.

"Look, Mommy." Gena pointed to the bent woman with stringy salt-and-pepper hair who was trudging along the road ahead of them. "It's Miss Jennie. We got to stop and give her a ride to church like we always do."

Great. She was not in the mood for Miss Jennie today. The woman would be some people's idea of a village idiot, but since

Harper Hollow was already filled with abnormal and eccentric people, she fit right in.

She wasn't an idiot by any stretch of the imagination. She knew the name of every person from the community, their ancestors, their children and all their birthdays, wedding dates, and dates of death. She was a walking census log. She was also a walking newspaper. If it happened on this end of the mountain Jennie knew about it, which was phenomenal since she didn't have a phone.

Laurel carefully pulled to the side of the road and leaned to call to the woman through Gena's open window. Jennie moved quickly for a lady her age, especially one with the dowager's hump she had slowly developed over the years.

"Hidee, Laurel. And little Gena. You sure are growing." She slung her navy purse straps over her arm, climbed into the back seat, and pulled the door shut. As Laurel pulled back onto the road Jennie leaned over the seat clutching her worn Bible in her right hand. "I'm much obliged to you." She always said that, and she always sat leaning over the seat talking to them. "Shoowee, it sure is hot." She always commented on the weather, too.

"How are you today, Jennie?" She didn't know what else to say, but she didn't have to worry. Jennie usually did all the talking during the drive to the church, and usually during that short trip Laurel learned everything that had happened in the past week whether she wanted to hear it or not. Sometimes she listened. Sometimes she didn't.

She didn't know Jennie's age, but she'd always seemed old. She could read and write very well, but she always got somebody else to write letters for her. She remembered the summer Mama pawned Jennie's letter-writing ritual off on her. She'd been twelve. Jennie dictated, and she wrote. The content was always simplistic. "How are you? I am fine." She always commented on the weather and her garden. It was never longer than a page.

"Make the letters real big now," Jennie would say. Once she'd stuffed the letter in the envelope, sealed it, and put the stamp on,

Jennie made sure every millimeter of the envelope flap and the stamp was glued tightly. Then she would ask in total sincerity, "Reckon it'll go?"

Mix obsessive-compulsive with eccentric and sprinkle it with a touch of autism, and you had Jennie Austin. She had been married twice, and she'd outlived both husbands, nice men and pillars of the community. Laurel had always consoled herself with the thought that if Jennie could find two husbands, she for sure should be able to find one. But it looked as if she couldn't have been more wrong about that.

Jennie talked nonstop, and even though Laurel tried to tune her out, she got the latest update on Harper Hollow gossip. The woman was more informative than the *Moore County Herald*, which Grandpa had nicknamed the *Moore County Can't Hardly* because it was mostly gossip. He always said, "You can't hardly find any news in that rag for the wagging tongue gossip."

She learned that Nellie Wagoner had given birth to a twelve-pound boy, her tenth child, and was out working in her garden the next day. The Wagoners were one of Mama's "poor families," as if they weren't poor themselves.

Mama had procured help for her poor from the rich families at the top of the mountain. Laurel had often thought that a lesson in birth control could have helped much more than free groceries and hand-me-down clothes given once a year. But Mama had her causes, and people loved her for it.

Maybe she was ungrateful, but she'd always resented Mama's work with the poor because of its influence on her life. It redefined her, exposed her, and even invalidated her most cherished memories. She would never forget that first visit from the rich Santa. He'd come with a bag full of toys to the little white church on the brow, the one she was headed for today. Although she'd loved the beautiful brown-haired doll she'd received that night, along with the gift came an unwelcome truth. If these strangers and their Santa had brought these gifts for the poor, then she must be one of them.

When she'd attended a Christmas program that same year at the rich Methodist church at the Top, she'd been awed by the site of the children dressed up like angels. They wore real halos that glistened far brighter than the tinsel garlands that she and the neighborhood children had always worn pinned to their hair. The rich children's gowns glistened with white sequins as opposed to the sometimes-graying white sheets that draped Harper Hollow angels. So, despite the beauty of the costumes, at the tender age of nine she'd decided that not only was she poor, but she was also one of God's lesser angels.

She thought she'd grown beyond the Christmas caste system until the year Mama's rich friends brought their Santa caravan to her end of the mountain. She'd been sixteen years old and long past believing in Santa. The caravan was crowded with kids her age and a few chaperones. Mama had dropped her off at Tucker's Grocery at the top of the mountain where she helped load the boxes of goodies stored there. Then she learned that Mama had chosen her to navigate the train to the houses of her poor. It wouldn't have been so bad had they dropped her off at the grocery once it was over, but they'd delivered her per Mama's instructions all the way down their rut-filled driveway in front of their dilapidated house amid her brothers' junk cars. Before that moment of exposure the kids from the Top had treated her as one of them, but she could see reflected on their faces that it all changed when they saw who she really was. From that humiliating day forward she vowed that would never happen again.

"Lon Green had another heart attack," Jennie announced bringing her back to the present. "He's out at Mountain General. He ain't expected to make it. I reckon it's a miracle he made it this far. Everything old lady Green cooks is swimming in lard grease." Jennie clucked her tongue. "It's sure a shame. Remember that time your mama give him first aid and saved his life?" She nodded, and Jennie continued. "Your mama is a saint. You ought to be proud."

She stopped at the intersection with the blacktopped highway and turned right. She *was* proud of Mama, and she loved her; but a part of her hated her, too, and she couldn't stand to be around her. She didn't expect anybody else to understand that.

Then Jennie told her that Mama's old Civil Defense unit, the one she had organized eight years ago, had rescued some climbers from the Moore Falls area where they'd been climbing on the rocky cliffs near the falls.

"Your mama sure was the stuff around here, but she just ain't doing no good, is she, Laurel? Poor little old Del just takes such good care of her. That's got to be hard on him, but I reckon he knows how it feels to be all stove up ever since he got run over that time. It looks like Gene can't quit that bottle long enough to do much to help." She reached to pat Gena on the head. "And Sarah just worries herself sick about Gena not having a daddy. Poor, poor Gena."

So Del was a saint; Gene was a hopeless sot; and she was an unfit mother. There would be no compassion in this place for those who struggled for a separate life, only for the one who molded himself to the insanity. Jennie's entire discourse may as well have come straight from Mama's mouth because she'd influenced it by spreading her venom throughout the community. Well, this was it. She was finding a church in the valley.

"Gena's just fine, Jennie," she snapped. She spotted Betty Jo's truck parked on the left side of the church as she approached the parking lot. She made a right turn off the highway and pulled in beside it. "Okay, here we are." She picked up her purse from the seat beside her and reached for Gena. "Come on, sweetie."

She knew she would have to give Jennie a ride home since she had to go back that way to stop by Mama's. She would feel like a heel if she didn't, but she seriously considered taping her mouth shut.

Chapter Nine

David's mind wandered as the choir at Tenth Street Presbyterian Church sang the prelude hymns to Pastor Finch's sermon. His thoughts went back to yesterday's lunch at the Pancake House. Gena had been her usual outgoing self. Watching her, he'd thought she had to be his child. She was an extrovert like him, and he hadn't detected even a shred of shyness.

"I've got a new friend, Mommy," she'd said to Laurel.

"That's great, sweetie. Where did you meet this friend?"

"At the swing when Miss Lucy took me to out to play."

"Does your friend live in our apartment complex, too, then?"

Gena nodded her curly head. "Yes. Can her grandma bring her over to play with me some day?"

"Well, uh, sure. I'd want to talk to her mommy and daddy first."

"Her mommy goes to work at the hospital like you do, but Sally's not got a daddy. Just like me." Laurel frowned, but Gena concentrated on pouring syrup on her pancakes and went on talking. "Her daddy went to live with Jesus. They put a flag over him so the angels could see him from Heaven and come pick him up, and they shot guns so Jesus would know he was coming. Sally's mommy got to keep the flag. I told her my Grandma Sarah says my daddy didn't go to be with Jesus, and someday she's gonna tell me all about him."

Gena nonchalantly took a bite of her pancakes while Laurel almost choked on hers. Her face colored, and she cleared her throat and took a sip of tea.

"We've talked about this, sweetheart. Remember?" He carefully assessed Laurel's expression as she spoke to Gena. She seemed frustrated, and she was clearly upset that the subject had come up.

"On my next birthday when I get to be five, we're going to have a talk about my daddy 'cause I'll be old enough to understand."

"That's right." He could see that Laurel was choosing her words carefully and that she was trying hard to keep her voice even. "This is not Grandma Sarah's business. This is our business. Okay? You and Mommy." Gena nodded, and Laurel continued. "I'll ask Miss Lucy to get your new friend's phone number from her grandma. I'll call her mommy then and see if we can arrange some visits. Okay?"

Gena flashed Laurel a smile and nodded. She wiggled around in her seat and glanced across at him. "You could get married to David, Mommy. Then he could be my daddy. I like him."

"Oh, Gena," Laurel moaned and colored again. "David doesn't—"

He leaned toward Gena, interrupting Laurel on purpose. "Sweetie, I would marry your mommy this second if she would say yes. I've known her a long time, and she's very special; but remember those things I did that I shouldn't have?" Gena nodded. "Well, Mommy needs some time to sort that out." He winked at her then. "That doesn't mean I'm going to give up on her. You can help me with that. See, every night after she goes to sleep I want you to go into her room and whisper, 'David is a good guy.' Maybe that'll soften her."

Gena giggled; and Laurel rolled her eyes at him, but she did smile.

Even though he'd handled that awkward situation and placated Gena without totally alienating Laurel, he wanted to know the particulars about Gena's paternity, too. He knew he deserved this secrecy. Laurel used to be as open and unguarded as Gena, but he'd been the one to change all that by hurting her.

It made him ache in some dark place inside to see how much she had closed off emotionally. Grady had warned him that life had stomped the sweet out of her, but he wouldn't describe the change in her exactly that way. The sweetness was still there. He could see it when she interacted with Gena. It was joy she had lost—and hopefulness—all because of him.

If only he could find a way to reach her. If only he could make her see the truth: he had loved her that night and he loved her now. Regardless of how things had turned out after that night, he felt that he was one with her, and that without her in his life, he would never feel complete.

He'd thought about going over to ask her and Gena to come with him to church this morning, but he'd seen her leaving before he'd even finished his coffee and taken his shower. He'd gone into his office and sat at his desk making out his tithe check. His apartment was an end unit, and that room had a window facing the parking lot.

As he stuffed the check into the envelope from the packet provided by the church, he caught a flash of light in his peripheral vision. He looked up to see that it was the sun reflecting off Laurel's car door as she opened it.

He watched. She still had the baby blue 1965 Ford she had bought new the year after they'd finished training. He'd bought his '65 red Mustang at close to the same time, and he still drove it, too. She was obviously dressed for church, but she was leaving so early. He figured she must be headed for Sunset Mountain.

Gena wore a frilly purple dress, and Laurel looked beautiful even at a distance in a sleeveless pink A-line. He watched as she lifted Gena into the passenger seat and closed the door. As she walked around to the driver's side the adoring smile she'd had for Gena faded to a pensive sadness.

She was too young to radiate such unhappiness. He vowed right then, sitting in that church pew, that no matter how many times she rejected him he would keep showing her his love. He'd let her vent her anger as much as she had to, but giving up on her was not an option. God had given him this second chance. He wouldn't let it slip away.

Chapter Ten

As Laurel drove into the rut-filled driveway of the house where she had grown up, she cringed at how much the place seemed to have deteriorated even in the two weeks since her last trip. That had been on the Sunday before last. She usually came for long visits on Sundays after church and made brief afternoon stops on weekdays on her way to pick up Gena at Mama Rita's.

She hadn't come at all the week before she started her new job. She'd worked late almost every evening that last week at Mountain General trying to assure a smooth transition of her department to the new chief. Every available minute after work she'd spent packing for the move to the valley.

She wouldn't come here at all if she didn't have to. It was too heartbreaking. If Mama had listened to her, she could be living in a nice house with plenty of money in the bank to handle her medical emergencies. If she'd planned better, this place wouldn't be crumbling around her. If she didn't have so much bitterness inside her, maybe she wouldn't be self-destructing, and maybe she wouldn't even have medical emergencies.

She pulled into the bare yard directly in front of the log cabin. Once there had been a lawn here. She reached for Gena and helped her from the car, holding her hand as they walked up the rickety front steps to the aluminum storm door with the initial *H* in the grillwork.

She'd once been so proud of this stylish door. She'd bought it brand new from Sears with her first paycheck seven years ago. After that she had opened a charge account at Sears and bought a new living room suite for her family. How naive to think she could change their status in any way. The door looked as shabby as the house now, and the new furniture inside was just as worn.

She squeezed Gena's hand tighter as they entered the foyer, which used to be an open porch. Daddy had enclosed it to make a freezer room back when she was a teenager. With the storm door attached there was about a six-foot wide entryway to the living room. Instead of the rustic foyer it used to be, now it was just another junk-filled entrance to hell.

Connie and Del had moved in with Mama immediately after Daddy died, and Gene routinely stayed in his tiny attic bedroom when he and his girlfriend of the moment had an argument. Gene and Del didn't get along. They'd never gotten along because Del had always been Mama's favorite child. Gene resented that fact since Del wasn't their real brother. She'd heard him express his jealousy many times. Only when he was drunk would he do it in front of Mama because criticizing Del was the one thing Mama wouldn't tolerate.

Laurel used to have a good relationship with Del. As far as she was concerned, he was her brother. She didn't remember when he hadn't been a part of their family. But as a grownup especially in the five years since Daddy's death, Del's personality had become increasingly caustic. Remembering the sweet little boy he used to be, she found it hard to accept this change.

She took in a breath preparing for confrontation and turned the doorknob. Mama's hospital bed commanded the living room.

"Why, it's my little Gena." Mama turned her head as far as the arthritic rigidity of her neck would allow and smiled.

Gena responded by bounding over and hopping onto the chair next to her. She bent to kiss Mama's cheek. Laurel didn't try to stop her. Mama desperately needed this kind of innocent love from someone she hadn't yet alienated with her manipulations.

Mama was so pitiful. Every time Laurel visited it broke her heart to see how much she'd lost. It also made her angry when she acknowledged that at so many points Mama had the option to get better and receive the medical expertise to stop her decline, but she always chose the path of pain and self-destruction.

She engaged in light conversation with Connie and bounced words off Del. You never really talked to Del. It was more like verbal Russian roulette. She never knew what comment had the potential to precipitate his anger because his eruptions of temper couldn't be measured against precipitating causes. It seemed he had a soul full of free-floating anger, so she'd stopped trying to get along with him. They never agreed on anything anyway.

"Gene had to go to the emergency room last night," Connie told her in a low voice. "He was drunk and got into it with Peggy again. Only this time her brother was there and hit him over the head with a whiskey bottle."

"Is he okay? Did they release him?"

"Yeah, but he had to have eight stitches," Connie whispered. "Banjo brought him home from the ER. He's up in his old bedroom sleeping off his hangover."

When he was a teenager, Gene's troubles had involved driving under the influence and public drunkenness, which more often than not had landed him in jail. Even with all his wildness and numerous wrecks, he'd walked away without a scratch each time. Now it seemed his addiction was killing him in degrees. Each new binge brought deeper wounding.

They visited for around thirty minutes, making small talk. Mama acted so unusually pleasant that Laurel wondered if she'd forgotten their phone conversation about David's letters, but then Mama never forgot anything.

"I need to go put some clothes in the washer," Connie announced abruptly. "Then I'll set the table for lunch."

"I want to help, Aunt Connie," Gena chirped, quickly hopping down from the chair where she'd been coloring a picture for Mama.

Connie laughed. "I wouldn't dream of doing it without you."

Gena slipped her hand into Connie's, and they headed for the kitchen. Then Del went to the back bedrooms to do whatever it was Del did, and she was left alone with Mama. As she flipped through Mama's bills and read through the explanation of benefits from her insurance companies, she heard the washer begin to fill with water. The washer and dryer were tucked in the kitchen corner against the wall behind her. By thc time she'd finished sorting and writing the needed check payments, the washer kicked into the agitation cycle, making the floor vibrate.

"I told her to take those clothes to the washateria," Mama said angrily. "She's had that thing going since you got Banjo's twins to dump your hand-me-downs on us.

Hand-me-downs? Her washer and dryer might have been four years old, but they were like new; and she'd thought she was helping. She could have used them herself and would have except that her apartment had a laundry facility in each section, and poor Connie spent half her life at the valley Laundromat washing clothes.

"One of these days my bed is going to drop straight into the cellar the way she keeps that thing shaking the floor. Termites have gnawed the underpinnings, and all it needs is a few more shakes."

She sighed. Everything she did to help, even when it was a sacrifice, somehow got devalued. "I thought Del took care of that, Mama. Two months ago he was supposed to have replaced those underpinnings and also sprayed for termites."

"Del has his hands full," Mama snapped.

"Really? Well, I already had Uncle Will and Uncle Joshua scheduled to take care of it, but he had a fit. Said it was his business and he'd take care of it. So, I guess that means he didn't do it, after all."

"He took care of replacing the beams, but I can't stand to smell that spray."

So that means it won't be long before the termites eat through them, too, she thought, and she decided to just drop it. What was the point? Mama and Del would have their way no matter what she thought.

Since things were already confrontational, she figured she might as well go ahead and follow up on their conversation about David's letters. There was no use in delaying it, so she got straight to the point. "I want my letters, Mama."

"I don't know why you're making such a fuss over a bunch of old letters, Laurel." She adjusted herself in her hospital bed and reached for the paper bag next to her. She couldn't fit her gnarled arthritic fingers around it so she picked it up between her palms and set it on the hospital tray that stretched over her bed.

As angry as Laurel was, that act almost reduced her to tears. She'd seen many cases of rheumatoid arthritis in the eight years of her profession but never one as severe as Mama's. Her case presented like a different disease altogether, one with no hope, no cure, and no let up from the pain she experienced or perpetrated.

Her first symptoms came within two days of Daddy's death. It was as if she couldn't stand the competition. Everybody was grieving over the enemy. So, even as he was being laid to rest, Mama was doing battle with Daddy.

Now in the five years since, Mama had gone downhill so fast that Laurel didn't know how she was still alive. Yet she *was* still alive, hurt and hurting everyone who had ever loved her. It seemed she lived to die and fought like hell to maintain the right to do it.

Laurel reached for the bag, inspected its contents, and cringed when she saw that every single one of the dozen or so envelopes had been opened. She jerked her head up to confront Mama. "You read my mail?"

"You had a chip on your shoulder when you moved back home. I needed to see what was going on."

"After you satisfied your curiosity why didn't you give them to me? They're addressed to me. It's the U.S. mail, Mama, and stealing it is a federal offense. They have laws against this."

"Oh, don't be ridiculous."

"You could've at least told me he called. Is there anything else about my personal life that you've kept from me?"

Mama didn't answer. Instead she stared at her as only Mama could stare. It was her silent command to confess all misdeeds. She had always been Mama's good little girl who vowed to herself that she would never do anything she couldn't look her in the eye and confess. But once she turned twenty-one and began supporting herself, she decided confession time was over even though she hadn't planned to do a thing that needed confessing.

"So, I guess that boy who ruined you is back in your life, or you wouldn't know about these letters."

She felt herself begin to tremble with anger, and the old heartache bubbled to the surface. *Ruined?* She didn't know what Mama had read in those letters from David, but she knew in her heart, down past the anger and the pain, that her one night with him had been the most beautiful moment of her life. She didn't know how she could have loved someone so purely, how it could have been so right, so sacred, and turn out the way it did, but she would never regret it.

"Did you let the whole family read my letters? Did you and Del call a family meeting?"

"This is between you and me, Laurel."

"I'm almost thirty years old. I handle my life and Gena's all by myself. In other words, I'm a grownup. No, Mama, this is my business. It's between me and only me."

"I raised you better, Laurel."

"You don't know anything about my life, Mama. All you know is you want to control it, and I won't let you."

"I know that you've got no business raising a kid. If I weren't in this bed, I'd take Gena away from you. I ought to do it anyway."

She had to grit her teeth to keep from yelling. She took in a deep breath and spoke in an even tone. "You wonder why I don't visit more often. Well, this is why." She clutched the bag in her left hand and headed for the kitchen to get Gena.

"You come back here, Laurel. Do you hear me?"

She kept walking, and behind her Mama was already in the theatrical throes of yet another gasping crisis. She heard the sound of Del's cowboy boots thudding on the short tier of steps that led down from the back bedrooms as he came to investigate. How could Mama do this, and wasn't she aiding and abetting her just like Del always did if she fell for it? Couldn't she have a justifiable disagreement with Mama without having coals of deathbed guilt heaped on her? She hated this!

As she entered the kitchen Gena glanced up from helping Connie set the table. She put her tiny forefinger to her lips and whispered, "We have to be quiet. Uncle Gene is up the steep steps sleeping."

The steep steps were the rough ladder-like stairs that led to the two attic bedrooms in the main cabin. Mama had built them, and she had roughly partitioned off the two tiny rooms above. Initially she had decorated the primitive stairwell with an unframed farm scene done in oils by a distant relative. It was a good painting but dark and dreary.

One of those bedrooms had always been Gene's, but since he was six and a half years older, he had occupied it intermittently between his liaisons, his marriage, his moonshine binges, and his jail sentences for public drunkenness.

The other bedroom had been hers. It was barely big enough for her mirrored dresser and the twin beds shoved under the eaves of the low-pitched roof. The only place she could stand to her full five-foot-six-inch height had been in the center of the room where the roof peaked.

It had been hot and humid in the summer, and on July nights she'd kept turning her pillow to the cool side to be able to bear the heat. In the winter she did her homework propped on her bed with a small electric heater sitting on a chair blowing toward her. She slept burrowed under layers of thick quilts that kept her warm even when the fires below in the wood-burning heater in the living room and the monkey heater in the kitchen had dwindled to embers.

She'd loved the privacy of that room. It was her space away from the rest of them. It had been just her and the night sounds: the whippoorwills who sounded as lonely as she felt; the rain on the tin roof, a different sound given the intensity of the downpour but always peaceful even in the midst of a storm; and hound dogs barking in the hollow engaged by their owners in a ritual she saw no sense in—possum hunting.

She stooped to Gena's level and looked into her eyes. "Listen, sweetie, we need to go." She was still shaking with anger, but she tried to keep her voice even.

As she straightened, she saw Connie's smile transform into a disappointed pout. "You're not going to stay and eat?"

If she ate a bite of anything right now she'd choke, and this place was suffocating her every bit as much as Mama's dictatorial control was suffocating her. "I'm so sorry, Connie. I hate to miss your good cooking." She meant that, and she liked Connie so much better than she liked Del; but she had to get out of here. "We'll have to grab something at home. I've got a lot to do with this new job. We need to get back."

Gena didn't protest, and Laurel held her hand as they walked out the kitchen door. One of Del's dogs yelped from a nearby pen. Laurel wasn't supposed to know they were fighting dogs, but she wasn't stupid. She felt sorry for the poor animals, yet she feared them, too. They'd been bred to inflict pain. She lifted Gena into her arms and hugged her closer.

The back and side yards were scattered with her brothers' junk cars in various states of disrepair as well as miscellaneous car parts: batteries, motors, and carburetors. She side-stepped a hubcap brimming with water from a recent rain and swatted at the mosquitoes that immediately spiraled up from their breeding spot to attack them.

Del's goats roamed freely, adding to the squalor. This place was like a museum of bad choices. Her family had always been poor, but this was different. This was apathy. This was just plain laziness. It was barbaric, and it didn't have to be this way.

If not for Connie the inside of the house would look as bad as the outside. The furnishings might be shabby. Del may have stacked two of the three new bedrooms full with his dog food, fighting paraphernalia, and miscellaneous junk, but as long as Connie had a broom, a mop, and access to water, she would have cleanliness around her.

She had to admire Connie. She couldn't live here and rise above it the way Connie had. She could barely stand to visit. It broke her heart and made her furious all at the same time, and she wondered if her life would always be like this, nothing but heartache and anger.

After Daddy died, Mama had sued Mitchell Logging Company. The accident hadn't been Daddy's fault. He'd been hit head-on inside a blind mountain curve when the logging truck's brakes failed and its driver steered away from the steep embankment. The police speculated that if he hadn't been carrying a load of brick, Daddy's lighter truck would have flipped, and he would have been killed instantly. Both Gene and Del had been working at the construction site where Daddy was headed. Daddy's brothers, his partners in the family business, had come along ten minutes after the accident. They'd called her at the hospital, and she'd rushed to the emergency room to wait for his ambulance to arrive.

Once the lawsuit had been resolved, Mama received $100,000, plenty enough that she could've lived comfortably for the rest of her life. Six months before the settlement Laurel had bought her house for only $15,000. She knew Mama could find a great house big enough to meet her needs for around $20,000 even if both Del and Gene lived with her. She could have one built on her eighty acres for even less. She'd tried to talk her into spending and investing the money wisely, but Mama wouldn't listen.

First of all, she gave Del money to start an ambulance service. He'd worked in Daddy's construction company since high school, but he didn't like the business. He quit immediately after Daddy died and moved in with Mama. An ambulance service was a good idea because there wasn't one on the mountain. Ambulances came up from the valley, and the delay in their arrival had often meant the difference between life and death. When Del had presented a service proposal to Mountain General, Byron eagerly signed a profitable contract with him for his exclusive services.

Del hired his redneck buddies as drivers and attendants. They excelled in swiftly navigating the back roads in bad weather mainly because most of them had gotten their experience outrunning county law enforcement agents. In spite of that and their lack of experience in anything but the most elementary first aid, things went well for two years. Then the people at the top of the mountain and a few from their end began to complain about disrespectful attitudes from Del's staff.

She remembered being mortified when Del told her about his last run-in with Byron that ended his contract with the hospital. "He told me he'd had complaints about my men not showing respect just because Virgil told one old, rich biddy to stop stuffing herself with jalapeños. We've picked her up once a month for the last six months, and we always have to fumigate the ambulance."

She'd remembered Mrs. Brooks. She had chronic gall bladder disease that they'd finally diagnosed and treated. "Maybe jalapeños weren't the best thing for her condition," she told Del, "but it's not the place of an ambulance attendant to badger her about it. It's unprofessional."

Her opinion had only fanned the flames of Del's anger. "You sound like that pansy-assed administrator. He said I needed to make my men keep to a standard—his standard, of course."

"You *are* under contract with him," she reminded him. "What you do reflects on the hospital."

"Bull crap. I told him where he could stuff it. He's not telling me how to run my business."

"Del, you need to work with him," she remembered pleading. "You've got a great thing going. Talk to your guys. Ask them to remember that they're transporting sick or injured people who need to be treated gently. Tell them to change their attitudes."

"Listen up, your highness, I ain't changing nothing."

Del wouldn't compromise, and the hospital cancelled his contract. He didn't even try to take his venture elsewhere. He quit a lucrative business and didn't try to sell the company or his expensive equipment to recover any of Mama's investment. His fleet of four ambulances now sat in the back field overgrown with weeds along with the other accumulated junk. Her whiz-kid brother, with his genius-level IQ, hadn't worked at anything since except for his goats and his fighting dogs.

He hadn't been the only one to squander the settlement. Mama had done her share. Daddy had long ago drawn up plans for his dream house. She remembered that he'd cut the trees from their acreage, hauled them to the Johnson Fork sawmill, and after the lumber was cut, had stacked it in the hollow. He stored the roofing and nails in the then-vacant attic. He even started building the foundation to the addition. The new part would consist of three bedrooms, a bath, a basement den, and a garage. He planned to tear down the old log cabin and replace its three rooms with a new living room, dining room, and kitchen.

Daddy completed the foundation for the addition the year Laurel turned eleven. The day he smoothed the final piece of mountain stone into place he and Mama got into an argument. She never discovered what the argument was about, but Mama and Daddy argued all the time so what did it matter? He threw a shovel at her and stormed out of the basement. He never went back. From that day forward Daddy worked in his construction business building other people's dreams and left the skeleton of his to rot and overgrow with weeds.

Once Mama got her money from Daddy's settlement, she decided to hire her unscrupulous cousin Cecil to finish the addition Daddy had started. Never mind that Daddy had once commented he wouldn't let his chickens live in a house that Cecil built. She'd tried to talk Mama out of it, and she did finally convince her to get an estimate from Daddy's brothers. They had, after all, been partners with Daddy in his construction company.

She'd been pleasantly surprised when Uncle Will and Uncle Joshua told her they would like to do the job for cost alone in memory of Daddy because as the oldest son he had mentored them and they'd always looked up to him.

To do the job free they would have to do the work on weekends and earn a living during the week. Mama grew impatient as always and let Cecil finish what Laurel's uncles had barely had the chance to start.

Halfway through the job Cecil took off with the substantial advance Mama had paid him. She hired a private detective to track him down. She prosecuted, and Cecil ended up in jail. By then he'd spent all her advance money, and she'd spent most of what was left of her settlement on legal fees to prosecute. At that point Cecil had only added the new addition, minus the basement den, and it fit the old log cabin like a tumor.

Now, five years later, the house was like everything else about her family, a disaster. Only one of the back three bedrooms in the new addition was used as a real bedroom for Connie and Del. The addition had begun to look as ramshackle as the original cabin where Mama stayed. All the settlement money was gone—all of it for nothing. Money poured into a bottomless pit.

* * *

That night, depressed from her visit with Mama, Laurel took strength from her nighttime routine with Gena. Bath time was always fun. It was filled with animated chatter, bubble foam mustaches and beards, and Gena's sweet giggles when Laurel pretended to be a friendly bee buzzing by to wash her ears and her fingernails.

Bedtime was their cuddle time. She cherished their special time when she hugged Gena close and told her how much she loved her. She read at least two stories, which Gena always chose, and the prayers they prayed together made her feel more connected to God than her own angry supplications. Gena in her fresh innocence kept her anchored and focused on what was real and gave her otherwise bleak life meaning and purpose that was not dead end.

After Gena went to sleep, Laurel sat on her bed and read David's letters. He'd sent two the first month and one a month for the next twelve months. In every one of them he said the same thing he'd said last Monday but in more detail. Also in every letter he told her he loved her.

He'd tucked a picture in one of the letters. The note on the back said it was his freshman class picture. She smoothed the tip of her finger across the photo. He looked every bit the doctor she knew he would be in this picture dressed in a white shirt and a black tie topped with a white lab coat.

His brown hair was longer now, mid-ear. Otherwise, he looked exactly the same with those blue eyes that could make love to her from across a room and the lips that just by their touch on hers could take her to Heaven. She glanced toward the wall that separated them, and she squeezed her eyes shut. "Did you mean those things, David," she whispered, "or was it my own delusions?"

She opened her eyes, sighed, and made herself snap out of it. He'd been a skirt chaser. That was a fact. Maybe she'd cut him more slack than he deserved, but she had known that he was an only child with over-protective parents. He was probably making up for lost time once he got some freedom away from them, but that didn't mean he couldn't fall in love. She knew how it felt to bounce off your parents. Hers had hated each other. For that reason she hadn't wanted to ever fall in love, but she had.

She hadn't regretted for one second that they made love, and that amazed her. She hadn't felt shame or guilt. She hadn't felt *ruined* as Mama had so sordidly put it. What she had felt was a different kind of regret, but not for the act that had been sweet and pure. She regretted that David hadn't really loved her, that he had lied with his words and his actions. She regretted that he wasn't capable of the kind of love she needed and that she could never love anyone else the way she loved him.

That night so many years ago she'd believed that he meant it when he said he loved her. She had seen it in his eyes and felt it in the way he made love to her, but after seeing Marilee's wedding announcement the next day nothing made sense to her. What she had known in her heart and soul was a lie, and nothing could make the pain go away. It was still there even now, buried beneath all her other pain.

"Once you were gone from my life," David had written in his last few letters, "I realized that you're the one I've loved all along from the beginning, and after making love to you, there can never be anyone else."

Last Tuesday when she had overheard the lab assistants talking, for once the gossip had supported everything David had told her about that marriage announcement: that Marilee had indeed used him to make another guy jealous. It seemed that he was considered a lone wolf now, too.

In his letters he'd begged for her forgiveness. It was the theme and content of all of them. As she gathered the envelopes and tucked them away in her dresser drawer, she wondered what she would have done if Mama hadn't intercepted those letters. Maybe she would've forgiven him. Maybe she could forgive him now, but her life was more complicated now than it had been five years ago.

She didn't know how to trust. She didn't know how to be optimistic. Love had failed her on too many levels. She knew only how to put one foot in front of the other and keep going. Plus she had the responsibility of a child now.

Gena was her life. Loving her had saved her, and she loved her with all her heart. Having her in her life had filled the void created by losing David and her beloved father and any semblance of family she might have once had. But she'd learned that all love was tenuous, and she lived under the cloud of fear that someday Gena would be taken away from her, too.

Chapter Eleven

On Monday as soon as the morning huddle ended, David left Stu's office and walked past the tissue lab. It already reeked of the toluene used to prepare tissue samples for microscopic observation. He headed for the lounge and the new coffeepot. Usually the place was crawling with lab assistants and techs, but at seven o'clock everyone was either out collecting blood specimens for the morning run of clinical testing or doing quality control on the machines.

He'd managed to dodge Stu's hug as he left the huddle, but Laurel hadn't been so lucky. He saw her try, but she hadn't moved quickly enough.

She entered the room a few minutes behind him and muttered as she reached for a Styrofoam cup, "Geez, Stu's a nice guy, but for a man who hates germs, he sure is touchy-feely. How did you manage to escape him?"

"Lots of practice. But sometimes I'm not awake enough, and he nails me." He handed her the cup of coffee he had just poured and took her empty cup to fill for himself. "Now, if he tries to kiss me, boss or not, I swear I'm going to coldcock him."

She almost smiled. It got as far as her eyes. "I don't think you need to worry. That would involve saliva, and he wouldn't risk the germs. I notice he doesn't touch Miles. Do we just look like we need a hug?"

"Miles has so much hair with that beard and shaggy mane I think he's afraid he'll get cooties." He filled his cup and took a sip. "Ah, now this is coffee. You did great."

"All things considered this is probably cheaper than the previous setup. Why do these doctors so underestimate the power of a good cup of morning coffee?"

He grinned. "Something you can be sure I'll never be guilty of doing." He took another sip. "How was your Sunday off?"

"Okay."

"Just okay?"

"Yesterday I took Gena to the Presbyterian church we've always attended on Sunset Mountain. She loves going. I hate for her to miss, but I wish I could find one closer."

"Go with me next Sunday. I've been going to one about two miles away. It's Presbyterian. I was raised a Baptist, but these people are nice. The sermons are thought-provoking, and no one gets in your business. Gena would probably like it. I see a lot of children her age every Sunday."

She didn't acknowledge his offer. Instead she stirred cream into her coffee. He leaned close. "I could take you and Gena to Henderson's Cafeteria afterward. She'll love that for sure. They have purple Jell-O."

"Alright," she finally said. "We'll give it a try. Gena seems to be adjusting, but I worry anyway. Everything about her routine has changed: the new apartment, our schedule, her sitter."

"Who kept her when you lived on Sunset Mountain?"

"My grandparents. My dad's parents. They doted on her. I owned a house in a subdivision just down the hill from Mountain General. It was about six miles from their house."

"Do you still own your house?"

"No, I sold it when I took this job. Having the equity money in savings makes me feel more secure with this move. I wanted to be sure I could afford good care for Gena—someone who could come to the apartment. My grandparents are hard to measure up to, but I got lucky. Grady recommended a wonderful lady. Gena likes her a lot."

"I don't think you need to worry about Gena. She seems well-adjusted to me and very gregarious."

She actually smiled then. "She's definitely outgoing. We had summer block parties in our little subdivision. She loved playing with the neighborhood children at those, and ever since she was a toddler we've gone to the hospital ball games held at the high school up the hill. They always have hot dogs and soft drinks. She enjoyed that atmosphere so much."

"I remember reading years ago in the *Sunset Valley Herald* that they turned the mountain army base into a high school. Is that the one?"

She nodded. "The house where we lived used to be officer's housing. It's a compressed little subdivision carved into the hillside below the old base with shoebox houses and postage stamp lawns. It doesn't have trees but real sidewalks, and it's pretty and orderly. Most of the residents are hospital personnel."

"I guess Laughlin lived there, too." He couldn't completely disguise the irritation in his voice. He wanted to know more about her relationship with this guy, although he had no right, and he knew it.

She shot him a puzzled glance. "Byron? He's old money. My entire house would probably fit into his bathroom."

"Old money?"

"Sunset Mountain has a definite caste system. The filthy rich live on the end with the highest elevation. Not only is it the highest point in altitude but also in status. The have-nots live down on the back side. My subdivision, the hospital, and the high school are neutral territory, the perfect no man's land. Not quite far enough back down the mountain to be a part of the world where I grew up and not close enough to the mansions to be a part of their world."

Neutral territory. That didn't make him feel one bit better about Laughlin. "So, I guess Laughlin felt perfectly comfortable in this neutral territory."

She shot him another bewildered glance. "Byron's family owned the hospital. Of course, he was comfortable there. I doubt that he ever went to a ballgame, though."

"And your subdivision?" He couldn't help it. The thought of that rich asshole dating her made his blood boil. Seconds ticked off, and finally she understood what he was asking.

He saw a definite flicker of unguarded pain cross her face. She tried, but she couldn't hide it; and when she spoke, the tone of her voice made him regret his jealousy. "Byron was a colleague and a good friend. That's all. We never socialized."

Despite being sorry for upsetting her, he couldn't quite let this go. "But he asked you out. He'd have been a fool not to. I remember how he was always attracted to you."

"Yes, he did ask me out, but I couldn't accept. Eventually he stopped asking."

"I see."

"No you don't. You don't see anything, David, not the way it really is. You never have."

She started to turn away, but he gently grabbed her arm. "I'm sorry."

She looked up into his eyes. "Are you?"

"More than you could ever know."

She glanced stubbornly away, and he knew he was about to strike out again. "Look," he said gently. "Could we start over? I was about to suggest that I take you and Gena to see the Chieftains play tonight since she likes baseball so much. They've got a great team this year. That might take the sting out of not getting to go to the Mountain General games."

A hesitant look crossed her pretty features. Of course it was too soon to expect her to risk trusting him, not to mention forgive him. His uncalled-for jealousy hadn't helped. He'd have to be patient.

"Listen," he said. "I know you hate the sight of me, but couldn't we at least try to be friends?"

"I don't hate you, David. I wish I could … but friends?" She shook her head. "I don't know how to do that anymore."

"You could at least give me a chance to redeem myself."

She chewed on her lower lip and concentrated on stirring her coffee.

"Please." He tried to infuse that plea with his old easy charm, not that he expected it to work. Nothing with Laurel was easy any more.

"Don't do that." She kept her eyes on her cup.

"Don't do what?" he asked, knowing she thought he was just being frivolous and flirty. All he wanted was to make a tiny crack in this wall she'd built around herself, and he'd grovel and get down on his knees if he thought it would help.

"Don't play little boy lost with me," she said. "I've seen this act before. Remember?"

He deserved that. He did. But he *was* lost, and she was the only one who could lead him out of the darkness.

"Laurel." He said her name softly with all the tenderness he felt, and she glanced up into his eyes again. "Throw me a crumb. Please. Now what do you say? I have free season passes for two. It's part of my perks as a resident. It's the hospital's way of making up for the lousy salary. Since the season's almost over, it would be nice to finally use them."

She took a quick sip of her coffee and looked up at him again. "I'll pay for Gena's ticket."

"Children under six are free."

"Then I'll buy the hot dogs and drinks."

"Deal. Be ready at five."

David couldn't remember the last time he'd had so much fun. He'd bought Chieftain caps for all of them as they entered the park, and Gena looked adorable with hers pulled down over her curls. For a four-year-old she certainly knew her way around a baseball game. She'd shocked him with her knowledge of the finer points of the sport. She even knew who Hank Aaron, Johnny Bench, and Roberto Clemente were, but she blew him away when she recognized the squeeze play that won the game for the Chieftains.

Serious fan that she was, she'd loved the antics of the Chieftains mascot as he worked the crowd. When the furry creature took a well-orchestrated pratfall on the grassy sideline directly in front of them, she'd giggled uncontrollably. It was one of those contagious giggles that infused the air around her and infected them vicariously.

She was a delightful bundle of energy, and in the presence of her gregarious spirit, the simplest things took on a new aura for him. With Gena even ballpark hot dogs tasted like gourmet fare. Laurel seemed to enjoy herself, too, and Gena with all her enthusiasm acted as a natural buffer to the estrangement between them.

On the way back to the apartment she fell asleep almost mid-sentence in the back seat of his car, all tuckered out from being in constant motion, he guessed. He scooped her gently from the car seat and carried her upstairs to her bed. Her tiny body curled against his chest, and her limbs relaxed in the curve of his embrace. He could hear her gentle breathing against his shoulder and feel her tiny heart beating close to his. He glanced at her peacefully sleeping face and felt goose bumps cover his entire body. He was holding pure innocence in his arms, pure faith that the world was a good place. He knew then that he had to always be around to protect her. He had to be the father she was looking for, and in that serendipitous moment she became indelibly a part of him.

He watched from the bedroom doorway as Laurel tucked her in after taking off her shoes. He felt a squeezing sensation in his chest when she leaned to kiss Gena's cheek and smoothed her curls back from her brow gazing at her lovingly.

He was still standing in the doorway when she crossed the room and turned off the light. She reached to pull the door halfway shut. When she turned, she was so close he could feel her warmth. He needed that warmth so much he ached for it. In a totally impulsive move that was probably a mistake, he bent to touch his lips against hers.

She didn't back away or resist, but she didn't kiss him back either. It didn't matter. The touch of her lips on his was enough, and it was the perfect ending to this amazing night. He didn't press his luck. He forced his lips from hers and whispered, "You're a wonderful, loving mother."

"She's so easy to love," she said.

He understood that. He knew he would love Gena even if she weren't part of him, part of Laurel. He wished he could find the words to express that, to express what he felt tonight, all of it, but it was too soon for Laurel to hear it. He reached to brush her cheek with his fingertips. She glanced away and spoke softly, "Would you like some iced tea?"

"Sure."

She edged past him setting off sparks in every place where she lightly brushed against him, and she headed down the hallway. He followed, admiring the curve of her hips in her snug jeans and chastising himself all the way. Tonight had almost been like old times, but he did realize that it couldn't have been without Gena's presence.

He made himself focus on the embroidered flowers that bordered the neckline of the peasant blouse she wore. "I'm sorry Gena didn't get to have her bath. I know you have a routine."

"It's okay. She usually falls asleep before we get back on evening outings, so I gave her a quick one before we left. A little mustard and relish can't do much harm."

"She certainly knows her baseball."

"Grandpa's responsible for that. They watch it together, and he's taught her everything about it."

"Maybe I should give you my tickets so he can go with you."

"That's sweet, but he'd rather watch it on the new color television my uncles bought him. He's a homebody anyway."

"Then maybe I could convince the two of you to go with me for the rest of the home games."

She glanced back over her shoulder as they walked through the living room, but she didn't comment. He hadn't expected her to commit to spending extra time with him, but he was surprised that she was prolonging his time with her tonight by offering him tea. He watched her as she popped ice from a tray into two glasses, refilled the tray with water placing it back into the freezer, and filled the glasses from a Tupperware pitcher.

"Here you go," she said handing him one of the glasses. "Let's go sit on the sofa." As he took the glass from her, their fingers touched, and she looked up into his eyes. He held her gaze for a few seconds. Then she glanced away and headed off to the living room. He followed.

As he sank down beside her, he set his tea on a coffee-table coaster and picked up the baseball hat she'd tossed on the sofa on the way in. He set it on her head. Before he withdrew his hand he couldn't resist tucking a strand of hair behind her ear.

"You look cute," he said. Beautiful was more like it.

She smiled and removed the cap holding it in her lap. "Thank you for tonight, David. You've won Gena's heart. Trust me. She'll sleep in the hat you bought her." She glanced down and traced her forefinger over the logo on her hat. "If the offer still stands, we'll go to the games with you. She would absolutely love that."

"Of course it still stands."

She glanced at him again, started to say something, but paused.

"I enjoyed tonight very much," he said quickly. "I hope you did, too."

She nodded. "It was nice." After another long pause she spoke softly. "Yesterday, I confronted my mother about your calls and letters. She and Del admitted that you called, and she still had your letters. I insisted she give them to me. She'd read them, of course."

"Did you read them?"

She nodded. "I'm so angry with Mama for keeping them from me and denying us the option to work things out five years ago before things got so complicated."

"What about working it out now?"

Ignoring his question she continued, "I owe you an apology. You were telling the truth, and I didn't believe you."

He reached to squeeze her hand. Surprisingly, she didn't pull away.

"I've overheard some gossip since I've been back." She paused and glanced over at him. "Usually I don't listen because, even though most of what is said is actually true, the way they interpret the facts is always so distorted."

"What'd you hear?"

She glanced away again. "That you didn't date those years you were in school. Someone supposedly overheard your med school roommate say that."

"It's true. My last date was with you August 13, 1966, unless you count the night I went to Marilee's house and threatened to strangle her if she didn't have the newspaper print a retraction to that phony wedding announcement."

"Did she?"

He nodded. "I hoped you would see it, but it was that Sunday after your dad's funeral."

"Oh," she said flatly. "I guess I owe you an apology for that, too."

"No. You don't. If I hadn't been such a philanderer to begin with, maybe you could have believed me. I don't know why I ever expected you to trust me after the way I took your love for granted."

"I never understood the audacity of that." Her voice was soft but bitter. "It was like you thought no one else could ever want me, and you could just put me on a shelf like a favorite toy and take me down when you got bored with the latest product."

"It was never like that."

She pulled her hand away from his and stared straight ahead. "Of course it was."

He winced. She was right but only half right. He placed his hand on her shoulder and rubbed the gauzy material of her blouse. "Don't shut me out, Laurel. Let's talk about this."

"Isn't it a little late for that?"

"I hope not." He rubbed her shoulder again making small circles with his thumb. "You're only half right about your toy analogy. I knew you were rare and special, and I was all too aware that there were many others who wanted you. I would have feared that they had the power to take you away from me except for one thing. I knew you wouldn't go."

She bit her lip, but her expression didn't change.

"You were mature. I wasn't, but I knew loyalty when I saw it. I needed that. I needed for you to keep on loving me while I grew up. Part of me always knew you were everything I wanted from the start. I didn't want to lose you. I've loved you from the beginning, and I'm sorry I took you for granted." He lifted his hand to stroke her shiny hair. "But that night we shared was love in its purest form. I gave you my heart forever then."

"It's hard to believe you own someone's heart if you don't see them for five years."

"But you do own my heart. I've paid for my mistakes, Laurel. They cost me those same five years, and I'll never be able to love anyone else. Not after you."

She looked into his eyes. He thought he saw a glimmer of belief.

"Look, I deserve your anger for the way I treated you before that night. I know that, and I understand that you need to vent that anger. Go ahead. Say all the things you need to say. Ask me anything. Sock me if you need to."

She shook her head. "I don't want revenge, David."

"Then let's work this out."

"Can we really do that? So much has happened." She picked at the stitching on the baseball cap as she spoke. The sadness in her voice stabbed at his heart. Then suddenly he had the painful thought that she might have found someone else, not Laughlin, but somebody she did have something in common with. Gena could be his child, and then again she could belong to some rebound guy. That guy could be the "so much" that had happened that could keep them from working things out.

"Maybe you found someone else," he said. "I deserve that."

She shot him a glance that let him know he'd struck a painful blow without meaning to. "I couldn't do that any more than you could, David. Not after that night."

This meant Gena had to be his child. Should he ask that question again? He had a right to know, but he decided to wait. He'd pushed her too much already.

"We could at least try this again. We work together. We live next door to each other, all of this after not being able to find you for five years. I think God's trying to tell us something. I know that seeing you again is the answer to my prayers."

She stared stoically ahead and spoke softly, "I've just about given up that God gives a damn about me."

Her face reflected such hopelessness that something inside him ached to the core. He took a deep breath, but the pain wouldn't go away. Then he said the first thing he felt, and the pain let up a little. "Give him a chance, baby. Give *me* a chance."

She didn't say a word, but she had every right to tell him off. He'd sounded preachy, and he hadn't meant to. Where did he get off doing that anyway? This whole thing was his fault, and the truth was, his faith was fragile, too. He'd tried to turn his life around and follow God's will, but so many days he felt like he was dying.

She concentrated on trailing her fingertip across the warp of her jeans. "I know you deserve another chance, David. I will try. I do want to try, but things are complicated now. I have to go slow with this. Please understand that."

"I can handle slow," he said gently. "I promise I'll do whatever it takes."

She looked so vulnerable that he wanted to take her in his arms and kiss her doubts away. But she wouldn't be ready for that for a long time, and he had just promised to go slow. Instead he reached for her hand, brought it to his lips, and kissed it. She looked up into his eyes then.

"Just keep remembering that I love you."

She took in a breath and nodded. He wouldn't press her for any more than that small gesture of affirmation. He could feel how fragile she was.

"I'll see you in morning huddle, angel, and I'll make sure Stu keeps his hug to himself this time. I'll tell him you've been exposed to the plague."

That won him a smile.

"My hero," she said.

"Have lunch with me tomorrow?"

"I'd like that."

Chapter Twelve

Laurel fell asleep that night thinking about David. She could still feel the warmth of his hand on her shoulder and the sensual feel of his thumb rubbing her skin through the thin material of her blouse. Nothing had changed in the power he had over her senses. As much as she had accused him of his arrogance about it, he'd never known what his touch meant to her. It was as if she needed it to breathe and to be connected to him was to be complete.

She wondered if it was wise to try again. Wasn't she just setting herself up for more heartache? He'd never met her family or been to her house. She'd lived in the hospital dorm the entire time she'd known him. What would he think if he ever saw that ramshackle place she called home? What would he say when he witnessed her family's craziness? Would he want her to be part of his life then?

Maybe he had missed her as much as she'd missed him. She now knew that he had been the person she'd heard playing Rachmaninoff's Concerto no. 2 the day she moved in. But could he ever love her enough to see past her decaying family, and could she recover from the heartache if he couldn't?

Maybe he'd run as fast as he could away from her, but how could she blame him? She had a hard enough time dealing with the heartache of that place. Well, she couldn't let him see it. It was too big a risk. If they had a chance at a new start, she had to be judged for herself.

She'd prayed before she fell asleep that she would do the right thing about him, that she'd be fair, and that he wouldn't hurt her again. She always tried to pray even if it was in the form of disjointed thoughts. She hoped God was listening. She hadn't felt his presence for a long time.

She wasn't surprised when an answer to her prayer hadn't come booming down by the next morning or even in the next several weeks—but she waited. She had just enough faith left to do that, to wait. After all, she'd endured five years without any kind of hope about David, and now here he was in her life again, and he wasn't backing off. Maybe that was the only answer she would get.

She was ready for some happiness. Her heart felt as if it had been shattered into a million pieces, and the last five years had almost broken her spirit. If she hadn't had Gena to love she might not have survived.

Even though she wasn't positive she was doing the right thing, she began to say yes to David's invitations. It soon became an unspoken date to go to the pool together on Saturday mornings, and after that first Sunday at his church they'd attended together regularly. She'd made that decision easily because Gena had loved it.

After that first visit she had talked all the way to Henderson's Cafeteria about her Sunday school class and children's church, something new to her because she'd always sat with her in the mountain services. That day she announced, "I told my teacher that we'll be back, Mommy."

Henderson's became a routine as well, but Laurel had insisted on paying for herself and Gena. David had finally relented but not easily. She didn't want to get too dependent on him. She needed to maintain her separate life, just in case.

Now in the three weeks since she'd promised to give their relationship another try, he hadn't pushed. He hadn't even kissed her again, although she felt the chemistry there as strong as ever. That allowed her to be comfortable around him although reining in her own emotions was another matter. That brief kiss the night of the ballgame in the doorway of Gena's room had torn down so many of her defenses.

Last Saturday, sitting on the edge of the kiddy pool, he'd reached across her to talk to Gena, and his bare thigh, hard and muscular, had pressed against hers. That innocent act had sent a surge of heat through her body, and she'd wanted to melt into his arms and make love to him the way they had that night. That hadn't been the only time she'd felt that way.

She had to make herself be constantly cautious. She wouldn't make the mistake of too much too soon with him again. It wasn't that she'd changed her mind about the purity of that night—she hadn't. When she'd finally allowed herself to dwell on it again, she'd realized that God made rules for a reason. Things taken out of order, no matter how pure, held the risk of unnecessary and far-reaching pain.

She began to put her unresolved fears aside because David's actions told her that he genuinely adored Gena. He was the positive male influence she needed. Through their interactions, his and Gena's, Laurel saw a side of him that she'd never seen before. She loved how he could always relate to Gena and how he never seemed to fear stooping to a child's level. When she watched as he taught Gena to blow bubble gum bubbles, she fell in love with him all over again. He'd looked so boyish and mischievous and just plain cute.

He was wonderfully calm in emergencies, too, the doctor part of him taking over she guessed. When Gena cut a gash in her leg on the edge of the metal slide at their playground, Laurel had panicked, but she'd been careful not to let Gena see her reaction. She saw emergencies every day; but this was her little girl, and she felt so helpless.

David stayed completely calm. He pressed his clean handkerchief over the wound to stop the flow of blood enough to assess it. He gave her a reassuring glance and took Gena from her arms still holding the handkerchief pressed over the cut. He spoke in a soft, calming voice to Gena as he carried her up to his apartment. There he gently tended her injury, which hadn't been as bad as it looked.

She didn't need stitches, and she'd already had a tetanus shot. He covered the wound with a butterfly bandage. Afterwards he cuddled Gena in his arms. She still had big tears in her eyes.

"You're good as new, sweetie," he said. "Would you like to go over to your place and play now?"

Gena shook her head and whimpered, "My tears aren't finished."

He hugged her closer and kissed her forehead. "I understand. Take all the time you need."

Later when she thought about the innocent wisdom of Gena's words, she realized that she'd never in her life allowed her tears to finish. She'd learned at a tender age to stuff down her pain because tears were a sign of weakness in her family. By the time she'd lost Daddy and David in that same tragic week, she'd had years of practice with her parents' hate-spewing arguments, Del's childhood accident, and Gene's self-destruction.

She'd been afraid to touch the core of her pain. She was still afraid, but maybe not allowing herself to mourn hadn't lessened the hurt. Maybe it had only made it worse. She could try to change. Having David in her life would help. She could use some happiness. She was still cautious about their relationship, but spending time with him again reminded her of the many reasons she'd fallen for him in the first place.

He was acutely intelligent, and she found herself going to him first with any problem she had at work. When she needed a pathology consult on an aplastic anemia smear, it was David she went to for confirmation. Because of his background in the lab, he knew hematology as well as Stu and Miles.

He was patient and kind with all the staff, except for the blatant predators, and he didn't abuse the power of his degree. When one of the pathology secretaries messed up his schedule and had him taking call three weekends in a row, he hadn't exploded. He quietly pointed it out so she could correct it. He didn't chew her out and humiliate her as Dr. Campbell would have done or wear her out with obsequious although well-meant kindness the way Stu would have.

He had a delightfully quick wit, and he was charming. He no longer used that charm indiscreetly the way he once had. She noticed that he didn't get sidetracked by the women around him the way he had all those years before either, and that had been the only thing she'd ever disliked about him.

Aside from their time together outside the hospital, every time he could break free, he joined her and Audrey in the cafeteria for lunch. She'd never seen him with another female.

Today he'd gotten paged and had to leave shortly after finishing his lunch. He grinned at them and teased, "Stu probably needs a hug."

She and Audrey both laughed, but after he left, Audrey started in on her. "You two have been spending a lot of time together, haven't you?"

She shrugged. "We live next door to each other. Gena adores him. We do things with her."

"Let's see. You've gone to all the Chieftains games together. I've seen you together at the mall a whole bunch of times, eating or window-shopping. Then last weekend I saw the three of you at the Baskin Robbins downtown after the street fair." She glanced up from cutting a bite of chocolate cake. "And you go to church with him every Sunday and out to eat afterwards, and these are just the things I know about."

She shrugged again.

"So, where're you going this weekend?"

"After we do Gena's swim lessons tomorrow morning, we're going to decide what to do. I went to visit Mama after work yesterday, so Gena and I won't be going to the mountain like we usually do on Saturdays. Gena was disappointed that she didn't get to go, but since she's had a cold I didn't want to expose my mother to it. Her health is too frail as it is."

"I don't blame you for that."

"Mama wasn't as understanding as you. She laid me low for not bringing her."

"Well, you did the right thing."

"My sister-in-law, Connie, was disappointed, too. She loves having Gena around. She has two daughters, twelve and eleven. Her first husband got custody. It broke her heart. She misses them so much."

She remembered how Mama had played a big part in the fact that Connie had lost her children. Instead of supporting her, she'd let it be known, ever so obliquely as only Mama could, that Connie leaned heavily on her mother's little helper in the form of the hard whiskey she hid all over the house.

Never mind that Mama's badgering was one of the reasons Connie drank in the first place, that and the fact that Mama had never accepted her children as part of the family. Connie didn't deserve having her daughters taken away, but they were better off living away from all that.

She glanced up at Audrey and continued. "I had Mrs. Archer stay over an extra couple of hours while I went to the mountain, but when I got back David was there, too. He and Gena had ordered pizza for all of us from that little Italian restaurant down the street. They were making salads to go with it and had even coerced Mrs. Archer into baking a chocolate cake. They're such cohorts."

"This sounds serious."

"We're working on being friends again. It's a good place to start."

"Don't look now, but I think it might be a tad beyond friendship already. I know one thing. That boy has changed."

"Yeah? In what way?" She tried to sound nonchalant. She knew he'd changed. She didn't fully understand it, but she was learning to trust him again. Maybe it was because to her the hallmark of a person was the way he treated a child. In that respect David was an angel.

"Oh, come on." Audrey kept her voice low. "Used to be he'd have a harem down here, and he'd go flitting from table to table. But nowadays, as you just saw, he didn't move an inch from right here with you."

"He was eating lunch." She tried to sound as if she'd missed the implication, and Audrey rolled her eyes.

"You know how women are in this hospital. If a mangy old hound dog crawled through that front door with *doctor* stamped on his butt, they'd be all over him. They'd be wanting to marry him, have his young'uns, and live the good life on his money."

"A mangy old hound dog, huh?" She had to laugh at that image.

"The point is, when he was an intern, they were all over that boy worse than they were when you two were techs. He's for sure not a mangy dog but just about the best-looking stud this hospital has seen in a long time. He ignored them, and you and me both know that's not the way he used to be. Something's got a hold of that boy. Honey, that something's you."

"He's committed to his profession. He's almost thirty, so maybe he just got bored with being a playboy."

Audrey rolled her eyes again. "That's not the reason at all. After you two broke up I'm the one he talked to. You're the one he's always loved even if he didn't know it, and, honey, that thing with that Marilee floozy was just bad timing."

"Bad timing," she scoffed. "I'll say."

"Okay, bad choice of words. It was more a delayed reaction. It was the past catching up with him after he'd already decided on his future, which happened to be you. You gotta remember he's an only child, and his parents were strict. When he got the least bit of freedom he went kind of wild. But he didn't count on meeting you before he got all them wild oats sowed. I know he took you for granted, but then he did see the light; and when he saw it, his past got in the way."

"What do you mean his past got in the way?"

"It's plain as the nose on your face. When it all of a sudden dawned on him that he loved you, he didn't have all the loose ends from his past tied up. It bit him on the butt when it made you doubt him."

"How would you feel if someone you'd loved for three years finally told you he loved you and proposed to you, and the next morning you saw an announcement that he was going to marry someone else?"

"I'd doubt him, but, honey, he tried to explain it. You were too hurt to listen. So, both of you ended up losing. But that's the past. What you need to see here and now is that he does love you. He cut himself off from that wild living. I'm here to tell you he hasn't had one single date since his last one with you."

"I've overheard some gossip about that, Audrey. And he says he didn't date, but how can you know for sure what he did when he was way off in Memphis?"

"Because he told me, and I believe him. Just like you told me you didn't date either, and I believe you."

She wanted it to be true that he loved her the way she loved him, but part of her couldn't quite believe it.

"I'll tell you something else about David," Audrey said in a sudden hushed tone.

She glanced up at her. "What?"

"Don't take this the wrong way, okay? I don't know what went on between you and him. He's too much of a gentleman to tell me intimate things, but I can read people, especially David Hudson."

"What are you trying to say?"

"I guarantee he thinks Gena belongs to him."

She felt the blood drain from her face. "Why do you think that?"

"Well, for starters, the day before you started as chief I mentioned that you were coming back. At the same time loud-mouthed Edna just blurted out that you had a child. He didn't think I noticed, but that knocked the wind right out of him, and I thought he was going to keel over right there in his tracks. Then before he left that day he asked me for your file. I figured it was so he could check out Gena's age."

She rubbed at her forehead with her fingertips. She thought about her conversation with him her first night here. He had asked her specifically about Gena's father, but she'd been in such shock from seeing him so unexpectedly that she had reacted cautiously the way she always did when people pried into her personal life.

"Maybe you and him need to talk."

"Maybe we do. I've heard the gossip. I know everybody wonders about Gena. You probably do, too."

"It's none of my business, and only you know if it's David's business."

Audrey had always been straightforward, so she didn't get upset that she'd pried into her personal life. She appreciated her candor. She knew everyone wondered if Gena belonged to David, but she hadn't thought David was one of those people.

She distinctly remembered telling him after seeing Marilee's announcement that their night together was a safe time. But she had been angry and hurt, and it was obvious now that he hadn't believed her. Being in the medical profession, he knew that there were no absolutes, only educated guesses. It didn't take a medical background to know that safe wasn't foolproof. Everyone knew that.

The other alternative was that he might think Gena belonged to some rebound guy like Byron. No wonder he'd acted so jealous when he'd questioned her about him. Because he was such a compassionate person, Byron had plenty to do with her parenting of Gena—but not in fathering her.

Because of the circumstances of her birth, she'd made it a practice not to discuss Gena with anyone who didn't already know the details. It was too big a risk. If David asked again, she'd have to address this with him, but she wasn't ready to initiate any discussion with anyone about Gena.

Chapter Thirteen

As he left the cafeteria, David thought about the weekend ahead. He would be spending all of Saturday and Sunday with Laurel and Gena. For the past three weeks they'd routinely gone to the pool on Saturday mornings. He'd been teaching Gena to swim, and she was learning fast. He was so proud of her.

After a couple of hours at the pool they always had lunch together, and afterwards Laurel and Gena made their weekly trip to Sunset Mountain to visit her family. He'd offered several times to go with them, but Laurel always made an excuse. It was obvious that she didn't want him to meet her family. He couldn't understand why.

He'd have to meet them someday if he realized his dream of making Laurel and Gena his family, but progress toward that was slow, even with all the time they were spending together. Slow, he could handle, but he hadn't expected this wall Laurel continued to keep between them. He wondered if she'd ever trust him again. He knew she was trying, but being guarded seemed a conditioned reflex.

She'd definitely changed in the past five years, but all the things he'd loved about her were still there. He'd always thought she'd be a success at whatever she chose to become professionally or personally, and he'd always thought she'd make a wonderful mother.

Reality hadn't proved him wrong on either point. The change lay in her outlook. Five years ago she had been filled with expectations and dreams. Now, she seemed afraid to dream. Even though he knew she still loved him, he wondered if she would ever allow herself to believe that they could move beyond the heartache.

He'd become painfully aware of her pessimism during a casual conversation last Saturday. After Gena's swimming lesson, she played in the kiddy pool with Sally, her new friend from the apartment complex. Meanwhile, he and Laurel relaxed in the chaise lounges nearby with his portable radio tuned to a pop music station. When "Hold Me, Thrill Me, Kiss Me" by Mel Carter began to play, it took him instantly back to their past.

He glanced at her and leaned forward. "Remember that night we danced barefoot to this song on the eighteenth green at the country club? Everybody else at that lab tech banquet was inside dancing to that awful band, but we had this radio and this song and a glorious full moon."

She was rubbing suntan lotion on her arms, but she stopped, looked up abruptly and laughed. Her smile took over her features, and for a moment he felt as if he'd gone back to 1965. "Yeah," she said. "And then the sprinklers came on and drenched us both."

"But we kept right on dancing." He laughed, remembering the pure bliss of that night, how pretty she'd looked with her hair hanging in wet strands, the water droplets glistening on her face, and the sound of their frivolous giggling.

"Even our shoes got wet although they were sitting several feet away," she said smiling. "You squished every time you hit the accelerator, the brake, or the clutch on the trip home."

"I distinctly remember suggesting that we take off all our wet clothes to make the night more romantic, but you didn't like that idea."

"We were already guilty of trespassing. We didn't need to add indecent exposure."

"My suit was never the same. It shrank about two sizes."

"My dress, too," she said.

He remembered how perfect she had looked before they got soaked. She had been a vision of beauty with every hair in place, the chiffon of the dress that so perfectly matched her blue eyes caressing her body in sensual flutters. The whole dancing-on-the-green escapade had been his idea. Yet she had been so gloriously uninhibited and had never once blamed him for her ruined dress.

He leaned back in the chaise. "Every time I've heard this song in the past five years I've thought about you and that night."

She went back to rubbing the lotion on her arms and didn't acknowledge his last comment.

"I guess the last thing you wanted to do was think of me."

The final trace of her brilliant smile completely disappeared from her face then. "I've tried not to dwell on the past. What's the point of being reminded of something that can't ever be again."

"So you never dreamed that someday our paths might cross again, that someday we might regain what we lost?"

"No." She rubbed lotion on her legs concentrating on her task.

"Well, I dreamed, prayed, and hoped enough for the both of us," he said feeling deflated. He knew she still loved him. Why wouldn't she admit that she'd missed him?

She kept applying the lotion. "I've learned that all the wishing and hoping in the world and even praying don't ever change some things. What else could I do but accept that?"

"So, you didn't miss me at all? You didn't regret that things ended the way they did?"

"I didn't say that, David." The pain in her voice was palpable. "It took me a long time to get past all that, but all I ever achieved was limbo."

"But you've moved on very well. You've become a respected professional. You're independent. You've bought a house all by yourself. You're a mother. You have a good life."

She shrugged. "It's not the life I dreamed of having."

"Not even Gena?"

A look of remorse swept instantly across her face, and she answered softly. "Gena is a gift. I love her with all my heart, but I live in fear that God will take her away from me, too."

He wanted to tell her how sorry he was that he had gone on with his life and left her to fend for herself with his child. He wanted her to know how much he had longed to have her with him and that she and this child were his dream.

She leaned back on the chaise, and as she screwed the cap back on the lotion bottle, she stared absently toward Gena and continued speaking. "You were the biggest part of my dream, David, because I loved you so much. Maybe if the thing with Marilee hadn't happened, if we'd gotten married, I would've been happy, but I think maybe that was my last chance at happiness, and I missed it."

He moved to sit on the side of his chaise closest to her. "What do you mean?"

"When my father died, my family fell apart. So many bad things have happened, not that there weren't moments where things could've been mended and life could've been a whole lot better. But they didn't choose the good, something my brother excuses as their God-given freedom, and I'm left to pick up the pieces." She rolled the lotion bottle back and forth between her palms. "My family is a house of broken dreams, David. It's like living inside a whirlwind. Once you're attached to it in any way you get sucked into its vortex, and your dreams get sucked into the void right along with theirs." She looked up into his eyes. "I can't involve anyone else in it. It wouldn't be fair."

He scooted closer and reached to hold her hand. "Let me decide what's fair for me. Okay?" Her stoic gaze softened, so he continued. "Getting another chance with you is the answer to my prayers, Laurel. You're my dream, too, you and Gena. I love you. I love Gena. Let me help you find your dreams again."

"You may decide you were better off staying away from me." Her voice held an edge of bitterness. "My family's hard to take. But then I guess you got a hint of that talking to them on the phone."

"I'll take my chances. You're worth it."

"We'll see," she said almost inaudibly staring straight ahead.

He paused in front of his locker marveling that he'd come all this way from the cafeteria without acknowledging any part of his surroundings and with no conscious memory of how he'd gotten here. He'd been too deep in thought. He twirled his combination and retrieved a couple of his pathology textbooks from inside the locker. It had indeed been Stu who'd paged him, and he'd asked him to help with an impromptu lecture to interns on clotting factors.

As he closed the locker door and headed toward the conference room, he reminded himself that this whole thing with Laurel was far more complicated than forgiveness and reconciliation. But he loved her, and he would do whatever it took to make her his wife.

Chapter Fourteen

Although Laurel tried to keep her renewed relationship with David from Mama, that hadn't been possible. Ever since the night of the baseball game, Gena had talked nonstop, telling Mama and Connie about all the things they'd done together. Even when Laurel tried to guide the conversation in another direction, Gena always came back to talking about him.

Laurel had eagerly told Betty Jo and her grandparents about him and wanted him to meet them, but she couldn't feel anything but trepidation about the prospects of his meeting her immediate family. She might not ever be able to share that part of her life with David—the dead-end squalor of the place itself and Mama and Del with their caustic attitudes. Their relationship had a chance now. Mama would try to destroy it.

It came as no surprise when Mama voiced her disapproval. "Nothing good can come of you seeing that boy again," she'd said sternly.

"He's not a boy. He's a man, and, like me, almost thirty years old."

"That's the problem. He's a man."

"You don't have much faith in my character, Mama."

"After the way it went before, do you blame me?"

She gritted her teeth and responded more harshly than she'd planned. She'd vowed she wasn't going to let Mama get to her. "This is none of your business, Mama, and I'm a big girl."

"When it involves Gena, it's my business. She'll get attached to him, and he'll take off again."

Bingo. She'd hit the spot she was aiming for, the one thing Laurel feared most: that this wouldn't last with David. Well, she wasn't going to let Mama have the satisfaction of knowing that.

"We're not going to talk about this anymore, Mama."

But Mama brought up the subject every subsequent visit starting with that Saturday she'd learned about it the week of their first Chieftain's game. Each time she punctuated her negative remarks with hoarse coughs that didn't get better even after Del gave her breathing treatments.

Now three weeks later and on the Saturday before Labor Day she assessed that Mama's cough seemed completely better, but she didn't voice her opinion because that was an open invitation for Mama to prove her wrong.

When Gena hopped up on the bed and gave Mama the picture she had colored especially for her, Mama seemed fine. She hadn't started coughing again until Gena told her excitedly that David was taking them to a Labor Day concert and picnic in the park that following Monday.

"David said they're going to have lots of pretty music, but I don't have to be quiet like I do in church. He's going to help us cook fried chicken to take. It'll be so much fun, Grandma Sarah. I wish you could come with us."

"You be careful and don't get lost."

"I won't." Gena scooted off the bed and scampered off to visit Connie in the kitchen. She could hear them laughing and talking. A few seconds later Del passed through with a sack of dog food on his shoulder to store in a back bedroom. She could hear him thumping around.

Mama fixed her with a scathing frown. "I asked you to bring Gena up here for Labor Day."

"Mama, don't make a big deal of this and spoil it for her. She has her heart set on it. Don't make her feel like she has to choose."

"No, you have your heart set on it because of that boy. You're using Gena to get what you want, and you're teaching her to disrespect her family the way you do."

That made her furious. Disrespect her family? It was more correct that she was the one who was disrespected. She was merely a puppet with Mama pulling her strings. "You know something?" she responded angrily. "I don't have to put up with this. I come up here every Saturday to visit. I do everything you ask me to do to help, but it's never enough for you. You want to own me, and I'm sick of it. I'm sick of it. Do you hear me?" She tried to keep her voice low, but she was shaking with rage.

Mama narrowed her eyes and hissed, "You're just like your daddy."

It wasn't a compliment, not with that tone of voice, and she already knew how Mama felt about Daddy. She didn't wait for her to play dirty and go into crisis mode. She wheeled around, went to the kitchen, scooped Gena into her arms, hugged Connie, and left without saying another word to Mama. If she'd said what she truly felt, she would never be forgiven. She loved it that she was like Daddy. As far as she was concerned he'd been the only sane member of the family.

Retribution was swift for that act of defiance because six hours later, after she had tucked Gena into bed at the apartment, Connie called.

"Your mama's in ICU here at Mountain General. They've put her on a respirator. Del told me to call and tell you. She had a spell right after you left. A treatment didn't help, so we finally called an ambulance. They say it's pneumonia. She's bad, Laurel. Del wants you to come."

She sank back onto the sofa after placing the phone in its cradle. As many times as she'd been through this she hadn't learned to control the panic and the guilt. She knew deep down that she hadn't caused this just like she hadn't caused all the endless crises before this one, but every single time it happened, she let herself get caught up in Mama's web of manipulation.

What was she supposed to do? Gena was already asleep. She didn't want to traumatize her by waking her to bad news. *She's a child, Mama*, she thought, *but oh, I'm expected to drag her through another deathbed crisis. It's my punishment for challenging you.* She sighed, closed her eyes, and leaned back.

"Laurel, what's wrong?" It was David's gentle voice, and she felt his hand on her arm as he sank onto the couch beside her. She'd forgotten for a few minutes that he was even there. He'd gone to the kitchen to fix them glasses of tea.

He set their glasses on the coffee-table coasters as she opened her eyes and turned to him. "My mother's in ICU at Mountain General. The doctors say it's pneumonia." She rubbed her face with both hands feeling instantly drained from the opposing emotions in her heart. "It's the last thing she needs with her illness. My sister-in-law says she's bad. My brother wants me to come."

"What illness does she have?"

"Rheumatoid arthritis. She's been bedridden for a little over four years. She has a severe crisis about every six months, sometimes more often." She let out a deep sigh dreading what she knew lay ahead tonight. "It's enough to wear out the synapses—mine in reacting to it. Sometimes I wish it *would.* I get so tired of feeling and hurting and worrying."

She thought about how selfish she sounded. David couldn't possibly understand how she felt without knowing the family history. Maybe he would think she was incredibly selfish, too, but instead of recoiling in judgment, he squeezed her shoulder and spoke softly. "I'm going with you. Call Lucy Archer. She can spend the night here with Gena since we don't know how long we'll be."

She didn't argue. She was too grateful to have him with her. This meant he would meet her crazy family, but at least he wouldn't see that place she came from.

At Mountain General Hospital he sat with her as they all waited for the specialist Mama's doctor had called in for a consult, and he held her hand when that doctor delivered his verdict.

"Mrs. Harper's arthritic condition is constricting her lungs, and the pneumonia is compounding that problem," Dr. Barnes said gently. "She's not getting enough air exchange. The respirator helps but doesn't solve the problem. The only hope is to do a tracheotomy. Without it she won't make it through the next twenty-four hours. If we do the tracheotomy, given her overall condition, the odds are fifty-fifty that she'll make it through the procedure. I have to go see another patient, but I'll be back in thirty minutes. Do you think you all can make a decision by then?"

She knew this doctor, and he looked to her for the answer to his question. She nodded numbly. As she tried to absorb his words, David stood and introduced himself to the doctor. He walked with him toward the doorway across the room. She knew he was using his position to get more detailed information.

Mama could die. She'd never been this bad before. These crises were always bad; she lost some vital function with each one, but she'd never been close to dying. Laurel couldn't help feeling that this was her fault. They'd argued, hadn't they? She'd known Mama had respiratory distress, but she'd challenged her anyway thinking Mama was exaggerating the symptoms to get her way like she always did. But how could she exaggerate pneumonia? She couldn't just conjure up the germs that attacked her lungs. Mama had really been sick, and she'd agitated her. So how could this crisis not be her fault?

She glanced at Del. He hadn't said much even when she'd introduced David. Connie sat quietly beside him. Connie had hugged her when they first arrived, and she'd detected the strong smell of alcohol. Over the years she'd often smelled alcohol on Connie and was certain that by now she was the full-fledged closet alcoholic Mama had accused her of being. She couldn't blame her. She was as much a victim of this whole mess as the rest of them.

Del retrieved a Camel from the pack tucked in his tee shirt pocket. He tapped the end of the cigarette against the boot sole of his right foot, which was crossed over and propped on his bony left knee. She cringed when she thought of what residue might be on that boot, knowing that one of the last places he'd walked before this crisis was probably inside his dog pens.

He lit the cigarette, took a puff, and exhaled. The smoke spiraled over his head in the opposite direction. Then he rubbed his tongue across his front teeth and made a squeaking sound. "Okay, little sister, what are we gonna do?"

"I don't believe we have a choice. She needs the tracheotomy."

"Oh, you always have a choice." His voice was mocking and condescending, and he shot her his crazy, green-eyed stare. "It's just that you Geminis can't ever make up your mind. It's the twin nature of your sign. So you give up trying and use the old no-choice excuse."

She sighed. Why did he always have to be such an ass during a crisis? Was that his way of coping with the anguish? Well, it made hers worse, and it made her angry.

"There's a lousy choice here," she blurted. "If we do nothing, she'll die. Her only hope is the tracheotomy. This is a life-saving procedure. I've seen it done many times." She might hold a desk job now, but she'd done her time working call doing ER emergencies. She always marveled, though, at how little all that experience helped on the flip side of the pain.

"Oh yeah, that's right," Del spoke in his most sarcastic tone. "I forgot. You're the educated one."

She hated it when he patronized her. It was his own fault he didn't get a college education. He'd thrown away a full four-year scholarship with living expenses. Mama had made the mistake of telling him that he'd tested at genius level on his high school IQ test, and that knowledge had an overall negative impact.

He boasted that he was smarter than his teachers anyway so why go to school. Then there was the factor that brainpower didn't figure into becoming a revered mountain man. That rite of passage involved the seedy side of their rural life: the moonshine binges; the trashy women; the dogfights; and the drugs.

She'd never known the results of her IQ test, but it hadn't mattered because she'd learned that in this world no matter how smart you were, the credentials of education were the key to financial success. For that reason she'd studied hard to earn her two-year scholarship and to qualify for government loans that she'd paid back all by herself.

Mama with her protectiveness and strict moral guidelines had guided her away from the seamy side of their environment, yet she supported Del's lifestyle. She might not approve, but she found it too easy to look the other way; and she blamed Laurel when she couldn't do the same. Sometimes she felt like she was the adopted member of the family, like the one who didn't really belong because her mindset was so different. Del was lucky. She wished she was the cousin instead of him.

"We have to sign the papers, Del," she said firmly. They were wasting precious time. "We have to tell them to go ahead with it. It's the only hope, the only choice."

"Not none of me. I abstain."

She glared at him. "You can't abstain!" She abruptly softened her voice when she realized that she was almost screaming at him. But Del was smiling and complacent now like the burden had just been lifted from his shoulders, as if by saying he wouldn't decide he was released from any responsibility.

"I see how it is," she said. "I get to take all the blame if she dies. For your information, you have as much responsibility here as me. You can't pull your distance card this time. She's been your mother, too. You can't just roll over and play dead and let me take all the burden and responsibility."

His eyes narrowed angrily. "Don't you talk to me about burden. Who takes care of her day and night? I ain't seen you doing bedpan duty. She's lucky if you stay thirty minutes on your piddling little weekly visits, and you always upset her."

Guilty as charged. She'd walked right into that one. There was no end to Del's manipulative abilities. He knew when to play brother, when to play cousin, and when to just sit the fence. He knew exactly how to get under her skin doing whichever tactic he chose. He was so much like Mama in that respect he might as well have been her child. She wondered what Gene's vote would be. She imagined he would abstain, too. No matter what he did, Del and Mama always interpreted it as wrong, but Gene was drunk as usual. He hadn't even been able to put a sentence together when she'd called him at Peggy's house to tell him about Mama.

"It don't matter anyway," Del said as he grimaced through the cloud of smoke he'd just exhaled. "Mama's got the power to heal herself. Like Great-Grandma Cowan. I've got that power, too, where you can make people sick or well."

Cora Lou Cowan was his great-grandmother, too, so maybe he *had* inherited her so-called powers. She didn't think he should be bragging about it. From what she'd heard, the woman was nuts, a crazy old midwife who used potions, herbs, and Indian mysticism.

"Mama has that power?" she asked. "Well, maybe you're right, but I've only seen her use one side of it. I've watched her make herself sick for five years now, but not once have I seen her try to make herself well. Why is that, Del?"

"Not being one of us, you wouldn't understand."

Oh, I'm one of you, she thought. *I just wish to hell I wasn't.*

It was as if he'd read her thoughts. "Oh, I don't mean you ain't a Cowan, but you ain't like us, never have been. It's our Cherokee heritage. We're shamans."

"What in the hell is a shaman?" She was totally exasperated now. Had he meant *shamus*, a private eye, and was mispronouncing the word?

"We're medicine people," he continued. "I'm one. Grandma Cowan was one and Mama, too. Shaman."

She lost it then. "You're a medicine man? Like those guys from the movies with war paint and potions and all that?" He nodded his head yes. "You're certifiable, Del. They're going to come and carry you off to the psychiatric ward. That is ridiculous."

She glanced at Connie who sat across from her next to Del. She looked embarrassed. She wondered how sweet Connie could live with her crazy brother. Abruptly she heard a movement behind her. She turned to see that David had returned. She'd been so exasperated with Del during their entire conversation that she wasn't sure how long David had been there or how much he had heard.

He was leaning against the room divider about three feet behind the group of folding chairs that they had arranged in a cluster of four with two facing each other. She exchanged a glance with him, but she couldn't read anything. He moved to the chair next to hers and reached to squeeze her forearm.

"I'll play your game, Del," she finally said. "I'll sign the papers. I'll take the blame for the outcome."

"Let's ask Mama what she wants to do. It is, after all, her life," he said.

"I didn't think she was responsive."

"She'll communicate with me."

Given the seriousness of her condition, she doubted that, but she agreed. They got immediate permission to visit. Connie stayed behind, and she, Del, and David were allowed to go inside ICU for ten minutes.

Mama was indeed awake, and her eyes darted straight for Del. Her chest heaved in cadence with the respirator. An IV snaked into a small vein on her right foot. Her arm veins had collapsed from too much use. Laurel thought of how frightening it must be to be conscious and to have breath forced into and out of your body and how scary to know what little control there was in having your life sustained by a machine. She ached for the fear Mama must be feeling and regretted with all her heart that she'd challenged her.

Professionally, she'd seen all of this many times before, but this was her mother. Now she was on the helpless side of the pain. She thought about the moral challenge of every healthcare professional to "*first, do no harm*." But that was impossible here. Each life-sustaining treatment was a risk in itself.

David checked the monitors, and he reached for Mama's chart and began to read through it. She knew Mama couldn't see him standing just out of the range of motion of her arthritic neck. Even if she had, she would probably think he was one of the Mountain General staff doctors. She wished she could be clinical, too, but she couldn't. There was too much pain in her heart. She'd caused this. It was her fault. It was always her fault.

"You're looking better, Mama," Del said, lying to himself, lying to her. Mama smiled with her eyes. The respirator in her airway prevented any other communication.

"Mama!" Del spoke again in a loud voice so he could be heard clearly over the machine's whooshing as it kept life pumping into her body. "We're gonna sign the papers so they can do a tracheotomy."

After the way he had stubbornly abstained on that decision, she didn't fail to notice his "we." He continued, "I need to know if this is what you want, Mama, 'cause I won't let them do it if it ain't."

It was touching the way he felt her pain as if he were part of her body, yet there was something wrong and scary about it. She couldn't decide what that something was.

Mama knew she was in the room, but even when she touched her arm and stood where she could easily see her, she wouldn't in any way communicate with her. She'd walked out in the middle of that argument with Mama this afternoon so maybe that was it, and this was Mama's way of reminding her that this crisis was her fault. Well, she didn't have to be reminded. What she saw before her was clear enough.

She was so tired of this endless pain with Mama, and she felt trapped with no way out. Fighting it didn't help. Today was evidence of that, and nothing she tried financially or medically reversed anything or made it better.

She scanned the monitors and then she glanced toward Mama again. Even though Mama ignored her, she had no problem communicating with Del, and she watched as Mama let him know in response to his prompting that she wanted the tracheotomy. Their communication was seamless, and she wondered what she and Gene had done wrong. Mama didn't love them, her own flesh and blood, the way she loved her sister's child.

Even when Laurel was a child Mama had discouraged flowery expressions. To say I love you was right up there with tears as a stamp of weakness for Mama, but she could die on that operating table tonight. Regardless of whether Mama loved her or not, she needed to express her own love. She did love Mama in spite of everything. In a flood of emotion that bypassed her brain, she told herself she couldn't let Mama leave this life without knowing that.

Abruptly the truth shot out of her, the truth she always had to guard for fear that Mama would use her weakness against her. "I do love you, Mama," she said softly, and she reached to gently squeeze her arm. "I love you."

She knew Mama had heard her. She could see it in her eyes, but after that unspoken communication Mama turned her eyes to Del. It was her deepest cut. She thought of all the times in the past five years when losing in a standoff with her that Mama would stab her in the back with her empty *I love yous* as she walked away. It was in this stinging moment of complete rejection that she realized what was wrong. Love didn't mean the same thing to Mama that it did to her. For Mama it was a weapon, and she knew exactly how to go for the heart.

An ache began to throb deep inside her, but she couldn't locate its center. Maybe it was her soul hurting because the pain metastasized to her heart and brain and limbs and left her trembling all over. Just when she thought she'd surrender to the choking tears, she felt David's arm slip around her waist. As he pulled her gently closer, she leaned into him. She desperately needed his support, and even though he was witnessing her family's craziness full force, she was grateful he'd come with her.

Mama's nurse appeared abruptly with a clipboard in hand. "The doctor's ready for your family's decision, Laurel. Have you all decided yet?" Nova Sue Brown asked gently. Nova Sue knew her well enough to guess that in a life-or-death situation her choice would be life, but she also knew this decision wasn't hers alone.

"I'll sign," she said. She scribbled her signature without even reading the form Nova Sue extended. Then she walked out with David while Del trailed behind still talking to Mama.

The wait for the procedure to be over seemed interminable. As they waited, Gray Lady volunteers brought them coffee and juice and offered magazines, pillows, and blankets. Some of those sweet ladies she recognized as prominent widows of businessmen from the top of the mountain, and she was struck by the irony of this act. These ladies, for lack of something better to do, were volunteering the very services for free that her end of the mountain had done for them for pay. Was death the great equalizer, or were they all really equal beneath their facades? Was it really true that God didn't care whether his angels wore sequined robes or dingy white sheets? Long ago when she was nine years old, Mama Rita had consoled her with that thought.

She wanted to think all that through—whether the perceived caste system on this mountain was real or just a dysfunction of her soul. She knew one thing for sure. This mountain had both given her life and wounded her, but maybe it wasn't the mountain, after all. Maybe it was Mama.

After an hour and a half the surgeon entered the waiting room to report that Mama was out of surgery and doing well. An hour later they were allowed to visit. Again, Connie waited while she and David and Del went into to ICU. They rang the bell, and Nova Sue lead them back to Mama's cubicle. Nova Sue was the nurse Mama didn't like, the one she couldn't manipulate. On her last visit to ICU Mama had used her last ounce of strength for sticking out her tongue at her while her back was turned, yet she was the best nurse in the unit and the one Mama had improved the most under.

They filed into the room the way they had before. David again assessed the monitors and studied Mama's chart.

"Mama," Del called, and Mama's eyes fluttered open. She could smile now that the respirator was gone and she was breathing on her own, and she smiled only for Del. Del chattered on happily although Mama was too weak to respond by having him manipulate the hole in her neck.

She spoke to Mama, too, but instead of reacting, Mama acted groggy and confused when seconds before she had been alert for Del. The estrangement between her and Mama was conspicuous. She couldn't transcend it, even now on the heels of this deathbed crisis, and suddenly she realized the truth. She was in no way wanted or needed. She was required to be here. It was her punishment.

Del kept talking. "We got to get them to bring the feed bag around for you, Mama. You hungry?" Mama nodded affirmatively, and he continued. "Well, no wonder. You ain't had no solid food since early this morning. I'll bet your stomach thinks your throat's cut."

He paused, she guessed thinking about the significance of the colloquial expression he'd just used, and he doubled over the rail of Mama's bed laughing that annoying rat-a-tat chuckle of his. She wasn't amused. It was a cruel comment, but Mama was grinning broadly. She was afraid to look at David to gauge what he thought. After this ordeal he'd probably run as far away from her as he could.

This was hell. She was in hell; but she had always thought that hell was hot, and this room was so cold her teeth were chattering. Then abruptly she had to acknowledge the obvious. This deathbed crisis was just for her. Somehow, some way, Mama had willed her body into crisis mode. She couldn't whip Laurel back into the family fold any other way, so she risked losing her life—and it truly hung by a thread—just to get back what belonged to her. How warped and wrong that was, and she had to acknowledge that it had nothing to do with love. Nothing at all.

Chapter Fifteen

Laurel's mother stayed in ICU for a week, and David went with her to visit every afternoon after work while Mrs. Archer kept Gena. They were both off on Labor Day, and he'd encouraged Laurel to stick with their plans for the picnic and concert. Gena was looking forward to it, and Laurel needed the relaxation. He'd pointed out that they were only allowed to visit for ten minutes on the even hours, and sitting in the waiting room all day wouldn't help her mother. She'd agreed to go, and in spite of the situation, they all had a good time. They drove up to Mountain General after the picnic, and Laurel visited her mother while he stayed in the hospital cafeteria with Gena.

On every subsequent visit to see her mother Del was the same smartass nutcase he'd been the night of the surgery. He couldn't believe the things Del had said that first night. If he was such a healer, why hadn't he used his powers that night instead of letting modern medicine bail him out? David could see why Laurel got so infuriated with him.

As for Mrs. Harper, she could talk now when the tracheotomy was covered. He knew it was an effort that tired her quickly, but she would expend the energy only for Del. She didn't seem to like him much, and she didn't have to say a word to get that point across. She completely ignored him even after Laurel had introduced them. He didn't let it bother him, though. She had been through a lot, and he took that into consideration.

It did bother him immensely the way she treated Laurel. That night of the surgery his heart had ached for her, and he wondered what had made her mother so bitter toward her. He knew one thing for sure. Laurel didn't deserve it.

He'd heard enough interchange between her and Del to know that she didn't get along at all with her brother, but she seemed to have no problems with her sister-in-law. He'd talked to Connie quite a bit during the visitations that Del and Laurel made together. In the privacy of the ICU waiting room Connie had told him that at the beginning of Mrs. Harper's illness they'd all thought she was exaggerating her symptoms.

"Imagine how bad we felt when they diagnosed this disease, but she could be a whole lot better off than she is. She won't follow the doctor's orders, and she's always got a fight going with somebody," Connie said. "She's awful to Laurel, and when Laurel bucks her, she gets sick. She's hard to live with. I can tell you that personally."

He'd gained much information from scanning Mrs. Harper's chart, and he didn't know how she was still alive. Her health had deteriorated much more rapidly in the last five years than any of the case histories of rheumatoid arthritis that he'd studied in medical school and that included the clinic cases he'd seen.

She seemed to harbor a venomous anger, and he couldn't help wondering if that had contributed to her illness. According to their chartings more than one resident at Mountain General had entertained that same question in the last few years.

Now almost four weeks after the ICU crisis, her mother was back home and things had gotten back to normal for Laurel—if you could call this situation normal. Laurel still went to visit every Saturday, but he had noticed how carefully she assessed the situation at her mother's house before she would expose Gena to it.

Many times after she'd returned he would learn from her conversation with Gena that she had left her to visit with her grandparents while she checked on her mother. Following those times Mrs. Harper never failed to make a follow-up call supposedly to speak with her granddaughter, but he could always tell from Laurel's side of the conversation that it was more a gripe session to punish Laurel.

He'd come to realize how much of her family's problems Laurel had absorbed in order to protect Gena. She was the reason Gena was so well-adjusted. She protected her with a wall of security and stability that she alone provided—sometimes at great emotional expense. It shouldn't have to be that way. Laurel deserved to be happy.

He wanted to help, so he tried to subtly point out the truth as he saw it about her mother's condition. That truth was that the source of her mother's continued decline lay within and was in no way Laurel's fault. He'd checked out books from the medical library that contained case histories of patients with autoimmune diseases. The similarities of some of the patients to what he knew of her mother's situation were striking. Some didn't appear to be like her at all, but he hoped that reading about the similar cases would lessen Laurel's unjustified feelings of guilt.

They had discussed one case history over lunch yesterday, and he decided to use it to voice his opinion on her mother's situation. "I saw from her charts that the doctors have tried gold salts shots and all the more traditional treatments on your mom," he said.

"Yes, but nothing's worked. She had knuckle and hip replacements early on, but ultimately none of that helped." She glanced up him. "Sometimes—most of the time—I don't think she wants to be helped."

He'd entertained that same thought, but he didn't say it.

Laurel continued. "She talks about her illness like it's an old friend. She always says, 'I hope none of you kids get this old arthritis.' I don't think she can wait for us to get it, especially me."

He nodded. "Do pain medications help?"

"When she'll let them. I've seen her fight the highest dosage they can give her until she neutralizes it. I don't begin to understand that. She couldn't possibly enjoy what she's been through, and yet she just keeps on pushing the envelope."

"I saw that they've started her on steroids. Has that helped?"

"Not appreciably. She's been on them a year, and I don't see the difference yet."

"That's an option I wouldn't use myself unless it was the absolute last resort, and it may well be since they've tried everything else. But steroids have some serious side effects."

"Like what?"

"Long-term use can cause a psychosis. How often does she see her doctor so he can regulate her?"

"Only when she has a crisis. Once she became bedridden, she couldn't tolerate going to routine visits, and if she could have, it would have had to be by ambulance."

"Does Del administer her medications?"

"Oh yes. He's always bragging about what good care he gives her and how he uses a two-year-old *Physicians' Desk Reference* to adjust the doses. Connie's cousin, Emma, found it in some doctor's garbage where she works as a maid. Del's like some New Age witch doctor using a *PDR* to enhance his magic." She shoved her tray of half-eaten food aside and sipped her iced tea. "I know you couldn't have missed hearing him talk about being a medicine man."

"I heard," he said. That piece of information about the *PDR* infuriated him. With his crazy practices Del had most likely caused every crisis that Laurel got blamed for precipitating. "Your mother strikes me as an acutely intelligent woman. Doesn't she see the danger in letting him do that?" he asked gently.

"I've warned her so many times about it." She glanced up at him. "David, no matter how debilitated Mama looks, she's not a victim. She's totally in charge. In his defense, Del does exactly what she tells him to do. Of course, he could tell her no."

"I'd be glad to check her on a regular basis and make sure the doses are right. I'd confer with her doctor first, of course, to get his permission."

She hesitated, and finally she spoke. "That's sweet of you and a great idea, but a new associate of Dr. Fuller's tried the same thing last year when she first started on the steroids. Although she was nice to the doctor, the minute he left she had Del undo everything good he did. I could never let them waste your time like that."

"I don't mind trying, and who knows, maybe I could reach her."

"David, my mother obviously wants to self-destruct. She wouldn't let your efforts make a difference anyway, and because of that I won't let her drag you into the craziness. She'd just end up blaming you for every good thing you did and only because I care about you."

She cared about him. That was good to hear. It was the first time she had admitted to any affection for him in present tense. Maybe they were making progress.

The next morning they went to the pool and practiced strokes with Gena. She was a natural. A few more lessons and she would be swimming on her own. After they wound up their practice session he lifted Gena to the edge of the pool where Laurel bent to wrap a towel around her.

As she patted the child's damp curls he admired her figure the way he did every chance he got on Saturdays. He couldn't help it, and it always aroused him. It was shameless, but he didn't make any attempt to subdue his libido. He was too grateful that it wasn't dead.

A couple of those Saturdays she'd caught him in the act of undressing her with his eyes, and she'd colored a bit, but every Saturday she wore that same luscious turquoise two-piece and gave him a repeat performance. He could feel the chemistry between them as strong as ever. He would allow himself this lustful voyeurism, but he wasn't about to act on it. She was too fragile, and the last thing he wanted was to hurt her again.

She threw on her cover-up, spoiling his view, and gathered her straw bag and Gena's hippo, and they headed to the apartment.

As she pushed her key into the lock of her door he squatted to talk to Gena, brushing a damp strand of hair away from her cheek. "You're learning fast, sweetie. You'll be swimming without your tube by next summer. The pool's going to close for winter after next week, but we'll take up where we left off as soon as they re-open in May."

Laurel beamed him a smile as she swung her apartment door open. Her phone immediately rang.

"Go ahead. Answer it. Gena and I will get your stuff. Won't we?" Gena nodded enthusiastically as Laurel rushed to the phone. Once he and Gena brought all their pool stuff inside he closed the apartment door behind them.

He assumed this was a lab problem that one of the supervisors was contacting Laurel about until he caught a glimpse of her shocked expression. She sank onto the sofa with the phone to her ear, and she spoke softly. When she ended the conversation she turned toward Gena.

"Honey, can you get changed out of your bathing suit by yourself?"

"Yes, Mommy, I'm not a baby." Gena then skipped off toward her bedroom.

He and Laurel exchanged a glance. Then she stood and walked over to him. "I need a favor." She hesitated. "And I hate to bother you."

"Anything. Just ask."

"I wonder if you could stay with Gena. There's been another emergency with my family."

"Your mother?"

"No," she answered softly.

She didn't seem to want to elaborate, so he didn't push. "No problem. I'll take good care of her. Don't worry."

"I know you will, and I won't worry if she's with you."

He could tell by the expression on her face that whatever this was, it was bad. "Want to talk about it?" he asked gently.

She heaved a deep sigh, and she looked so distressed he wanted to take her in his arms and make it all go away. "My brother's been taken to the state mental hospital."

"Your brother? Del? The one I met when your mom was in ICU?" If you asked him, the guy was nuts alright, but the last time he'd checked, morbid stupidity wasn't grounds for being committed.

"No, the other one. Gene. He's the oldest, thirty-six. They're both older than me. Del is the middle child."

"What happened?"

"Gene's divorced, and he usually stays with his girlfriend. He and Peggy haven't been getting along, so he's been staying at Mama's the last few weeks. According to Mama he got high on PCP this morning and went crazy. She said he was running around naked picking at imaginary bugs on his body. Then he supposedly hit her in the face with his fist."

"Supposedly?"

"You saw Mama's condition and how brittle her bones are. If he hit her the way she made it sound, she'd be in ER again and most definitely not calling me to tell me about it."

"And you don't think she's telling you the whole truth about what happened?"

"No, as coldhearted as that sounds, I don't."

He didn't say anything. He didn't think she was being coldhearted at all. She was being a realist. Judging from the evidence he'd seen, her mother was a master at manipulation.

He reached to squeeze her shoulder, and she looked up into his eyes.

"Gene is usually the gentlest person you'd ever want to meet. I know alcohol and drugs make him aggressive. I've seen it for myself. It's just that I don't think he would do this even under the influence of mind-altering chemicals. Mama has a way of making people angry. I can see him getting so mad at her that he would knock her glasses off into the floor and stomp them to pieces. I've been that mad at her myself, but I can't see him ever actually physically hurting her."

"And you need to go check it out?"

"I'd like to see the situation for myself, and I'd like to hear Gene's side of this if they'll let me see him. I'd take Gena, but I don't want her exposed to any of this craziness. I've managed to keep her away from the worst of it so far."

"I'll take care of her. You go."

"Are you sure you don't mind?"

"Of course not. I'm not on call so we'll stay here in your apartment with her toys and books. I don't think she'll be bored."

"Thank you. I owe you for this."

"No you don't." He reached for her hand, brought it to his lips, and kissed it. "You be careful. Promise me."

"I'll be okay. My place in the family is to be the audience to their destruction. Maybe Daddy's the lucky one. He doesn't have to watch it anymore and think it's his fault."

Her expression grew so sad he thought she was going to cry. This time he reacted to his feelings and pulled her into his arms. She didn't resist. Instead she wrapped her arms around him and lay her head on his shoulder. He kissed her hair and spoke softly into it. "Don't worry about Gena, baby. Do what you have to do."

He went to his apartment to change out of his bathing suit while Laurel changed and got ready to go. She walked out the door at eleven o'clock as he was fixing lunch for Gena, her requested peanut butter and jelly sandwich. He had one, too, and marveled that he had forgotten how good peanut butter and jelly tasted.

He occupied himself totally with entertaining Gena. He read to her. They played Old Maid, her version of it, at least. They sat on the floor and built a village with Lincoln logs, and they played tea party with her dolls. They even listened to some of her story-time records. He'd never known how short a child's attention span was.

As he entertained her, she talked very intelligently for a four-year-old. "You're keeping me 'cause Mommy doesn't want me to see her argue with Grandma Sarah, aren't you?"

"Well, no, sweetie, I think your grandma is not feeling real good, and Mommy had to go check on her."

"Grandma Sarah gets sick a lot. She can't get out of bed. Mommy bought her a TV so she has something to do."

"That was nice of Mommy. So, see, they don't always argue."

"Nuh-unh. Mommy told her she better not give it away this time. The last one Mommy gave her she gave to Miss Jennie who Mommy says would probably talk to it instead of listen to it." She leaned toward him and whispered. "Miss Jennie talks a whole lot, so I think Mommy is right."

He laughed. "Miss Jennie sounds like an interesting lady."

"Mommy gets mad at Miss Jennie, too, 'cause when we used to give her a ride to church with us, she always patted me on the head and said poor Gena 'cause I don't have a daddy."

That brought a sharp twinge to the pit of his stomach. He knew Laurel was proud of being Gena's mother and the thought that someone would pity her or Gena because she didn't have a husband smarted. He should be that husband. He should be Gena's father.

"But Grandma Sarah did keep the TV 'cause this one she can turn on and off from her bed and change the channel, too."

"That's good. A remote control. You know that Mommy was only trying to help, don't you?"

She nodded her head up and down, and her shiny brown curls bounced. The shade of her hair was exactly the shade of Laurel's; but Laurel's hair was straight, and he remembered so was her father's. "Where did you get those pretty curls?" he asked automatically.

"Grandma Sarah has curls 'cept her hair is falling out now, and Uncle Gene's hair is curly like hers and mine."

"So, how do you feel about your uncles? Do you like them?"

"I like Uncle Gene. Mommy, too, even though he drinks that bad stuff and gets silly, and sometimes he's grumpy. Mommy tells him to get help, but he's nice. He's Mommy's favorite. I'm named after him."

"You are? That's nice."

"He carves things for Mommy and me." She reached to show him the cedar heart that hung around her neck on a purple velvet ribbon. "Uncle Gene carved this for me 'cause I like necklaces, and I like purple."

He rubbed the intricately carved heart between his thumb and forefinger. "It's very pretty."

"Grandma Sarah says Uncle Gene's mean, but he's not. Mommy says he wouldn't hurt a flea. Uncle Del is the one who's mean. I don't like him. He makes Mommy real mad."

"How does he make her mad?"

"He makes Grandma Sarah's house messy, and he won't keep the stuff Mommy bought for my grandma's house nice. And sometimes he makes Mommy cry, just not in front of him."

That immediately got his attention. "What does Uncle Del do that makes Mommy cry?"

"He says he's gonna tell somebody to take me away from her 'cause I don't have a daddy." She zeroed in on him with those intense blue eyes. "Don't tell Mommy I know she cries."

Hearing that, he wanted to beat Del's ass. "I promise, sweetie. I won't tell."

"Marita says nobody's gonna take me away, and I don't need a daddy. She says my Mommy loves me enough for ten people."

Laurel called her grandmother Mama Rita, but she had never mentioned anyone named Marita. She obviously was important in Gena's life as well as being very wise. "Marita is right," he said. "You remember that."

"I know my mommy loves me no matter what. She would love me even if I didn't be her little girl. She always tells me that, and I always believe her. Mommy never tells lies."

His conversation with Gena set off a dilemma inside him. He had to be a father to his child. He couldn't let her go on thinking she didn't have a father when he was right here. He would talk to Laurel again soon when she wasn't so overcome with family problems. He didn't want to hurt her any more than he already had, but he couldn't let the subject drop. He had a responsibility, and he loved this child.

When he hadn't heard from Laurel by five thirty he began to worry, but surely she'd be home any time now. He and Gena went over to his apartment to get ingredients for dinner and to retrieve the Walt Disney *Peter and the Wolf* record he'd bought especially for Gena earlier in the week. He decided now was the best time to give it to her. He thought she would enjoy hearing it while dinner cooked.

He fixed a salad, drizzled French bread with melted butter and wrapped it in foil, and put together his favorite spaghetti sauce recipe. He let Gena help him prepare all of it. She helped him tear lettuce, and she added the radishes and tomatoes he'd sliced to the bowl. After she helped him measure the ingredients for the sauce, he let her swirl the spaghetti into the pot of cold water. Throughout the entire process she was a charming mix of mischievous giggles and efficiency. He'd never had so much fun preparing a meal.

As they worked he told her about the record he'd given her. Then while he kept watch over the cooking spaghetti noodles and sauce and browned the ground beef, she listened to it and colored as she sat at the drop-down kitchen bar close to where he worked.

He'd already explained what she would be hearing even though the record explained it, too. "This is a story about a little boy named Peter," he'd told her. "He has a lot of little creatures as friends, and the story tells what happens when they all meet up with a wolf at his grandfather's place. It's a little different from your story-time records. You see, it's by this talented man called Prokofiev who made up this musical story for his children. He uses musical instruments to tell the story. It's cool. I think you'll like it."

As he set the table hoping Laurel would arrive soon, *Peter and the Wolf* played in the background punctuated with Gena's giggles when she recognized the various sounds he'd told her to listen for and expect: Peter sneaking into the forest with Sasha the bird, Sonya the duck, Ivan the cat, and Sonya encountering the wolf.

He went back to the kitchen, took the noodles off the stove, and drained them. He added the ground beef. As he poured the sauce over the noodles he heard a key turn in the door lock, and Laurel entered the apartment. When Gena spotted her, she made a dive for her and stretched to wrap her arms around her waist. "Listen, Mommy, Sonya's okay. The wolf didn't really eat her."

Laurel flashed him a smile that warmed his heart. "*Peter and the Wolf*. How nice." She lifted the child into her arms and hugged her close, closing her eyes as if she were trying to absorb her sweetness. He understood that feeling. She was a wonderfully sweet, unspoiled child.

"Are you okay?" he asked when she entered the kitchen carrying Gena.

She nodded. "Something smells great."

"David cooked for us. He let me help with *everything* like Marita does." Gena then took Laurel's face in both her tiny hands, her eyes glowing with enthusiasm. "We tasted it, Mommy. It's yummy."

"It's ready when you guys are," he added.

"Great. I'm hungry. Go wash your hands, sweetie." She set Gena on the floor and patted her behind lightly before she scampered toward the bathroom.

"We'll listen to your record again with Mommy after dinner," he called to Gena as he walked over to the record player and turned it off. He walked back to the kitchen to finish getting the food ready. While he talked to Laurel he moved back and forth taking food to the table. "Who's Marita?" he asked. "Gena talked about her the whole time we were fixing dinner."

"My grandmother. We call her Mama Rita, but Gena couldn't say it at first, so it's 'Marita.' Did you all do okay? I know she's a handful."

"A handful of sweetness. We did great. I've got everything ready. Go ahead and sit down."

Gena scampered into the room and took her seat at the table. "I want to say the blessing, please."

"Sure, sweetie," Laurel said.

He took the chair at a right angle to Laurel and bowed his head.

"Dear Fodder, thank you for this food and for David 'cause I love him a whole lot. Amen." Everything about Gena's simple prayer gave him goose bumps from the way she pronounced *father* to the inflections in her voice to the pure sincerity of her words.

During dinner they made casual conversation with Gena doing most of the talking as she told Laurel about all the fun things they had done while she was gone. After dinner he didn't make any move to leave, and Laurel didn't ask him to. As they listened to *Peter and the Wolf* again, he loaded the dishwasher and cleaned the kitchen. He wouldn't let Laurel help. Later after Gena's bedtime ritual they tucked her in together, and Gena kissed them both.

She blessed him again in her prayers. In fact, he was second only after Laurel on her list. "Bless Mommy; bless David …"

As she drifted off to sleep sucking her thumb and clutching her beloved teddy bear, they headed for the living room. "I brought some wine over from my apartment when Gena and I went to get the stuff for dinner. Would you like a small glass? It might relax you."

She nodded, so he poured the wine and joined her on the sofa leaning to set her glass on the coffee table before he took his seat.

"How did it go with your family?" he asked softly.

She reached for her glass and took a sip of wine, but she didn't answer.

"I'm sorry. You may not want to talk about it. I can understand that."

"It's just that it defies words." She took another sip and leaned her head on the back of the sofa. "I went to see Mama first. Just as I suspected she doesn't have a mark on her. Her glasses were crushed to smithereens though. Luckily, she has an old pair. I have to call the optometrist Monday and get her a replacement prescription. Gene supposedly threatened to kill them, all of them, so Del was standing guard with a shotgun. He looked terrified. I felt sorry for him, and Del is hard to feel sorry for."

"So, do you think your mother was lying about the whole thing?"

"I think she twisted the truth like she always does."

"How so?"

"Mama can be infuriating. I've been mad enough at her to want to stomp something into oblivion the way he stomped her glasses. I know he didn't hit her because of the lack of physical evidence. He may have started to but pulled back and stopped himself. I can see the drugs releasing his inhabitations that much, but drugs or not, I know my brother. He'd never hit her."

"Do you think he actually threatened to kill them?"

"Probably not in those words. I've seen enough arguments that I can picture how it went. She probably taunted him when he stopped short of hitting her, telling him he wasn't even man enough to do that just like she always did with Daddy. What did he have left but idle threats and destroying the closest inanimate thing? He knew she had the upper hand by then and that Del would get involved and he was headed for jail. I can believe he said he ought to kill them, but he would never carry through. I've seen him cry inconsolably when he ran over a cat. It was an accident, but he wasn't so high that it didn't devastate him. He can't get bombed enough on anything to block out his sensitive side even though he tries."

"Why would your mother lie about all that?"

She shrugged. "For the same reason she does anything. For control."

"What about Gene? Are they going to keep him in the mental hospital?"

"That was the worst part," she said softly. "They had him in a straitjacket. When I told them I didn't think that was necessary, they were so hateful. They acted like he was some dangerous, rampaging bear."

She swirled the wine in her glass and finally took a sip. Then she continued.

"He's more like a poor, wounded deer, and he's just so lost. He's been divorced for over four years, and he just can't keep a relationship. He has nobody to love him. Any love Mama has to offer is such a hurting thing. He uses alcohol and drugs to insulate himself from her. I'm not saying he's right to do that. It's just that I understand him."

She turned to look at him then, and he couldn't bear the pain in her blue eyes.

"Mama, in some way or the other, puts all of us in a straitjacket. Gene's is just literal. I love my mother; but sometimes I hate her, and I really hate her for this." She looked away. "I'll never understand her. It's like she gave birth to us to hurt us."

He reached to set his glass on the coffee table. "You don't have to go through this alone. You've got me. Please don't forget that. I'm a wall away. Just say the word, and I'll be here any time night or day."

She looked up at him, and her expression softened. "I won't forget. I don't know what I would have done without you today, David."

"It's been my pleasure. Gena is a wonderful child."

"Mama actually got mad at me for not bringing her. I just let her rant. They were all supposedly in fear for their lives—and she wanted me to bring a child into that?"

"Has your mother always been this way?"

"Yes and no." She set her wine glass on the coffee table next to his and turned toward him, gathering her legs under her. She rested her arm on the back of the sofa and traced her fingers over its pattern. "I guess it's time I told you about what makes my family tick. Understand that I don't want to, but you deserve to know."

He turned toward her. "Nothing you can say is going to change how I feel about you."

"I hope not." She took in a deep breath and began, "A long time ago there was an accident. Our family wasn't the best one around before it happened, but afterwards we didn't stand a chance."

"How old were you when this accident happened?"

"Six. Del was seven, and Gene was twelve. Before that day we were like everybody else except that our parents argued all the time. We didn't know that wasn't normal. Gene and Del were playing in the yard. I was on the porch playing with my doll. Daddy flew out of the house in a rage, mad at Mama, but that wasn't unusual. He had a temper, but he never let it go over the edge. He'd walk away first. Gene's like that. Daddy headed for the car. Mama got there before he could close the door. They scuffled over the keys. The car got knocked out of gear. It lurched back. Del was crouched behind it, and it ran over his right arm pinning him beneath the back right tire."

Her face reflected so much pain that he knew she was reliving that day—not just chronicling it. He reached to rub the arm she had propped on the back of the sofa. "He doesn't show any evidence of the injury. He looks to be totally recovered."

"That's on the outside. What it did to his soul you can't see."

"What was the extent of his physical injury?"

"His radius and ulna were broken. The country doctor who had an office in Johnson Fork, the next community over, took care of him. He was a quack, and he set the arm haphazardly. Del had a lot of pain, and his arm was twisted. Mama spent two years searching for a doctor brave enough to try to undo what the quack had done. After the new doctor operated the set was perfect, but rehab was painful."

She moved her arm from the back of the sofa and concentrated on braiding the tassels on the pillow between them. "You see, my mother felt guilty because she was as much to blame as Daddy in what happened, so she just had to fix Del so she'd be off the hook. She badgered him and made him fight the pain until he did go back to being normal on the outside."

"She badgered him in the therapy after the surgery?"

"Yes, and what you can't see is that underneath the physically robust man lies a little boy who never understood why he had to be the one who got hurt by somebody else's war and why one of the main perpetrators of his pain was also his healer."

She paused and hugged the pillow to her as if it held some balm to the trauma she was walking back through. "I think Del is forever in debt to Mama for giving him back a normal life, but he hates her, too, for the pain. He can only handle the ambivalence by molding himself so close to her that he's almost one with her psyche. At least that's the way it looks to me."

"What was your dad's relationship with him?"

"Daddy was crushed with remorse. He babied Del from that day forward, something Del both loved and hated—that old ambivalence again. And it set Del at odds with Gene."

"In what way?"

She sighed and paused. Finally she looked up at him. "Del is not really our brother. He's our first cousin, our Aunt Dorothy's son. She was Mama's older sister."

"What happened to your aunt?"

"She and her husband were killed when a train hit them at a crossing. I don't remember them, but we lived in the valley with them while Daddy was in the army. I was two when it happened. Del doesn't remember them either. He was only three. Mama and Daddy are the only parents he's ever known."

"Was Gene jealous because he came to live with you?"

"Not until the accident and only because afterwards Del was Mama's favorite child to the point that Gene and I didn't feel like she loved us at all. Daddy had always loved Del the same as he loved us, but the way he babied him after the accident made the whole jealousy thing worse for Gene." She picked up her wine glass again, took a sip, and held the glass with both hands. "Maybe Daddy didn't pay enough attention to Gene. Maybe it was that he was too lenient on Del. But Gene was hurt by the favoritism he thought he showed Del. When he got older he developed bad ways of getting attention like drinking and running with a wild crowd."

"Where were you in all this?"

She twirled the stem of her wine glass back and forth between her thumb and forefinger. "I was always their audience, naive little Laurel who could always see the big picture. I loved them all and never blamed anyone. I always tried to fix them, but somehow I never could."

"I'm so sorry, baby," he said. "You've been though a lot."

She set her glass back on the coffee table. "Daddy did genuinely love all three of us. As long as he was alive there was some semblance of balance, and I felt free to have a life. Now it feels like I'm trapped taking his place, and I see why he was so sad all the time."

"Come here," he said gently, coaxing her into his embrace.

"It's crazy stuff, David. I won't blame you if you don't want to be part of it. I don't know if it's ever going to change."

He settled her into his arms and murmured, "Hey, look at me." She shifted her head against his shoulder and looked up into his eyes. "You're not getting rid of me that easy."

"Why would you even want to be associated with such craziness? It's like visiting hell."

"Hell was the past five years without you, thinking I'd never get another chance at your love. Heaven is having you and Gena in my life whatever that involves. You're going to have to start believing that, baby."

"I want to."

"Then do because I'm not going anywhere."

Chapter Sixteen

On Thanksgiving Eve after over six weeks of therapy, the mental hospital released Gene. By then Mama had made up with him through phone conversations, so he planned to go home to the mountain. While Laurel picked him up at the hospital, David kept Gena the way he'd kept her almost every Saturday while she visited both Gene at the hospital and her family on Sunset Mountain.

As she guided her car from the hospital parking lot she glanced at her brother. Regardless of the anger she felt at Mama and the hospital itself over the straitjacket episode, she'd come to realize the time spent here had actually helped him. At least they'd forced him into sobriety. He looked healthier than she had seen him in a long time.

"Guess you're glad to leave this place behind."

"It wasn't so bad. My social worker was kind of cute." He shot her a grin that for the first time in years wasn't tired around the edges. "She was a whole lot better than that shrink. He slapped me in that straitjacket the minute I came through the door. The asshole was always calling me a mama's boy."

"Aren't we all Mama's little boys and girls? And she has all of us in straitjackets."

"Not precious Del."

"Del's situation is much worse than a straitjacket. He's joined at the psyche with Mama."

He grinned again. "You sound like one of them." He nodded back over his shoulder at the hospital, the red brick facade of which was receding in her rearview mirror.

"If you ask me, Del's the one who needs psychiatric help," she said. "Have you ever heard all that shaman stuff he spouts?"

"Yeah, he's full of it. But he just wants you to think he's crazy. He's crazy like a fox."

"Mama's just outright manipulative. She's not going to change, and neither is Del. Are you sure you want to go back home?"

He shrugged.

"You can stay at my place," she added. "You can drive my car to that new heavy equipment job the social worker helped you get until we can get yours fixed at Moore's Service Station. I can sleep in Gena's other twin bed, and you can take my room. We can look for a place for you after you get settled into your job."

"Wouldn't that cramp your style with this new boyfriend you've been telling me about?"

"Of course not. David's a great guy. I want you to meet him."

She did want her brother to meet the man she loved now that things were going so well. She'd let down her guard with David, and he hadn't disappointed her. The past six weeks had been wonderful, and relaxing in the knowledge of David's love made it easier to cope with her family. She had more energy, and she felt joy for the first time in a long time.

"Would you mind if we dropped by my apartment for a few minutes on the way? You can see Gena, and meet David, too. He's keeping her for me."

"Sure. Are you bringing him up tomorrow for Thanksgiving."

"No. He and I decided to have Thanksgiving at my apartment. He's thawing the turkey in his refrigerator as we speak. Neither of us has ever cooked a turkey. Come stay with me. Have Thanksgiving with us and critique our efforts."

"Nah, I'd feel like a fifth wheel."

"Chicken. You just don't want to risk not getting a good meal after all that hospital food."

He laughed. "Has he met Mama and Del yet?"

"He went with me the last time Mama was in ICU."

"I kind of missed that one." He grinned sheepishly.

"Del was his usual crazy self. Mama was recuperating from pneumonia and the tracheotomy, but she'd already decided she didn't like David sight unseen."

"That's our Mama."

They stopped briefly at her apartment. He and David seemed to like each other even though Gene was unusually reserved. When she thought about it, she realized that she hadn't seen her brother totally sober for so long that she'd forgotten he was basically shy. It was just one more reason he'd hidden in his addictions.

Gena gave him a tour of their apartment and chattered on about the new storybook David had bought for her and had been reading to her when they arrived. They'd made chocolate chip cookies while she was gone, so Gena insisted on giving him some to take with him along with a picture of a turkey she had colored.

As they left her apartment parking lot Laurel glanced at Gene. "Just one more stop. Connie asked me to pick up a turkey and some other things for Thanksgiving. Can you handle the grocery store? I'll hurry."

He nodded, and they stopped at the Kroger's at the foot of the mountain. He seemed restless as he walked around with her while she selected the items on Connie's list. She accomplished the task quickly. At the checkout when she noticed the cigarette display, it hit her that he hadn't smoked since she'd picked him up. He wasn't a chain smoker like Del, but he smoked a lot. He was probably about to have a nicotine fit.

She reached for a carton of Luckies, his usual brand. "You need some of these, don't you?" she asked as she added the carton to her cart.

He nodded.

Once she paid for the groceries they headed to the car with the buggy, and he helped her load the paper sacks into her back seat. As they settled into her car he reached to retrieve the cigarettes from one of the sacks. He tore open the carton and took out a pack.

"Care if I smoke?"

"No, go ahead."

He grinned as he dangled the cigarette from his lips, reached into his pocket for his lighter, and lit it. "One bad habit at a time," he said.

"Hey, if I was going home to Mama's house, I'd learn to smoke, too."

He laughed. They made small talk as they drove up the mountain, but she wanted to know if he had dealt with the hard feelings with Mama and Del regarding the PCP crisis. If they hadn't at least talked about it over the phone, she worried that, therapy or not, he was going back into a situation that could quickly turn sour. She decided to come right out and ask him about it.

"So, have you, Mama, and Del resolved things about that day they took you to the hospital?"

"I wouldn't say we resolved it, no," he answered. "Mama thinks what she wants to think, does what she wants to do." He shrugged. "My conscience is clear no matter what the gospel according to her and Del is. I didn't hit her, but she sure as hell showed me who's boss. I got thrown into a straitjacket and punished for all my sins. So now that I done been put in my place, we can be one big happy family again."

"You need to get out of there, Gene. Our home is not a home anymore."

"You worry too much. Everything's gonna be fine. Mama feels guilty for what she did. I could tell by the way she talked. She'll be kissing my ass at least until after Thanksgiving is over, maybe even longer depending on how guilty she feels." He flashed a boyish grin. "I plan to milk it."

As far as she was concerned, buying into Mama's games only meant more heartache. Games were her territory. You couldn't win, and too often the losses were so costly you were better off walking away. She wished she could make Gene see that. She wished she could convince him that he should get as far away from their family as possible.

Once they were headed down Harper Hollow Road she decided to make her offer one more time. "After we drop off the groceries and you visit with Mama please pack up your clothes and go back with me. Gena would love it. You saw how happy she was to see you."

He studied his hands. "You're a good mama. David's good with kids, too. The shrink at the hospital says I'm not good with them because I can't stop being a kid myself. Do you think he's right?"

"I don't know. Maybe none of us has stopped being a kid. That doctor would have to be a member of our family to understand how hard it is to become a separate person. He'd have to know Mama to understand that you can't have an adult relationship with her. She beats the life out of independence with her guilt-whipping. It's her way, or you pay for it."

"Oh, yeah, the great god Mama."

"Do you think she's ever actually loved us?"

He shrugged. "That shrink at the nuthouse says it don't matter whether she does or not. He says you gotta learn to love yourself in spite of her."

"Still, it would be nice if our mother loved us."

"Yeah, but Mama is Mama. Ain't nobody gonna change her."

"So, why are you even coming back here?"

"It's what I'm used to. Look, it's not that I don't appreciate you inviting me, but I'd feel like a fish out of water in a city apartment."

She sighed. "You'll let me know if you change your mind."

He nodded.

When she parked in front of Mama's log cabin, she reached to touch her brother's arm before they got out of her car. "If you won't come home with me, please at least take this. All I ask is that you don't spend it on drugs or alcohol."

She handed him a wad of bills. She'd decided before she went to pick him up that she would prove she had faith in him by making an investment in his future. So she had gone by her bank on the way and made a withdrawal from her savings account. She'd opened the account with the forty-five-hundred-dollar equity check she'd received for her house.

She watched him count the bills. Abruptly he glanced up with a shocked expression on his face. "It's two thousand dollars. I can't take this, Sis. You might need it."

"It's part of the equity money from my house. I can spare it. It's a gift. You don't have to pay it back. It's enough to live on for a long time while you get on your feet. You're starting that new job on Monday. You can get your car fixed. You can get your own place. Just please make it as far away from here as you can get."

"Thanks," he muttered as he folded the money into his billfold.

She knew he was touched by her unexpected gift, but she also knew that he didn't know how to express it with any more than the word he'd just uttered. She wanted to hug him, but that would make him uncomfortable. She understood. She was every bit as guarded when it came to displays of affection, and in that vulnerable moment sitting outside her mother's house she suddenly realized why.

Too many times in their lives Mama had used displays of affection or hollow words of love to lure and trap them in the course of her manipulations. When they'd been foolish enough to express genuine love in return they would be left holding their hearts in their hands chastised for their weakness and feeling like fools. No wonder they held suspect any expression of emotion. No wonder they found it hard to believe anyone else could ever love them if their own mother couldn't.

Being always on guard was a conditioned reflex for her and Gene, but not Del. He'd molded himself to Mama for so long that he'd become like her. To Del sincere words of love, given or received, were a sign of weakness. He used to say if you had to say you loved someone then it didn't mean anything. Hugs were alien to him. He touched only to inflict pain.

She couldn't change her family, but she could change herself. Knowing that she had to start somewhere she decided to risk the words that she felt in her heart for Gene. She wouldn't make him uncomfortable, and she wouldn't do it in a way that made him feel he'd have to reciprocate.

They got out of the car, and he opened the back door on the passenger side handing her a bag of groceries. She hugged the bag to her left shoulder, but before she reached for the mesh bag that held the turkey she touched his arm. "You're my brother, Gene," she began softly. "I love you, and I want to help. I want to see one of us get out from under Mama's thumb. Get away from her, and don't let her guilt-whip you into coming back."

He nodded, and she knew he didn't know how to respond, so she changed the subject as she reached for the turkey. "Can you get the rest of it, or do we need to make another trip?"

"I got it covered," he answered grabbing the two remaining paper sacks, pushing the car door shut with his knee.

When they stepped inside the living room bearing the grocery sacks and turkey, Mama greeted Gene as if nothing bad had ever happened between them. "Connie and Del made up a room for you in the new addition. It's got your bed and all your stuff in there. They moved it from your attic room. Tomorrow Connie's making us a big turkey dinner. It'd be a great homecoming if your sister wasn't too good to celebrate with us."

She ignored Mama's comment and headed toward the kitchen following Connie who had retrieved the bags Gene held. As she passed through the doorway she saw Del sitting at the table smoking a cigarette and drinking coffee. Connie set her two sacks on the floor and removed a rack in the refrigerator to make room for the turkey.

"Well, well, ain't this nice? The prodigal son returneth. Connie, put on the fatted calf."

She set her sack of groceries and the turkey on the table with a thud and turned on Del. "Can't you be positive about this?" she said in a low hiss. "He's sober for the first time in I can't even remember when, and he's beginning to work through his problems. Don't mess with that. Give him a chance. Don't provoke him."

"Provoke him? Hell, I ain't the one who knocked the crap out of my mama."

"Maybe Mama exaggerated that a little bit, huh, Del, because she didn't have a mark on her when I got here that day. In her condition? Explain that."

"I ain't gotta explain nothing, little sister. You don't know nothing 'cause you ain't never around."

It never failed to irritate her when he called her *little sister*. It was his way of showing superiority, not a term of endearment. "I'm around enough to know when the truth is being stretched."

"You calling us liars?"

"You know only what she told you, Del. You weren't there either. I'm not denying that he stomped her glasses, but her bones are brittle. If he'd hit her, she would have shown some injuries—some pretty bad ones—and she didn't. I was here."

"Well, bully for you. You're never here any other time. How long are we gonna be blessed with your royal presence this evening?"

"I'm leaving as soon as I tell Gene good-bye. Does that make you happy?"

"Delirious."

He could be such an asshole. Even though she understood why he had become the person he was, it was hard to accept it. Their true kinship didn't matter when it got right down to it. Cousin or not, he had been her brother for her lifetime. She did love him, but loving him and Mama was like trying to love a couple of porcupines. The closer you got the more they hurt you.

When she got ready to leave, Gene walked her to her car. Before she opened her door to get in, he surprised her by enveloping her in a bear hug. She responded by releasing all her affection into the embrace as she hugged back. It said the words that neither of them knew how to say.

Chapter Seventeen

David had loved Thanksgiving since first grade when he'd been a pilgrim in the school program. He'd wanted to be an Indian, but Mom wouldn't allow it after he'd sliced his finger trying to split a stick to make a tomahawk. She'd overreacted, as usual. He hadn't even needed stitches.

He'd enjoyed everything about autumn as a kid like jumping into mounds of raked leaves and scattering them. That hadn't earned him any points with Mom. He remembered helping his grandfather haul pumpkins in from the field on his farm and helping watch his booth at the county fair. His fondest memory had been of helping him gather peanuts and waiting with great anticipation while his grandmother roasted them. He couldn't remember a single Thanksgiving Day as a child that hadn't been filled with warmth and a feast from Grandpa's harvest.

As happy as those celebrations had been, he'd been looking forward to this one more than any he could remember. After having an early breakfast with Laurel and Gena Thanksgiving morning, he brought the thawed turkey over from his refrigerator, and he and Laurel began preparations for their meal. As they worked, Gena watched cartoons and then the Macy's parade. She bounced back and forth between the adjacent living room where the television was on and the kitchen where she watched them.

When he took the wrapper off the turkey, he set it in a pan in the sink. He inspected it as he ran water over it to rinse it. "What's this stuff inside?"

Laurel grabbed a wad of paper towels, reached to pull out the packet and held it out for them to inspect. "It looks like the neck, the gizzard, and the liver."

"Liver is the cesspool of the body, and who eats a gizzard?"

"Don't look at me. It's disgusting, and the neck is not worth the effort. This whole packet looks about as appetizing as an autopsy."

He laughed. "Well, we don't want an autopsy anywhere near our prize turkey. Let's throw it away. Put it in a separate sack and I'll take it down to the dumpster later."

She kept the packet covered with the wad of paper towel and promptly transferred it to a heavy paper sack she had reached under the sink to retrieve. He stepped briefly aside to allow her access to the area, and he went back to rinsing the turkey cavity.

"That's where Mama Rita puts the dressing."

"Where? Under the sink?" He'd awakened with great expectations and plans for this day, and he felt lighthearted and playful.

"No, silly." She pointed to the cavity he was rinsing. "Right there."

"In its butt?"

She nodded. "That's where it's supposed to go. Is that not where your mom puts hers?"

"She's always made it in a separate pan, which is good because I'm not about to eat anything that came out of a turkey's butt."

"Picky aren't you?" She grinned. "So your mom didn't stuff your turkey, huh?"

"Maybe she did. I don't know. I never paid that much attention, but the dressing I ate was always separate. So what about our dressing? We need to make it, just not in there."

"Not to worry. We always celebrated Thanksgiving at Mama Rita's house, and it was my job to make the extra batch of dressing without onions for Daddy and Grandpa." Picking up a can of chicken broth that sat on the counter along with the rest of the ingredients for today's meal, she grinned mischievously. "But instead of using broth from the turkey, today I'm going to cheat."

"So, the turkey will cook okay bare-butted, you think?" he teased.

She giggled. "I guess. I've never cooked the turkey."

"What? You're no help."

"Hey! This was your idea, David Hudson."

Gena bounced over and leaned on the bar. "How long before our turkey cooks?"

"Oh," Laurel hesitated. "Um, let's see. I think I remember reading it takes eighteen minutes per pound. Or maybe it was thirty minutes a pound. How much does it weigh, David?"

"I don't know. I threw away the wrapper with the weight sticker." He bounced it up and down in his hands. "Maybe nine or ten pounds?"

"Hmm," she mentally figured. "A little over four hours? Oh, but that can't be right. It never takes Mama Rita more than three hours." She flashed Gena a too-confident smile that anyone could tell was pure sham as she absently ran her hand across the pop-up indicator of their self-basting turkey. He could tell she was searching for a believable answer when she had absolutely no clue. Then abruptly she announced, "Wait! It's got one of those pop-up thingies that tells you when it's done."They turned to Gena and said in unplanned unison. "It's done when the pop-up thingy pops." Then they looked at each other and burst into giggles.

Not to be fooled for a second, Gena rolled her eyes. "We're gonna hafta eat peanut butter and jelly."

"No. No, honey." Laurel straightened and reassured her. He loved it that she was acting so giddy. She'd been like this for the past six weeks. This was the old Laurel before all the pain. "We're going to have a great Thanksgiving turkey with all the trimmings," she said.

"Yeah, listen to Mommy, sweetie. We've got it covered. It'll cook even quicker since we're not putting all that dressing up its a—"

Laurel wheeled around and clamped her hand over his mouth before he could actually get the word *ass* out. "David!" She started giggling again.

He respected and supported her rule of not making off-color remarks that Gena could repeat; but he was in a frivolous mood, and that one had just slipped out. He decided to tease her some more. "You just infected me with autopsy juice. I didn't see you wash your hands after handling all that stuff that was in the butt."

He knew she hadn't touched the packet with her bare hands; but her giddiness was infective, and he was in the mood to play. He started such exaggerated sputtering that she planted her hands on her hips and rolled her eyes. He could tell she was trying not to smile. "I never touched the stuff. I used a towel. You saw that."

"Well, okay. You're off the hook then. I guess." He winked at Gena, and she giggled; but she abruptly turned her attention back to the television when she heard the Macy's parade come on.

Laurel started working on preparing the dressing, and he finished rinsing the turkey. As he worked he wondered how Stu was handling Thanksgiving and whether he would allow himself to be exposed to the bird at all before it got cooked. For a pathologist he had a baffling aversion to animal parts and germs. Pathology had its risks, but with proper precautions you had nothing to fear. Stu was Phi Beta Kappa and plenty smart enough to know that, but the man was morbidly germophobic.

Just two days before he'd had an obstetrician friend's hospital privileges temporarily suspended for the joke he'd played on him.

A janitor had killed a bat on the obstetric floor, and Dr. Shaw confiscated it and sent it in a specimen cup to pathology to Stu's attention. Stu opened it in good faith thinking it was as the label touted: products of conception of Bella Batman. When he saw the true contents, he got livid. Even though he was gloved at the time, he hadn't been working under a hood and hadn't used a mask. For a man who was a stickler on protocol for infectious disease prevention, that set his world on tilt.

When Miles related the whole scenario to them at lunch that day, he and Laurel couldn't help laughing. "Don't get me wrong," Miles had said. "I like the egghead, but the risk of airborne rabies is almost nil on top of the fact that the health department hasn't reported a case of rabies in this city in well over twenty years. The old man is losing it."

Unfortunately, things didn't end there. Stu made the incident the entire focus of morning huddle the next day. He'd come to the meeting masked, gowned, and gloved and had passed out an advisory that he and Miles follow suit. Laurel, too. He'd even offered to give them all a shot of gamma globulin, which he had already given himself. He and Laurel and Miles had barely made it to the privacy of her office afterwards before they collapsed in hysterical laughter at his paranoia.

With that in mind he turned toward Laurel. "Can't you just see Thanksgiving at Stu's house? Right now he's probably got the whole family gowned and masked and that poor turkey shot full of gamma globulin. I guarantee there's no monkey business in that kitchen. If his wife did to him what you just did to me, he'd put the bird in quarantine, culture every square inch of it, start on a massive dose of antibiotics, and hole up reading everything he could find on avian-transmitted diseases."

She started giggling uncontrollably at that, remembering the previous day's episode he was sure.

"It makes you wonder how his wife ever conceived," he continued. "Three times, no less. Given his need to sterilize everything, that's a miracle."

"Stop!" she gasped between giggles. She was laughing so hard she bent over holding her chest. "I can't breathe."

"I can fix that with a little mouth to mouth," he offered thinking that wasn't a bad idea.

"Opportunist," she said as she slowly recovered her composure.

Gena chose that moment to bounce back to the kitchen, and she stood watching them. He lifted the rinsed turkey into the foil roaster pan they'd bought. He paused to wash his hands, and before he turned to put the turkey in the oven, Laurel moved to open the door for him. Maybe he should try to snap himself out of his giddy mood and be the adult that he was, but even though Gena was eyeing them both with increasing suspicion, he didn't want to do that. It had been too long since they'd had this much fun.

"The oven's still on from when I baked the cake," Laurel said. "I adjusted the temperature for the turkey."

"Geez, this thing is going to take up the whole oven. Where are we going to put the pumpkin pies, not to mention the yams?" He glanced up at her.

"You can use the oven in your 'partment," Gena chirped as she leaned her elbows on the drop-down bar, resting her face in her hands.

"Great idea. You're a brilliant kid. Did you know that?"

"Yes."

"And not proud of it at all," he teased.

She giggled.

Laurel moved back to the counter opposite the stove. She covered the pan of dressing with foil and transferred it to the refrigerator. "I'll put the dressing in the oven when the turkey's on its last hour. Don't let me forget." She transferred one of the cooled layers of her white cake to a plate and started spreading peppermint candy frosting on it. "This is a mix so I know it's going to turn out good."

He took two big steps across the cozy kitchen and reached to scoop his finger into her frosting. He tasted it and mumbled, "Yum, it's going to be good, Gena."

Laurel swatted at him with a kitchen towel, but he was ready for her. He dodged the swat. Gena abruptly focused her attention back to the parade. "It's a purple hippo like mine! Yea!" She went to stand in front of the television, watching spellbound.

He sneaked another fingertip full of frosting as Laurel glanced at Gena, but she caught him before he got it to his mouth. "Thief! Give me that." She grabbed his finger and licked the frosting off in one movement. As she rolled it around in her mouth she smiled triumphantly up at him.

This was war, sweet, seductive, foreplay war and his best game. He planted a hand on each side of her on the countertop, trapping her. He grinned, feeling deliciously wicked. She had started something he was going to finish, and she knew it. "That's my bite of frosting. You asked for this."

He bent to kiss her, sliding his tongue into her mouth to do battle over the frosting, but suddenly neither one of them cared about the frosting. She swallowed. He swallowed, and as he went in search of sweeter confection, she draped her arms around his neck and got lost in their kiss exactly the way she used to.

Abruptly the timer she'd set for the yeast rolls dinged and brought them both back down to earth. He pulled slightly away, letting both hands drop to her waist. "Yum. That was good icing. Maybe I could have some more later?"

She giggled. "If you haven't spoiled your appetite already."

"Never happen." He licked his lips. "Not in a million years."

"You and Mommy are so silly." They turned abruptly to see that Gena was regarding them sternly, her hands on her hips.

They started giggling again, and Gena rolled her eyes as if to prove her point that they were beyond silly. He let go of Laurel and lunged for Gena. He caught her and lightly tickled her tummy. "Silly? Silly? What do you mean silly?" She squealed and giggled.

When he lifted her into his arms, she touched his chin with her forefinger. "You and Mommy don't know how to cook Thanksgiving dinner, do you?"

"Never cooked one in my life, but I've eaten plenty. Does that count?"

She shook her head. "You should've asked Marita. She's old. She knows everything."

"Well, we're learning, honey. Think of it as a fun adventure."

She giggled. "Was kissing Mommy a 'venture?"

"That was my dessert." He wiggled his eyebrows at her. "Just like this is my dessert." He started kissing her cheek making loud smacking noises.

She giggled again. "You're silly!" Then she looked into his eyes still smiling. "You like my mommy a whole lot, don't you?"

"I love your mommy, and I love you. Is that okay with you?"

"If you don't be so silly and eat all the icing." Abruptly the parade caught her eye again. "It's Tweetie Bird!" She wriggled out of his arms and skipped over to watch.

He moved toward Laurel then and draped his arms around her waist. "That kiss just told me it's okay with you."

She traced her finger along the line of his shirt buttons. "I can't resist you. I never could, and I couldn't possibly find anybody else who could make cooking a turkey so much fun."

Their turkey turned out great even though they hadn't known what they were doing, and it finished cooking in perfect time for their one o'clock meal. The side dishes tasted good, too, especially Laurel's dressing. Everything tasted even better as leftovers for dinner, but the best thing about it was that Gena liked it. It seemed that her great-grandmother Marita was a force to be reckoned with when it came to cooking and the standard she held them to. She gave them high praise for their efforts anyway.

Both his and Laurel's giddiness lasted all day. It was a welcome change from the cautious relationship they'd had her first two months back at City General. He'd finally succeeded in getting beyond her sadness, and the past six weeks had been like the old days. She was especially relaxed and unguarded today, and it set the stage for the question he wanted to ask her tonight.

After they'd tucked Gena into bed and she'd charmed him into reading three bedtime stories, he and Laurel relaxed in the living room with glasses of wine.

"You do know we're going to have enough leftovers for this whole week, don't you?" She grinned at him after taking a sip of her wine. "That turkey was twelve pounds if it was an ounce. I think I owe you some more money for my half."

"You owe me nothing." Then he shrugged feigning innocence. "Well, I guess you could give me another big taste of that dessert as payment."

"Nice girls don't pay their debts like that."

"You have your mind in the gutter, young lady. I was talking about your cake."

"Sure you were. Don't forget how well I know you."

He leaned toward her. "Then how about you forget your straitlaced principles for a second and pay up?"

She was still smiling. The game was still on, so he leaned to coax a short kiss from her luscious lips. He tasted a trace of wine and much more than a trace of their passionate past, a past he ached to revisit. He moved closer and deepened the kiss. She didn't resist so he let go of all restraints and kissed her until they were both breathless. "I love you," he whispered when he came up for air. "I know you love me, too."

"I do. Oh, I do love you, David," she whispered, and this time she initiated the kiss.

She'd never known how crazy she drove him with her tentative moves. Her lips touched his, cautious in approach, tantalizing in their delicate lightness but filled with such pure nectar that it made him drunk with desire. As he tasted her sweetness, she touched his face as if she were trying to memorize each place her fingers had been—gently, reverently. She didn't have to say she cherished him. Her touch said it for her. She hadn't kissed him this way since that night over five years ago, and he felt his self-control fading. He made himself pull away gently. He'd vowed he would never hurt her again with too much too soon, and it was time to show her how committed he was to their future.

"Marry me, sweetheart," he muttered against her lips as he pulled away. "Make me the happiest man in the world."

She took in a ragged breath as they disengaged and looked up into his eyes.

He wondered if she could tell how nervous he was. The last time he'd done this, things had ended badly. He reached into his pocket and withdrew the small velvet box he'd kept for five years. He held it between them and opened the lid so she could see the ring. "I got this for you that Sunday afternoon five years ago. I was so sure I could make you see the truth that I went ahead and bought it that day like we planned." He looked into her eyes again. "Will you marry me, Laurel?"

The changes in her features came so quickly it made him dizzy. Passion faded to realization and then to sadness, and all traces of the day's giddiness disappeared. She sat stiffly looking at him with that cautious wall of hers abruptly back in place. "David, I'm sorry. I—I can't. There are too many things that aren't resolved."

He heard her words, but he couldn't understand that she was actually turning him down, not after today, not after the trust they had built between them over the past three months and especially the past six weeks.

She took in a deep breath, and her voice caught as she spoke. "You said we'd go slow with this."

"It's been over three months. You just told me you love me. You've told me all day how you feel about me."

"I've always loved you, David, but that doesn't mean things will work out."

"You're punishing me," he said softly staring at the floor. Maybe that wasn't fair, but that was the way this felt. Hadn't he suffered enough? Couldn't she see that he'd been running on empty ever since she'd left his life?

She reached for him and held his face in both her hands. "No. Oh, please, David, don't think that. I'm afraid. I'm so afraid. You don't know how my life has been for the past five years. You don't know what you'd be getting yourself into. You may think you don't care, but you would—and I do."

"You've told me about your family. I've seen a lot for myself. Why won't you believe that it doesn't matter to me? You're what matters, you and Gena."

"You haven't seen them in all their glory."

"It won't matter if I do."

"You can't promise that. You don't know everything."

"I don't expect you to turn your back on your family no matter how bad things get if that's what you're worried about. But can't we have each other? Can't we be something wonderful for you to escape to—you, me, and Gena? I know she's my daughter. We didn't use protection that night, and she was born exactly nine months later. I want to be the father I should have been all along. I don't want her to go through life thinking she doesn't have a daddy. I want to take care of you, Laurel. I want to take care of my daughter.

She pulled away, dropping her hands from his face and flailing at the space between them like she was fighting her way through cobwebs. She stood and turned away. And then her words, spoken barely above a whisper, pierced his heart like a dagger. "She's not your daughter, David."

Chapter Eighteen

She finally turned toward him, and she winced at the pain on his face. She had to explain this. Even if he didn't understand, she had to wipe away some of that hurt.

"I wanted her to be yours, David. When she was a newborn, all those nights that I rocked her in my arms and fed her, I would pretend that she was, that she was mine and yours from that sweet night. At least then I would have a part of you forever if I couldn't have your love."

He was quiet for a long time, staring at her. She couldn't tell what he was thinking, and her heart ached at the inevitable. Even though he loved Gena, she wasn't his child, and that would matter. He would be angry that she hadn't told him the truth from the beginning on that first day when he'd asked her.

Her protective secrecy seemed to have accomplished nothing but more pain. She'd meant it for good. She'd been willing to be labeled an unwed mother for Gena's sake, knowing that the truth could hurt Gena more than the gossip could hurt her reputation. And she would do it all over again if it meant protecting Gena.

Finally, David got up and walked over to stand in front of her. "There's no way I'll believe you slept with anyone else. No way."

At least he knew that about her. "There's never been anyone but you, David."

"And I've never heard of a single documented case of spontaneous generation in humans," he said gently. He wasn't being sarcastic. She could tell he was thinking this through. She wanted to blurt out the truth so everything would be okay between them again, but would it? Would he understand?

He became so quiet again that it scared her. What was he thinking?

Finally he broke the silence, speaking in a soft voice. "Gena told me that she's named after Gene."

"Yes."

"You said Gene is divorced, and that happened a little over four years ago."

It wasn't really a question, but she nodded.

"What was his wife's name?"

"Renee," she answered, and she knew he was putting all the pieces together.

"I saw on your application that Gena's middle name is Renee."

She nodded again.

"Your resemblance to Gene is striking, and Gena looks just like you—" He paused and made unwavering eye contact. "She's your niece, isn't she? She belongs to your brother Gene and his ex-wife Renee."

"Yes," she answered, feeling both relief and trepidation.

Five years of heartache had taught her to never expect the best. She waited for him to turn and walk out of her life, but he didn't. Instead he moved closer and reached to cup her cheek with his palm. A tender expression spread across his face.

"Sweetheart, why didn't you tell me?"

"It wasn't because I was trying to hurt you. You have to know that. I didn't realize you might think she was yours until Audrey mentioned it the Friday before Labor Day, and that was only her hunch. I never thought you'd seriously think that because I told you that next morning it was a safe time. I guess you didn't believe me."

He moved his hand to her shoulder and rubbed it. "I guess I wanted her to be our child as much as you did."

"But you see, I was at the end of my cycle, and I started a few days later. So when our paths crossed again thinking that I could have had a child by you was ancient history. I didn't realize how fresh it was for you. I wasn't trying to hurt you. Please tell me you know that."

"I do know that, sweetheart." He motioned toward the sofa, and they both went to sit back down. He reached for her left hand and held it in both of his.

"Did you adopt her?"

"Yes, but there's so much uncertainty with that. I live in constant fear that someone's going to take her away from me."

"Who? Gene?"

"No, he asked me to take her. Renee rejected her at birth. He wasn't capable of taking care of himself much less a newborn. I took her without hesitation, but I made him agree to let me adopt her and to not tell her the truth until she was old enough to understand."

"But I don't understand. You adopted her. She's yours."

"Renee didn't give her consent, and my attorney said that could be a problem anywhere down the line even though she abandoned her. She never wanted a child. She would've had an abortion if she could have found the money to pay for it. Gene's never been drunk enough to do something like that. When Gena was born, she wouldn't hold her. She wouldn't even look at her. Gene had to name her."

"How old was she when you adopted her?"

"She's been with me from the beginning. She was born at eight o'clock at night, and Renee sneaked out of the hospital somewhere during that night. I took her home with me as soon as the doctors released her."

She felt a rush of tenderness then, and she glanced up at David. "I loved her instantly. I'm the one who held her first. She's been a part of me since she took her first breath, and I couldn't love her any more if I'd given birth to her."

"Has Renee ever made any threats that she's going to take her?"

"No. Nobody's seen her since the day Gena was born. When she served Gene with divorce papers a month after that, we learned that she lives here in the city. My attorney checked a year ago, and she was still here." She chewed on her lower lip. "It's like waiting for the other shoe to drop."

"Did you get the fact that she rejected her at birth witnessed?"

"Yes, by the doctor and three nurses, in writing and notarized."

"Then she'll have a fight on her hands if she challenges you, and you'll win."

"Renee's not my only problem."

"Who else would have any say in the matter?"

"My mother. She never wanted me to adopt Gena in the first place. She wanted control of her even though she was already in a wheelchair by then. She threatens to take her away from me all the time. Many times she's threatened to contact Renee and tell her about the fact that I adopted Gena."

"Would Renee even care? She abandoned her."

"No, but Renee hates me. She'd just love to hurt me."

"Your mom is just venting. Hate is not grounds to recover a child you abandoned, and your mom doesn't have that kind of power."

She placed her free hand over his. "Don't underestimate my mother, David. You don't know how manipulative she can be. If she can't find something to use against you, she's not above twisting the truth so that it can hurt you."

"Why would she do that?"

"I don't know. Maybe because she's so unhappy herself, but it's what she always does. She collects scraps of other people's mistakes and vulnerabilities and stores them away. When she needs control, she sifts through them and gives them back crafted into one of her crazy quilts. It's not a gift you want to receive. Somebody always gets hurt."

"She doesn't have anything to use against you."

"She does. I just haven't been aware of it. Up until I realized that she's had your letters for five years, all I feared was that she'd tell Gena the truth before I thought she was ready. I guess she's just been saving our night together for one of her special crazy quilts because if Renee knew about it, she'd have a field day with it."

"Why does Renee hate you? I can't see anyone hating you."

"Three years before Gena was born I caught her in the act of cheating on Gene with one of his drinking buddies. They were in the living room on the sofa. Everyone else was gone. I didn't tell Gene because I didn't want him to self-destruct. I gave her such a high-minded lecture that she called me cold and frigid."

"There's nothing cold or frigid about you," he said.

"Yeah," she said softly acknowledging their passion, "and I can just hear her reaction if Mama ever tells her about that night."

"Baby," he said softly. "It's not the same thing. We love each other."

"That wouldn't keep Renee from using it. I've had to walk a fine line between Mama's threats to take Gena away and defying her when it comes to telling Gena the truth. Everyone on Sunset Mountain knows, and I'm afraid they'll tell Gena before I get the chance to tell her properly. Mama started nagging me to tell her the minute she turned four and said she'd do it if I didn't. I won't have Gena traumatized. I've been gradually preparing her for the truth, and when she turns five I'm going to tell her."

"And that's why you left the mountain and came back to City General?"

"Yes. Mama had a fit about it, too, but it's her own fault. She doesn't think about anything but what she wants. She's already spread her influence in the community. That last time Gena and I went to the mountain church the town gossip was leading up to mentioning it to Gena and would have if I hadn't stopped it."

"So, you're afraid if we become engaged your mother will hold my letters over your head as a threat to take Gena away from you."

"Yes, and she'll choose a time that will hurt me the most."

He pulled her into his embrace then. "Baby, you'll win if she challenges you. I'll help you win. Gena's special, and you've done a wonderful job with her. This doesn't change a thing about how I feel about her or you. I want to be her father. I want us to be a family—you, Gena, and me."

She snuggled against him consoled by his tenderness and touched by the way he'd again surpassed her expectations. She tried not to think about the fact that Mama wouldn't easily give her up if she agreed to marry him. She worried, too, about how he would react when he saw that place where she had grown up. It would make a difference. It always made a difference.

"I know you want to go slow with this, sweetheart," he said softly, "but how I feel is not going to change no matter how long we wait. Marry me, baby, or at least take the ring and promise me you'll try hard to get past whatever it is that's making you doubt me. I'll do everything I can to help."

"You don't want to be a part of my crazy family, David. You've seen some of it, but you can't know how awful it can be. I can't separate myself from it, but I couldn't ask you to put yourself through it. It would kill your status as a doctor. People would say I trapped you with Gena; and once you were a part of my family for awhile you'd feel trapped, trust me, and maybe you'd start to believe them. I couldn't bear that. I love you, but I couldn't bear your pity or your scorn."

"Is that why things are so complicated for us? You think if I couldn't love you enough before when you didn't have all these problems that I can't possibly love you enough now to put myself through your pain."

She nodded hesitantly. That was a big part of her problem, but not all of it. The pain was too interwoven to separate it into well-defined increments even to herself.

"Well, you're wrong. I love you, and I don't care what people think. This is my life, and I want you in it, forever."

"Oh, David," she said touched by his sweetness. How could she resist such devotion?

He pulled away slightly and reached for the ring box he'd left on the coffee table. He plucked the ring from the black velvet crevice and slipped it on her left ring finger. It was a beautiful solitaire and exactly what she would have chosen that Sunday over five years ago.

"I'll give you all the time you need, sweetheart. Just say you'll marry me."

She issued herself a reminder. *You're not on safe ground yet. He hasn't seen that place. Mama doesn't like him. She'll declare all-out war.* But she was too dazzled by his sweetness to listen to the voice of her insecurities, and it was too wonderful to realize that he had always wanted her to be his wife.

"Yes, I'll marry you, David." He bent toward her, and she felt the heat of his lips before they touched hers. She let herself become lost in the tenderness as he pulled her deeper into his embrace.

When they withdrew from the kiss, she whispered, "I've missed you, David. I've missed you so much. I love you."

"Come here, sweetheart," he said softly as he stretched back to lie on the sofa and pulled her into his arms. She snuggled against him. "Five years ago we became one, Laurel. It was my past that put a barrier between us, but we're still one because neither of us has broken that oneness."

"There was never anything between Byron and me in case you're still worried about that. I know you don't like him, but he's a nice person."

"I don't know him well enough to dislike him. I was just jealous. Maybe someday I'll make a fantastic living, but right now it's not even as much as my tech salary. And here's this guy who's got it all: looks, money coming out of his ears, and he's crazy about you. He's the worst kind of competition."

She lifted her head so she could look into his eyes. "You forgot the most important attribute of all, and that's why I could never date him."

"What's that?"

"He's not you."

He squeezed her closer. "You might be insane to prefer me over him, but don't think I'm going to try to challenge that."

"David, I'm grateful to Byron because he made life so easy for me when it came to Gena—and he didn't ask for a thing in return—but gratitude is all I feel for him. I took three week's vacation when I brought Gena home from the hospital so we could bond. But I had to work, so he let me set up a crib and a playpen in my office and bring her to work with me."

"That was nice of him."

"Yes, and not even Grady would have done that. I balanced things well because she was such a good baby. I did it the whole first year of her life. When she was a year old, Mama Rita and Grandpa started taking care of her."

"I see why you're grateful to him."

"Because he saw the need with Gena, he's set up a daycare for children of employees. It's well staffed with highly competent retired nurses, and he makes it an employee benefit at no charge. By the time the daycare opened Gena was already bonded with my grandparents, so I didn't use it except for rare occasions."

"I'm sorry I was jealous."

"It's kind of nice that you cared that much about what I did those five years." She snuggled against him again and tucked her head into the curve of his neck.

"Someday I'll tell you the gory details about how much I cared. I wouldn't have made it if I hadn't buried myself in studying and working part-time." He brought her left hand to his lips and kissed it. It was an act of sweet possession that filled her with warmth. "I thought the regret and yearning would bleed my heart and soul so dry that I'd wake up one day and find that my body had turned to a hollow shell."

"I know," she said softly. "I felt the same way."

"From now on it's you and me and Gena against the world. Deal?"

"Deal," she answered, and although she meant it, a part of her held back even as she said the words. He didn't know everything about her life yet. He hadn't seen or experienced that house that held all those broken dreams—that place with all its emptiness that could never be filled.

Chapter Nineteen

David felt as if all the cares of the world had been lifted from his shoulders. He and Laurel were finally going to have a future, and he had the gift of Gena now. That made up for so much of the past heartache. That Thanksgiving night after he went to his apartment, he lay wide-awake reflecting on their situation. Then slowly, in a serendipitous revelation, he saw the blessing behind the pain for both of them. The next morning he shared his thoughts with Laurel after they had breakfast together in her apartment.

They sat at the maple dining table, sipping their coffee while Gena played in her room with her new playmate, Sally, whose grandmother had just dropped her off for a visit.

"How do you feel about our engagement now that you've had time to sleep on it?" he asked. He hoped he already knew the answer to that. Gone was last night's hesitancy, and she'd been so affectionate that he was positive she had no regrets.

She held out her hand and gazed at the ring he'd given her. "I love the ring. It's exactly what I would have chosen that day five years ago." Then she glanced up at him. "Most of all, I love you.

I'm so sorry I didn't believe you about Marilee, and I'm sorry for all the wasted years it's caused us."

He leaned toward her taking both her hands in his. "They weren't wasted. Last night I gave our situation a lot of prayerful thought, and I saw God's plan for us."

"To punish us harshly for our sins before we're allowed to be the tiniest bit happy the way my mother does?" she muttered with a sarcastic edge to her voice.

He squeezed her hand. Knowing her mother, he could certainly see why she felt that way. Parenthood was supposed to be symbolic of the way God loved, but her mother was a poor symbol. She dangled the false hope of love always out of Laurel's reach.

"The sins were mine, Laurel."

"Not according to my mother. According to her I got just what I deserved for letting myself be ruined."

"I hope you don't believe that. You don't, do you?"

She looked up into his eyes. "I know that I never regretted it. I know that it was the purest thing in the world to me, and not having a ring on my finger didn't make it any less pure. I loved you, and I believed you loved me."

"And I did. I do now. The mistakes I made before we made that commitment to each other can't ever change that. I'll admit I've thought that all these lonely years of not having you in my life was my punishment for messing things up to begin with."

"I don't blame you for that anymore. It was my fault, too, for not believing in that pure love that I knew passed between us."

"God doesn't blame us either, sweetheart, and these past five years haven't been about punishment. It's all been about God taking our mistakes and making something wonderful from all the pain."

"What do you mean?"

"It's about Gena. Don't you see? If we'd gotten married, you would have been in Memphis with me when she was born. You wouldn't have been here to even know the need to rescue her. Who could have taken her if you hadn't?"

A look of sudden comprehension crossed her face. "My grandparents are too old to have taken her on a permanent basis. They would have tried, but Mama would have demanded custody simply because she thinks of her offspring as possessions. When she became bedridden, that would have left Gena living with her, Connie, and Del and all that life in Mama's house entails."

She shuddered, and a look of anguish crossed her features. "She wouldn't have stood a chance of being the happy child she is today."

"We made the decisions that caused our own pain—me mostly. I take full responsibility. But look at what God did with all of that. We got another chance. We have each other, and we have Gena, too. Laurel, I couldn't love her any more if she did belong to me."

Tears glistened in her eyes. "I haven't liked the pain. I have to be honest about that, but having you in my life again makes it worth it. Maybe God *was* watching. Maybe it *was* his plan because Gena saved me every bit as much as I saved her, and I can't imagine life without her. I'm so glad you love her, too."

"I do love her, Laurel. God made a place in my heart especially for her, and from the moment I met her, we connected. She's part of me now, and she's my daughter in every way that matters. I want to adopt her when we get married. Do you think Gene would approve of that?"

She nodded. "He told me Thanksgiving Eve how good he thinks you are with her. I'll ask him."

"Another thing, when we tell her about our engagement today, I'd like to ask her to be my daughter. Is that all right with you?"

She nodded and rewarded him with a glowing smile, that same smile he used to take for granted before all the pain.

Before lunch he made a quick trip next door to his apartment to pick up Gena's engagement gift. He'd searched for a month before he found exactly what he wanted. It was a special necklace made of purple rhinestones. Immediately after lunch Sally's grandmother picked Sally up, and once the three of them were alone, Laurel showed Gena her ring. They told her the ring meant they had made a promise to each other.

"That means," he explained, "that since we love each other so much, Mommy and I promise to marry. And it means I need to ask you a question."

"Okay," Gena said.

"You know how special you are to me, don't you?"

She nodded.

He then got down on one knee in front of her as she sat on the sofa next to Laurel. "This is my promise present to you." He extended the box, opened it, and placed the glittering necklace in Gena's palm. He pointed to the letters the purple rhinestones formed. "This says, 'Daddy's Little Girl,' and that's the question I want to ask you. Will you be my little girl? Could I have the honor of being your daddy?"

Clutching the necklace, Gena immediately threw her tiny arms around his neck and hugged him. "I knew God would answer my prayer," she squealed. "I prayed for him to let you be my daddy."

Tears filled his eyes. When he blinked to focus, he saw that Laurel had tears in her eyes, too. But Gena was already lifting her hair for him to fasten her necklace, which he managed to do even through the blur. She turned and hugged him again, and he lifted her into his arms as he stood. "I love you, sweet Gena," he managed to say in spite of the knot in his throat, but tears trickled down his cheeks.

Gena noticed, and she reached to swipe at them. "Don't cry, Daddy. I love you, too." That finished him off.

He couldn't wait to tell Mom and Dad his good news, so that afternoon he took Laurel and Gena to meet them. His parents already knew the past situation between him and Laurel minus their passionate night. He'd told them the truth about the whole thing five years ago. Once Marilee's bogus engagement announcement hit the newspaper, he'd had to explain. They knew, whether they understood the situation or not, that it was Laurel he loved. His celibacy and bachelorhood during the past five years on the heels of his womanizing had to be proof of that.

He'd told them about dating Laurel again, and they knew about Gena. Once they met Laurel he knew they had no doubts about how he felt about her. They were happy about his good news, and Gena sealed the deal. She charmed them immediately, and before their visit was over they had her calling them Granny and Pop.

While Mom and Dad took Gena to the enclosed back porch to see their new kittens, he suggested going to visit Laurel's family the next day to announce their engagement. He realized that her mother and Del wouldn't be happy, but he wanted to meet her grandparents and the cousin she talked about so much.

"Let me tell them all by phone," she pleaded. "Mama is much easier to take from a distance, and that way Gena won't hear all her negative comments. She's not going to be happy that you want to adopt Gena. Maybe we shouldn't mention that part to her just yet."

He agreed; but it was postponing the inevitable, and they had to visit her mother someday.

Chapter Twenty

It amused Laurel that for the entire week after Thanksgiving the lab buzzed with gossip about her engagement to David. She would enter a room; the talking would stop; and all eyes would focus on her. She'd overheard tidbits of a conversation between Trudy and the young assistant who had a thing for David. She had learned her name was Danielle.

"They've been spending a lot of time together," Trudy said. "I'll bet she's pregnant again, and I'm sure now that little girl is his. Have you seen the way he acts around her? Like a proud peacock."

She'd smiled to herself. Let them talk, but it was interesting to note that she wasn't the only one who saw the bond between David and Gena. He was going to be a great father. Donating genes for the creation process was not the foremost requirement for being a loving parent. She knew that from experience.

Stu and Miles hadn't seemed at all surprised when they announced their good news in Monday morning huddle. Audrey was ecstatic, and for that entire week she pestered them to start making wedding plans. Telling her they planned to wait until spring to set the date didn't deter the feisty woman one bit.

When David dropped by her office at noon that Friday to go to lunch with her, Audrey started in on them again. She got up from her desk and walked over to confront them.

"Now listen, you two. I have five girl cousins and two kid sisters, and I know how to do this stuff. If you're putting this off because you don't know what to do first, let me at it. You won't have to lift a finger." She opened her spiral dictation tablet and poised her pencil over it. "I'll need a list of guests. Tuxedos are easy. We can rent them. Oh … and Gena would be adorable as a flower girl. Let's see." She pressed her lips together. "Hackney's! They sell children's bridal stuff and—"

"Take it easy, Audrey," David interrupted. "The bride-to-be will tell us when she's ready." He winked at her. "She's a sensitive girl. She won't make me wait too long."

Laurel smiled up at him as he sat on the edge of her desk. She would marry him this second if only she could be positive that he wouldn't regret it the minute he saw that place she came from. She'd been wrong in anticipating his reaction to meeting Mama and Del and to the truth about Gena, but this was different. That place stamped clichés on her that she'd been trying to rise above her whole life: redneck, white trash, ignorant. Deep inside, she wasn't sure if she'd transcended all that. She'd tried her best, but she was still tied to it by the love she had for the people trapped inside the lifestyle.

Also, she dreaded the escalation in her battle with Mama for autonomy. Marrying David would surely augment that. It had already begun. Mama had been nothing but negative since she'd told her the news of their engagement. You'd think she would embrace having a doctor in her family, someone who could help solve the mystery of her disease. David was in a position to find the cutting edge in treatment. Instead, Mama felt threatened. As always, she chose turmoil over peace and pain over healing.

"Are you ready for lunch?" David asked bringing her away from her troubling thoughts. "You can come, too, Audrey, but you can't nag Laurel about the wedding. You hear?" He beamed Audrey one of his most charming grins.

The office phone rang abruptly, and Audrey went to her desk to answer it. It had rung all morning. They'd had a deluge of salesmen descend on them after this week's lab products convention at a local hotel. If she had to wade through another sales pitch, she'd go batty.

Audrey put the call on hold and turned toward her. "It's for you. She says she's your cousin Betty Jo. Do you want to take it, or do you want me to take a message."

"Betty Jo?" Why was she calling her at this time of day? She should be in class. "I'll take it." She reached for the phone feeling a strong sense of foreboding. "Betty Jo, hi. What's up? Are you between classes?"

"Today's exam day. I finished early." Betty Jo's usual calm voice held an edge of panic. "Laurel, I don't know how to tell you this gently, but something awful has happened." Betty Jo paused, and her apprehension kicked up a notch. "Del stabbed Gene. Laurel, he's dead. Gene's dead."

Her heart almost stopped, and then it started racing. Panic rose in her chest. She struggled to get her breath. "Wait, no, you have to be mistaken. It couldn't be. Are you sure?"

"I'm sure. Daddy and I got here right after it happened. I tried to do first aid. It was too late. I'm so sorry. Aunt Sarah got hysterical and went into respiratory crisis. The ambulance just left taking her to Mountain General. Del's on his way to jail with the sheriff."

The phone slipped out of her grasp, and she heard it make a soft thud on her desk. She buried her face in her hands, and the words ripped out of her. "Dear God, no!"

She could hear Betty Jo's voice calling her name, but she couldn't react; she became aware that David was picking up the phone. "Betty Jo, I'm David Hudson, Laurel's fiancé. What's wrong?"

It seemed forever before David spoke again and finally he said, "I understand. Yes. Okay. We'll be there. Bye."

She made herself straighten, and she swallowed her panic. David hung up the phone and knelt in front of her cupping her face in his palms. "I'm so sorry, baby. I'm here. I'll be here for you. I'm not going anywhere."

Audrey brought a cup of water from their office cooler and set it in front of her. "Drink this, honey. Just sip it."

From then on she felt like a zombie, as if her mind and body had separated. She'd always known something like this was going to happen. But knowing it was going to happen and dealing with it when it did were two entirely different things. Nothing could have prepared her for this massacre to her heart. Gene was dead. Mama was on her way to the emergency room in shock, and Del was charged with murder.

When they reached Mountain General, Mama was still in ER. As soon as the staff recognized Laurel and learned that David was a doctor, they allowed them to go back to the treatment room to visit. The emergency room doctor was all too familiar with Mama's case, and he had already diagnosed exacerbation of a chronic inflammatory disease by acute anxiety. He'd given her a sedative, and they were just waiting for a room assignment.

"Mama, we came as soon as we heard," she said. "You remember David."

David reached to gently touch Mama's shoulder. "Mrs. Harper, I'm so sorry about all this."

"Where's my little Gena?" Mama completely ignored David as if he hadn't spoken. She was in shock, so maybe she wasn't being rude.

"She's with the babysitter, Mrs. Archer. We were at work when Betty Jo called. But she doesn't need to be in the middle of all this."

"You wouldn't come Thanksgiving. You could have at least brought her and your new fiancé up to visit us Sunday. Connie fixed a nice lunch from Thanksgiving leftovers. I guess you don't care about your family anymore."

There she went again trying to make her feel guilty."I told you we'd come up soon, Mama." She didn't need this. The grief of this tragedy was bad enough. She sighed and forced herself to overlook Mama's manipulations. How could she not be in total shock? "What on earth happened, Mama?"

She knew what had happened. Mama had pitted Del and Gene against each other for so long they'd finally pushed their conflict over the edge. She just needed to know the details.

"Ever since that PCP thing Gene and Del just couldn't get along." Mama started crying as she began relating the incident between rasping breaths. "I thought they'd smoothed things over when Gene moved back home after he got out of that mental hospital. He didn't remember anything about what went on when he attacked me and broke my glasses. He and Del talked about it some. I thought everything was okay."

That wasn't exactly the way Laurel had heard it. When Gene had talked to her about it Thanksgiving Eve, he remembered everything, and he had been adamant that he didn't touch Mama. Maybe he'd told Mama and Del what they wanted to hear to keep peace.

Mama continued. "This morning Connie was back cleaning the bedrooms, and Gene and Del were supposed to be changing the carburetor on Gene's car."

She wondered why Gene hadn't taken his car to Moore's Service Station. When he'd walked her to her car Thanksgiving Eve, he'd told her he was going to do that with some of the money she'd given him. She remembered also how that night he'd enveloped her in an uncharacteristic bear hug, and she was grateful now that she'd taken the risk to say she loved him. It was the last piece of love to pass between them.

She focused her attention back to Mama who was still speaking. "I was watching television when I heard a commotion outside. Next thing I knew a bunch of crows went by my window cawing and flapping their wings. One of them landed in the pine tree outside my window and just sat there. I figured Del was after them again. You know how he hates crows. Then I heard the porch door open. Somebody was coming in—and I don't know why—but it didn't sound right. I didn't know exactly what was wrong until I heard Gene call out to me."

She broke down again, and Laurel felt the anger drain from her heart. Maybe Mama had helped set this up with her manipulations, but she couldn't see that she had. The end result was still tragic. Mama was still heartbroken. She reached to gently squeeze her arm and fought back tears that were building from so many pent up places inside her.

"I tried to turn my head to see," Mama sobbed. "And just out of the corner of my eye, just as he said, 'Oh, Mama,' he fell forward. He grabbed at the phone stand. I could see the blood then, and it all came together. Del. Gene. The commotion outside. They just couldn't get along. They'd been snapping at each other since breakfast."

She bent to pat Mama's shoulder and became aware that David was watching her. When she glanced up into his eyes, he placed his hand on her back and rubbed letting her know he supported her.

"The phone was sitting on my bed. I pulled it over and called Nathan. He's still a constable, you know, and I told him to bring Betty Jo since she's going to nursing school. I figured she'd know what to do. I told him to hurry."

Quite and stoic Uncle Nathan, Mama's brother and Betty Jo's father, always handled their family's emergencies.

"I tried to turn my head to see Gene. All I could see was his body slumped on the floor. Somehow I knew he was still alive, so I started to pray. 'Dear God, you spared him once when he was born. Please spare him now.' But he started to shake. He trembled so hard the floor shook. I knew then he was dying. I've heard the sense of hearing is the last thing to go when you die, so

I told him I loved him. Over and over again, I said it. Then his body went still."

Laurel shuddered. Poor Mama. Poor Gene. How could any of them forget Mama's story of how Gene almost died at birth and how she'd prayed so hard that God spared Gene's life against his better judgment? If Laurel could remember that story so well, how much better had Gene remembered it? She couldn't help thinking that she would have gone ahead and died, too, and it hurt more than she could ever form into words that those were the last words her brother heard as he lay dying.

"Then Del came into the room." Mama was sobbing so hard now she could barely get her breath. "He had a pistol, and he was crazy in the eyes. He pointed it at Gene lying there helpless on the floor. I screamed at him. 'Don't you shoot him! You've already killed him! You stop it, Del! You've already killed him!' He stood there for a minute like he didn't hear me."

Mama took in several gasping breaths. Laurel bent to place the oxygen mask back on her face, but Mama waved it away.

"Del went white as a sheet. I guess he finally realized what he'd done. 'Call an ambulance, Mama,' he screamed. 'Call Nathan.' 'I already did,' I told him. 'I called Nathan and Betty Jo. They have the ambulance on the way. You help him, Del. Give him first aid. Do it! Now!' But all Del could do was cry. He dropped that pistol and went down on his knees beside Gene and cried like a baby."

Laurel felt a burning pain inside her chest. It went so deep she couldn't locate it so that she could rub it or soothe it to make it stop throbbing. She'd always loved these people. She'd loved them for as long as she could remember, and deep in her soul, in spite of Mama's manipulations, she'd thought they loved each other. How had it all turned so deadly? Had Mama set Del and Gene so at odds with each other that they each perceived dangers that didn't exist? She hated to blame Mama for this, but she couldn't overlook her part in it.

"I can't go back home where it all happened," Mama sobbed. "I can't live in the same house with Del. I'll never forgive him for this. Why did he have to kill him?"

She doubted that Mama was serious about leaving her place. This had to be hysteria talking. Del might not even be coming home. He was already in jail and would be prosecuted for murder. It wasn't fair. She couldn't believe that he was actually capable of murder. Mama needed to mentally step back and give this whole tragedy some soulful thought. She doubted that she would. She had much guilt to purge, and her history of purging guilt was to either condemn or to embrace. Who would she condemn this time, and who would she embrace? Right now it looked as if it was Del she condemned, but who would it be once this stage of shock had passed?

Mama's sedative took effect, and she drifted off to sleep. Her room was also ready. As Laurel and David left the ER, Larry Arthur, one of the attendants she had known for years, wheeled Mama out to the elevator to go to her room.

As she walked to the parking lot with David, a litany of urgent things to do bombarded her mind. There were funeral arrangements to be made, and she was the only one left standing. She would have to take care of it, but Gene's body wouldn't be released from autopsy until early tomorrow morning. She needed to talk to Del, and there was Gena. She needed to tell her something to explain this. She wasn't sure yet what that something would be.

As David guided his car out of the hospital parking lot and onto the curving mountain road directly below the hospital he broke the silence. "Do you want me to help you tell Gena?"

That wasn't a bad idea. Gena already accepted David as her daddy.

"I'd like that, but how much do we tell her, David? I don't think now's the time to tell her Gene's her birth father, but I don't know how to tell her that he's dead either."

"We don't have to give her any details. We can simply tell her that her Uncle Gene went to Heaven to be with God."

"I hope he did," she said barely above a whisper, and suddenly her throat ached with the sobs that surged upward.

He reached for her and pulled her closer keeping his eyes on the road and his left hand carefully on the steering wheel. She let her head rest against his shoulder. "Sweetheart, I'm so sorry," he said softly.

"I wish you could have gotten to know him. When you got past his addictions he was a sweet, gentle person. Del's not like that. He's cold and calculating. He's covered his emotions for so long that sometimes I wonder if his heart has turned to stone."

He rubbed her shoulder gently.

"Del used to be such an innocent little boy. He had a lot to overcome after the accident. The force of it warped all of us, but I just can't believe he'd commit cold-blooded murder." She closed her eyes and tried to shut out the confusing emotions. Finally, she continued. "I can't let all this confusion touch Gena, and I for sure don't want to tell her in one breath that Gene is her father and in the other that he's dead."

"You don't have to tell her until you feel she's ready, Laurel. That's your choice. No one knows her as well as you do."

"Then I'll have to keep her away from the wake and the funeral. If I don't, someone else will tell her. I don't want her there anyway. When I was a child Mama dragged us to every funeral in the community. I hated it. I could never figure out why people were screaming and throwing themselves across the casket one minute and laughing it up at some redneck joke the next."

"Maybe it was a way of handling the pain," he suggested gently.

"I can see that now, but I wish someone would have pointed that out to me then. I was a sensitive kid. It bothered me. All I could feel was this gaping sense of loss that was so dark and haunting."

"Mom wouldn't mind keeping Gena for as long as we need for her to. They've hit it off well, and my parents love it that they finally have a grandchild."

She nodded numbly. She liked David's parents. They seemed to totally accept her and Gena, but his family was normal. "I should've known this would happen. I should've expected it. How could I believe that Gene's therapy alone could make a difference in this insane family?"

"Honey, I'll do anything I can to help. I'm not going to let you deal with this alone."

That was the thing she feared most. To help her deal with it he'd have to experience it in all its heartbreaking devastation.

The next morning when David came over to her apartment at seven o'clock, she'd been up for hours. What little sleep she'd gotten had been fitful, but at least she'd showered and dressed and was ready to face the awful day before her.

David insisted on making them breakfast, and Gena insisted on helping. As they all sat at the table with the oatmeal and toast the two of them had prepared, Laurel thumbed through the newspaper. The incident of Gene's death was reported on page 10 of the *Sunset Valley Herald's* Saturday edition. When she saw the bold caption and the five-inch-square, two-column article beneath it, the bite of toast she had made herself take almost came back up. The caption read: "Sunset Mountain Resident Charged with Murdering Brother."

As she concentrated on reading the article, she knew she couldn't take another bite.

> A thirty-year-old Sunset Mountain man, Jonas Delaney Harper, was charged with murder yesterday afternoon following the stabbing death several hours earlier of his brother, thirty-six-year-old Gene Sinclair Harper, at the suspect's residence

> on Harper Hollow Road on Sunset Mountain. The victim apparently died from a stab wound to the chest at about 11:45 AM yesterday during an altercation between the brothers according to the sheriff's investigators. The alleged weapon, a large kitchen knife, was found at the scene.
>
> Both the suspect and the deceased lived with their mother who was reportedly in the house when the stabbing occurred. Mrs. Sarah Harper, who is bedridden from a long-term illness, reportedly became hysterical following the altercation and was transported to Mountain General Hospital for treatment.
>
> The suspect is being held in the county jail where he was questioned until late last night before charges were filed. Autopsy results are pending.

As if the pain of this situation weren't enough, it was humiliating to have her family's craziness splashed across the newspaper for everyone to see. She dreaded trying to explain this to Stu and Miles. Most of all, she hated it that David as her fiancé was now tied to the craziness. Maybe he would be just as embarrassed as she was and regret that he'd asked her to marry him.

Abruptly he reached across the table to squeeze her hand interrupting her thoughts. "I'll call Stu about both of us needing more time off next week. While you were talking on the phone to your grandparents, Gena and I decided that she would stay with

Granny and Pop. I called them last night, and they offered. They're looking forward to it. I'll take her out there after breakfast."

"Granny told Daddy we can make gingerbread men together." Gena licked a glob of butter off the side of her lips and smiled up at her with jelly rimming her mouth. "It's gonna be lots of fun, Mommy."

Laurel reached for her napkin to wipe the stickiness away, but Gena swiped her left pajama sleeve across her mouth taking care of most of it. She smiled as she folded the newspaper and placed it on the table. She reached for Gena and pulled her into her arms pressing her cheek against her sweet, sticky face. "Of course you'll have a great time, sweetheart. Be sure to save a gingerbread man for Daddy and me."

"I will, Mommy. I'm going to swing, too. Pop said he'd push me in the swing next time I came."

"Dad went out and bought a new swing to replace the one I had as a kid," David said. "That should tell you how much my parents are looking forward to having Gena around."

Gena wiggled in her arms. "I'm done with breakfast. Can I go get my dolly ready to take with me?"

"Sure," she answered as she got up and carried her into the kitchen. "Let's get the sticky off you first." She set Gena on the counter and cleaned her face and hands with a wet towel. Then she kissed her cheek and set her on the floor. As Gena skipped off to her bedroom she called after her. "Don't forget your mittens and hat so you won't get cold when you go out to swing."

She walked back to the table and took her seat again glancing across at David. "I don't know how to explain this to Stu, or Miles, or anyone else for that matter—even you."

He reached for her hand again and squeezed it. "I'll handle Stu, and I'll be discreet. But no one could ever think less of you for this, especially not me."

He brought her hand to his lips and kissed it. She could read the concern on his face, and for the first time since this nightmare had begun, she realized that she could let herself rely on his strength. She wasn't used to depending on anyone, but she knew he would be there when she needed him. She could feel his love.

"I'll drop back by here after I get Gena settled," he said. "If you're not here, I'll catch you at Pike's." That was the funeral home, and she knew he was being careful about calling it what it really was for Gena's sake in case she could hear their conversation.

"Okay. Call Pike's before you come. I'll leave a message there if I get finished early. When I'm through I might go on up to see Mama at the hospital and meet you there."

The funeral arrangements didn't take long primarily because Mama had already called ahead early this morning and made the arrangements herself. She'd selected the funeral package, the minister, the pallbearers, the time and date of the funeral, and the wording of the obituary. All that was left for Laurel to do was pay for it. She'd come prepared to do whatever it took to lay her brother to rest. She had twenty-five hundred dollars left in her savings account, and she hoped that would be enough. She and David had discussed it last night, and he told her she should follow her heart.

Mama had chosen a nice but economical package, one Laurel would have chosen herself. If only Mama had been this nurturing when Gene was alive. Pike's was the funeral home of choice for people on her end of the mountain, and Mama had long ago planned her own funeral with them. She'd paid for it when she could least afford the extra expense. Laurel just couldn't understand her fixation on death and dying when she hadn't expressed a single bit of interest in celebrating life or love.

Mama had chosen denim pants and a western shirt for Gene to wear. She had to agree it was appropriate. It was what he always wore and what he would've wanted. She told the funeral director that she'd bring Gene's favorite turquoise belt from home before visitation.

She waited with her pen poised over her checkbook while the director totaled the costs. "It's two thousand dollars even, ma'am," he said gently. Then abruptly he paused and handed her a paper bag. "These are your brother's personal items. They were in his pockets."

She took the paper bag and tucked it into her purse. As she wrote the check, the funeral director kept talking. "We have the body ready now, but public visitation is scheduled for tomorrow. The coroner said the cause of death was loss of blood from a severed artery. I'm sure they'll be sending a copy of their findings to your family."

She nodded numbly and handed him the check.

"Would you like to view the body now?"

She nodded again. He handed her the receipt and stood. Without saying anything further he led her to the door of Parlor A, and he slipped away. She glanced at the sign above the door. It read "Mr. Harper." She shivered. This had been Daddy's room. Every dismal nook of it would be etched in her memory forever. She hadn't come here in the five years since his death, not even when her cousin Adam, Uncle Will's son, had been killed in Vietnam. She'd had to make herself go graveside. At least Adam had died fighting for freedom instead of this insane mountain code.

She paused inside the doorway and took in a deep breath. Tucking the receipt into her purse, she glanced around at the bleakness of the room. It hadn't changed a bit. This was history repeating itself, and she wasn't ready for it. She would never be ready for it, but she had to get it over with. Propelling herself forward, she concentrated on the far wall until she was standing in front of the silver casket. Only then did she let her gaze drop, and when she did, the flimsy wall she'd built around her heart shattered. She swallowed a sob and reached to stroke Gene's forehead. He was so cold, and his flesh felt like wax. Something squeezed tight inside her, and it was hard to catch her breath.

Jennie Austin had once told Mama that all Gene needed was for someone to love him—wise words from an otherwise ignorant woman, falling on deaf ears. It was truer than anything anyone had ever said about her poor brother. He'd been born against God's better judgment because Mama prayed too hard, and once it was done he became the scapegoat for everything that went wrong in her life. Now he was gone, and she questioned why God had answered Mama's prayer in the first place to allow him to lead such a tortured life. But then this wasn't God's fault, and she knew it.

She smoothed her hand across the cold metal of the casket and gazed at the lines of pain etched into her brother's once handsome face. She knew he was gone from this body, but something about him was still here, hovering, somewhere. She talked to that presence.

"It's over now," she whispered. "She can't hurt you anymore."

She wanted to tell him that it was over for her, too, but she knew it wasn't. She knew if one of them could die, it was dangerous for her to stay, but she had to try one last time to change things.

"Your shrink was wrong," she said choking on the words. "It does matter whether Mama loves us or not. This couldn't be happening if she really loved us. So, it matters. You had to pay the price to prove that, and it's just not fair." Her chest and her throat ached with the sobs she held back, but she was afraid to let go, afraid she would drown in her sorrow. She took in several deep breaths, but she couldn't stop her tears. They trickled down her face. A stray one dropped on her hand and splattered on the metal of the casket. "None of this whole mess is fair," she whispered as she swiped at the shiny surface, "but just so you know, Daddy *did* love you. I love you, too."

After that she had to leave. She couldn't swallow any more pain. She paused at the main desk and asked to use their phone. She'd promised Mama Rita and Grandpa that she would call about the funeral arrangements.

"I'll get Joe Bob Drake to bring his backhoe and dig the grave," Grandpa said softly after she'd filled him in on the arrangements Mama had made. "Gene's already got that plot your mama gave him across the path from Sinclair. Joe Bob won't charge anything."

"Thanks, Grandpa, I hadn't even thought of that part."

"Oh, and I ought to tell you Will and Joshua bailed Del out of jail. They brought him home about an hour ago."

"I'll come up to see him then."

"Stop by and see us while you're here."

She couldn't see how Del wouldn't be heartbroken about this tragedy, so she decided to go see him before she visited Mama. She left a message for David at the funeral home telling him where she would be and asking him to meet her at the hospital. She could have given him directions to Mama Rita and Grandpa's place, but that was too close to home. She couldn't handle the turmoil of his seeing that place on top of everything else. He had to see it eventually, she supposed, but not today.

Chapter Twenty-One

When David returned to his apartment after taking Gena to his parent's house, he made a brief call to Stu's home since it was a Saturday. He explained that Laurel's brother had died suddenly, but he didn't give any details. Then he told Stu that her invalid mother had been hospitalized from the shock and that Laurel had her hands full dealing with it all. Stu couldn't have been more supportive, and he told David that both of them should take all the time off that they needed.

He knew Stu would understand if he knew the details of this tragedy. For all his teasing about Stu's fear of germs and his touchy-feely behavior, the man had a sincerely compassionate heart. So did Miles, but Laurel's nature was to keep her pain to herself. He respected her need for privacy. He felt blessed that she'd finally learned that she could trust and lean on him. He wouldn't do anything to betray that trust.

He called the funeral home to learn that he had just missed Laurel. She'd left a message for him saying she was going by her mom's house because Del was out of jail and at home. The message also said that she would meet him after lunch at the hospital. Glancing at his watch he decided he had time to head on out and try to intercept her at her mother's house. She'd given him the general directions once, and it didn't sound too hard to find. He figured he could ask for directions at a service station if he got lost.

As he pulled the door to his apartment shut, he turned to see a tall, slender girl standing in front of Laurel's apartment getting ready to knock. She looked vaguely familiar. "Are you looking for Laurel?" he asked.

"Yeah," she answered zeroing in on him with her intense blue eyes. "I'm her cousin Betty Jo Cowan."

That was why she looked familiar. He'd seen several pictures of her in a family album Laurel kept. He extended his hand. "I'm David Hudson."

"Laurel's fiancé, I believe," she said looking him up and down as she shook his hand. "I've heard a lot about you."

She grinned and cocked her head, swinging her curly auburn ponytail. In person she looked exactly the way Laurel had described her—cute, feisty, and tomboyish. She wore brown corduroy slacks and a flannel shirt beneath a well-worn leather jacket. The jacket had military patches on the sleeve and looked like the one Uncle Rick kept from his time in World War II.

"I hoped I could catch up with Laurel so we could go to the funeral home together," she said not waiting for him to respond. "I hate for her to face that alone."

"She's already finished there. I just talked to the lady at the desk at Pike Funeral Home. She said Laurel's mom had called ahead and made most of the arrangements."

"That figures. Good old Aunt Sarah. She's the boss of both the living and the dead. Where's Gena?"

"Mom and Dad are keeping her. I just came back from taking her to their house."

"Is Laurel coming back here?"

"No, she's on her way to see Del. He's out on bail and at home. I'm going to try to catch her there."

"You should ride up with me. I'm headed that way since I can't help at the funeral home. Laurel's going to be in no shape to drive after going to the funeral home and seeing crazy Del all in the same morning. And there's no point in having two cars up there."

"Sounds like a good idea. Lead the way." He followed behind her as she headed back down the hallway and entered the stairwell. "Nice jacket," he said.

She glanced back over her shoulder and grinned. "It's Daddy's from when he fought in World War II. Can you believe he had it stuffed away in a trunk? Hippies hate it. I wear it just to tick them off."

He laughed and followed her down the stairs and out the back door to the parking lot. "Crazy Del? Why do you say that?" He thought Del was a bit off-kilter himself, but he wanted to hear what someone who knew him well had to say.

"I was there yesterday right after it happened, you know, and he was just plain weird. I know you gotta have a screw loose to kill your brother, but he was out there. I'm not kidding you."

Betty Jo motioned to a red 1963 Chevrolet truck. She unlocked the passenger door for him and went around to the other side and hopped in.

"What does 'out there' mean? Is Laurel in danger?" he asked as he settled into the truck's roomy cab.

"I don't think so." She put the truck in reverse, backed up, pulled the gear into low, and guided her truck toward Tenth Street. "It's just that he was saying weird stuff about Great-Grandma Cowan being a shaman and that he was a shaman, too. I'm standing there thinking, 'Well, shame and disgrace sure describes this sad, awful mess.'"

His sentiments exactly, but he would never voice that. Laurel felt bad enough about this tragedy. Betty Jo built up her speed, went to second gear, then to high, and took a sharp right at Central Avenue.

"Now, how exactly are you related to Laurel?"

"We're double first cousins. That's because my daddy is Aunt Sarah's brother, and Mama is Laurel's daddy's sister. You've probably heard her and Gena talk about Mama Rita and Grandpa Harper."

He nodded.

"Well, they're my grandparents, too. We live across the road from them."

"I see."

"We're not inbred or anything, so don't you be worrying about yours and Laurel's babies having two heads." She flashed him a grin.

He laughed. "I hadn't given that a thought."

"Laurel said you haven't set the date yet."

"You must have talked to her recently. Well, except for yesterday after the tragedy."

"Yeah, Laurel may come up only once a week, but she calls Mama Rita and Grandpa every day to check on them—her mama, too. She and I talk several times a week. I don't blame her for not visiting much. Coming home to her house is like visiting a prison and the nut house all rolled into one."

"What do you mean?"

"For starters, Aunt Sarah can be the Wicked Witch of the North. She's always on Laurel's butt about something, and Laurel's the best kid she's got. Always has been. Gene's been an alcoholic since he was sixteen. I think mostly he drank because he got caught in the war between Aunt Sarah and Uncle Sinclair." She flipped the truck heater to high and glanced at him. "Has Laurel ever told you about the accident?"

"Yes, a couple of months back."

"Well, according to Mama, Aunt Sarah and Uncle Sinclair's marriage was rocky from the start, but the real biggie came with that accident. After that day Mama says they quit trying to get along. They lived under the same roof and slept in separate beds, but it was *not* a peaceful house. Uncle Sinclair wasn't a violent man, but he had a temper; and Aunt Sarah was always goading him."

"Laurel told me that Gene and Del have never gotten along. She thinks the accident was indirectly responsible for that plus the fact that he's not their real brother. Is that the way your parents see it?"

"Pretty much, but a lot of it was jealousy pure and simple." She shifted the truck into low gear as she turned onto Bluff View Road and started up the steep mountain grade.

"Jealousy about what exactly?"

"Everything, but mainly because Gene grew up to be a ladies' man and Del didn't date that much. I mean, he's good looking enough, and he wasn't a nerd. It's just that he didn't have Gene's charm, and he was a big smart-ass. Still is for that matter."

"How did he get together with Connie?"

"They went steady in high school. Their senior year he broke it off to date a new girl—to prove he could be a ladies' man, too, everybody thought. It hurt Connie a lot, so she started dating an encyclopedia salesman. You know, one of those guys that go door to door. Mama said next thing they knew she eloped with the guy and moved to Florida with him. Everybody says Del was hard to be around after that, but the dope asked for it by breaking Connie's heart."

"How did he and Connie finally get together again?"

"After two kids and six years of marriage, she divorced the encyclopedia guy. When she moved back home, she and Del picked up where they left off."

"I haven't heard Laurel or Gena mention her children. Where are they?"

"Four years ago Connie's ex hired a lawyer and took them away from her. So Julie and Amy went to live with their dad. Julie's twelve, and Amy's eleven."

"Connie seems nice. Why would the judge choose the father over her?"

"Because their mother's a closet alcoholic and Del's a sleaze." Betty Jo downshifted and slowed for a hairpin curve.

"How so?" He'd sensed sleazy from the word go with Del, but it didn't please him to be right. This was Laurel's brother, and he knew that in spite of his faults, she loved him.

"He dabbles—if not downright wades—in what I'd call the dark side. The good old mountain boys think he's cool with his dogfighting and his self-proclaimed shaman status. Plus, he's into all that hippy crap with herbs and astrology charts and moons in somebody's house. Mix all that with mountain Indian lore, and you've got some real loony stuff. While all that might raise him a notch in status in Harper Hollow, it didn't make points with the court system in a custody case."

"Dogfighting is illegal in the Carolinas, not to mention cruel and inhumane. How does he keep from getting arrested?"

"He's too smart to get caught. On the surface his dogs are better cared for than his family, so it just looks like he's a breeder. All that shady stuff he keeps well hidden even from Aunt Sarah. She knows, and yet she doesn't."

"Then how do you know for sure that he's actually doing it?"

Betty Jo shot him a glance. "We know. There's an underbelly in Harper Hollow. When you're a native, it's not hard to put the pieces together. Proving it is another matter."

He could see how overwhelming this was for Laurel. Its many facets overwhelmed even him. "I hate this for Laurel. She tries so hard with her family."

"Yeah, it's been hard for her trying to make their lives better without going down the drain with them. She feels guilty if she enjoys two seconds of her hard-earned separate life, and, believe me, she got where she is all by herself. They make her feel guilty on purpose, and they let what she does help them only to the point that they can make her feel bad about what she does."

"What do you mean?"

"Let me put it this way. If she'd done for anybody else what she's done for them, they'd let it make a difference instead of biting the hand that fed them. But, no, they do what they want and squeeze the life out of her because they know she loves them."

"Has it always been this way?"

"Mama said it wasn't. Aunt Sarah's always been controlling, but she used to have a life that didn't center on being sick. Oh, she's always had big illnesses about every decade according to Mama, but in between she did some cool things."

"What kind of cool things?" On the seat between them a neat stack of nursing textbooks fanned out as they rounded a sharp curve. He reached to pull them back into place and anchored them with his left hand. Other than Betty Jo's purse, which she'd tucked under her seat as she got in, the books were the only clutter anywhere in the spotless truck cab.

Betty Jo kept talking. "Aunt Sarah was always helping Granddaddy, her daddy, to circulate petitions for better roads and schools. We didn't even have a high school on the mountain until she started a movement to get the county to buy the property from the army. And she drove our grammar school bus up until five years ago when Uncle Sinclair got killed. She's the only woman who ever did that."

"On these mountain roads that's pretty awesome." He wouldn't be too eager to take on these curves with a school bus. He doubted that the roads farther out would be any better.

"Once in 1963 she got her bus stuck in the mud on Harper Hollow Road. She called the most popular valley television station and got them to come up and film it for the six o'clock news. The county road commissioner got so mad at her for the bad publicity he almost blew a gasket."

He grinned. "She sounds fearsome."

"It was best not to mess with her alright, and if you wanted something done that required guts, Aunt Sarah filled the bill. I always thought she was cool when she did those things, but

Uncle Sinclair thought she should've been home with supper on the table."

"What was he like, Laurel's father?"

"A workaholic like his brothers and my mama and the rest of the family. He was a real good man though, quiet and easygoing, unless you backed him into a corner. Aunt Sarah was always backing him into a corner."

"The way she backs Laurel into a corner?" he asked.

"Exactly. Laurel always stands her ground, but she feels guilty about it, which defeats the purpose. I'd hate to think what her life would be if she hadn't had Gena to love and protect. With you in her life she has a chance at real happiness, but don't expect Aunt Sarah to like you for that."

He already knew that Laurel's mother didn't like him. It didn't bother him, but he didn't want her to take out her wrath toward him on Laurel.

"What do you know about Renee?" he asked abruptly. He hadn't mentioned it to Laurel, but he worried that Renee would read about Gene's death and show up.

Betty Jo eyed him. "You want the truth?"

He nodded. Renee was the enemy, and the more he knew about her, the better he could build a defense against her.

"She was a hussy from the word go. She thought she was better than us hillbillies, but she was just a tramp. She'd do anything for a buck except work. Gene was blown away by her looks, but that didn't last long. When he found out how devious she was, it spoiled the looks thing for him. He hit the bottle even worse after that."

"Has anyone in your neighborhood heard from her since she abandoned Gena?"

"Not a single word, but she'll show up when she hears that Gene's dead. When she smells social security benefits for Gena, she'll try to claim her."

This wasn't what he wanted to hear. He would consult with his attorney friend Roger very soon about how to fight Renee if that happened.

"Renee's one money-hungry barracuda," Betty Jo added. "Like I said, she's pretty—beautiful, even—if you can forget what a wench she is. She can really turn on the innocent charm when she wants to, and judges are only human. It would kill Laurel to lose Gena."

He understood the power and wiles of female predators. He'd survived one of the worst in the form of Marilee. He wasn't about to see his and Laurel's happiness destroyed again by another emptyhearted manipulator, and he'd do everything in his power to prevent it.

Betty Jo glanced sideways at him as she adjusted the truck heater to a lower temperature. "You know, you're much nicer than I figured you'd be. I knew you were handsome with thick brown hair and killer blue eyes. I saw a picture of you. Laurel kept it tucked in her dresser drawer."

That was nice to know. He'd kept all his pictures of her, but he figured she would've thrown away all of his.

"I'm a little nosy, but when somebody as pretty as Laurel won't even date and acts offended like she did if you even mentioned she should, you go poking around to find out why."

"I guess I'm *persona non grata* with you."

"Nah. She never badmouthed you. I just put two and two together by myself—a picture here, a scribbled note there, a longing look. Just tidbits. Sometimes she'd get so sad when a song played on the radio that I thought she was going to cry. She probably did cry in private, but it's an unwritten rule in her family that you're weak if you cry."

He felt a twinge of deep regret. He wished he could have prevented those times for her. He remembered too well how he'd felt the same way.

They reached the plateau of the mountain where they drove through an area of opulent homes and the small business district.

This part of Sunset Mountain had changed very little in the past fifteen years since he'd attended Boy Scout jamborees at the baseball field here. He saw that they had added a post office where the hardware store used to be. The drugstore next door looked exactly the same, and he fondly recalled all the cherry Cokes he'd drunk at its fountain. Tucker's Grocery was still at the end of the strip, and the Sinclair Gas station was still next door. There were several other small businesses but only one that he didn't remember.

After a few miles the opulent homes thinned out, and the road curved around the hillside below Mountain General Hospital. He remembered that Laurel's house had been close by, and he assumed it was past the hospital. "Where's that subdivision where Laurel used to live?" he asked.

"I'll show you. It's at the bottom of the hill past the hospital. We have to drive right past it." She paused. "Warning. You are now entering the real world. That place we just passed through was fantasyland." She grinned and shifted into low gear.

When they headed down the grade past the hospital, she pointed to the left. "That's my old high school. The football field used to be a landing strip. I think they were training soldiers for fighting in mountain terrain because when it was a base we used to see helicopters all the time landing and taking off. Daddy was army in the World War II, and he said the place was more a training facility than a real base. No families lived here except for the officers who ran the place, and it was much smaller than a real base."

As he glanced left he clearly saw the military influence in the barracks-type buildings lined across the neat expanse of well-kept lawn.

Betty Jo continued. "When I was in junior high I'd walk down the hill to Laurel's house and do my homework until she got off work. She'd pick me up and take me home when she went to get Gena. She gave me my own key and left snacks for me. I always felt welcome there. When I got old enough to work she gave me a job in the lab drawing blood."

She started slowing the truck as they headed down a steep hill. At the bottom she stopped and turned left. "We'll just swing by her old house."

She entered the subdivision, took the second street off the main entry, and drove past a row of attractive one-story houses. At the end of the street she pulled the truck over in front of a pale blue bungalow with white shutters and trim.

"This is it. Laurel loved this house, and she was always working on it. I thought it was the prettiest house in this subdivision."

It was indeed a nice house. With its pristine white gingerbread trim and neatly landscaped yard, it looked like a cottage out of a storybook. The backyard was fenced, and he could see a swing set.

"These houses were all electric when the army built them which shows what they knew about mountain winters. First thing Laurel did was get Uncle Will and Uncle Joshua to build her a fireplace as insurance against the power going out.

"You get a lot of bad weather then, huh?"

"It's like a different world up here. We can have a foot of snow, and the valley will only get flurries. Laurel's first winter here the power went out in the bad snow we had January of 1967. She was the only one with a fireplace and a big stack of logs. She invited her neighbors over until the power company got the power back on the next day. That spring and summer our uncles were covered up building fireplaces for the subdivision."

That was Laurel, generous and compassionate. He wondered what was wrong with her mother and Del that they couldn't see that and where they got off criticizing her so much.

Chapter Twenty-Two

As Laurel navigated the same shaky steps up to the same dilapidated doorway at Mama's house, she noticed the red-bowed Christmas wreath that decorated the storm door. Connie made and sold wreaths every year using holly and spruce gathered from the hollow, but this year the festive decoration seemed so out of place that it almost reduced Laurel to tears. When she spotted the flocked "peace on earth" banner taped to the inside door, tears did sting her eyes. There would never be peace in this place.

Once she reached the living room just beyond the entryway door, she paused and took in the room. The log cabin bore no visible signs of the stabbing, not even Mama's bedside—the crime scene. Connie had obviously scrubbed the place clean of blood. If she couldn't clean up the pain, she would at least try to manage the mess it created.

Connie came in from the kitchen to greet her like nothing had happened. Had she dreamed this? Had it all been just an awful nightmare? But when she got a closer look at Connie's face she realized that her sister-in-law was one step away from hysteria.

They headed for the kitchen, the only reasonably nice room left in the house thanks to Connie. Del was sitting at the table and seemed lost in his task of rolling a cigarette. Connie offered coffee and refilled her and Del's cups. There was an awkward silence. Then Connie asked about Gena. Laurel told her that David had taken her to stay with his parents.

"So where is this fiancé of yours? Is he invisible?" Del muttered.

She bristled. Was he trying to pick a fight? She gritted her teeth and made sure her voice was pleasant. "I just said he took Gena to his parents for me, and he had to touch bases with our boss about being off for the next couple of days. I'm meeting him at Mountain General."

"He's that doctor boyfriend that came to the hospital with you, huh." It wasn't really a question, and he continued. "I reckon I talked to him on the phone, too, about five years ago, didn't I?"

He was actually smiling, and it was such a mocking smile it made her fighting mad. She wasn't going to provoke him on purpose, but this was the one thing she wasn't going to tiptoe softly around. She was still mad at him for his life-changing interference.

"He wasn't a doctor back then," she said, "and I believe you told him to get lost. I'm certainly glad he didn't take your advice."

"Well, well, ain't that nice? Little sister ain't gonna be a old maid no more." His lips curled in a smirk, and he took a sip of his coffee.

She made herself push her anger aside. Why did she expect him to be different just because he was charged with murder? Buying time before she confronted the issue, she told Connie she needed Gene's turquoise belt. When Connie left to look for it, she took in a deep breath and began. "What on earth happened up here, Del?"

She watched him gather his thoughts. He was beginning to show his age even at thirty. His red hair was thinning like Granddaddy Cowan's had. He looked a lot like Granddaddy. He shrugged. "We were working on Gene's car when he brought up that PCP thing again. He said he'd talked to you about it Thanksgiving Eve, and the way you and him figured it, Mama was just trying to cause trouble."

"That's exactly what I think because it's just the kind of thing she does, Del, and I don't think she sees the danger in what she does."

He narrowed his eyes at her and frowned. "Do you want to hear what happened, or do you want to tell it?"

She held up her hands in surrender, and he continued. "Well, that ain't the way I see it, little sister. See, 'cause I was here, and your mama was scared to death that your big brother was gonna kill us all. He said he was going to. I don't care if he was high on PCP. That's all the more reason to take his threat to heart. I made up my mind after that PCP thing that I'd always keep my weapons ready." He patted the bulge under his tee shirt, and she could see the outline of a pistol tucked into his waistband.

"And you actually heard him make that threat?"

He glared at her with an even darker frown that made her sigh in resignation and motion for him to continue. "Mama's word was enough for me. She can't take care of herself, and you won't do it. It's up to me. Some of us care about family. I'll defend mine with my last breath."

When Del said "family," he meant Mama. They'd always been close, but since Daddy's death he'd held a blind allegiance to Mama. Also he'd become openly hostile to Laurel the way he'd always been hostile toward Gene.

He took a sip of coffee and another couple of slow puffs off the cigarette he'd lit when she first sat down. He went on. "Yesterday when Gene and me kept on arguing, neither of us would back down. He said he didn't threaten to kill us, which was as much as calling Mama a liar, and I told him so. He made some smart-ass crack like, 'Well, if the foo shits.'"

She picked up the can of Pet condensed milk and added a splash to her cup. As she stirred it into her coffee, she remembered how as a child she'd gazed in wonder at the logo on this can. It was a cow in a can inside a cow in a can inside another cow in a can *ad infinitum*. Life in this family was like that, but she couldn't decide whether the dark point of infinity was their beginning or their end.

"Now that clearly pissed me off," Del was saying. "We really went at it then, and some other things came up. Then your precious big brother pulls a knife on me. I'm not armed, so I take off to the house; and it clearly ain't over between us. I come in to get my pistol, but I no sooner hit the kitchen than he's coming in the door right behind me."

He motioned toward the solid wood door to his left. She could almost see it happening. She had seen them argue so many times. As they got older the anger escalated, but it always stopped at the edge. Until now.

"I don't see the knife; but he had it last time I seen him, so I ain't taking no chances. I pick up the butcher knife. He sees it, and tries to take it away from me. We get into a big scuffle, and I don't know how it happened—"

He paused and tapped cigarette ashes onto the edge of the saucer of his coffee cup. She thought he might start crying from the look on his face, but then he hardened and continued. "I don't know he's hurt 'cause he turns around and goes back out the door. I know he's got a gun in his car. I figure he's gone to get it, so I go get my pistol and get ready for him. I don't remember much after that except for when Nathan told me what happened."

There was a long silence, and she watched as he methodically rolled another cigarette. Her heart ached for him. She was convinced that this had been a tragic overreaction, a miscalculation that came from years of thinking the worst of each other. When two people spent the biggest part of their lives being pitted against each other, any agitation had the power to push their conflict over the edge.

She broke the silence. "I want you to know, Del, that I don't blame you. Okay? I know it could be you lying in that funeral home. You and Gene have been at odds with each other since that awful accident, but you were both victims. We're all victims."

"I don't know how you figure that. I'm the one who got run over. I'm the one who lived with a bum arm for two years. Hell, it still bothers me."

"Can't you see how that day changed everything? Mama pulled all of us into her war with Daddy after that. Don't you remember the awful things she used to say about him? But Daddy's gone now, and she won't stop the war. We need to work on fixing that. We need to heal this sick family before more tragedy happens."

"There's plenty you don't know about that day, and it ain't got nothing to do with anybody but me." He lit the cigarette he'd just rolled from the stub of the one he was smoking and leaned back in his chair.

"I know everything you do. I was there. Remember?"

"Oh yeah? Well, did you know that Mama and Daddy were fighting about me that day? Mama told him a secret he didn't know, and he stormed out 'cause he couldn't accept it."

"What secret? What couldn't Daddy accept?"

"Mama told him I was her real kid by another man she was with while he was off building barracks. He got mad as hell, and then he ran over me."

She couldn't say anything for awhile. She was too shocked. Was this the truth? One thing she did know. Daddy did not run over Del on purpose. "Daddy was heartbroken that you got hurt. You know that. I remember it well. I don't care what Mama told him or how upset he got. He was not a violent man."

"What upsets you the most, little sister, that your daddy was not what you thought he was or that I'm your half-brother?"

"Daddy did not run over you on purpose." She couldn't help raising her voice. Daddy wasn't here to defend himself. "That accident was Mama's fault as much as it was his. And for your information, you've always been my brother in my heart."

"Touching," he said as he flicked more ashes onto his saucer. "Gene didn't believe me either."

"I didn't say I don't believe you. What's the difference? You've always been my brother, and I love you. What I said is that Daddy didn't run over you on purpose. I don't care what Mama told you. She hates Daddy, and it's not fair for her to speak for him. Daddy always loved you. You know that."

She wondered if he and Gene had argued about this, too. "So, you told Gene about this?"

"Yes, I just told you he didn't believe me either."

"That was the biggest part of your argument, wasn't it?"

He shrugged. "I reckon you could say that. Gene said it sure explained why I always had my head up Mama's ass."

She cringed. They'd always argued like that, saying one crude thing after the other.

Del continued. "The subject of this property came up next. Being just a cousin, I always felt like none of this land belonged to me, but it ain't just Harper land anymore. I get the Cowan part."

"If you think I want any part of this acreage, forget it. I don't."

"Of course not. You're too good, too citified, and I reckon Mama's right that you've got above your raising. Gene—now, he was a different matter."

"I can't see him being unfair about it. There's eighty acres here, plenty enough to share."

"You can't, huh? Well, we had us a tear-down, drag-out about it. That's how fair about it he was."

"Had he been drinking?"

"No. That's what made it so bad. I could have made allowances if he was drunk. He said Daddy left him the acreage next to the house. Mama says it belongs to me no matter what Daddy said."

She couldn't believe anybody would fight over this tainted land. "Was it really worth somebody dying?" she asked.

Del ignored her comment and took a sip of his coffee.

She leaned toward him. "What difference does it make who has what part? But Del, I remember that Gene always said he wanted the land next to the house, and you said you wanted the other part. When did you change your mind?"

"When I found out I had some rights. When I found out I'm part of this family, too."

She sighed. "Well, this secret explains one thing for me. It explains why Mama has always loved you more than us. She obviously loved your father. She never loved ours."

"Well, I guess that makes us even because your daddy never loved me."

"That is not true, Del. Gene was jealous because he thought Daddy loved you more than he loved him."

"He felt guilty for running over me. That's all."

"He felt bad, not guilty, and he did love you. Don't you remember how he stayed right there beside you when the doctor set your arm? Don't you remember how he rocked you every night until your pain medication took effect and how he slept right next to you on a cot in case you needed him? Don't you remember how he made Mama back off when she pushed you too hard in your rehabilitation?"

Tears filled Del's eyes, and the muscle in his jaw twitched. Maybe she'd succeeded in making him remember. She, for sure, remembered all those times. Daddy hadn't been an expressive man, but she remembered hearing him tell Del he loved him. She'd had to assume that he loved her by his actions. With Del he'd crossed his comfort barrier to reassure him, but she'd never been jealous of that. She'd understood.

"Did Mama tell you all this secret stuff?" she asked.

He nodded and took his time dragging on the cigarette and exhaling the draw. The vulnerable expression on his face gradually hardened.

"When?"

"After Daddy—your daddy—died. That day of his funeral she told me."

She wondered why Mama hadn't bothered to tell her and Gene, too, but this was so like her. "Did you ever wonder why she waited until Daddy wasn't around to defend himself to tell you he hated you and ran over you on purpose? Del, just because she didn't love him, that doesn't mean he wasn't a good man. Think about this. Don't hate a man who didn't deserve your hate."

"Don't tell me what to think."

"Don't tell me to believe something that's not true."

"There you go calling Mama a liar again, just like Gene did."

"Because it *is* a lie. Be reasonable about this, Del."

"You know, you might ought to think before you speak, Laurel Elaine. You don't want to end up like Gene."

Her heart began to pound. Was he threatening her? She had come to offer peace and to console him, and he was threatening her? How dare he? Did he not realize the situation he was in? He was charged with murder. Even though she truly did not believe this tragedy was premeditated, he was making himself look guilty. She made herself take calming breaths. Anger wasn't going to help. Anger had caused this mess in the first place. Maybe this was just remorse, the shock of all that had happened.

"Come on, Del. This is grief talking."

He fixed her with a threatening gaze. "You heard me. Don't be stupid."

Her mind raced with more emotions than she could separate. She was angry, and yes, she was afraid. He was crazy. He couldn't have done this and have this attitude about it if he weren't crazy. Despite her fear, she couldn't hold her tongue.

"What are you going to do, shoot me with that pistol you have tucked in your waistband and call it self defense when I'm not even armed?"

He laughed. He actually had the nerve to laugh, but it might as well have been another verbal threat. It was that contemptuous.

"I don't think it's a good idea for you to be carrying a gun, Del, not after what happened yesterday."

"You can't ever tell when I might need it."

It was another threat—a veiled one—but still a threat. She pushed aside the cup of coffee she'd barely touched and stood. "I think it's time for me to leave."

He shrugged and took another sip of his coffee. This was it. He was crazy, and Mama had infused him with so much of her venom that hate pulsed from him. She was the object of that hate now just because she existed, and she would be his next victim. She went to find Connie and to retrieve Gene's belt. Then she would get the hell out of there and never go back.

Chapter Twenty-Three

Betty Jo talked constantly on the rest of the trip from Laurel's old house, but David genuinely liked her. She gave him a lot of useful family information during those six miles. It kept him from being quite so shocked when they pulled down the rut-filled driveway of Laurel's homeplace.

Still, he was stunned to see the squalor. Now he totally understood Laurel's disgruntlement with her family, especially after hearing Betty Jo's story of how her mother had gone through a hundred thousand dollar settlement in a year with nothing to show for it.

He opened the truck's passenger door and glanced around as he got out. A '60 Chevy sat in a parking space under a dying elm tree. Its hood was open, and car parts lay scattered on the fender. Laurel had parked her car directly behind it. Toward the side of the house he saw two black and white goats look up from gnawing at a patch of grass to bleat in their direction. Near the goats was another older model car sitting in weeds up to the hubcaps. It looked to have been landlocked for awhile.

"Watch your step." Betty Jo balanced on a rickety stone step and reached to open the front storm door.

He followed and stepped up inside. As the wreath-laden door closed behind him it made a grating sound that let him know the glass was loose. He followed Betty Jo through a dark, dusty foyer. Various car parts lined their path. Straight ahead was a wooden door with three diagonal rectangular windows covered by a curtain on the opposite side. A flocked "peace on earth" banner was taped to the wood beneath the windows.

Betty Jo turned the knob and stepped inside. "Nobody around here ever locks their door," she said over her shoulder. "And in this house what you'd have to fear would be inside anyway."

He scanned the room and saw a worn sofa to his right, and to his left a hospital bed sat by the room's lone window. In the far left corner stood a brown stove that had to be propane-powered judging from the tank he'd seen outside. Directly ahead in a straight line with the bed was a color television. Some televangelist was on, but the volume was turned down. Next to the television sat a wooden rocking chair and a green recliner that looked almost new.

Betty Jo crossed the badly worn linoleum floor toward a doorway where he could see wood stairs of about five steps to its left. Coming down them he caught a glimpse of Laurel. She had her purse slung over her arm, and as she walked toward them, she glanced back talking to Connie.

"Look who I found," Betty Jo said cheerily as she walked ahead of him.

Laurel turned abruptly, and when she saw him standing behind her cousin she turned ashen. He made eye contact, but she took in a breath and glanced away.

Betty Jo didn't seem to notice, and that kept it from being an awkward moment. "David, you've met Connie, I believe, Laurel's sister-in-law," Betty Jo said.

He moved forward to take Connie's hand and squeeze it. "Yes. Hi, Connie. It's good to see you again."

Betty Jo explained his presence. "I went by your apartment to see if I could help with the arrangements, Laurel, and I ran into

David on his way to come meet you. I figured why have two cars up here, so I gave him a ride."

He moved to Laurel's side and placed his hand gently on her back. "Looks like you're on your way out."

Still not looking at him she answered. "Yes, I came to get Gene's favorite belt. Thanks, Connie."

"Well, if it ain't the fiancé." The gruff words came from the doorway Laurel had just passed through. It was Del. He moved into the room and stretched his wiry body to grab a can of Prince Albert tobacco from the top of the television. "He ain't a figment of your wishful thinking after all," Del added.

Laurel's ashen expression colored with anger. "You're not funny, Del," she said bitterly. He started to counter with his own sarcastic comment, but Laurel guided him toward the door as she frowned at her brother. "And we were just leaving."

"Don't let the door hit you in the ass on the way out." He grunted and turned back toward the doorway.

He didn't like this guy's attitude, but from the look on Laurel's face she didn't need any more hassle. He decided to let the comment slide.

"See you, Connie," Betty Jo said as she walked ahead of them into the entryway.

"Where to next? The hospital?" he said to Laurel.

"I need to go to Mama Rita and Grandpa's."

"Okay, I'll drive. Just tell me where to turn."

"Follow Betty Jo," she said. "When she turns left, you turn right."

He turned to Connie. "Bye, Connie."

Laurel didn't say a word to him from the time they made their way to her car until he pulled out of the long driveway onto the main dirt road. She wouldn't even look at him. She glanced out her window the whole time. He had no idea what was wrong, but he knew he was the reason for this sudden, stony silence because she'd been at least amiable when she was talking to Connie.

He reached to squeeze her shoulder. "Laurel, have I done something wrong?"

She took in a ragged breath but still wouldn't look at him or respond.

"Honey, please, look at me."

She turned her face to him then, and he saw the tears and the bitter expression. "Welcome to Dog Patch, David." She wiped at her tears and stared straight ahead again. "I never wanted you to see it."

"But we'd planned to come up this weekend. I would have seen it then."

"I didn't want you to, and I dreaded it so much I would have found some excuse not to come."

"Honey, my family's not rich. I didn't grow up with a lot of money either."

"But the people in your family don't go around stabbing and killing each other. They're not stuck in a dead-end lifestyle because they have no aspirations. They don't take the assets God gave them for granted and squander them. How could you see that place and not regret proposing? How could you not run as far away as you can get from me?"

He glanced at her but he kept one eye on the road, paying attention to Betty Jo's truck. "This doesn't change how I feel about you in any way. I love you. I want to marry you. I'm not going to leave you."

She chewed on her lip and stared at the road ahead. He wasn't sure she believed him, and he searched for the right words to convince her.

"I couldn't blame you if you left," she said. "My life is such a mess."

He reached for her hand and squeezed it. "But it's not your mess, baby. This is not your fault. This is not you, and even if you still lived here, it wouldn't be you."

"I'd probably be better off if it was. I hate this life, but the farther I get away from it, the more it hurts me."

"I don't understand."

"I can never soar high enough to rescue anyone but myself. I can earn just enough to patch things for my family and to buy myself a separate life but never enough to help them find their dreams, only mine. The guilt of that takes away all my victory."

He suddenly understood why she'd lost so much of her joy and hopefulness. "That's not fair," he said.

She shrugged, and before he could point out that her family had a responsibility for their own dreams, she continued. "I can never catch my breath before something else bad happens. And now, now my mother's having another medical crisis. Gene is dead, and Del could go to the electric chair for murder. But oh, he's still passing out judgments. He just reminded me that I don't take responsibility for my bedridden mama, and it's true. If I had to stay around her, I'd suffocate and die."

"You don't have to be someone's human sacrifice to be responsible. I just got an earful from Betty Jo about how you take responsibility, not that any of it surprised me. She told me how you got her into nursing school this fall and helped her get a scholarship."

Betty Jo took a left at a fork in the road, and he followed passing a row of mailboxes. "She also told me how you've paid your mother's pharmacy bill for the past five years. And that you've paid her heating and electricity bill every month even though your brothers and sister-in-law have all been as ablebodied as you." It infuriated him to see how her family emotionally abused her, especially Del. "I'll kick Del's ass if he keeps harassing you about it."

"But you can't, David. Don't you see that has the potential of ruining you? I can't let that happen. I have to fight this battle myself."

"Don't think for a minute that I'm going to stand by and watch them hurt you."

"I love you for defending me, but I don't want this to touch you. Please. I don't."

"That's how it is when you're one with someone, baby. What touches them touches you. It's part of those vows we're going to take."

"I know." She gave in just a little, but he knew it was only temporary. She hadn't fully accepted this part of their relationship, the part where she shared her pain with him. She was getting better about it. He knew she was trying, but absorbing pain for the people she loved seemed a conditioned reflex for her.

Abruptly Betty Jo gave a left-turn arm signal and waved. Laurel motioned him toward a short driveway to their right. As he pulled into the grass and packed-dirt parking area, Laurel spoke again. "My grandparents asked me to stop by. They're upset about this, too."

He nodded, and as they got out of the car he looked around. His first glance of the place reminded him of the Marlboro ad he'd seen in last week's issue of *Life* magazine. The only thing missing was the snow.

The cabin was built of rough-hewn logs faded to a rustic gray. The front gable framed a large rock chimney with a window to its right, and its roofline extended to cover a porch on each side. Wings jutted to each side of the main cabin recessed behind those porches. The left wing held a rectangular window, and the right one held a door. Smoke curled in gray, translucent spirals from the front chimney and from a smaller one tucked at the back of the cabin.

They stepped onto the left porch that held a wooden bench, a neat stack of logs, and two wooden rocking chairs. When Laurel's grandfather opened the door to her knock, David breathed in the pleasant aroma of the cozy interior. It was a mixture of burning wood, the clean scent of soap, and the smell of cookies baking. Although the furnishings weren't sophisticated, he couldn't think of a single other place he'd been that looked more warm and inviting.

They hung their coats inside a pine wardrobe to the left of the thick plank entry door, and Laurel's grandfather directed them to the sofa across the room. The sofa had a wooden frame with overstuffed cushions draped with a red and yellow wedding ring quilt. In the seating area the wide plank floor was covered with a hooked rug in muted earth tones. A Shaker-style rocking chair with floral patterned cushions of bright primary colors sat perpendicular to the sofa just off the rug but close enough to catch the warmth of the fire.

Lewis Harper had a firm handshake, and his blue eyes radiated warmth. He looked to be in his mid-seventies. He was as tall as David's six feet with thick gray hair. Mama Rita, who had just entered the room and greeted him like she'd known him forever, barely came to his shoulder. She was roundly plump with smooth skin, welcoming blue eyes, and a head of neatly coifed hair that looked like white cotton candy. She wore a dress in a tiny floral print topped with a solid-colored bibbed apron.

Mr. Harper took a seat in a comfortably worn leather chair to the right of the rocking chair, facing them. Tucked in the corner to the left of the front window and close to his end of the sofa David noticed a desk sprinkled with an open Bible and several other open hardback books. One of the books was a Strong's concordance. A simple bookcase holding two more shelves of thick hardbacks hung above the desk. An oak chair on rollers sat pushed back from the desk as if it had just recently been vacated.

"It's right chilly outside," Mr. Harper said. "The weatherman on channel four says it might snow tonight." He gestured toward the large console television that sat turned off in the opposite corner near the wardrobe. "I'm gonna lay him a wager on that one 'cause these old bones don't ache."

"Hot cocoa is just the thing for this kind of weather," Mama Rita said. "I'll go make us some." She was out of the room before he could ask her not to go to a lot of trouble, although hot cocoa did sound wonderful.

He exchanged a smile with Laurel. She seemed totally at ease in this house unlike in the one where she grew up. "Gena sends her love," she said loud enough that her grandmother could hear from the nearby kitchen.

Mama Rita stuck her head around the door. "Tell Little Miss Sunshine that Marita and Grandpa love her, too. I made her favorite chocolate-glazed cookies this morning. I'll send her a batch." She disappeared from the doorway, and he could hear her humming above the muted clinking and more pronounced clanking as she moved around in her kitchen.

Mr. Harper got up from his chair and grabbed the poker that hung on the wall behind the brown enamel stove. He opened the door and stoked the fire. Then he reached into the massive steamer trunk in the corner behind the stove for a large chunk of wood. He added it and two smaller pieces to the fire, stoked some more, closed the stove door, and hung up the poker.

He dusted his hands on his overalls and took his seat again. "This is sure a sad time. Betty Jo says your mama's better this morning. Will said Del didn't have a whole lot to say when they bailed him out of jail. Joshua felt sorry for him. He thinks he was just reacting to that PCP thing when he was holed up and scared."

"I just talked to him, Grandpa. I was trying to tell him I don't blame him for this. I know Mama's kept him and Gene at odds with each other when it hasn't exactly been called for. Now it seems on top of everything else she's even told him that Daddy ran over him on purpose. When I told him that wasn't true, he accused me of calling Mama a liar. He said Gene called Mama a liar, and look what happened to him and did I want to end up that way."

She'd failed to mention that part of her encounter with Del to David. That greatly concerned him. He'd be sure to find out more about it later.

Mr. Harper sighed and leaned back in his chair. "Sarah just can't leave well enough alone. I don't know what's wrong with that girl."

"Is it true that Del's my half brother? Did Mama really cheat on Daddy while he was in the army?"

The room became totally quiet. All David could hear was the crackling of the fire and the ticking of the wall clock. Mama Rita appeared in the kitchen doorway and exchanged a glance with Mr. Harper. David saw her nod toward her husband then disappear back into the kitchen. Mr. Harper leaned toward them rubbing his hands over his knees.

"Alright, I'm going to tell you about this, honey, because I think it's time you knew. Ma and me wouldn't even know about it, but after that accident with Del, Sinclair was heartsick. He came and talked to us. He talked to us a lot back then. You should know that nobody else in the family knows this, not even Nathan. Now that your mama's told Del, I reckon it'll leak out soon enough. Things like this usually do. I'm surprised the secret's been kept this long. Tell me what you do know and we'll start there."

"That's it. Del said Mama told him the day of Daddy's funeral that he was her real son by a man she was with while Daddy was in the army. It seems he told Gene about it yesterday. It was one of the things they argued about."

"It's true. Del's your half brother and not your cousin. You see, Sinclair got drafted into the army with that first bunch of soldiers in October 1940. He was so good at building they put him in the Army Corps of Engineers right off. They built barracks to house the soldiers they'd be drafting, anticipating we'd get in the war. He was gone that whole first year. During that year Sarah took Gene and went to live in the valley with her married sister. Dorothy and Peter didn't have any kids. They had a lot of friends coming around, and your mama got hooked up with one of them. She got pregnant right away. None of us knew a thing about it. She never came home, and she had Del in the valley hospital. After he was born she pretended he belonged to Dorothy and Peter. He was a couple months old when Sinclair came back home for his first leave. He never suspected a thing. We didn't either."

"She just left her child with her sister?"

"No, they all lived together. There was a housing shortage in the cities back then. Sarah lived with Dorothy and Peter until your daddy came home from the army. She had that job in the valley. She, Peter, and Dorothy all worked different shifts in that munitions factory, and they took turns babysitting. Sinclair got more leave time after that first year so you were conceived in the fall of 1941."

"How could Daddy even be sure I belonged to him?"

"Well, for starters, you look just like him, the way Gene looked just like him."

"Did Dorothy and Peter really get killed at that railroad crossing in 1944?"

"That part was true. Your mama stayed in their valley apartment until your daddy came home in 1945. Most of the women in the apartment building worked so she swapped out babysitting with them."

"When did Daddy learn the truth about Del?"

"The day of the accident when Del got run over. I don't know what started the argument that day. They didn't need much, but Sarah got so mad at your daddy she blurted it out. She showed him Del's birth certificate that listed her as his mother and Sinclair as the father. She *was* legally married to him. When Sinclair saw Del's real date of birth, he knew he wasn't around to conceive him. And, too, Sarah rubbed it in about the real father. Her boyfriend was married, too. Sinclair was fighting mad because she'd cheated on him. That's why he stormed out. It just about killed him that Del got run over because of their fighting. I never saw your daddy cry much as a grown man, but he cried a lot over that. He loved Del. As far as he was concerned he belonged to him even when he thought he was Dorothy and Peter's boy."

As Laurel took in everything her grandfather was telling her, she looked overwhelmed. It was shocking stuff. David would never have figured that Sarah Harper would have this particular skeleton in her closet.

"There's more," Mr. Harper said.

"What else, Grandpa?"

"There was another baby."

"What! When?"

"Sarah had a stillborn baby girl in 1944 just before her sister and brother-in-law got killed. She told everybody the baby was full term when she lost her."

"But she belonged to Daddy, right? He was coming home on leave a lot by then."

"He thought she was his until Sarah told him better. You see the truth was, the baby was not full-term. Sarah knew she was only seven months along, and counting back there was no way the baby belonged to your daddy. It was that same married man who was the father. I reckon your mama hadn't got him out of her system yet."

"When did Daddy find out the truth?"

"When he was building the foundation to his dream house, they got into it about something. He didn't say what, but like Sarah always did, when she got mad, she went for the heart. When she told him about it, it just sucked the will right out of him. He quit that dream house and never went back. He told me he was doing it for you kids; but your mama kept working against him, spending their money, and he was tired of beating his head against a wall."

"I remember that day. He threw a shovel at Mama and walked away. He wasn't trying to hit her. He was just mad."

Mr. Harper sighed and leaned back in his chair. "Sarah and your daddy should never have gotten together. They didn't suit each other. I reckon they thought it was love at first or Gene wouldn't have already been on the way before they married, and they did do alright for awhile."

"They had to get married!" Laurel sounded more angry than shocked. Intuitively David knew it was because of her mother's hypocrisy. This information made him wonder why she'd reacted so judgmentally about their one night together. But he'd seen that mindset before. Usually it was the people with the wildest pasts who were the most judgmental.

"It happens," Mr. Harper said. "We didn't let it make any difference. Everybody knew it, and that didn't help matters. Sarah showed a lot of remorse because the whole thing disappointed her daddy. She was her daddy's baby girl. When Gene almost died at birth Sarah figured it was God's retribution for her sin." He shook his head. "God don't work that way. Sarah should have known better than that, but I reckon guilt warps the thinking."

"So what happened to make Mama and Daddy hate each other so much?"

"Your mama was always a dreamer. I think she dreamed Sinclair into something he never could be. She started trying to change him into what she wanted right off, and that's when their fighting started up. I reckon it took her awhile to realize she'd made a mistake; and when she did, all she wanted to do was get out of the marriage, but she couldn't find a way. A fling with another man didn't help. He didn't fill the bill either. He just complicated her life with something else for her and Sinclair to argue about. When she told Sinclair about it just to taunt him, it was the end for them. He only stayed with her for you three kids."

"Why didn't she divorce Daddy if she hated him so much?"

"She didn't have anywhere to go."

"But when Mama finally got the money from Daddy's settlement and could be independent, why did she just blow it? Daddy was already gone. She didn't have a bad marriage anymore. Why did she throw it all away and self-destruct?"

He shook his head. "Guilt maybe, for cheating on him, for what happened to Del. She was as much to blame in running over him as Sinclair was, but she shoved it all off on him. Maybe in some deep part of her she knew it takes two to make the kind of fight that makes you so blind with rage that you forget what you're doing to your kids. Or maybe she couldn't stand coming face to face with her dream of being independent and seeing it couldn't make up for the love she was missing. She finished their dream house and it didn't help."

"That place is a nightmare, Grandpa. It's not what Daddy planned. I remember his cardboard model and how proud he was of it. Why did she let Cecil botch it when Will and Joshua could have made the dream come true? It would have cost her nothing but the building supplies."

"I can't answer that for sure, but misguided dreams have caused mankind more than a few tragedies that didn't have to happen. It's sad. Sarah just gets sicker, and now we've got all this."

Laurel's grandmother entered the room bearing steaming cups of cocoa on a sheet cake pan draped with a yellow tea towel. "Sarah learned a bad way of getting attention from the time she was Gena's age," she said picking up the conversation. "I reckon that has a lot to do with what's going on with her right now."

Laurel glanced up at her grandmother. "What do you mean, Mama Rita?"

"Jonas and Elaine went through some hard times when Sarah was a kid. They argued a lot, and Jonas wouldn't go to church. Then Sarah got scarlet fever and almost died. That brought her daddy to his knees because he loved his little girl more than life itself."

She paused to serve David one of the steaming cups of cocoa. He took it and the cloth napkin she extended. "Thank you," he said.

As she handed Laurel a cup she kept talking. "Jonas straightened up, quit drinking, and became a God-fearing man, and Sarah got well. I think that warped her idea of love, even God's love. I reckon she thinks she has to sacrifice herself by getting sick to make everything go the way it ought to go. But her ought to and God's will don't always fit."

He watched as Laurel set her cocoa on the table beside her. Then she got up and paced, wrapping her arms around herself. This was a lot to assimilate especially in the middle of this tragedy.

"Remember when you used to rescue hurt birds when you were a little thing?" her grandmother asked after handing a cup of cocoa to her husband and setting her makeshift tray on a clear edge of the desk. "You were always trying to heal things, and you helped most of those little creatures."

Laurel nodded. Her grandmother moved closer and rested a hand on each of her shoulders. "Do you remember that robin that broke its wing? When you went to try to help it, I remember it was so scared it pecked you so hard it drew blood."

"Yes," Laurel answered softly biting her lip. "It died because it wouldn't let me near it to help. It thrashed around so much when I tried to splint its wing it made the injury worse and impossible to heal."

"Your mama's like that, honey. Only God can heal her. You have to let him. All you can do is pray that he'll hold her in his arms and pour his love into her soul, that he'll cradle her and not let her go until she's not scared anymore and until her bitterness melts away. You may not get to see that happen, honey, but God can do it."

"I don't know how to let it go, Mama Rita. I want God to be in control, but Mama expects so much from me. No matter what I do, I never meet her expectations."

Laurel's grandmother hugged her against her ample breasts as if she were consoling a child even though Laurel stood almost a head taller. "Giving things over to God takes awhile, honey. Just keep praying and giving it over." She patted Laurel's back, and she withdrew and smiled. "Now, I'll have lunch ready in about thirty minutes, and I want you and David to stay and eat. Why don't you show him around outside after you have your cocoa? Bossie's new calf has grown so much you won't know him."

* * *

When they stepped off the kitchen porch into an expanse of thick grass that led past a small well house, David took in the two outbuildings made of weathered wood. They were in good repair. One stood just behind an expanse of wooden rail fencing and looked to be a small barn. The building to its right had a chicken-wire fence surrounding it, and he could see hens and roosters inside.

They walked up to the wooden fence where three cows grazed inside, and a baby calf trotted over. Laurel reached through the fence and rubbed the calf's head. When the brown and white animal nuzzled her arm she held out the sugar cube she'd brought for him.

"David, meet Milky Way. Gena named him."

"For the constellation?" he asked.

She laughed for the first time since this whole nightmare had started. "No, for the candy bar. You of all people should know how much Gena loves them. You're always spoiling her with treats."

"I'll spoil both of you for the rest of my life. All you have to do is set a date."

She smiled at him as the calf licked the last of the sugar from her palm. He leaned his elbows on the fence rail and gazed around him. "This is a nice place."

She dusted off her hand and reached to pet the calf one more time before turning to lean against the fence.

"Grandpa made his living farming, and he still has a small working farm. Every summer he has a nice garden. He's got fruit trees back there in the meadow: apples, peaches, and pears plus a Japanese walnut tree. Mama Rita cans and freezes the produce in the fall. They have these chickens for both meat and eggs and their cows for milk and butter. They have a couple of pigs, too."

"My grandfather has a farm. I loved going there as a kid."

"Gena feels the same way about this place. When my grandparents kept her, Grandpa would take her out to gather eggs and let her help him feed the animals." She glanced up at him and smiled. "She's named all the chickens. She loves it here. I always did, too. It was like home."

"Gena's very much like you. The physical resemblance is uncanny."

"I guess the Harper genes are so strong they don't have to go in a straight line. I look more like my Aunt Clara, Betty Jo's mom, than she does."

"Betty Jo told me she went to high school at the old army base and that after school she used to walk the quarter mile from school to the hospital to catch a ride home with you."

"Yes, when I'd come here to get Gena, I dropped her off."

"She said you trained her to be a phlebotomist and got her out of her last study hall so she could work a few hours for extra money. She said that's how she got interested in becoming a nurse."

"She was better than my seasoned phlebotomists. Patients loved her. She saved to buy her truck with the money she earned there after school, weekends, and summers. She helped me move in that truck."

He turned to lean backwards against the wooden fence and pulled her against him settling his arms around her. "Your grandparents are wonderful. I like them a lot."

She rubbed her hands against his chest. "Thank you. They've been an oasis in a desert of pain."

"Why didn't you tell me Del threatened you?"

"He might have just been letting off steam."

"I doubt it from what you told your grandfather and the way he acted when I was there. I don't want you around him unless I'm with you, Laurel. Promise me."

She looked up into his eyes, and her expression softened.

"I'll kick his ass if he ever hurts you. That's a promise. But I don't want you hurt in the first place, so please stay away from him."

She snuggled against him, wrapped her arms around him inside his jacket, and lay her head on his chest. "I love you. You know that, don't you?"

"Yes, I do. Sweetheart, don't ever apologize for where you came from. It made you the wonderful person you are, and you should be given accolades for how far you've come all by yourself. You're my hero."

Chapter Twenty-Four

Even though Laurel felt drained from her emotionally challenging morning of funeral arrangements, confronting Del's craziness, and visiting Mama at the hospital, she decided to go ahead and tell Gena about Gene's death. Up until now all she knew about this whole ordeal was that Gene had been hurt by what Laurel had described as an accident and that hearing about it had made Grandma Sarah sick. David agreed with her decision and promised to give her moral support.

After they picked Gena up at David's parents' house, Laurel gave her time to settle and play with her doll and dollhouse. About an hour before dinner she decided to go ahead with their discussion.

"Gena, sweetie, could you and your dolly come sit by Mommy and Daddy?"

Gena hadn't needed a ceremony to seal David's proposal to her. He was God's answer to her prayer. She recognized that and embraced it. As far as she was concerned, he became her daddy the second he proposed. Laurel didn't confuse her with legalities. She wished it could be that uncomplicated for her.

Gena bounced over immediately and crawled up between them on the couch. "Daddy and I love you very much, sweetheart. I'm sorry we've been away so much yesterday and today." She couldn't do this without prefacing the whole thing by emphasizing how important she was. She ran her fingers through the child's soft curls. "Did you have fun at Granny and Pop's house?"

She nodded. "Granny showed me pictures of Daddy when he was a little boy. And she told me he would never be quiet in church, and sometimes he got spankings." Her eyes sparkled with mischief.

David laughed and bent to tweak her cheek. "Now, don't you be listening to Granny about that. I was an angel."

She exchanged a smile with him and continued. "We had an extra special Thanksgiving this year, didn't we? The best thing about it is that Daddy asked us to be his family, asked you to be his little girl."

"And now he's my daddy. And I got Granny and Pop, too." She paused and looked up abruptly. "I didn't get to see Grandma Sarah though and take her some plum pudding. Is she okay? Is Uncle Gene okay?"

"We need to talk to you about that, sweetheart," she began softly. David reached across the back of the sofa and squeezed her shoulder in support. "Remember that I told you Uncle Gene got hurt and worrying about it made Grandma sick again?" Gena nodded. "Well, Grandma is getting better, honey, but Uncle Gene got hurt real bad."

"Is he at the hospital where you used to work, where Grandma Sarah is?"

She exchanged a glance with David. "No, honey, he was hurt so bad that God took him to Heaven so he wouldn't be in so much pain." Her voice broke, but she quickly controlled it.

"Is God gonna take Grandma Sarah, too, since she has so much hurt all the time?"

Laurel hadn't expected that question, and she hesitated searching for the right thing to say. But David rescued her. "God has a time planned for everyone to come live with him. It's not your grandma's turn yet."

"Did you get to tell Uncle Gene bye, Mommy?"

She thought about Gena's question. The literal answer was no, but in her heart she'd been telling him good-bye since she heard the news of the stabbing. "I didn't get to say the words with my mouth, but I said it with my heart."

Gena grew unusually quiet. She fidgeted the way she always did when she was thinking about something, and Laurel exchanged a wary glance with David. Abruptly Gena looked up at her again. "If somebody makes you promise to keep a secret, can you ever tell?"

She felt a strong sense of foreboding. "You should never keep secrets from Mommy, honey. It's okay to tell Daddy and me any secret you have. Who told you a secret?"

"Grandma Sarah."

She grew even more apprehensive. What had Mama done now? Leaning toward Gena, she spoke very gently. "What did Grandma Sarah tell you?"

"She said Uncle Gene's my real daddy, and a bad lady's my real mommy."

Even though this was the threat Mama had held over Laurel's head for six months, the one she had taken such pains to guard against, she hadn't expected this. Not really. She'd thought that even Mama would consider the damage she could cause Gena and keep quiet. It seemed she had given her too much credit. She leaned toward Gena. "When on earth did she tell you that, honey?"

"The last time we went to her house when you talked to Uncle Del in the kitchen."

That had been the Saturday before Thanksgiving, two weeks ago. She'd thought she was being careful. She'd been trying to talk some sense into Del about sticking to the prescribed dosages for Mama's medications, and she'd made sure that Connie would be present while she was out of the room. Mama would never say something like that in front of Connie because she knew Connie would tell her about it immediately.

"But Aunt Connie was with you," she said gently. "Did Grandma Sarah tell both of you?"

"She made Aunt Connie go up the steep stairs to get the manger scene. She told me while Aunt Connie was gone. She said not to tell."

She knew why Mama had done this. She was mad at her for taking Gene's side in the PCP incident, and now she'd created a dilemma for her at the worst possible time. Even though she'd been planning what she would say since the day Gena was born, right now she wasn't sure any of it was good enough. Then David rescued her.

"Sweetie, do you know what it means that Uncle Gene is your real daddy and another lady is your real mommy."

"Uh huh. God gave me to them first, but they didn't want a baby so he gave me to Mommy. Now she's my real mommy."

Laurel reached to clasp Gena's hand in both of hers. "Uncle Gene loved you very much, sweetie; but he didn't know how to take care of you, and so he asked me to. I loved you from the minute I saw you, so he didn't have to worry about you being loved."

"What about that mean lady?"

What could she say about Renee? She could barely stand the thought of her. She didn't want to lie to Gena, but neither did she want to tell her the awful truth. She bent toward her and smoothed the locks away from her forehead.

"Her name is Renee, and Uncle Gene named you after her and himself. She was very pretty, but she wasn't grown up enough to be a mommy. When God sees that first mommies and daddies can't take care of his babies, he finds somebody who can. I was so happy and proud that he chose me because the minute he put you in this world I fell in love with you. I love you with all my heart, and I always will."

"And God choosed David to come and be my daddy?" Gena glanced at her first and then at David. David answered this time.

"That's right. I loved your mommy before you were born, and she loved me. God chose us for each other. But sometimes grownups can't see what God is doing, and we get mixed up and don't follow his plan. But, see, God was watching over all three of us the whole time. When he saw that the time was right, he got all of us together again so I could have the honor of being your daddy."

"Since Uncle Gene's in Heaven, God probably already told him what he did so he won't have to worry about me."

"I'm sure he did, honey," David said.

"Sweetie," Laurel said, "I'm sorry Grandma Sarah told you before I thought you were ready to know, but this doesn't change what's between you and me. You're my little girl. You're part of me. Do you remember what I've always told you about where you grew inside me?"

"Right here," Gena said reaching to place her tiny hand over her chest, "in your heart." Then, undaunted and resolute, she added, "Marita says the bestest things come from your heart."

That almost reduced her to tears. "That's exactly right," she said. She leaned forward and touched Gena's cheek with her palm. "If you have any questions at any time, I want you to ask Daddy or me. Okay?"

"Okay, Mommy."

Before long they had dinner and spent their typical evening together. She kept waiting for Gena to show signs of trauma, but she didn't. After they tucked her into bed and before David left for his apartment, the two of them sat at the dining room table going over the plans for Gene's funeral. It was scheduled for Tuesday afternoon. She'd never done this and hoped never to do it again, but she needed to be sure she didn't miss anything.

"Mama had already called the funeral home before I got there this morning. She planned everything in detail down to the pallbearers. All I did was pay for it."

"The lady at Pike's told me she'd made most of the arrangements. So, Gene didn't have a burial policy, after all?"

"No. Mama said she couldn't get him interested in taking one out, not that I blame him. Maybe if Mama spent more energy on relationships that are alive, my family wouldn't have turned out the way it has."

She reached for her purse to fish out her notes and the receipt the funeral director had given her. When she groped inside the purse, she also saw the paper bag he had given her. It held the items that had been in Gene's pockets. She laid it on the table in front of her and toyed with it not ready to confront the last things that had touched her brother's body before he died.

"What's that?" David asked.

"Everything Gene had on his person when he died. The, uh, man at the funeral home gave it to me."

"What's in it?"

She shrugged. "I don't know. I can't bring myself to look at it."

"Would you like for me to? It's probably his billfold with driver's license, pocket change, keys, and things like that."

"Please do."

David emptied the contents of the bag onto the table and began sorting through it. She averted her eyes. She'd had enough for one day. She couldn't take any more. She tried to consciously suspend her brain in limbo, but abruptly she became aware that David was speaking to her.

"Laurel, honey." He reached to squeeze her hand. She looked into his eyes. "He signed a paper giving me permission to adopt Gena. He even had it notarized."

He passed the wrinkled and creased sheet of paper he'd just unfolded across the table to her. She scanned it and looked up. "Even though he and I talked about it over the phone the night after Thanksgiving, I didn't think he'd get around to actually doing it. He was all for it, but he tends to put things off." She paused abruptly and thought about her words. Then she repeated softly. "He used to put things off."

David squeezed her hand again. "Another thing. There's two thousand dollars in cash in his billfold." He spread the billfold to reveal the bills, and he removed them and counted them out for her.

"It's the money I gave him to start over, to have his car fixed and find an apartment, to keep him going until he got stabilized." She flipped absently through the stack of bills and saw that it was the exact increments she had given him, twenty one-hundred-dollar bills. "He didn't jump to immediately change his life the way I would have if someone had done this for me, so I thought he might use it on booze or drugs. What was he waiting for, David?"

"You said your mom was hassling him to stay at her house. Maybe he was waiting until after the holidays because of that."

"But why was he working on fixing his car himself when he had the money to pay for having it done? Mama said he and Del got into the argument while he was changing his carburetor."

"Maybe he was trying to prove that he could still do it. You said he liked to tinker with cars. Maybe it was a small way to prove himself after the humiliation of the mental hospital."

She picked up the stack of bills and laid them on the funeral home receipt. Tears filled her eyes at the irony of the situation. "I wish he hadn't waited. Two thousand dollars could have saved him. Instead it buried him."

"I know it hurts, baby, but you tried your best," David said softly.

"I don't understand it. I couldn't wait to get out of that house away from Mama. What made my brothers and me so different? Is it because I'm female? Did I get more chances than they did?"

"I think it has to do with your choices."

"In what way?"

"Betty Jo told me that Gene was so smart they let him skip a grade in grammar school, but he got bored and quit in tenth grade so he could get a job and buy a car."

She nodded. "Our parents were fighting a lot around that time." She drew endless figure eights on the back of the funeral home receipt. "Not that they didn't always argue, but I thought he was trying to escape to a life of his own. He burned his bridges when he quit high school. That made it hard to find a good paying job although Daddy and my uncles did hire him to work in their construction business. He narrowed his options even more when he got addicted to his escape mechanisms—booze and wild women. He missed a lot of work because of his lifestyle. Anyone else would have fired him."

"Betty Jo also said that Del turned down a four-year scholarship to college."

"That was after Connie married the door-to-door salesman. That broke his heart, and he just gave up on life. He finally settled into a job with Daddy, but he hated it."

"I understand that he broke up with Connie and moved on to another girl. That she married the other guy on the rebound because he broke *her* heart."

"That's true."

"And he could have gone to college even later. It would have been easy to qualify for another scholarship with his IQ. I understand he tested at genius level."

"Yes."

"And there's the fact that your mother set him up in that ambulance business. I understand it was highly successful when he just walked away from it and threw away both its potential and the money your mother invested in him when he could have sold it and lived well."

"Yes, he did that," she acknowledged.

"And when Connie came back into his life he didn't cherish the second chance he got. He did nothing but diminish her until she became so dependent on him she couldn't ever leave him again. She lost her children. She got addicted to hard liquor, and he didn't try to help her with any of it. He's most likely the cause for most of it."

He knew a lot more than she'd ever told him, and she cringed. "Betty Jo told you a lot."

"I see a lot for myself, too, Laurel. "You had the same parents they did. You experienced the same heartache. You thought we'd lost each other, but you didn't throw your life away. Instead you funneled your love and energy into Gena. She wouldn't have had much of a chance without you, and because of you, she's a happy and well-adjusted child. You thought nobody could ever love and respect you because you came from the have-not side of that mountain, and yet you had the fortitude to work hard and became a success all by yourself."

"Something my mother calls getting above my raising."

"But your grandparents don't think that or Betty Jo and her family. Can't you see that your mom and Del both diminish your success and use it to their advantage? They punish you for the freedom you've earned by making you pay rent on your existence, and that rent is in the form of making you watch and pay for their self destruction." He reached to squeeze her hand. "Honey, you can't rescue people who don't want to be rescued, and you're not responsible for fixing them. That's their responsibility."

She couldn't begin to understand how he could empathize so well when his family was so normal. She'd known for a long time that her family didn't want to be rescued, even Gene, or he would have been gone from Mama's house on Thanksgiving Eve. He could have been well on his way to healing his life instead of lying dead in that funeral home.

So many times she'd thought of her family as drowning victims. When she tossed out a rope to rescue them, because it wasn't the type of rescue they wanted, they forced her to stand on the shore and watch them drown. "I can't believe you understand," she finally said.

"Well, I do. And I know the next few days are going to be hard, but I'll be there with you. Please don't forget that."

"I won't forget, David. Thank you for offering to be a pallbearer, but Mama had already chosen them. It's probably just as well that you're not. Having your name listed in the obituary as a doctor would be too much of a red flag for Renee."

"Do you think she'll come to the funeral home or the funeral?"

"I don't know what to expect, but if she thinks there's easy money in it for her, she'll come around eventually."

"I have an attorney friend. I went to high school and college with him. I'll call him soon and see where we stand. We need to be prepared for the worst."

Chapter Twenty-Five

At the funeral home visitation David met Laurel's extended family. Since visitation was for two days, Sunday and Monday, he got on a first-name basis with most of them. Unlike her immediate family, they were normal—at least as normal as his extended family. He met quite a number of the neighbors from the community, too. That was an eclectic bunch.

He met Banjo Whitt, Gene's best friend and drinking buddy, and his twin sons, Ben and Bobby. The Moore County Civil Defense unit visited on Sunday. They came as a unit and dressed in full uniform out of respect for Laurel's mother. Betty Jo told him that Mrs. Harper was a founding member of the group.

He stayed close to Laurel the entire time. He realized how much she hated the gossip and small talk. It did seem inane in the face of her grief. Betty Jo was exceptional. She stayed close to both of them and did the introductions they both knew Laurel didn't have the energy for.

Given her age Betty Jo was a master at moving people along. He'd been most grateful for that talent when he met the eccentric Jennie Austin. The woman had almost talked his ears off while Laurel went to get her mother a glass of water. Betty Jo, who had taken a bathroom break at the same time, reappeared and quickly rescued him.

The service was held at eleven o'clock Tuesday morning at the funeral home with Reverend Jimmy Powers officiating. David had met him at the first visitation. The twenty-five-year-old pastor was Laurel's one choice in the arrangements as the minister Mrs. Harper had chosen suffered a recent stroke and couldn't officiate.

Laurel told him she had chosen Jimmy because of his pure heart. She said if anyone could bring peace and meaning to this awful situation it would be Jimmy. Once the eulogy began he understood her choice.

Jimmy was neither formally educated nor ordained, and his diction was simple and unaffected, full of verb-subject disagreements and colloquialisms. Yet it was the most touching eulogy he'd ever heard, delivered so sincerely, so imbued with God's mercy and love for his fallen children that David had a hard time holding back his tears.

He wondered who could walk away from that chapel and condemn Gene Harper to hell for the pain-filled life he'd led after that moving reminder that "*all have sinned and come short of the glory of the Lord*" and none but by the grace of God would be saved.

When the quartet sang the words of the closing hymn, "Softly and Tenderly," a soft sob escaped from Laurel's throat, but she quickly swallowed it. He draped his arm around her shoulder. She needed to allow herself to grieve. She couldn't keep stuffing this pain down much longer.

Immediately following the service he pulled his car in line and followed behind the funeral motorcade as it left the valley and began winding its way up the curving Sunset Mountain highway. Along the entire route vehicles pulled over whenever the terrain allowed it. It was those individual acts of anonymous respect that finally reduced Laurel to tears.

As she sobbed openly, he pulled her closer with his right arm. "It's okay to cry, baby. He was worth your tears. Your pain is worth your tears."

They arrived at Harper Memorial Baptist Cemetery thirty minutes later. Following immediately behind the hearse was Sarah Harper's ambulance. Laurel's grandparents followed in the family limousine along with Nathan and Clara. He and Laurel rode immediately behind them in his car. Her Uncle Joshua and her Uncle Will along with their families drove behind them in their respective cars. Betty Jo and the Whitt twins trailed behind the rest of the family in her truck.

As Laurel emerged from his car, she shoved her sunglasses on and took his arm. They followed the procession from the hearse to the grave plot. Directly ahead of them two ambulance attendants pushed Mrs. Harper's stretcher. Beside her walked Del and Connie. They'd been waiting at the graveyard when everyone else arrived, a fact that made Laurel instantly apprehensive.

"This is not good," she'd commented as they parked. "He's so off-center anything could happen."

He didn't think she was being paranoid at all, and he wondered if they were the only people who thought Del's presence was a tragedy waiting to happen. Laurel's mother seemed to accept his being there. That didn't fit with the comment he'd heard from her immediately following Gene's death. He'd heard her vow to never forgive Del and to never go home again as long as he was there.

When he caught a glimpse of the fully armed county sheriff standing on the fringes of the crowd, he realized that someone else actually had recognized the potential for danger. In addition another armed officer sat in the nearby squad car. He felt Laurel relax when she saw them.

It was frigidly cold, and Laurel's grandfather had told them they'd had some sleet this morning. Before they left the funeral home Laurel had tried to convince her mother not to come graveside. Pneumonia was the last thing she needed again. When

Mrs. Harper adamantly refused to listen to her, Laurel spoke with Jimmy and made sure the graveside service would be brief. They'd already paid their respects, she told him. Nobody could do any more for Gene.

Once they'd all gathered at the grave plot, Jimmy delivered a short but heartfelt prayer. Afterwards, the pallbearers, Banjo Whitt, his twin sons and Laurel's uncles, Will, Joshua, and Nathan, lowered Gene's coffin into the grave and began to shovel in the dirt. Laurel had told him earlier that she dreaded this part of the service. She hated the finality of it, and it was the part that reminded her most of her father's funeral. He pulled her closer hoping to give her some comfort.

He expected Mrs. Harper to erupt into hysterical tears the way she had at the funeral home, but she didn't. Connie cried, maybe for Gene, maybe for her husband who faced life in prison or the electric chair, or maybe for herself, but who could blame her? None of this was her fault. Del didn't shed a tear, and he didn't say a word to anyone.

In less than ten minutes it was over, and the hospital attendants shuttled Mrs. Harper back into the ambulance. He and Laurel walked alongside her stretcher on the way. Del and Connie walked on the opposite side, but they didn't communicate.

When the driver backed the ambulance up and headed out to the hospital, Del and Connie got into their car and followed. He and Laurel and the rest of the mass of mourners filed back down the graveyard path toward the parking lot.

"A lot of people came to pay their respects," he said softly noting the number of people who had been waiting at the graveyard for the procession to arrive.

"Funerals are social events in this place," she said bitterly. "I spent my whole childhood trying to figure out why."

Laurel's grandparents left in Will's car, and Clara and Nathan planned to ride with Betty Jo in her truck. As the family left the cemetery, Betty Jo draped her arm around Laurel and hugged her gently. "We'll see ya'll at Mama Rita and Grandpa's." She hurried to catch up with the rest of the family who were already getting in their vehicles.

As he opened the car door for Laurel, he heard a female voice from behind them. "Well, they told me virginal Laurel Harper had a boyfriend, but I didn't believe it. Life is a surprise a minute."

Laurel instantly wheeled toward the voice. "What are you doing here?"

"I came to pay my respects like everyone else."

"Oh, I'm sure," Laurel said bitterly. He didn't know who this was, but he had a strong suspicion.

"Well, aren't you going to introduce me to this handsome man?" The girl's lips curled into a smirk. "I promise, honey, I won't take him away from you."

He slid his arm around Laurel's waist and pulled her close. Then he glared at the stranger. "Just who in the hell are you?"

"Renee Harper, Gene's ex-wife, honey." She glanced from him to Laurel and back again, smugness dancing in her brown eyes. "And Gena's mother."

"There's a lot more to being a mother than a roll in the hay," Laurel said angrily.

"Tell me about it," Renee said.

Laurel shrieked at her then. "You never had morning sickness. You were never the least bit uncomfortable, yet you spent the whole nine months scheming to get rid of her, and when you couldn't, you abandoned her. You wouldn't even look at her much less hold her. That's not a mother. That's a monster."

"But I am her mother. Judges always award babies to their mothers."

"You're not getting her," Laurel said. "You're not dragging her through your sleazy life. That'll happen over my dead body."

Renee smiled haughtily. "My, my, the power of suggestion, and I'm so sleazy you never know what I might be capable of doing."

He spoke gently to Laurel. "Get in the car, sweetheart. Let me handle this." He could feel that she was shaking from anger, but she did as he requested. Then he turned on Renee. "You watch it with your threats, or I'll have that sheriff over there deal with you. And, by the way, a word to the wise: stay away from my fiancée. If you come anywhere near her or Gena, you'll answer to me, and make no mistake, that won't be a pleasant experience."

He walked around to the driver's side and got into the car. By the time he fit the key into the ignition, Renee had lost her haughty demeanor. It must have come as quite a shock to her that she couldn't flirt with him and have him grovel at her feet because she was now shaking her fist in the air yelling, "You haven't heard the last of me!"

"I knew she'd challenge us," Laurel said as he pulled from his parking space and headed down the road toward her grandparents' home. "I didn't think even Renee was classless enough to do it at Gene's funeral."

"Try not to worry, honey. She can't win. She abandoned Gena. No judge in his right mind would give her custody."

"I hope." She twisted the strap on her purse and continued. "I have Mama's situation to deal with right now. I don't have the energy to do that and try to guess what Renee's next move will be, too. I'll just have to deal with that when it happens."

They'd discussed Mrs. Harper's circumstances extensively, and Laurel was torn with unjustified guilt over the whole thing. Regardless of her mother's graveside truce with Del, she'd made it clear that she would never forgive him. That left her with no one to take care of her even if Del did go free. Just last night Laurel had confessed painfully that everything inside her rebelled against taking care of her mother herself. She told him the month she'd lived with her at the inception of her illness had been bad enough.

She wanted to maintain her separate life, and she wanted them to have a chance at their dream of marriage. If she became her mother's caretaker she was certain she would sabotage that dream.

Aside from that she didn't want Gena living in the atmosphere of her mother's orchestrated turmoil. Yet she felt guilty because without Del her mother had no one but her.

Whatever his motivation had been, Del *had* taken care of her mother. His future, however, would be in the hands of the court. His pre-trial hearing was scheduled for this Friday morning, just three days from now. According to Laurel, the Moore County judicial system was brutal. She felt that even if Del got a reduced sentence he'd be gone for awhile. He certainly didn't expect that Connie would stay. According to Laurel her mother had made Connie's life hell.

Laurel had less than a week to work things out. He'd talked to Mrs. Harper's doctor himself, but he hadn't yet nailed down a definite time for her release. The best her doctor could tell him was that it wouldn't be until early next week, maybe Monday.

Laurel had decided to discuss her mother's future care with Nathan since he was her brother and her closest living relative other than her or Del. Nathan had suggested a family meeting at her grandparents' house right after the funeral. It would be the two of them, Nathan, his wife Clara, Betty Jo, and her grandparents.

When they all congregated in her grandparents' living room a short while later and began the discussion, David wasn't surprised when all of Laurel's relatives upheld what she felt before she even had the chance to express it.

"You've done plenty for your mama," Nathan said reaching across him to pat Laurel's arm as the three of them shared the sofa. "You've paid her biggest bills, kept her warm, and kept her medicine coming. That's amounted to a lot of money. You've sacrificed a lot of your life for her. You've got David now, and he comes first. Truth be told, Sis is in a place that's hard for any one person to cope with. Connie calls Clara all the time crying about how hard taking care of her is. Sis can be downright ornery."

Sarah Harper was much worse than ornery. He figured Nathan knew that, but he was being what he'd learned was his usual kind self.

"That rest home Pa was in is a good one," Nathan added. "Maybe you could try to get her in there. I talked to Sis at the funeral home. She's the one who mentioned wanting to go there, or I probably wouldn't have thought about it."

"I agree with Daddy," Betty Jo said as she leaned forward in the chrome and red vinyl chair Mama Rita had brought in from the kitchen. "I've seen what you've done to help. Don't let Del's badmouthing bother you. He's had as much benefit living with Aunt Sarah as she has, probably more. He couldn't pay rent when he had his own place because he didn't want to work that hard. I mean, why else would he throw away his business and Aunt Sarah's investment in it when it was at its peak. He's a dumb-like-a-fox jerk and a lazy shit to boot, that's why."

"Betty Jo!" Clara reprimanded, rolling the desk chair forward until she was even with Lewis Harper's leather chair. "That's not pretty language." David noticed that Mr. Harper turned aside so his daughter couldn't see him chuckling, but he didn't miss it. Apparently neither did Clara.

"Dad, don't laugh at her," Clara protested. "She's loudmouthed enough."

"Mama, it's the truth. I sure haven't heard Aunt Sarah griping at Del about that, not one time. She's on Laurel's butt all the time. She should be proud of Laurel. She takes care of herself and Gena and does all that stuff for them and expects nothing in return. How does emptying a few bedpans compare to that? Besides, Del makes poor Connie do all the real work anyway."

Betty Jo glanced at Laurel and continued. "Just so you know, Laurel, Uncle Joshua and Uncle Will agree with us about this whole thing. They think you've more than done your duty for your family."

He watched as Laurel took in the comments. Finally, she spoke. "I appreciate the support, all of you, but I feel like such a fraud. If you only knew what's in my heart. You're giving me too much credit. I should be more nurturing. If I was a good person, don't you think I'd want to be there helping my poor mother?"

"From the beginning of her sickness you've seen to it that she got the best medical care," her grandfather said. "And you knew where to find that since you worked at the hospital."

"But it hasn't helped. She gets worse and worse," she said. "She lets Del change her medications like he knows what he's doing, but he doesn't. I should have moved back in and controlled the situation myself."

Betty Jo rolled her eyes. "Nobody can control Aunt Sarah. Not even Del does that. She's in control of everything that goes on in that house especially her medications. You used to know that."

"Your mama's strong-willed, and Del does exactly what she tells him to do," Aunt Clara said. "You couldn't change that. You would've just been beating your head against a wall trying if you'd moved back in. And, like Nathan said, you've taken care of the money part."

"But it doesn't help. Nothing I do helps her. It's like she fights me for her right to get worse and worse. And she's so pitiful. She can't feed herself. She can't *even* scratch her nose if it itches. Her rib cage is so caved in that the breath is slowly being squeezed out of her. Not in days or months, but years. Long, painful years. Why? Why?! Why does she choose such pain?"

He watched as her face twisted with emotion, and he knew she was trying to hold back her tears. She got up abruptly and paced in front of the woodburning heater.

"I pray for her every day, but she just gets worse. Why is God not listening to me? Is he punishing me for not doing my part? Am I the one who doesn't fight hard enough, or it is her? Should I give up my life and be at her bedside every day the way Del is? Would that help her or just destroy me? It sounds so simple, just love her, but it's not that easy. She won't let me. Or maybe it's just that I'm too selfish." The more she talked the more frustrated she seemed, and abruptly she dissolved into tears.

He stood and started moving forward to comfort her, but Betty Jo got there first. She draped her arms around Laurel. "Stop this. Stop beating yourself up. You don't deserve it. You don't have a selfish bone in your body."

"But I *do*. I don't *even* want to be around her. She sucks the life out of me."

"That's self-preservation, not selfishness, and exactly the reason you shouldn't be her caretaker. Listen to me." Betty Jo made Laurel look at her. "The medical caretaker who can help the most is the one who does the job without getting emotionally pulled into the disease. You taught me that. Laurel, Aunt Sarah is in a league all by herself. She uses her disease to punish you for being the very things she taught you to be. That's so wrong. If Mama treated me that way, I'd have her shipped off to Siberia, and she could rot there for all I cared."

He could see why Laurel considered Betty Jo her best friend. She was precocious and wise beyond her years, and her sense of humor was always well-timed.

"She would do that, too. Don't think she wouldn't," Clara announced, and even Laurel laughed through her tears.

"Listen to your family, sweetheart," he said gently draping his arm around her waist while Betty Jo hugged from the other side. "They've known you all your life. They know the loving person you really are."

Laurel's grandmother got up from where she'd been sitting in the rocking chair listening to the conversation. She walked over and stood in front of Laurel. She patted her face and spoke softly. "Little Laurie, your mama's sick inside her heart. She can't be healed from the outside, and she's the one who has to do it. Remember that when you're trying to fix her."

Chapter Twenty-Six

On Wednesday morning, with her family's support buoying her spirits, Laurel started the process of investigating nursing home options. Uncle Nathan had assured her again before she and David left the meeting that this was what Mama wanted. She would do her best to make it happen.

Knowing all too well Mama's history of changing her mind, she'd called her last night at the hospital and talked to her at length about this. Uncle Nathan hadn't misunderstood. Mama specifically asked to go to Northwoods Nursing Home.

First, she called Mama's doctor to obtain a referral. Next, she went through a maze of subordinates and finally got to speak with the key authority at Northwoods. By lunchtime her head was pounding. At fifty-five Mama was too young for Medicare, and she didn't qualify for any sort of aid because she owned eighty acres of land.

She could qualify only if the state could attach her property. Without that attachment, cost for her care, not including medications, would come to fifteen hundred dollars a month. Laurel had a good job and her twenty-five hundred dollar savings, which might barely pay two months, but she couldn't afford it after that. The head of the nursing home referred her to a county official who could tell her the process involved in getting county aid.

By the end of her conversation with the Moore County official, she'd given him the go ahead to appraise Mama's property. At least she would have an idea how much aid she could count on from their attachment. Also there was the possibility that once they gained that appraisal, if it was worth enough, Mama could actually sell her property.

It wasn't doing her any good just sitting there. She didn't have anyone to leave it to with Gene gone and Del headed to prison or worse, and she didn't want it. If Mama invested the proceeds of that sale, she could afford her care for the rest of her life. Laurel had already vowed that she would have no part of this if Mama didn't plan wisely this time.

As if this problem with Mama weren't enough, her nerves were on edge because of the confrontation with Renee yesterday. She was going to make trouble. It was just a matter of when and how. She closed her eyes and massaged her temples.

Abruptly she heard David's soothing voice. "Hi, baby."

She opened her eyes and smiled up at him. He was early, and she hadn't heard him come in. "Hi."

"Doesn't look like you've had a good morning. Did you hear from Renee?"

"No. Have you heard anything? She's not above bypassing me to try to get money from you."

"No. Let's go eat lunch. Do you feel like it?"

"I think it'll help. I have a splitting headache from the red tape of trying to make arrangements for the nursing home for Mama. Audrey's been running interference for all my usual duties this morning."

He reached into his pocket for a tin of aspirin. "Take a couple of these once we get to the cafeteria." She tucked the tin into her lab coat pocket, stood, and walked around her desk to meet him.

He draped his arm around her waist. "You can tell me on the way to the cafeteria how far you've gotten with the nursing home."

She leaned into him breathing in the subtle aroma of his aftershave and savoring the comfort of his embrace. He'd been wonderful throughout this whole ordeal, and he hadn't judged her by her family's situation the way she'd feared. Not one time. She'd worried for nothing. It was such a gift to have his love, and the instant this situation with Mama was settled she would marry him.

She spent the rest of Wednesday and all day Thursday catching up on the backlog of duties that had accrued in her time away from the job. By Friday morning she'd caught up, and she hoped it would be a slow day.

Nursing her second cup of coffee, she sat at her desk and flipped through her calendar to make sure she hadn't forgotten anything. The only entry for the day was the note she'd penciled at the top of the December 10th page. It read, "Del's pre-trial hearing." She'd made the notation to remind her, although she'd kept that thought tucked in the back of her mind all week.

She felt sure that Del wasn't going to be free after this morning's hearing. He'd be in jail awaiting his fate. He was charged with murder one, after all, and that charge left only two choices, the chair or life in prison. As far as she was concerned, he needed professional help, not prison. He was clearly over the edge. Prison would make that worse, and death wasn't fair.

Del's imminent absence made it all the more crucial that she get the red tape blocking Mama's admission to Northwoods out of the way, yet Mama seemed complacent about the whole thing. Just last night when she'd spoken with her by phone, Mama informed her that she was to be released from the hospital tomorrow morning and that she'd arranged to go home by ambulance.

"I'll need to speak with Dr. Fuller and have him extend your stay a couple of days until I can work out something with the rest home. There's no one at your house to take care of you, Mama."

"Connie's going to do it," Mama said, "And Del is still out of jail."

"But for how long? His pre-trial hearing is tomorrow morning, and depending on that outcome, his freedom is subject to change."

But Mama didn't seem the least bit worried. Laurel assumed that she'd somehow managed to guilt-whip Connie into staying with her regardless of the outcome with Del. That wouldn't be so surprising. Connie had no other place to go, and Mama wasn't above capitalizing on that fact.

Connie would self-destruct taking care of Mama all by herself even if Laurel did pick up the tab on major expenses. She needed to make firm arrangements about the nursing home soon. If the county didn't call her by two o'clock this afternoon, she'd call them. How long did it take to appraise property anyway? It should've been done by the end of day Wednesday, two days ago. She needed to know the county's decision. Northwoods was holding a place for Mama pending that appraisal.

The calm of her uncluttered day fell apart within thirty minutes of her second cup of coffee, and she got so busy she didn't have time to worry about the appraisal. The SMA-6 broke down before the morning run of electrolytes finished, and the techs had to perform the tests by older backup methods. It was up to her to get the machine back up and operating.

The auto-analyzer manufacturer gave her the run-around the better part of the morning about sending a repairman. She'd finally diagnosed and fixed the problem herself, and by noon she had the machine up and running. She'd learned a lot flying by the seat of her pants at Mountain General, an experience she couldn't have been more grateful for this morning.

She relaxed in her office unwinding from the crisis. She was starving, but David would arrive any minute to go to lunch.

She'd no sooner sat down when Audrey buzzed from the front office where she'd gone to post the assistant's schedule.

"Laurel, I've got a call for you on line two. He says it urgent, and that he's your brother."

"Thanks, Audrey, I'll take it."

As she reached to press the flashing button, she wondered why Del was calling her. It was unusual; but maybe it was about this morning's hearing, and he wanted to discuss Mama's situation. She picked up the receiver. "Hello. Del?"

"What in the hell do you think you're doing, Laurel Elaine?!"

"Excuse me?"

"Don't play dumb with me. What in the hell gives you the right to give the county a lien on this property?"

"I didn't. Only Mama can do that, but they're appraising it. It's the only way Mama can get the care she needs. I can't afford a nursing home long-term. I don't make that kind of money. They said maybe she can qualify for aid through her assets. I thought it was worth looking into."

"Well, you thought wrong."

"Maybe you should talk to Mama about this. She's the one who wants to go to Northwoods Nursing Home."

"Oh yeah? I just talked to her, little sister, and you've got some explaining to do. Let's hear it."

"I just told you!" She raised her voice, but she immediately made herself take a couple of calming breaths.

"Well, for your information Mama don't want to trade her property off to the county 'cause she ain't going to no rest home."

"Really? Well, who's going to take care of her, Del?

"I am, damn it!"

"You!"

"Yes, me. They dropped the murder charge. Got that? I'm gonna be here. I'm taking care of Mama, and nobody's attaching this land. You'd do well to remember that I'm your brother, not your cousin. I've got a legal say in this, and I've got the birth certificate that says I'm a Harper."

"Does Mama know all this?"

"Damn straight she does, and she's mad as hell at you for trying to take her land away and send her to the poor house."

"Mama's mad at me? Really? Because I did exactly what she asked me to do? Well, that figures, but I'd like to hear this from her, if you don't mind."

"Be my guest. And by damn, you call off the county or else."

"Or else what, Del?!" she yelled.

"You heard me!" Then he slammed down the phone. After that all she heard was a dial tone.

Shaking with fury she paced. Then abruptly she stopped, picked up the phone, and dialed Mountain General Hospital. She took several calming breaths as she waited. Then she asked for Mama's room. It rang five times, and finally Mama answered.

"Mama, I just got a call from Del, and I would like for you to explain it to me."

"What needs explaining?"

"First of all, did you or did you not ask me to get you into a nursing home?"

"Well—"

"Answer the damn question, Mama." She didn't usually swear, but she could tell by Mama's hesitation that something was up.

"I didn't mean you could give them my land!" Mama's formerly weak voice was plenty forceful now.

"I didn't. I can't do that. You're the only one who can do that, but you can't qualify unless you let them appraise it. If it's worth enough, once you agree they can attach your assets, but you have to agree before they can do it. All they're doing is an appraisal to see if it qualifies to pay for your care. I don't know what land in that area is worth. Nobody ever sells."

"I thought you were going to pay." Mama's voice had a sarcastic edge.

"I don't have that kind of money, Mama, and I don't make that kind of money. I just used a big chunk of my house equity to pay for Gene's funeral."

"But you're marrying yourself a doctor."

She fumed. She wasn't involving David in this, and how dare Mama assume that she could run roughshod over his life through her. "He doesn't have that kind of money either. He's a resident, Mama. I make more than he does, and any money he had he spent on school. And before you even say it, his family is not rich either. They just planned well, unlike you."

"What's that supposed to mean?"

"You went through a hundred thousand dollars, Mama. You wouldn't listen to my advice about planning and investing. You just threw it away, and I've picked up the tab on a whole lot of things ever since. Because I care. Because I love you. But I'm telling you, Mama, I haven't understood why Del couldn't contribute a cent to keeping himself warm."

"I'm not giving my land away!" Mama almost screamed into the phone.

"You wouldn't be giving it away, Mama, but that's fine. That's up to you. So, we're back to square one now. What are we going to do?"

"I'm going back home. Del will be there. We've done fine so far."

Yes, except that I've paid your utilities, your pharmacy bill, and your balances after insurance, she thought, but she didn't say it. No matter how used she felt, she couldn't bring herself to be that mean. She knew Mama couldn't afford it.

"And I take it Del's not going to prison," she said.

"They let him go. They should have. He told me Gene was crazy drunk, and he didn't have a choice but to defend himself."

"That's strange because when I asked him if Gene had been drinking, he said not at all."

"You talked to him the day after it happened. He was still in shock."

It sounded more like double talk than shock to her, but it was pretty clear that Mama had finally made her choice of who to condemn and who to embrace in this tragedy.

"I don't think Del belongs in jail either, Mama, but he needs help. He's off-center. You know that."

"I don't know anything of the kind."

"So, you've forgotten what I told you about how he threatened me?"

"Oh, you just misunderstood, Laurel. He said he didn't threaten you. You're too high-strung."

She was high strung? What did Mama think she was with her academy-award-winning hysteria?

"Okay, Mama, I'll call the county and tell them to forget it, and I hope you and Del live happily ever after because this is the last time I get involved in your manipulations. And it's the last time I set foot in your house. Whether you'll admit it or not, Del has big problems, and I won't risk my well-being or Gena's over your need to pit us against each other."

"If you really loved me, you'd walk through fire for me."

She didn't say anything. What was the point? The only right answer for Mama was for her to lay down her life and die for her the way Gene had, and how could that help anybody, least of all Mama? As for walking through fires, she'd walked through plenty of them for her, enough to prove her love ten thousand times over. That was all part of Mama's game, too. Mama was the one who set those fires in the first place, testing her, always testing her.

"I had a visit from Renee today," Mama said abruptly in a voice that was suddenly as calm as if she'd just stated that it was raining outside. Her heart began to pound.

"Lovely, Mama. I hope you had a nice visit."

"Renee has her good points."

She exploded then. "Good points!" She yelled into the phone. "She abandoned your newborn grandchild and your son, Mama. She wouldn't even look at Gena. She wanted to get an abortion.

Gena wouldn't even be here if she'd had her way. You know it's true. You were there."

"But she *is* Gena's mother. She told me she hired an attorney, and she's filing for custody."

So this was how it was going to be. For the zillionth time, Mama was meddling and manipulating. She wondered how she could even say she loved Gena and aid and abet the person who could harm her the most.

"I know this game you're playing, Mama. So, listen up. That woman is an unfit human—let alone mother—and she is not getting Gena." With that she ended the conversation. It took all her self-control to keep from slamming the phone into the receiver.

She willed herself to be calm. She flipped her phone index until she found the county number she'd called Wednesday and dialed it. She told the representative as calmly as she could that Mama had changed her mind.

"We know," the county official told her. "We spoke with her yesterday morning and early this morning. We appraised her property at $75,000 after the appraiser went out Wednesday, but we told her that in an outright sale she could probably get substantially more."

She'd been standing by her desk when she placed this call, and now she sank into her chair. She had a bad feeling about this. Why hadn't Mama mentioned talking with the county? Prior to today she hadn't mentioned the appraisal to Mama hoping to spare her the worry.

She wasn't trying to hide anything the way Del had made it sound. She hadn't mentioned it to him because she hadn't expected him to be around to even be involved in the decision-making. She was certain he'd learned about the whole thing when the appraisers arrived on the property Wednesday. Why he'd waited until this morning to call and gripe about it she didn't know.

"You talked to my mother about this yesterday?" she asked. "I'm surprised that she contacted you since she asked me to handle getting her into the nursing home. As I told you she's had a severe setback in her illness from the shock of my brother's death."

"One of the ladies in our office knows your mother. She called her home Thursday morning and got her hospital room number. She wanted to be sure your mother knew about the appraisal. She didn't seem to be aware of it. It's against the law to dispense with property that doesn't belong to you, Miss Harper."

She bristled. "It would be, I suppose, had I done it without her signature, but I hadn't planned that."

"Well, you should be aware that she doesn't want to qualify for any sort of aid and won't be going to the rest home. She told me she wanted to sell half of her property now that she knows what it's worth and keep the rest of it. I would have called you, but from the way she talked, we thought you already knew her plans."

"And you believe she can actually find a buyer?"

"Oh, she already has, for forty acres of it, at least. I put her in touch with a gentleman yesterday morning who's been looking for some rural land for the purpose of starting a cattle farm. All he needs is a caretaker. Your mother volunteered your brother for that. She said his lawyer was certain he'd be released since the incident with your other brother was clearly self-defense. Last I heard the buyer took her an eighty-thousand-dollar cashier's check to the hospital yesterday afternoon. He even brought the officer of her bank to the hospital to notarize the documents and take her check back to the bank to deposit it."

After she ended the conversation, she fumed. Mama had again left out part of the truth, the most important part. She wasn't going to be destitute after all, and it looked as if she had kept that little tidbit from Del as well as from her. Otherwise, he wouldn't have been so upset. It wasn't enough that her manipulations had ultimately killed Gene, now she was pitting her and Del against each other in the same way. Well, she wasn't going to play her deadly game. Not anymore.

She knew Mama well enough to know that she had sold the twenty acres each that Daddy had always promised to her and to Gene. She'd keep Del's promised twenty acres to assure his allegiance and, of course, the twenty that surrounded her house. More power to her. She'd never wanted the land to begin with. All she'd ever wanted was to be free to live her own life without having to feel guilty about it.

She picked up her phone and dialed Mountain General Hospital again. All kinds of alarms were going off in her head. Mama and money spelled opportunity for major manipulation. When the operator rang the room and Mama answered, she dispensed with the salutations.

"Mama, why didn't you tell me you sold part of your land?"

"You didn't ask. Is there a problem?"

"Oh, nothing except for the fact that Del thinks I went behind your back trying to sell it. Why haven't you told him the truth?"

"I just made the sale yesterday, for crying out loud. I'm in a hospital. I'm not exactly in a position to be calling around reporting to everybody."

"So, you'd rather let Del think I'm the bad guy and get us at war with each other before you'd waste a few breaths on telling him the truth?"

"If he thinks that, it's not my fault."

"You did this on purpose, so don't lie to me. I don't care if you sold your land. Just don't make it into a war between Del and me. And Mama, I've got another question for you."

"What's that?"

"You called Renee didn't you? You made sure she knew about Gene's death so she'd smell social security benefits for Gena and show up. We both know she'd never come around if money wasn't involved."

Mama's silence was the only answer she needed.

"She won't win, Mama. I have witnesses to the way she rejected Gena. I have documentation to prove she willingly abandoned her the night she was born."

"She had postpartum depression. She told me she planned to come back, but by the time she got better you'd already gotten legal custody of Gena. She didn't have the money to fight you."

"And she does now? I don't understand why she's doing this. Social security benefits won't amount to that much, and where's she going to get the money for a lawyer. Did a rich relative die and leave her money? Does she have a sugar daddy now or—" She stopped talking the instant the thought crossed her consciousness, and then she reacted. "You gave her the money to hire an attorney, didn't you? The whole thing was your idea. You just got a windfall by selling your property, and you're already throwing your money away. Why, Mama?"

Mama didn't answer.

"I know you did it, Mama, but why? Gena doesn't even know Renee. She's a total stranger to her."

"She's no more a stranger than that husband-to-be of yours is. At least Renee's flesh and blood."

"Flesh and blood is better than someone who loves her? Someone she loves?"

"I won't have my grandchild raised by an outsider," Mama said.

"So you'd rather have a totally immoral woman who just happened to donate a few genes and unwillingly supplied her body as an incubator? Why, Mama?! Why?! Don't you even care about Gena?"

"Renee is Gena's mother. A child ought to be with its mother."

She felt a hot seething anger build inside her chest. Mama didn't love Gena, and she already knew she didn't love her. It was time she asserted her freedom. It was time to cut through Mama's web of guilt.

"She's with her mother. I'm Gena's mother," she said willing her voice to remain calm. "You and Renee have a fight on your hands, Mama. She's *not* taking Gena."

She hung up again without saying good-bye. This was the final blow. Mama always found a way to blame her no matter what she did to help. She was used to it, but she wouldn't let her drag Gena into her manipulations. It was time to draw a line in the dirt.

She was sitting at her desk tapping her pen on its blotter trying to calmly think the whole thing through when David entered.

"Hey, sweetheart, ready to go to lunch?"

She glanced up at him and took in a deep breath. "Do you mind if I get Audrey to run down and get us something from the grill so we can talk in private?"

"No. Why?"

"Before I fill you in, do you think your attorney friend could see us today after work?"

"I'll call. Why? What's happened?"

"In a nutshell, they set Del free because murder's justified in kangaroo court. Mama's not going to the rest home. She's sold half her land so she and Del can live happily ever after on the other half. Renee and Mama are new best friends, and to punish me for trying to put her in the poor house, she's in cahoots with her to take Gena away from me."

Chapter Twenty-Seven

David had placed an immediate call to Roger Willis, and his friend made room in his schedule for them that afternoon of December 10. When they dropped by Laurel's apartment after work to retrieve her adoption documents and to ask Mrs. Archer to stay a little longer, they saw that a registered letter had arrived from Renee Harper's attorney only an hour earlier. She was officially suing Laurel for full custody of Gena. The papers had been filed the previous morning, the same morning Laurel's mother had made the deal on her land. For someone who had been hospitalized for an acute setback in her health, Sarah Harper had certainly been busy.

Their initial visit with Roger had been a somber one. He'd presented all the negatives for them and the positives for Renee. It wasn't an optimistic picture. David realized that attorneys had to cover all bases, but this was devastating news. It felt like the bad guys always won. Laurel was furious with her mother and the entire process and devastated by even the possibility of losing Gena. He didn't know how much more she could take, and he didn't know how to make it all go away.

Five days later on the following Wednesday, December 15, they again sat across from Roger in his downtown office a mile from the hospital. As a personal favor to David, his friend had spent the days since their first visit giving Gena's case priority.

Roger leaned back in his chair after spreading several documents on the desk in front of him. "The good news is that you've got a great case. We can prove abandonment by the birth mother from the father's statement and from the notarized statement of witnesses present at the child's birth. You'll have no problem proving the great care you've given Gena, Laurel. The fact that you're getting married gives you an even better advantage. The document Gena's father signed giving permission for David to adopt her is the icing on the cake. Regardless of all this, we're still going to have to go to court."

Laurel leaned forward, her brow creased with worry. She'd been so upset about this that she could barely concentrate on her job. It had been hard for David, too. He couldn't believe this latest twist her mother had delivered, and he couldn't help believing that none of this would be happening if she hadn't interfered.

"What's the bad news?" Laurel asked cautiously.

"Renee could get temporary custody of Gena while we're challenging her."

Laurel shot to her feet. "No! Roger, that can't happen. She's a total stranger to Gena, and she doesn't really want her. All she wants is money."

Roger leaned forward. "I didn't say it was a sure thing. I just want you to be prepared for the worst-case scenario."

"How can I prepare for that? She's four years old, Roger, and you don't know what this woman is like. She doesn't care about anyone but herself. Can't you do something? Can't you talk to the judge? Can't you make him understand that Gena would be in danger living with that woman even for a day? She's a lowlife."

Roger softened and motioned to Laurel to sit. She reluctantly sank back into the chair. "Look, I'll do my best to see that it doesn't happen. I can see how much you love this little girl."

David spoke up then. "What grounds does this woman have for doing this, Roger? After all these years of total abandonment, what's her excuse for this sudden interest?"

Roger flipped through several pages of the document in front of him and paused to scan one of the pages. "Let's see. It states here that she had postpartum depression when she gave her daughter up and that later when she recovered, she couldn't afford the legal fees to get her back. Now that her ex-husband is deceased and since the child's grandmother is in failing health, she's concerned that a spinster aunt is not a suitable guardian. She feels her child needs a male influence in her life."

Laurel rolled her eyes. She was totally exasperated. "With Renee there would definitely be a constant stream of men passing through. That's what I fear the most. I can't let her subject Gena to her sordid life."

Roger continued. "It also says here that she's in a common-law relationship and that they've been together since she divorced your brother. She was reluctant to try marriage again after the way things turned out with her alcoholic first husband."

"The little hypocrite." Laurel's voice was bitter. "Gene was her second marriage, and she only married him in the first place because they both were drunk. Roger, this is ridiculous. How can any court not see right through her? How can they even waste taxpayer time and money honoring her whim?"

"Stranger cases have been presented. Look, I seriously doubt that any judge would award her permanent custody, birth mother or not. The Child Custody Act of 1970 speaks to that. We have issues of abandonment and estrangement and the added fact that she wouldn't even recognize Gena if she passed her on the street, but please bear in mind, that won't stop her from trying."

"She's only doing this for money. You have to realize that," Laurel muttered bitterly. "She didn't want to be pregnant in the first place. She tried to abort Gena by drinking something some idiot friend told her to try. I'm not even sure what it was."

David glanced at her. "Honey, you never mentioned that before."

"Because I've been afraid to let it cross my lips. I don't want Gena to ever know that, and I didn't want to risk that she would hear me say it. Gene told me right after it happened, and nobody else knew but him, Renee, and me, although Renee has never known that I knew. It's a miracle it didn't thwart Gena's development. Instead she's a beautiful, brilliant child."

"This Renee person is definitely something else," Roger said.

"What else can we do to fight back?" David asked.

"I'll want to speak with Laurel's grandparents who kept Gena and get their statements and any other relative who can attest to Renee's actions while she was married to Gena's father."

"You can also speak with my Uncle Nathan and Aunt Clara and my cousin Betty Jo," Laurel said, her voice infused with a glimmer of hope. "They live across the road from my grandparents."

"How about your parents?"

"My father died from injuries sustained in an auto accident in 1966, and my mother has severe debilitating rheumatoid arthritis. And to be perfectly honest she would do more harm than good."

"How's that?"

"Oh, she knows the truth, all of it. She professes to love Gena, but my mother is manipulative. Right now she's upset with me, so she'll do her best to hurt me."

"Why is she upset with you?"

"She's bedridden, and she asked me to get her into a nursing home when the tragedy with my brothers happened. When I tried and she learned that in order to get aid she'd have to let them attach her eighty acres, she backed out. Never mind that because of the appraisal I had the county make, she's now sold half her land and made a lot of money. Still, she found a way to blame me even though it all ultimately helped her, and she's got my brother thinking I was just trying to take her assets for myself."

"Well, I'm sure we won't need her with the other relatives and your grandparents."

"But she may actively work against us," David added.

"Why would she do that?" Roger glanced from him to Laurel.

Laurel sighed. "You'd have to know my mother. She's controlling. When she can't call the shots, she guilt-whips and manipulates until she gets her way. She's not above lying for Renee."

"Then we'll leave her out of it."

"But what if Renee calls her as a witness?" Laurel asked.

"She's just one person."

"Don't underestimate her, Roger. I have reason to suspect she's prompting Renee and probably even backing her financially. That postpartum depression thing came straight from Mama's soap operas. Renee may be stupid, but my mother is not. Given her debilitation, she's formidable. You won't even know what hit you when she sways the judge."

Roger leaned forward. "Why would your mother do that to you?"

Laurel grew still. She sat staring at her hands. Finally she looked up at Roger. "I wish I knew."

Roger studied her, and finally he spoke. "I'm good at what I do, Laurel. I promise you I'll give this case my very best efforts."

"I appreciate that," she said softly.

"Thanks, Roger." David stood and reached across the desk to shake his friend's hand; but Roger hadn't moved from his spot behind his desk, and he knew him well enough to see the gears turning in his mischievous but brilliant brain.

Laurel stood, too, but before she could speak again, Roger grinned up at them. "There's something else I could try as a last resort if it comes to that, if all our other efforts fail." He made a tent with his fingertips and pursed his lips.

"What?" he asked. He'd seen this look many times before. This was the guy who'd made panty raids infamous at the Baptist college they'd both attended. He wondered what was going on in his devious mind.

"It's back-door stuff, and I'd rather not tell you until I try it."

"This is not going to get you disbarred, is it?" He'd never known what Roger was going to do next in college, but he was a highly regarded attorney now.

"I'm too smart for that." Roger looked up at Laurel. "You said Renee hasn't seen Gena at all since she gave birth to her and wouldn't look at her even then. And she still goes by Harper. Right?"

Laurel nodded and exchanged a glance with him. Roger continued. "Sorry I can't elaborate, but if this works, I can save you a whole lot of time, trouble, and money. It'll be my wedding present to you. If not, we've got the traditional route to pursue. Just in case I've lost my touch, don't get your hopes up."

Once they were inside his car Laurel turned to him. "I'm relieved that Renee didn't drag our night together through the mud and use it against us. She has to know about it. It would be out of character for Mama not to tell her. But spinster? I guess she thinks I'm incapable of passion because I wasn't a slut like her."

"Forget what she thinks. You and I both know she's wrong. Your passion comes from your heart where it counts."

"What do you think Roger's planning?"

"I don't know, but judging from my college experiences with him, I see a panty raid in somebody's future."

She laughed. Her laughter was good to hear. She'd been through so much heartache. He thought a little lightheartedness would benefit them both. He was furious with her mother for the way she'd manipulated the property appraisal to make it look as if Laurel were the bad guy. She hadn't even thanked her for arranging it in the first place even after it turned around instantly to greatly improve her life.

He couldn't imagine any mother treating her child this way. Mom had once been overprotective to the point that he'd perceived her actions as controlling. He'd been so resentful when he was younger that they'd had more than a few standoffs. Eventually, when he'd confronted her in an adult manner, they'd worked things out. She had finally realized that it was appropriate and more loving to let him live his own life and make his own mistakes. Sometimes she still overstepped her boundaries, but she always backed off when he reminded her he was a grownup.

Sarah Harper seemed threatened by the autonomy of her children. It seemed she was capable of anything when it came to keeping them submissive. That was wrong, and to use Gena as a pawn in her manipulations was unconscionable. He wondered what really made Sarah Harper tick. Was she basically mean-spirited, or was she developing the psychosis that went along with steroid treatment? From what Betty Jo had told him she hadn't always been like this. He got the idea that she had always been controlling, but not so tyrannical. What she had set in motion regarding Gena was beyond tyrannical.

He couldn't love Gena more if she *had* been his child. He would do everything in his power to keep her with them where she belonged, but right now he felt powerless. Short of disappearing with her and Laurel if the judge decided in Renee's favor, he couldn't think of a solution. He would try that, but Gena would suffer the most from that sort of action. He knew this had to be done legally, so all he could do was stand firm and pray. In his soul he knew that God hadn't put the three of them together to have them torn apart like this. He had to have faith. He tried, but every day that week his faith was tested.

From their first visit with Roger, he'd called daily to check the status of the situation with Roger's secretary, Teresa. On Thursday, the day after their last appointment, Teresa had given him some unsettling information about Renee's common-law husband. On Friday he learned even worse news. Renee's cutthroat attorney was demanding temporary custody of Gena for the holidays.

According to Teresa, Roger was doing everything he could think of to prevent it. So far it didn't look good because the presiding judge had a reputation for being crooked and for conceding to the worst of birth mothers.

As it stood, there was a great possibility that they would have to surrender Gena to Renee on Christmas Eve. That was a week away. If that happened, it was going to be a heartbreaking Christmas. The deck seemed stacked against them. Not only was the judge sympathetic to unfit birth mothers, but also, per Teresa, he was a good friend of Renee's attorney and always decided in his favor. It was hard to have faith, but he kept praying that God would intervene.

Laurel refused to tell Gena about the custody battle. She felt that Gena was too young to understand, and she didn't want to frighten her if there was even a slim chance that it might not happen. Even though their lives had been turned upside down, Laurel was determined to keep things as normal as possible for Gena. She insisted that they go ahead with their planned festivities.

After work that day he took them to his grandfather's farm to cut a Christmas tree. Gena had been looking forward to that adventure all week. She got to meet his grandparents, and she thoroughly enjoyed tramping through the woods with them to find the perfect tree. That night they trimmed it together the way they'd planned, with Gena's dough ornaments decorating the most prominent branches.

They'd spent the previous evening making those ornaments. They'd worked between sips of hot chocolate topped with marshmallows. Carols played in the background punctuated by Gena's sweet giggles as they helped her form the dough into various Christmas shapes. Her Santa was the masterpiece of the evening. She squeezed white dough through a garlic press for his beard and pressed it onto the misshapen blobs of red and white dough that formed his fat body. He and Laurel used a toothpick to etch "1971" on the back of all the ornaments before popping them in the oven to harden.

That Friday night as he got ready for bed in his own apartment he reflected on the fact that they'd just made their first Christmas memories as a family. He'd taken bunches of pictures to commemorate the occasion, and he was still basking in the glow of the wonderful evening. When the realization hit him that it might also be their last Christmas together, he sank to his knees beside his bed and begged God for a miracle.

On Saturday they took Gena to visit Santa and to look at the animated storefront displays downtown. He and Laurel had already done their shopping, but Gena wanted to buy gifts for her new relatives on his side of the family, his parents and his grandparents. They accomplished all that with a visit to Woolworth's where she bought an apron each for Mom and Grandma and Old Spice aftershave for Dad and Grandpa.

After they finished shopping, they had lunch at the mezzanine at Baxter's Department Store. Gena looked adorable in the red-plaid taffeta dress Laurel had made her. She'd worked on it every evening the week after Thanksgiving while he sat on her sofa nearby reading to keep current in his specialty.

To complete the day they spent the afternoon at his parents' house and had dinner there. Gena, Laurel, and Mom baked and decorated Christmas cookies after dinner. On the way back to the apartment complex they drove around to see the Christmas lights and decorations. Gena sat in Laurel's lap thoroughly captivated by the sights.

"This is the bestest Christmas," she said abruptly. "I told Santa I don't need any presents."

"You did?" Laurel said softly as she cuddled her close. "That was very sweet, but I'll bet he brings you something just for being such a little angel. Anyway, it's okay to wish for something for you."

"Then I wish Christmas is always like this one is right now."

He wished that, too.

Chapter Twenty-Eight

On Sunday morning Laurel got up at six o'clock after a sleepless night of tossing and turning. She would have called David and asked him to come over, but she didn't see the point in his losing sleep, too. He'd be up in an hour anyway. This wonderful week had been overshadowed with an unshakeable sadness for both of them. If not for Gena's high spirits, neither of them could have made it through. David was as worried as she was. The way he loved Gena warmed her heart. As far as he was concerned, she was already his daughter, and it was wrong that custody battles were more about rules of law than about love.

This lawsuit was her worst nightmare realized, and the threat of it hung over their lives like a menacing shroud—one of Mama's ugliest crazy quilts. She understood why Mama had set this in motion. She had to regain control. She'd lost that control in the tragedy with Del and Gene. She hadn't intended for things to go that far. Their battle was supposed to stop at the edge but not go over, and Mama was supposed to save the day by dictating who was to be punished and who was to be absolved. Instead, all she had accomplished was to manipulate herself out of her home.

She realized now that Mama had never intended to go to a rest home. She'd been buying time, sending Laurel on a wild-goose chase while she regrouped and looked for a way to salvage things. And she'd gotten lucky. With the proceeds of her property and by retaining the portion of her land that Del wanted most, she'd bought his loyalty. But to ensure Laurel's she'd have to resort to more drastic measures. Hadn't she seen a lifetime of Mama's schemes played out?

Mama chose her unwitting warriors and laid out her battle plan, and only she was privy to the details. She initiated the battle, and then she maneuvered and manipulated. Usually when the fighting got to a peak, before an inalterable assault was triggered, she would step in and salvage everything, taking the credit for aborting an attack that she had subversively directed in the first place. She always came off as the peacemaker, but peace bored Mama and diminished her control. So, she would repeat the process.

Most of the time she accomplished her goal because usually her manipulations had a rescue point. It was the genius of her strategy. She wondered if Mama had a rescue point in this mess she'd set up with Renee. It would be out of character not to have one. Abruptly, she decided she would try to find out exactly what it was and push Mama toward it.

She glanced at her kitchen clock. It was six thirty. She would give Mama a call now. She awoke early. Del didn't, so she wouldn't have to waste time arguing with him.

Mama answered the phone on the third ring. "Hello, Mama," she said.

"Well, she condescends to call," Mama said. Laurel let her vent and get her fill of demeaning her. Gena was worth it.

Finally, Mama stopped talking, and Laurel took advantage of the lull. "Mama, even though you won't admit it, I know you're backing Renee in this lawsuit. I don't know what you hope to accomplish by doing it, but have you even thought about what this means for Gena?"

"She'll be with her real mother. It's the worst thing in the world for a mother not to be able to acknowledge her child."

Suddenly she realized that Mama must be talking about her situation with Del.

She'd wondered about Mama's secret, and she wanted to know more about it. Still, she hadn't mentioned it. The past couldn't be changed, so why dwell on it. However, she felt she had to point out that Mama's situation and this one weren't even similar.

"Del told me that he's your real child, Mama, but this is not the same thing. Renee abandoned Gena. You didn't do that with Del."

"That's my business, and it's ancient history," Mama snapped.

"It must not be if you're identifying with Renee. Obviously you loved Del's father; but, Mama, Renee didn't love Gene, and she didn't love Gena."

"I'm not talking about this with you. That happened a lifetime ago."

"But you told Del about it five years ago. It would have been nice if you could have shared it with Gene and me, too."

"What for? It didn't concern you."

Oh, it concerned them alright. The fact of the other man's existence had hurt Daddy and turned all their lives upside down, but she decided to let it drop. "Okay, Mama, that's your business. I'll give you that. But Gena's situation is entirely different. Renee's a total stranger to Gena. And while I know you object to David not being flesh and blood, what about this common-law husband of Renee's. He's not flesh and blood. He doesn't know Gena. David does, and he loves her. I love her. Renee will neglect her, Mama. Gena won't have her basic needs met. She won't be paid attention to. She won't be cherished. She's your granddaughter. Do you want that for her?"

Mama didn't say anything, so she pushed on. "You know Gena's happy with me. You know I protect her the way you always protected me."

As a child Mama *had* protected her from predators and unsafe situations even though she'd caused her enough pain since she'd become an adult to balance that protection. Still, she'd been grateful. Mama's nurturing during her childhood had kept her from being wounded beyond repair by the seedier side of their community.

"Do you know anything about Renee's common-law husband, Mama?"

"I know his name's Max."

"Did you know that he's been in and out of jail for the past six years?"

"Your brother's seen the inside of a jail a time or two."

"For public drunkenness, not armed robbery. Not rape of a minor."

"Where'd you get all that?"

"My attorney. And don't even bother telling me it's not true. Lawyers have access to legal records. Mama, you can't want Gena around this man! Don't you see the danger? You protected *me* from people like that. Why would you want to subject your innocent granddaughter to it?"

There was total silence on the line.

"Mama, did you hear what I said?"

"You don't have to worry. Renee won't win," she said.

"Really?" she responded sarcastically. "Unless my lawyer can find a way to stop it, we have to let her have Gena Christmas Eve. That's five days from now. I think that shows she's got a big chance of winning."

"Her money won't last."

"It'll last long enough that Gena will be exposed to that horrible man."

Mama grew silent again.

"Just how much money did you give her, Mama?"

"A thousand dollars. She's not getting any more. She thinks she is, but that highfaluting lawyer will drop her when he finds out that's all that's forthcoming."

"The damage will be done by then. She'll already have Gena." She wanted to scream at Mama for supplying the money in the first place.

"No judge is going to give her Gena when they find out she swallowed some concoction trying to get rid of her when she was pregnant."

Was this Mama's rescue point? She was losing her touch if it was.

"How did you know about that?" she asked.

"Gene mentioned it when he was drunk that week after Gena was born."

"We already know that Mama. Gene told me about it when it happened. You're not going to save the day with this information. We can't prove it, so it's not going to undo the harm you've done."

"I didn't file the lawsuit, Laurel. Renee did."

"But she wouldn't have if you hadn't called her and told her about Gene's death. If you hadn't dangled the fact that my fiancé, who happens to adore Gena, is a doctor. If you hadn't goaded her with that cash carrot knowing that she's too greedy to see beyond the moment. This is another one of your games of control, Mama. How dare you put Gena's well-being on the line like that, just so you can be in charge?!"

There was another long silence.

"You just can't see the danger in your manipulations, can you? Love to you means controlling us like chess pieces in a lethal game. Gene's dead because of that game."

"Gene caused his own death."

"But he and Del were arguing about you. About your manipulations. About which of them you were going to give that prized land to, probably even about which one had the most right to be called your son."

"I can't help that."

"You could have helped the way you exaggerated the PCP incident. That's what started their argument that day in the first place. Gene didn't hit you, Mama. I saw you right afterwards. You set up that whole tragedy by making Del believe he did. If you didn't have Del so brainwashed, he could have seen the truth like I did. Instead, from that day forward Del was intimidated and frightened by Gene and a hair trigger away from exactly what happened."

"You saw my glasses to prove what Gene did."

"But your face didn't have a mark on it."

"I didn't *say* he hit me in the face. I said he came at me with both fists and he stomped my glasses to pieces. I can't help it if Del misunderstood."

Laurel wanted to scream. She couldn't believe the twists and turns of Mama's conscience and how she so blindly justified her half-truths. "*My God, Mama*, can't you even see how you manipulate the truth, or is it just a conditioned reflex? You were crying your eyes out like you were terrified when you told me that."

"I *was* terrified."

"No you weren't. You were totally in control, and you knew it. Can't you see how wrong that was? Can't you see how deadly it turned? I can't take these games of yours anymore. Gena's on the verge of being taken away from me. Gene's dead, and Del's gone crazy. And all of it's your doing."

"Del's not crazy."

"So, it's normal to talk about being a shaman? It's normal to threaten me just because I disagree with the two of you on anything. He stabbed Gene just because he disagreed with him. That's the definition of crazy in my book."

"Well, he's not crazy no matter what you think."

Maybe he wasn't crazy, but if he wasn't, he definitely was the closest thing to evil she'd ever seen. Worse, Mama enabled him. Maybe she even directed him. Whether he was evil or insane didn't matter. He was deadly. She had to get out of this family. Somehow she had to keep from losing Gena, and then she could have a life with her and David, one that didn't include Mama's craziness, one that wasn't deadly. Mama had money now. Money was all Laurel had ever been able to contribute anyway, and now she wasn't needed. It was time to walk away.

"Mama," she began, forming her words from the desperation she felt as she went along, "I can't be a part of this family anymore. There's no love. We only hurt each other. Our family's sick, and nobody wants to change it but me. I've tried so hard to make things better, but nothing works. You and Del don't want it to work. I've loved you with all my heart. I still love you, but I have to walk away. It's over."

"You'll be happy when I'm dead," Mama said sounding as if she were going to cry.

"That's not true!" Her voice caught on a sob. "You could've been happy, Mama. You could be happy now. With the money from your land you've got a chance to make some of your dreams come true. Do it. Go for your dreams, but unless things change, I can't be a part of them. I'm sorry." Her throat ached with the sobs she was holding back. "Good-bye, Mama."

She started to hang up, but abruptly Mama spoke. "Maybe you and David and Gena can come up Christmas Day. Connie can fix a nice meal."

She felt like a wind-up toy that had been wound too tightly too many times—like her spring was going to strip, and she'd come flying apart.

"Didn't you hear a thing I just said? And I can't see that we'll have anything to celebrate on Christmas Day because Gena will most likely be with Renee."

"You can stop all that."

"What!"

"Give her five thousand dollars, and she'll walk away. You're right that she doesn't want Gena. She thinks she can get money from you and David."

"We don't have five thousand dollars, Mama."

"But *I* do."

It dawned on her then. Mama's windfall was her rescue point, and she'd just moved in to save the day. It would work, too, and she almost said yes. She wanted to. She'd do anything to keep Gena, but abruptly she realized that Mama's offers always had strings that created endless heartache. She had to do this the right way, the legal way, the way that had the best potential for a healthy and irreversible resolution.

"I can't do that, Mama. It's tempting, but I can't. I appreciate the thought, whatever your reason for offering, but no. I have to go."

When she hung up the phone, the tears she'd stuffed down erupted. When she could speak without sobbing she picked up the phone again and dialed David's number. He answered on the second ring. "David," she said softly. "I'm sorry to wake you."

"You didn't. I couldn't sleep. I just got out of the shower."

"Can you come over? I need you."

"I'll be right there, sweetheart."

He came immediately dressed in jeans and a tee shirt, his hair still damp from his shower. As they sat at the kitchen bar, she told him about her conversation with Mama, and all the things they'd said to each other.

"Maybe I should have taken Mama up on her offer to give Renee the five thousand. Part of me says it's the easiest way, the sure way, and I should take it, but it never stops with Mama. What would she want from me in return? What interest would I have to pay? Or you or Gena? Gene paid with his life, and it wasn't enough. I have to learn from that."

"You made the right choice, honey. We can't let ourselves be blackmailed. It would never end. Gena belongs with us. I have to believe this is going to work out. Roger's the best attorney in this town."

"Mama almost had me thinking she was just trying to help, but she set this whole mess up to begin with. It wouldn't be happening if she hadn't contacted Renee and made her think she was going to get rich. She just refuses to see the danger in the situations she's set up with her manipulations and the part she's played in the tragedies."

He rubbed her arm. He looked as weary and sad as she felt. She hated to burden him with any more pain, but she needed a friend. She had just made the hardest decision of her life.

"I'm so tired of this pain, the way it's hurting you, the way it could hurt Gena and only because I'm my mother's child and she won't let me go. I told her it's over, that I can't be a part of our family anymore." She tore small pieces off the paper napkin she'd used to dab her eyes. "She says I'll be glad to see her dead." She swallowed hard and looked up into his eyes. "It's not true, David. I love her, but I can't keep letting her do these things. If she would risk Gena, no one is safe."

"You know I'll support you in whatever you decide," he said.

"I know you will, and I need that so much. I don't want to walk away from my family. What I want is for the pain to go away. I want Mama to let go of whatever it is that's eating her alive. I want her to get better and really live. But she won't, and I just don't see why I have to go down the drain with her to prove my love."

Her voice grew hoarse as she continued, and David squeezed her hand.

"She can't even see how much she's hurting me. And she can't see that she's even done anything wrong about Gena's situation. She actually thinks that she did a good thing by offering to rescue her from something she set up in the first place. I can't understand that. I can't."

She paused, took in a ragged breath and finally continued. "Loving her is too dangerous. I had to end it, but she's my mother, and it's ripping at my insides—"

She sobbed then, and her tears came from a place so deep she lost her breath and couldn't finish.

David stood and gently coaxed her off the stool into his arms. He held her until she could finally control her tears, and when she reached for another napkin to dab at her face, he finally spoke. "What can I do to help, baby?"

"Just love me. I need you, David. I can't make it without you, but I won't ask you to fight my battles for me, I promise, and I won't suffocate you with my grief."

"You've got my love for as long as we live, and in every battle I'm going to be right there beside you. I'm going to do everything I can to give you so much happiness that you'll have the strength to face all this. I love you and Gena so much. We'll get through this together, you, Gena, and me. God won't let us lose each other. He didn't bring us through all this pain to let that happen."

Chapter Twenty-Nine

By Wednesday morning, December 22, they hadn't heard any news regarding Renee's lawsuit. The last time David had spoken with Roger had been the previous Sunday morning. Before church he'd called him at home to tell him about Laurel's conversation with her mother. He felt Roger should be aware of what Mrs. Harper had told Laurel about Renee—that she didn't really want custody of Gena and she hoped to get money for backing off instead. They hadn't heard anything from Roger since. David had decided he would call his office this morning at nine o'clock. He felt so frantic he thought about calling the answering service the minute he awoke, but he made himself wait.

Time was running out. They had only two days left. Neither he nor Laurel could bear the thought of handing Gena over to Renee. Laurel had been sharing her cuddle time with Gena for a couple of months now. He cherished that nighttime ritual of bedtime stories, prayers, and conversations. Not having Gena in his life would leave a big hole. He and Laurel tried to have faith that they wouldn't have to give her up, but so many times this past week both had regretted not taking her mother up on her offer to pay Renee off. They'd even fantasized together about disappearing with Gena, but they'd just been blowing off steam. That would only make things worse.

Only a few people at work knew what he and Laurel were going through. They'd told Stu and Miles, and, of course, Audrey knew. All three of them had been very supportive. After they left the huddle at 7:30 AM, they hadn't even made it to the coffeepot before Audrey met them in the hallway. There was a serious expression on her usually jovial face.

"Your lawyer wants to see the two of you. He's waiting in your office."

He prayed this wasn't bad news, but his heart rate kicked up a notch knowing that it had to be. Roger would have called if this was good news.

"I gave him coffee," Audrey added, "and I'll bring yours in. I'll give you a few minutes."

"You're a doll, Audrey," he said. Even he could hear the false bravado in his voice. He'd tried to keep Laurel's spirits up, but he was as worried as she was.

As they stepped inside her office, Roger glanced up from where he was sitting quietly drinking his coffee. "I've got some news," he said.

David couldn't read anything from his friend's expression. He felt the blood drain from his face, and he exchanged a frantic glance with Laurel. This was it, the day they'd been dreading.

"Oh, come on already with the long faces," Roger said abruptly. "Don't you have any faith in your attorney?"

He stared at Roger trying to decide if this was good news or bad. Roger didn't joke about things like this, and it sounded like it could be good news. He was afraid to hope. Then she saw a little smile play at the edge of Roger's mouth, and he knew everything was going to be okay. "I brought you that wedding present." Roger shrugged. "You can consider it a Christmas gift, too."

"Which is?" David asked as he walked over and paused in front of Roger.

Laurel followed close behind him, and Roger handed her a document. "What is this?" she asked accepting the two-page document.

Roger grinned smugly. "Renee Harper's affidavit relinquishing all rights as a parent to one minor child, Gena Renee Harper soon to be Hudson. You won't hear from her again. Your little girl is legally yours. Once you and David get married we have all we need for him to legally adopt her, too."

"Are you serious?" she asked.

After all the turmoil, this sounded too good to be true. He eyed Roger suspiciously. "How did you get her to sign?"

Roger leaned back in the chair and propped his left ankle over his right knee. "I just reminded her of the incident where she tried to abort her daughter by drinking a noxious substance. I gambled that she wouldn't know what noxious means. She didn't. Then I elaborated on medical case histories of similar failed abortion attempts."

"Case histories?" David asked. He wasn't aware of any such medical literature.

Roger ignored him and focused on Laurel. "I summarized the documents for her. She didn't seem too interested in reading the actual documents I presented. She was too busy making provocative moves to try to seduce me."

That was Renee alright, David thought. In just that one encounter, he knew what she was.

Roger kept talking. "I told her that these children, although perfectly normal at birth, had shown developmental problems in grade school, and in some cases their health had deteriorated so much that the expenses had bankrupted their parents. That got her attention especially when I told her it was a shame that she had done a similar thing to her child, and who knew what could come of it in the next couple of years. But I did have sympathy for the fact that she now wanted to make amends for her actions and care for her daughter no matter what the cost. The little lady couldn't sign that document fast enough to wash her hands of the responsibility."

He and Laurel exchanged a hopeful glance. "And she can't contest this?" Laurel asked.

"She could, but she wouldn't get very far. It was her idea to give you her consent. Just a lovely young lady. Not much of a heart. Not too swift in the brain department and certainly no match for me."

David laughed. "You are so full of it. I've never heard of any medical case history that would presume so much with so few concrete facts. Where did you find these so-called case histories? They couldn't be real."

Roger shrugged. "My wife types fast and takes dictation very well. I thought I was rather creative. Like your wedding present so far?"

"Do we have to worry about Renee ever challenging us again?" Laurel asked. The reality of what Roger was telling them was finally sinking in.

"Not in this lifetime."

She beamed Roger a smile. "Thank you so very, very much." Then she reached for him and engulfed him in a hug. "Oh, David, this is wonderful!"

"Hey, I'm the one who got the signature," Roger protested spreading his arms playfully.

David hugged her closer. "If you expect a hug, Willis, you're in the wrong place."

Roger laughed and got to his feet. "You're still the same old killjoy, Hudson. Some things never change, I guess." Then he winked at Laurel. "Set the date already, and put the boy out of his misery." He squeezed her shoulder as he sauntered past them. He paused at the office doorway and pointed his forefinger at them. "Oh, and I expect to receive a wedding invitation." With those words he turned and left.

David squeezed Laurel closer. "We have some celebrating to do."

"We sure do," she responded, her eyes sparkling with happiness. "Why don't we make it a huge celebration? David Hudson, will you marry me? Right away? As soon as possible?"

"Baby, I thought you'd never ask," he said laughing. "Are you kidding? Right now wouldn't be too soon."

"Your mom has her heart set on a small reception. We can't elope anyway because ever since Thanksgiving, Gena's talked about the 'day we marry Daddy.' It's her day, too. We can't disappoint her, but," she continued playfully, "if we keep it sweet and simple, we could do it right away. Definitely no more than a week from now."

"How about New Year's Eve?" It was Audrey's perky voice. They turned to see her entering the office bearing their coffee. "I can get you fixed up before the day's over." She set their coffee on the desk and stepped back to her own desk to retrieve a steno pad. "Your attorney told me the good news, so let's pull out the stops. No time for mail. I'll call the invitations. I have relatives in the bakery business, and like I told you before, I know how to do this."

"In that case, how about Christmas Eve?" he said. "I can't wait another week."

"Perfect," Laurel said. "We're off the rest of the week after today. What a great Christmas present that would be for all of us."

"Let's see," Audrey said, not skipping a beat at the date change. "You want Rachmaninoff's Concerto no. 2 played. Your mother says her church pianist can handle that. We can get engraved napkins in a day, and my uncle is a whiz with wedding cakes. We'll use the fellowship hall at your parents' church for the reception and have punch, cake, mints, and nuts."

This was sounding way too complicated already. "Forget your list, Audrey. All we're going to need is that music on my reel to reel, a preacher, and a bed, in that order. If the preacher's long-winded, we might have to switch it around to him coming last."

"Pervert. What's your mother going to say?" Audrey scolded.

"She'll get over it."

Laurel laughed and cuddled closer. "Did I ever tell you how much I love you?" she said.

"Yeah, but you can't say it too often." She kissed him then, a deep, sweet kiss that made him wish they were eloping immediately.

"Time out." Audrey's voice interrupted their passion. "Do that later. Laurel and I have work to do." She planted her left hand on her hip then. "That means, Dr. Pervert, if you'll get out of here, we'll have this taken care of by the end of day."

"You can really do that?" He glanced from Laurel to Audrey and back again. "Wedding cake, reception—all that stuff?"

"She can," Laurel said. "She's bugged me since we got engaged for our preferences, lists, and details. She's even talked to your mother a couple of times. All she has to do is push a few buttons, and we're all set."

He reached for his coffee cup. "In that case let's make it the morning of Christmas Eve. I have stockings to fill that night."

Laurel giggled, but Audrey rolled her eyes at his double meaning.

He took a swig of coffee and winked at Laurel. "Don't waste your money buying a negligee, baby. You're not going to need it."

She giggled again, but Audrey, phone in hand and already caught up in implementing her list, peered at him over her half glasses. "Don't you have a dead body to go take care of? This is girl stuff."

He moved away from Laurel. "Don't let her get the preacher at Mom and Dad's church, baby. He's too long-winded. Pastor Finch is precise and to the point. Don't forget now."

Audrey pointed toward the door. "Out, and don't come back until noon. Bring lunch."

Laurel flashed him an apologetic smile. "Sorry. I'll make it up to you Christmas Eve."

He saluted Audrey and left the office whistling "Get Me to the Church on Time."

Epilogue

November 11, 1972

Laurel cuddled eight-pound-two-ounce David Andrew Hudson, Jr. in her arms. Her heart filled with love for this tiny angel she and David had made. He looked very much like Gena exactly as David had predicted except that his hair was going to be straight like hers and David's. Right now it was downy tufts of dark brown covering his perfectly shaped little head.

"I love you, Davy," she said softly, "and when you and your sister grow up I'm going to set you free so you can fly. I'll always love you both, and you can come home anytime; but I won't make you feel like you have to stay."

She bent to kiss his tiny forehead. "You get to see your big sister in a couple of minutes. Daddy's gone to get her. You're going to love her. She's going to feed you. We promised her she could. Can you hold off a few more minutes for that?" Davy squirmed and tried to suck on his fist. He was getting impatient alright but not fussy. "She's been waiting almost nine months for this moment, sweetheart. Hang on just a bit more."

David had gotten special permission to bring Gena to her room to see their baby. She was already in the waiting room with his parents. She heard them approaching before she saw them.

As she listened to their loud whispering and hushed giggling she smiled to herself. It was a toss-up as to who was more excited, David or Gena.

"Mommee!" Gena bounded into the room, and David lifted her onto the bed beside her.

She planted a kiss on Gena's cheek. "Hi, sweet angel, your brother's been waiting to see you."

"Davy, meet your sister, Gena," David said proudly. He helped her settle Davy into Gena's arms. She demonstrated how to hold the bottle, and she and David hovered over them to watch.

"Hi, little baby," Gena said softly. Davy seemed to take her in as his eyes followed her movements while he sucked on the bottle. "It's okay that you're a boy even though I told Daddy and Mommy I wanted a sister. I'm gonna take real good care of you 'cause I'm five years old now."

She and David exchanged a smile, and he reached to touch her cheek with his palm. "Are you sure you're okay, darling?" he asked softly.

She nodded. "I'm sad, but I'll be okay. I have such love around me here with you and Gena and Davy."

It had been that kind of day, one taken straight from a Dickens novel, the best of times, the worst of times, but she hadn't expected anything else. Life had already taught her that bad and good came mixed together. She wished that Mama could have celebrated this precious new life with her, but not having that was part of the price of her decision.

That decision to separate herself from the danger and heartache of her family had been the hardest one of her life. The only peace she'd gotten had been when she decided to take Mama Rita's advice to turn Mama over to God. Her grandmother had told her that only God could heal Mama with his love, so Laurel had finally stopped trying to do it herself.

She took that advice one step further and turned over to God all the emotions she had faced in that giving up. She had turned over the unrequited love itself, those emotions that pulsed out of her like a desperate S.O.S. that was never answered. She had given up her anger at Mama's bad choices and Del's support of those bad choices. She'd given up her fear of the craziness and her resentment of the needless pain, and she'd given up her memories. The giving up was an ongoing process. She gave them up, and she kept giving them up. It was like love dying a thousand times, and it hurt. Dear God, how much it hurt.

Turning her back on them was alien to every belief she had ever held about family and love. Maybe someday she would be given peace about her decision, but right now she wasn't sure that she had done the right thing. She knew only that she had done what she had to do to protect her own family.

So, now on one of the happiest days of her life and right on cue, she faced Mama's ultimate retribution for daring to break away and be so giddily happy in her separate life. It was just one more thing she'd have to get her heart around, one more thing to hand over to God. This morning a few hours before dawn Mama had died.

She should have expected it, and now she believed she had been given a sign. Yesterday morning after she'd awakened at 6:00 AM to the first pre-labor twinges, a strange thing had happened as she sat in the den of their new house timing the twinges to determine whether they were real or not before she woke David. A robin came and perched on the rail of the deck. Then it repeatedly slammed itself against the window of the den, retreating each time to set off again on its kamikaze mission. She'd tried to shoo it away, but it wouldn't be frightened off. It seemed intent on slowly and methodically bashing itself to death.

Was it bitterly coveting the warmth inside? Angry at its own reflection, or was there a more benevolent reason for its presence? She didn't know. She'd heard it again this morning thumping its deadly cadence just as her real labor pains had begun. By the time she and David woke Gena and headed out to the hospital, it was gone.

Surely that had been an omen, for it was sadly symbolic of the way Mama had lived her life. To Mama, love was control. She had to be the puppet master controlling the strings that made her children move so they would always need her. She could never see that she didn't have to be needed to be loved. She slammed herself against life, thinking, Laurel supposed, that the pain that followed would be worth the control and the warped sense of love she would gain.

She'd hoped that the money Mama had gotten for her land could give her some sense of the independence she seemed to be missing so she could heal, but it hadn't mattered at all. She'd learned from her grandparents that Mama hadn't blown the money this time, and she'd bought some comforts; but she'd kept self-destructing. Staying away had been heartbreaking, but to continue to be an audience would have been telling Mama it was alright to kill herself for attention and love.

It had been hardest to explain it all to Gena—why they never visited her grandmother. She was a child who loved purely. How could Laurel make her understand something she had known only in her soul but couldn't put into words and square with her heart?

So now, her broken dream, taken away from that house of all those broken dreams was that her family would never be a family filled with peace and love. She'd tried so hard to make them a family, to rescue them all from the consequences of the craziness, but her attempts had failed because it wasn't up to her to make it happen. The truth was that none of it was her fault. She'd thought for so long that it was. Somehow she just wasn't loveable, or Mama would have loved her. Somehow she was incredibly selfish, or Mama would have respected her separateness as a person.

She could see now that Mama had set her on an idealistic course that she'd never really believed in herself. But she had gone for the stars that Granddaddy Cowan said Mama had her wagon hitched to and caught them. She'd done everything expected of her, but she could never make Mama proud of her. By withholding approval Mama had made her feel that she was always striving and never arriving when it came to the voice in her head that defined success, even when she had gone farther that most people on that mountain ever went. She would never do that to Gena and Davy. It was the cruelest thing a parent could do.

"I think Davy looks like me." Gena's voice pulled her away from her sad thoughts.

"Isn't that great? I told you he probably would," David said. "You look like Mommy, and Harper genes are real strong." David beamed a smile so loving that it seeped around the sadness inside her, cushioning its sharp edges.

Tears filled her eyes. This was her wonderful family now. Maybe that other family had failed, and maybe that would always hurt, but God had given her this chance to start over and do it right. And it had been so right. David had kept his promise to fill her life with so much happiness that it balanced the sorrow, and he'd done it just by showing his love every day in little ways.

He was holding Davy now and feeding him. As he leaned against the headboard close beside her, their shoulders touching, Gena snuggled between them. "Davy's little. Was I that little?"

"You were one whole pound smaller," she said.

"And you looked like a baby angel, all frilly and sweet," David added. "Remember all those pictures in your baby book?" David bent to kiss her curly head. "You get that angel part from Mommy. The mischief part, you get from me."

Gena giggled. Laurel draped her arm around her, hugging her, savoring her sweetness. David smiled at her over Gena's head and leaned to kiss her cheek leaving healing warmth in the wake of his tenderness. She would have missed all this if she hadn't risked loving again. If only Mama could have taken that same risk. A tear escaped and rolled down her cheek. Gena noticed and reached to wipe it away.

"Mommy, don't be sad about Grandma Sarah. It's her time to go live with God. And Pastor Finch says we get new bodies. So, you know what? She's in Heaven in her new body, and she won't hurt anymore. And, Mommy, she can fly."

"Yeah," she said softly. She rubbed her cheek against the top of Gena's head and thought about that and about her confusing omen. Could it be true? Was Mama with God? Had her sorrowful prayers finally been answered and she was just too earthbound to see it? Had Mama's body been such a prison of mistakes that God had chosen to heal her spirit instead?

Most of her prayers had been for Mama's body, but the spirit was all that mattered. Maybe God had reached into Mama's soul and found that one receptive place that could still say yes to love and bonded it to him before she could slip past the point of no return.

Maybe he *had* set Mama free from her cage of bitterness. Maybe, like the wounded birds Laurel used to tend as a child, God had cradled Mama in his arms healing her with his love so that now her spirit could be free, and maybe the robin at her window had been an angel sent to tell her so. She knew in her heart and soul that it was possible.

She didn't understand Mama or her choices. She didn't understand her family, and she didn't understand the pain; but she did still believe in miracles. Maybe some things you never got an answer for. Maybe some things would always hurt, and maybe miracles weren't meant to be understood, just accepted.

"Fly free, Mama," she whispered. "Fly free."

The End